ISLAND ODYSSEY

Ghetto Flowers in Paradise

Francis O. Lynn

Seagull Publishing Company

Princeton, New Jersey

First Edition: December 12h, 2011

Editor: Randy Istre

Cover Photo by Suzanne Caimi Lynn

Author Picture by Hazel Hankin

Dedication

Island Odyssey is dedicated to Suzanne Caimi Lynn, my creative consultant, and most importantly my one love & one heart!

CHAPTERS

BROTHERS AND SISTERS
Spiritual Psychedelic Carnalism ... or not

September is the best month to be at the Jersey shore. The scorching sun of summer has waned, the water is warm, and once Labor Day has passed, the throngs of vacationers flee back to their city lives of work and mundane routines. My peer group, known as the Ghetto Flowers of South Philadelphia, had lived together in a cozy apartment throughout the summer. Everyone, except for Patrick O'Malley and me, had left for the city and other destinations. The two of us stayed in our Wildwood, New Jersey abode for as long as we could remain undetected by our landlord – the lease was up on Labor Day so we could be tossed out at any moment. We spent the days enjoying all of our usual Wildwood leisure activities of swimming, fishing, and strolling along the water's edge. It was a special time to reflect on every aspect of our lives, especially the experiences of personal transformation that the South Philadelphian Ghetto Flowers had gone through. We were seeds that had been planted in the concrete, asphalt, and redbrick row homes jungle of the inner city ghetto. Through many trials and tribulations, the Ghetto Flowers had blossomed and not withered.

Patrick had spent the summer employed as a lifeguard. He had that classic athletic swimmer's physique – tall and lean with well-defined muscles and skin bronzed by the sun. His curly golden blond shoulder length hair added to his sex appeal, and the beach beauties frequently flocked around his lifeguard stand, thrilled whenever he flashed his green-blue eyes their way. These ladies met with disappointment since Patrick was head-over-heels in love with Chrissie, the twin sister of my sweetheart, Sandy. That's not to say he wasn't tempted to indulge in carnal pleasures. In fact, it took an enormous amount of self-discipline and more than a little support from me to keep him from going astray. I was envious of Patrick's ability to tan - my skin was scourged with freckles, a malady that often accompanied Irish lads with the classic strawberry blond hair and sky-blue eyes. I, too, was a good swimmer, although not as muscular as Patrick, a bit on the thin side and a little taller, but I had no interest in basking in the sun all day in a lifeguard stand – I preferred swimming in the ocean, not staring at it. Besides, I had no interest in working during the summer months whatsoever – I was a genuine beach bum.

Patrick had purchased a small book from a garage sale an elderly lady was holding in her seaside home. The book was called, *Ocean of Love,* written by an Eastern philosophy teacher who found favor with many alternative-worldview-seeking young people. My dear friend and mentor, Ellen of Stone Harbor, New Jersey, had told me of her travels to India and of what she learned from Eastern meta-physical thought. It was a fortuitous coincidence that Patrick found the book she had mentioned in such an unlikely place. The teachings were simple and essentially said that universal love is the primary cause and energy at the very center of creation, and throughout the summer, Patrick and I discussed the teachings espoused in the book. The prose was poetic and lovely to meditate upon during our long walks along the seashore. The writings were a refreshing way to view the world since we had worked so hard to unshackle our minds from the programming of religious dogma that permeated our childhood – we were exploring new ways of seeing and being.

One evening we stayed up all night, strolling on the boardwalk and beach, accompanied by my faithful dog, White Shepherd. We had become accustomed to being night owls while living in Wildwood. It fit our natural late adolescent biorhythms. We started out foraging for food deals to fuel our hungry bodies. Most places on the boardwalk were closed. Fortunately, we found a pizza joint that had reduced their prices, since it was off-season and nearly all summer vacationers were gone. After eating our pizza on a bench facing the ocean, and feeding the crust to White Shepherd, we decided to take a walk on the beach that lasted throughout the night. We strolled along the U.S. Coast Guard owned and protected beach where there was no boardwalk or buildings, only a long stretch of undisturbed dunes, providing a sanctuary where a variety of shore birds safely nested and raised their young.

It was a pristine place to sit and watch the sunrise. Patrick fired up a joint, and soon the sweet smell mingled with the scent of salt air. There was a fine mist along the coast and as I scanned my eyes along the water's edge, I saw moving in the mist a group of people coming in our direction. White Shepherd noticed them as well and wagged her tail; she wanted to run up to them but I held her back. White Shepherd was just a puppy when she was given to me seven years ago, and now this quite large and exceptionally beautiful animal lived with my friend Ellen in Stone Harbor throughout the year because the city was no longer a suitable place for her. It was the darkest hour of the night, just before the arrival of dawn, so I couldn't make out the details of the approaching group until they were almost standing directly in front of us. They were young people approximately our age – late teens, early twenties - six of them, three females and three males. The males were dressed in knee-length brown robes, wore sandals, and they had long hair and beards. The females wore sleeveless brown tunics, no make-up and their legs and armpits were unshaven. A notably distinctive characteristic of their appearance was a simple four-inch wooden cross hanging on a leather lace around each of their necks. They looked like monks and nuns straight out of the fourteenth century.

"Good morning brothers. May we join you?" The person had a booming voice and he held a Bible in his huge hands. His long shiny black hair fell in curly ringlets over his shoulders and reached the middle of his chest, and he had a full beard that touched his collarbone. I was reminded of the character from the Bible, John the Baptist. White Shepherd had a low growl in her throat and slightly bared teeth. I placed my hand on her neck and she immediately calmed down.

"Hello. Of course, please pull up some sand – there's plenty of it – and make your selves comfortable. I'm Oliver James and this is my friend Patrick O'Malley. This furry white animal is White Shepherd – she is quite friendly and perhaps slightly more intelligent than your average human." I tried to be cleverly humorous, not one of my strong suits.

"We are pleased to meet you. I am Michael and we are Brothers and Sisters of The Holy Order of Light, followers of the original teachings of Jesus Christ, the One True Son of the Paradise Father of all Creation." My stomach churned. Michael spoke these words with an air of authority, as if he were making a pronouncement that the world could hear, and his almost black dark-brown eyes radiated with intensity. He tried petting White Shepherd but she growled, revealing her menacing teeth again, causing him to quickly step back – I placed my hand upon her neck.

Patrick extended his hand to Michael as he began to speak. "I heard of young people seeking the original teachings of Christianity. They are commonly referred to as Jesus Freaks, which sounds negative. Do people refer to you as Jesus Freaks?"

"Yes, we get that a lot. The intention is to ridicule our faith. However, we are steadfast in our convictions and unshaken by the ways of this world. Jesus teaches that we are in this world but not of this world. Followers of Jesus have been persecuted for two thousand years and Jesus Christ performed the ultimate sacrifice: he laid down his life so that we may all be forgiven our sins and gain entrance into the Eternal Kingdom of Heaven. We have been spat upon, chased, and some of us have even been physically beaten, and several of us have been denounced by our family and friends. It is a powerful experience to devote your life to sharing truth with all of humanity and to be despised by some in return. It opens the eyes to seeing how blind the ways of men are, and how clear, simple, and straight is the path to God." Michael sounded proud of his experiences with mistreatment.

I continued to stare into the horizon as I mulled over Michael's discourse. I wanted to blast apart the concept of Jesus being required to die for humanity's sins, but I decided to be more tactful. "Persecution and sacrifice is not an easy path. It is my understanding that the teachings of Jesus stimulated the mind to obtain knowledge and compassion for the human condition and that the lessons of love would eventually lead to the manifestation of a more civilized world. Persecution and sacrifice are not what Jesus taught. His was a message of love and joy through service."

After I made my comment, our group sat quietly looking at the sea. The sky began to glow with the first light of dawn, although the stars were exceptionally bright because it was a new moon evening. A flock of seagulls flew in front of us and settled on the water's edge several yards away. White Shepherd ran after them, causing them to take flight over the sea.

Michael's booming voice broke the reverie. "There will be no heaven on earth until Christ comes again. Have you not read in the scriptures where it says: *The Kingdom of Heaven is at hand.*"

I looked Michael directly in the eyes while responding to his pronouncement. "The capacity to be good ethical people exists as a potential within all people, and as we learn to love and serve each other through good works, then we experience the reality of what you refer to as the kingdom of heaven, *now*, and we share it with all who are receptive. It is a goodness that is manifested the instant people make the choice to do no harm. It is not dependent on the actual materialization of a messiah or belief in a set of religious doctrine – we are all messiahs each time we perform an act of kindness." Oliver the prophet of South Philly had spoken – look out – I was on a roll, hopefully giving Michael and his merry band of Holy Order folks grist for the mill! I was enjoying the exchange with Michael and so were the devotees of the Holy Order of Light. Patrick and I spent an entire year exploring philosophy, psychology, sociology and anthropology as we discovered key after key that unlocked the gates of our inner city prison and freed our minds from a childhood saturated with religious doctrine. Good people had reached out to the Ghetto Flowers of our concrete jungle garden.

Social workers and mental health professionals from all over the Philadelphia area had special interest in the unique circumstances of our neighborhood peer group, and in turn, we reached out to others. In the process, we grew in mind and heart – and many lives were saved – literally, including mine.

"You speak well, Oliver. You have a unique interpretation of the scriptures, although I don't follow your reasoning. The most important question is this: Have you been baptized and reborn in the Holy Spirit?" Michael's words were meant as a challenge to my philosophical perspective. I was feeling slightly amused.

Patrick turned his head abruptly toward Michael and his group, causing the curls of his golden mane to lift from his shoulders like light feathers. I was reminded of the gentle and self-assured character, Kane, the Kung-fu master in the popular television series. He slowly grazed his piercing greenish-blue eyes over the flock of evangelists as he spoke. "Michael, you are passionate in your beliefs, and obviously motivated to convince others to walk your path of salvation. I respect that you have found a way of life that works for you and your friends. For me, the world is full of a great deal of diversity; there are many religions with long standing traditions and each one of them has a prescription on how to live and what to believe. The world of religion is like a garden of flowers with a variety of colors, shapes, and sizes; it is this variation that creates wondrous beauty. There are many paths to choose from to walk through the corridors of life. It is my perspective that each individual must work out his or her own salvation. The one universal truth, I suggest, is that we respect one another, even love one another, which, to me, simply means to do no harm - or, to say it more positively, is to perform acts of kindness towards each other. It is not realistic to expect all people of the world to think and believe alike, and all attempts to do so have turned religious teachings into justification for hideous acts of violence – truly an ironic phenomenon that has rightfully turned many inquiring minds away from spiritual pursuits. However we can have the universal experience of love, for we are one human family."

Whew! That was a bit of a new twist coming from Patrick. I had never heard him speak with such authority, clarity, and succinct directness in revealing his own thought system. Patrick and I shared the importance of open mindedness – acceptance and tolerance towards religions, race, and philosophical perspectives. I had experienced what I consider to be a spiritual awakening - an epiphany of sorts - but the only absolute I took from my experience was the reality of the power and beauty of universal love. The reality of the experience was undeniable, and I fully understood that it was not scientifically verifiable – but it was as real as the freckles on my nose! What Patrick had just said rang true.

"Whoa! Far out and praise Jesus. You just made it clear to me why I have joined this Order. Thank you Brother Patrick O'Malley!" The long blond haired blue eyed female spoke, the first other than Michael to say anything. She was tall, slender, well proportioned – and if she lost the religious garb, she could be a Marilyn Monroe look-alike. "This Holy Order is my family and God is our Father and each of you is my brother and sister – my real family!" The young woman hugged the man next to her and proceeded to hug each person in her family of believers. She then went to Patrick and startled him by throwing her arms around his lean muscular torso, knocking him off his serene perch, causing them to roll in each other's arms along the sand. I laughed out loud. When they stopped rolling, the woman was on top of Patrick and they stared into each other's eyes as the tips of their noses touched. "Hi, Patrick, I'm Colleen – your new sister." She then kissed him lightly on the lips, surprising everyone, especially Michael, who looked perplexed and unsure how to respond, as though he felt the need to do or say something in response to this spontaneous expression of affection that was obviously more than a brother-sister exchange.

"Colleen, sister of my blood and spirit, you are exuberant in your expression," said Michael in a tone that let his blood-sister know he disapproved. There was something about Michael's style of speaking that was disturbing. Every word was expressed with a tone of holy resonance. White Shepherd sensed the tension in him and expressed her disapproval by growling every time he spoke. I decided that if he and the holy order were to come to our South Philadelphia neighborhood, they wouldn't last a day before high tailing it back to a pristine beach. Heaven, or the beauty that lives in the human heart, as I preferred to think of the concept, is indeed very present in our neighborhood, but you have to look past the insanity, and physical ugliness of the claustrophobic narrow streets and buildings, poverty, ignorance, substance abuse, and the violence of racism, and peer directly into the hearts of people to see that heaven is alive and well.

"Brother Michael, it is so sweet how you look after me." Colleen rolled off the bewildered and enamored Patrick. "Are you all in agreement that these two handsome young men know what it means to be a disciple of Christ and that we should ordain them into our Holy Order on this lovely morning?" Colleen's face was radiant with an angelic quality. I wondered if I was seeing a spiritual aberration. She really was pretty and completely sincere in what she was expressing – especially the part about us being handsome. "Are you two willing to take the vows of the Holy Order of Light and bear the cross of Jesus and join us in our spiritual quest?" She asked. White Shepherd responded well to Colleen's energy as she frolicked up to her and showered her face with slobbering kisses – much to Colleen's delight.

"Excuse me, brothers. I am Sister Linda. I encourage you to accept Sister Colleen's invitation." Her kind hazel eyes peered directly into the depths of my psyche, giving me a pleasant feeling. I liked the roundness of her face, the thickness of her rose pink lips, the freckles dusting her nose and cheeks, and the way the bangs of her short red hair framed her eyes. She asked, "What is your name?" I took particular notice of the glow in her eyes – in fact every member of the Order had that same look, which struck me as a bit eerie as well as enticing. I was perplexed that she needed to ask for my name, causing me to think that she was spacing out this whole time, not paying full attention to the conversations.

"I'm Oliver James. I am pleased to meet you, Linda."

"Likewise, Brother Oliver. You know, I have a brother who has the same wavy strawberry blond hair and bright blue eyes, and he is tall like you. Although he is not as blessed with angel kisses – freckles. You are very cute." Her voice had an erotic tone, and I liked what she had to say and the way she looked at me. I felt a slight twinge in my loins. "So what do you say, would you like to take advantage of the coming sunrise and be baptized in the ocean? We do it all the time as an affirmation of our faith. Like you and your friend have said, once initiated into the heart of the spirit, we live in the ocean of love. So, why not take a dip into the infinite?" That isn't exactly what we said but I wasn't about to argue.

Sister Linda stood up and completely disrobed. She was naked – raw naked – voluptuous in every area, a deeply religious person in her late teens or early twenties in all her natural beauty. Her firm round breasts with pointy pink nipples, red pubic hair, shapely legs and hips mesmerized me as she motioned toward the water's edge. Then, all of the people of the Holy Order rose, disrobed and walked into the ocean. Patrick and I watched in total disbelief. These people really were Hippie Jesus Freaks, no doubt about it. I couldn't help but wonder what their view of sex was. Did they believe in *free love,* and if so how did they practice birth control, or did they leave that up to the spirit? It was apparent that Patrick felt inspired to join them as he stood up and started taking his shirt off. I suspected that his motivation wasn't to re-affirm any baptism - he wanted to be with the naked women.

I placed my hand on his foot and said, "I think it would be better for us to let them enjoy their time without our direct participation. This is obviously one of their special rituals and if we share it with them they will only experience disappointment once they learn that we will not join their Holy Order."

"Holy Order or not, I want to be in the water with those naked women." Patrick stripped off his shirt and kicked off his shoes. Again, I warned him.

"Patrick, this is very, very special to them. Unless you truly want to join their religious order, I think you should consider your motivation, which I suspect is less than spiritual."

"Bro, screw all this religious stuff! You and I know the spirit is the spirit whether we wear robes, or no robes, and preach this or that. So we wouldn't be doing anything wrong by sharing in their religion. Who says you have to be a member of any religious group to appreciate what they have to offer? In fact, I know that allegiance to religious forms is not necessary to enjoy the benefits. I mean, think about my relationship with the Catholic Church. I was a Catholic from the day I was born. Hell, I was even an altar boy all the while not believing most of the mumbo jumbo."

"It's amazing how our minds can justify anything. It's obvious that what you are appreciating about this group of believers is through the eyes of the flesh and not the spirit."

"Hey Oliver, don't get all sanctimonious on me, not when there are goddesses right before our eyes who obviously want to share the beauty of creation with their new-found brothers. They are free spirited people and I sense they practice free love. I am curious how that works so I'm willing to do a little experimentation, and who knows, maybe it will make me more spiritual."

"Patrick, you could end up hurting them."

"Impossible! I think we could end up adding something special to their spiritual experience. After all, spiritual awareness is an evolving process and we could have a good influence on their religious unfolding – and they on ours!" Patrick's words clearly indicated that I wasn't getting through to him.

"And you want to add to your carnal knowledge. I say let them evolve without extensive input on our part. We don't know all the forces that have brought them to their cultural brand of religious expression. If we spend more time with them discoursing about Eastern philosophy as well as the extent of our explorations of Christian concepts, we would most likely offend them. And it's quite possible that there is nothing sexual about this ritual at all and you'd end up making a fool of yourself by offending their sacred ceremony." I was passionate on this point.

"Hey, I can read cues pretty well. If they are not interested in sharing spiritual love through physical expression, then we are not Nordic-Irish. The biggest cues I see right now are three gorgeous female bodies wading in an ocean of love, and I'm definitely cued into that. And speaking about ocean of love, man, there it is in glorious flesh, live and in color, not just some high-minded philosophical ideas." Patrick really wanted to be in the water next to those naked beauties. White Shepherd did not hesitate, she ran directly into the surf, frolicking in the sea foam and swimming around the merry group of naked beauties. She was particularly fond of Colleen.

"Yeah, right, and the female naked sirens are calling your higher nature. You sure are persistent on this free love thing. There is no such thing, for there are always consequences, especially when it comes to sex, which can be very heavy. And what about us offending their religious beliefs?" I was a little surprised by my moralistic mood, a state of mind that was a little unusual.

"You mean like the concept of original sin where God requires His only son to be crucified in order for humanity to be absolved from the sin of Adam and Eve? You know, that whole convoluted atonement doctrine that says we are all sinners and will be eternally punished unless we acknowledge our guilt and ask for forgiveness, that God required his only offspring be put to death and take on our sins before He'd forgive us even though the so-called original sinners lived thousands of years ago and listened to a talking snake and ate an apple?" Patrick really thought that the Biblical teaching about original sin and atonement was totally ridiculous – and I had my doubts and often wondered about the meanings of what I thought to be metaphors and allegories.

"Well, Patrick, I wouldn't put it like that, although I think the Adam and Eve story may be an allegory for something that had to do with sex – then again, most teachings related to sin and Catholicism has something to do with sex, maybe that's why they're so big on celibacy. Anyway, I sense that our open perspective would confuse them. They need each other and they have found something special. If I did not sense strongly that we would only interfere with their seeking rather than add to it, then I too would join them in their so-called baptism ritual. I just know in my heart that it is not the right thing for me. We are sharing goodness and mutual respect with them and I think that is what matters. Perhaps for you, ahem - Brother Patrick O'Malley, it would be different."

Patrick and I had concluded from our study of the Bible, Old and New testaments, that there were so many inconsistencies that God was either schizoid or the book was not the word of God but the words of men expressing their understanding and misunderstandings of God. I once worked in a textile mill for a Jewish family. The elderly owner had escaped Nazis Germany when he was a boy. I had a conversation with him about Nazis and Christianity the day I told him I was learning to be a Catholic, a decision I made in order to go to their schools to be safe from the prevalent racial violence of public schools – I was thirteen. He looked at me with sadness in his eyes and said, "The Germans were a nation of people raised in the Christian religion, and it did nothing to prevent them from becoming monsters." His words influenced my view of Christianity specifically, and religion and human nature in general. If we shared with this holy band of sunrise baptismal Jesus Freaks the full extent of our views on religion surely they would think we were heathens, and they might think we were doing to them what they were attempting to do to us – trying to indoctrinate them to our way of thinking.

"You may be right, Oliver, the risk to them probably isn't worth it, although it might be a healthy challenge to their set of beliefs. Hey, it's okay to sit here and appreciate the view. They are beautiful. Look, they are standing in an arc holding hands facing the sun. Well, this isn't the first religious service containing a bunch of asses that we have ever witnessed." We looked at each other and busted out laughing.

"*But,* it is the only religious service with naked people that we've experienced!" I replied. We continued laughing.

As the sun was just about to rise, the holy group dipped in unison below the water's surface, disappearing for a moment as the first rays of the fully risen sun reflected upon the sea in direct line to where these religious people submerged their bodies beneath the waves. They gracefully broke the surface of the water - a lovely sight to behold. They stood with their heads bowed in reverence of their faith ritual and their wet glistening bodies reflected the golden glow of the sunrise. Indeed, they were bathed in rays of the light of the risen sun. Even White Shepherd had sensed the sacredness of the moment, standing still in the surf beside Colleen apparently staring at the sun on the horizon.

They came out of the water and put on their robes. There was nothing sexual about what they did, other than being naked.

They moved about quietly as they dressed and then they sat down, flanking Patrick and me on both sides, placing us in the middle of an arc. White Shepherd, as was her practice after swimming, stood directly in front of me and shook the ocean water off her body, spraying our faces.

"Christ is King of the Earth and all its creatures. The sun is His crown and the light of His love shines upon us all. Why didn't you join us?" Linda asked. I was impressed with her poetic metaphor. Although, I was more attracted to her mostly exposed breast than the meaning of her words.

"It would have been presumptuous of us to join you since we are not members of your Holy Order of Light. Your baptism ritual is very beautiful and you are indeed Children of the Light of the Sun, which was so exquisitely evident in what we just witnessed. You have a beautiful religion." Patrick was impressively eloquent.

"Yes. Thank you for sharing your faith with us. You are beautiful people." I added my appreciation.

Linda noticed Patrick staring at her breast and to my surprise she shifted her robe slightly, fully exposing one of her nipples. Patrick's eyes were bulging out of his head and without realizing it, he began leaning towards her, obviously mesmerized by her beauty. I lightly kicked his foot. He straightened up and stopped staring. Linda frowned.

"Perhaps we can meet again and discourse on the teachings of our Lord," said Brother Michael.

"If our paths cross again, indeed that would be a blessing," Patrick added. Again, I was surprised by the religious tone of his words. "Hey, how about coming back to our place and we'll fix you breakfast?" Patrick wasn't quite ready to let these religious beauties slip away.

"That's very generous of you, but we must be on our way. Brothers and Sisters, we have completed our 100th baptismal of the Rising Son of Light. Now, we must go on and proclaim the Good News of the Risen Son to all who have ears to hear and eyes to see. Farewell my brothers, until we meet again, and prepare yourselves for the Second Coming of our Lord and Savior Jesus Christ!" White Shepherd was growling at Michael, causing him to look uneasy.

With the completion of Michael's pronouncement we all rose, and they each gave us a warm, wet hug. Linda and Patrick were enjoying their embrace so much and for so long that everyone else stood staring at them waiting. Patrick wasn't wearing a shirt and Linda's now fully bare breast pressed against his chest. Linda swiveled her pelvis against his groin. She stuck her hand in his pocket and whispered something in his ear.

Michael coughed loudly, causing them to break their embrace. And away they went to bring their truth to all who would receive their message. White Shepherd walked for a distance beside Colleen. I whistled and she returned to me.

"Oliver, that was far out and bizarre. Linda is one hot holy sister. I would love to do some spiritual body surfing with her! They are a nice bunch of people, although quite fanatical, and I think there is more going on with them than meets the naked eye, or beyond the eyes, or something like that. I'm glad they didn't throw us any guilt, or the-devil-is-going-to-get-you, if you don't believe our teachings crap. It's interesting how people who discover truth in a particular form are convinced that others must receive it in the same manner, be they Catholic, Protestant, Hindu, Buddhist, Jews, Muslims, or a new cult group. The phenomenon is the same - their way is *the only way,* or at the very least, *the best way.*"

"Patrick, do you mind telling me what Linda whispered in your ear?"

"Not at all. She said, *I placed in your pocket the universal communion of Christ that heralds in a new era of consciousness.*" Patrick reached in his pocket and took out what Linda had given him. It was a small leather pouch. He opened it and there were two small pieces of paper with a stamped image of a hippie-looking guy, with the words *Keep on Truckin'* printed in very small letters around the image. Patrick knew immediately what it was.

"Oliver! They use LSD as their Eucharist." He showed me the LSD paper.

"Wow! They were tripping the entire time and we didn't notice. I knew there was something strange about the look in their eyes. It makes me wonder how much of their spirituality is really psychedelics; you know, a big illusion." I was slightly amused and fascinated by our discovery.

"Well, it doesn't take a psychedelic chemical to believe in things that aren't real, after all isn't that the danger of all religions? Hey, maybe it was just Linda on LSD, and perhaps not all of them were tripping. She was acting a bit freer than the rest of them." Patrick's comment about religion, and Linda, was an understatement.

"Most people would interpret naked group baptism as exceptionally strange, not to mention the costumes. Linda told you it was universal communion and they call themselves *The Holy Order of Light*, and *Son*-rise baptism is their big ritual, so it wouldn't surprise me if ingesting LSD is a part of their ceremony, and perhaps they do perceive it as the Eucharist … which is a very strange perspective, to equate the body of Christ with LSD." My view of our holy encounter had taken a shift.

"Well, Oliver, I suppose you're right. But I'm not sure it makes the reality of their spiritual experiences any less real, in fact, it could make it more real, or at least more heightened."

"You have a good point, Patrick. After all, Aldous Huxley's essay, *The Doors of Perception*, makes the claim that psychedelic drugs, like psilocybin mushrooms, peyote, and LSD can open up the spiritual center of the brain, causing insights into other dimensions of reality, hence opening doors of perception, possibly into the spiritual realm. Maybe they use LSD responsibly as a way of making their minds more spiritually receptive like some American Indian cultures that use the hallucinogen peyote cactus. However, as far as we know, the only drug Jesus used was wine and from what I understand, it was symbolic of sharing the spirit of truth during the Last Supper. He never said anything about communing together by ingesting a substance that alters our state of consciousness. Through communal sharing, Jesus taught that people are able to enhance their awareness of others, self, the world, and the spiritual dimension of reality; chemicals aren't necessary to accomplish that. No doubt that it could be fun, and may lead people to self-discovery, but as a sacred ritual, well, I can only definitively say it isn't my cup of tea."

"As you know Oliver, my mind-altering substance of choice is marijuana. I'm not sure it gives me insights into the nature of reality, but it sure does feel good and it heightens my senses as well as stimulates creative thinking!"

Patrick was a big pot smoker, and he is normally cautious about putting non-organic substances into his athletic body. Discussing the use of chemical substances was not a new topic for us. We explored this issue on many occasions. My perspective was strongly influenced by our friend, Ellen. She had spoken with gurus about the use of psychedelic drugs during her travels to India. Her advice was to not use them. However, she did acknowledge the usefulness of hallucinogens for some people in some cultures and under special circumstances – and we just encountered special circumstances. Besides, wine does alter our state of consciousness, and Jesus, supposedly, even turned water into wine. Also, the Bible says he even changed it into his blood – the reasons for Catholics being blood-sipping devotees – arguably a form of spiritual cannibalism – man, I have some weird thoughts about religion. Although, I do believe that I possess a healthy skepticism, a trait that enables me to look carefully at claims of truth and determine from personal experience what's real or not. I wasn't completely convinced that altering one's consciousness through ingesting substances was inconsistent with Biblical teachings - I even wondered if the *manna from heaven* held mind-altering qualities. Still, I felt ambivalent on the topic, and Patrick was more than a little curious.

"I'm tempted to find out what it's like. How about you Oliver, are you willing to try LSD?" Patrick asked.

"I thought about it quite thoroughly on more than one occasion and I am not willing to take the risk. In the first place, we have no way of knowing exactly what's on those pieces of paper; for all we know it could be poison and that is a gamble not worth taking. It amazes me that people just blindly trust that what people give or sell to them is not going to hurt them. It could be rat poison and we wouldn't know it. I understand the curiosity, but it is not worth the risk. I suggest that you stick with organic substances, like pot, and not man-made chemicals."

Patrick stared at the stamp-sized pieces of paper. All he had to do was place it on his tongue and he would discover exactly why so many young people around the world were experimenting with psychedelics. I looked at Patrick, my eyes expressing concern. I hoped that Patrick trusted me more than our merry band of religious friends and two pieces of paper that dubiously held the promise of enhanced consciousness. Patrick smiled at me and proceeded to tear the LSD into little pieces and scatter them in the wind. White Shepherd went chasing after them, causing me concern that she would actually catch a piece and eat it – fortunately she hadn't. She could have been the first dog to trip on acid, and who knows, maybe it would have changed her DNA and she would have carried gene mutations for the next stage in canine evolution – for a brief moment I wondered if hallucinogens could alter human DNA.

"Good move, Patrick!" We got up and started walking. We were silent for a while. I broke our silent reverie. "I wonder about religions perceiving themselves as being *the one true way to God, or as a way to live life and view reality.* I think it's the social-psychological dynamic that happens whenever people experience something powerful. It's how cultural groups bond, enabling each other to meet the challenges of life by giving them a sense of security and purpose. We saw that in many forms in our neighborhood with the street gang mentality – it has striking similarities, although a group of people dedicated to loving all humankind with a message of hope and love will likely have better outcomes than being a part of a street gang. Unless they start brandishing swords in the name of their god, or getting into politics to legislate morality."

"If they approach the wrong people and start taking off their clothes and handing out LSD, they're bound to stir up trouble, and then again, it could be a lot of fun." Patrick responded.

"Well Patrick, I hope they are highly selective about who they choose to share their sacred rituals with. I think they sensed our goodness as people before inviting us to witness their ceremony. Michael is very protective of his flock and even though he may be completely encapsulated in the intensity of his religious convictions, he comes across as having a very good heart. Can we accurately judge whether or not he has discovered spiritual truths?"

"Our guesses regarding the validity of spiritual truth are no more or less valid than any person dabbling in the realm of things unseen. Yeah Oliver, we're the kind of people not to take advantage of others, although I felt the power of primal physical energy more than the power of the spirit. Other folks may not be able to resist the pleasures rising from the human drive to procreate. And we do have the right to discern if what they believe contains truth or not – as you said, each of us needs to develop our own way of seeing the world – I think you said that."

"In other words you were horny. If I wasn't here to dissuade you, you might be merrily prancing off with them like a hound dog in heat being lead by your little head, high on LSD," I said, humorously.

"Well, yeah, Einstein. I suppose you saved me from a venture into hedonism disguised as religious fervor. I think their faith is genuine, regardless of their odd hallucinogenic and sexually suggestive ritual, which, in my opinion, has a very unique appeal. What do you think will happen to them?" Patrick asked. Before I could respond, he answered his own query, "My prediction is that their religious group will serve them well for a spell and then they will disband, each going off on their own path. I surmise that it is rare that groups like that build into an enduring movement. I think that they are a surrogate family for each other and once this need is met to the fullest extent possible within their social structure, their group will disband. We experienced this phenomenon within our own peer group, the Ghetto Flowers, as they went through a similar process."

"You never know, Patrick, most established religions of today began as small movements, the first one taking place over two-thousand years ago, and that is only the Christians. There are a multitude of world religions with completely different historical cultures and prophets that have endured for thousands of years. Gee, Patrick, there was a young man who had a group of followers back in the fifth century and he created one of the most dynamic and famous religious movements within the Catholic Church."

"Who?"

"Your namesake, Saint Patrick of Ireland. He is the patron saint of leprechauns. In fact, I think I see a halo around your head and a leprechaun dancing on your shoulder. Who knows, maybe there is a pot of gold – or some golden pot at the end of a future rainbow." I laughed as I tussled his mane of golden curly hair.

"Oliver, it sounds like you're high on LSD. Saint Patrick O'Malley and Oliver James the Prophet - hey, maybe we should start our own cult of bare naked sunrise dipping beauties and see how long we can make it last," he said laughing. "We could live on a paradise island and everyone would be free to believe whatever their personal experiences lead them to – that would be a far out spiritual trip! I could make marijuana a sacred ritualistic herb that promises enhanced consciousness ... and clothes would be optional."

"Patrick, you have to be the most sensually-spiritually oriented person I know. I hope that tendency never bites you in the derrière."

"And you're not? Hey, at least we're not held captive by our Catholic upbringing with all those do's and don'ts of the evil flesh - *The Holy Order of the Celibates* and their subsequent sexual hang-ups. Fortunately, for me, the Catholic indoctrination had no deleterious influence on my sexual development."

"Amen to that, Patrick. It didn't hurt my sexuality any either, although I do not agree with the Church requiring their strongest devotees to denounce the most beautiful gift of all – and the most powerful drive in all of nature. Yet, celibacy is a religious practice of many religious cultural traditions, not just Catholicism. Supposedly, the intention is to channel all physical desires into a spiritual discipline and become closer to God. It appears to work for a lot of people, otherwise there wouldn't be so many priests and nuns and Buddhist monks, forsaking the most beautiful gift of all."

"What's that?" Patrick asked.

"What's what?"

"The most beautiful gift?"

"Creating life, Patrick, weren't you listening?"

"Ah. Sex! You're right about that. When I am making love with Chrissie, it feels like a powerful spiritual experience for me. I feel not only love for her - I also feel love for all of life. You know, that universal oneness that you and I have talked about. I think intimacy with others enhances spiritual development. Hey, maybe starting a religion that has a sexual-communion ritual is not such a bad idea after all. It even fits with the theory of evolution as well as Biblical teachings, you know, *net reproductive capacity* of the species, and *be fruitful and multiply* – they coincide - we could be on to something here!" Patrick wasn't joking.

"Universal, ha, that's a truism that holds up to scientific scrutiny. More like orgasmic love – something most human beings experience. Come to think of it, most animals do too, so I suppose that can be regarded as universal. And there you go again." I replied.

"Go again, what?"

"Never mind, Your Horniness!" We busted out laughing again, "Do you plan on being a father someday, Patrick?"

"Definitely! What about you Oliver?"

"There are a lot of hurting children in the world. I was, and to some extent still am, one of them, and I have seen too much suffering. I don't think I want to bring more children into our world." There was a hint of sadness in my voice.

"I understand, and part of me feels that way too. The world has always been insane and cruel. Then again, if our parents felt that way we wouldn't be here and I am deeply grateful for their courage. I think I'll let nature take its course." Patrick made an excellent point. "It sure does take a lot of courage to live in this world, and good ganja," he said, grinning, as he lit up another joint.

"That it does, and a little self-constraint now and then." I replied.

"You're talking about my interest in the naked baptismal angels, aren't you?" Patrick smiled as he let out a stream of smoke through his nose.

I nudged him on the shoulder and glint of light appeared in his eyes. I asked, "What got into you anyway? I never heard you speak in such an eloquent religious tone."

"I'm not completely sure. Perhaps reading that book, *Ocean of Love,* had a strong influence on me, and the vibes from the hippie Jesus Freaks were definitely an influence."

We reached the end of the peninsula and sat down on the sand. White Shepherd sat by my side. Patrick took out yet another joint from his shirt pocket and lit it up.

"Hey man, you sure are smoking a lot of dope this morning." I said.

"Where there is dope there is hope!"

"How come you didn't offer to smoke with the hippie Jesus Freaks?" I asked.

"If I had known LSD was their sacrament, I would have. Like you, I was worried I'd offend their religious sensibilities."

"Man, maybe we were wrong about that."

"Maybe, Oliver – no telling how they judge marijuana – for all we know they could consider it the devil's weed."

"It's possible. Religions can be strange like that."

"No one knows that better than Catholics, I suppose." Patrick handed the joint to me. To his surprise I accepted – a rarity for me.

"You know, Oliver, I feel at home living by the ocean. It's like looking out on infinity – that endless open space. I'd love to live by the sea, be a fisherman and live like the Native Americans did. Create our own shelter and stuff – live without money.

"Sounds good to me. Winters would be a problem, though."

"Not on a tropical island." Patrick's face now held a perpetual grin. The marijuana was shrouding his brain.

"Now that would be really far out. I often fantasize about living on an island. Some of my favorite books are Swiss Family Robinson, and Robinson Crusoe." I love the romantic ideal of living on a beautiful island.

"Yeah Oliver, I am a big Errol Flynn fan – all those pirate movies. Did you ever see the one about the English sailors who take over the ship and stay on an island, mating with all of those beautiful island women?"

"That's a great movie. Errol Flynn doesn't play in that one, though – *Mutiny on the Bounty* with Marlon Brando. Oh, and the original had Clark Gable. I heard it's a true story."

"Far out! I wonder if they had pot on that island," mused Patrick as he took another toke on his joint, and then passed it to me.

I stretched out my body, took off my shirt, rolled it into a ball and placed it under my head, took a long draw on the joint and drifted off into a dreamy reverie. I imagined being on a paradise island, living with a group of far out people from many cultures, entertaining all kinds of philosophical thinking, and sharing the beauty and goodness of life – naked babes included!

HITCHHIKING

South Philadelphia was not an exciting place to be after spending an extended summer vacation at the seashore. Patrick had by-passed the discomfort of transitioning back into the neighborhood by traveling to Canada. He had developed a friendship with a Canadian dude who was a member of the Wildwood lifeguard squad, so he decided to pay him a visit. It was a rainy October evening and I was sitting in my bedroom staring into the pages of Organic Chemistry, the textbook for one of the four science courses that weren't happening. The teachers at the Community College of Philadelphia went on strike seeking a fair contract, and there was no end in sight. I had changed my major from Mental Health to Chemistry because I needed a break, big time, from the social and psychological analysis of my life that had consumed so much of my energy during my first year of college. I decided to get a jumpstart on reading the textbooks before the courses actually began. Boredom was consuming me and I was in dire need of something that would shift me out of this oppressive mood when the phone rang.

"Yo?"

"Hey, Oliver, it's Patrick O'Malley."

"Whoa, Patrick, far out man, when did you get home?"

"A few hours ago, how the hell are you?"

"Bored. The college is on strike so I'm just sitting around wasting time."

"Ah man, sorry you're so down. Too bad we got kicked out of our Wildwood apartment. It would have been great to spend all of September and October there," Patrick responded.

"So, how was your trip to Canada?" I asked.

"Fun! I love hitchhiking. I met some really cool people and visited some far out places. I even visited a commune on my way back into the U.S. It's called Earth People's Park. It has 600 acres situated in the Green Mountains of Vermont with the Canadian and U. S. border running along its northern boundary. John Sebastian, Joan Biaz, the Grateful Dead and other rock and folk musicians under the organization of Wavy Gravy, the Hog Farm hippie of hippies, raised money to buy the land. I think it might have come from the cash they got from playing at Woodstock. The far out thing is that the deed states that the people of planet Earth own the land so anyone who wants to live there has the right to build a home. It would take a Martian or some other alien to bring it back into the capitalist monopoly game - free land for free people. Far out, eh?"

"Yeah, if I ever need to run and hide, that sounds like the place to go, but I'd prefer an island paradise. It certainly would have been an option if I needed to disappear into Canada as a last resort if my military draft deferment didn't go through," I replied. During this past year I went to battle with the U.S. military establishment to get conscientious objector status. They didn't buy it so I got what was called a Four-F status instead, a quadruple fuck-up – lucky for me, but not so lucky for thousands of other young people. A therapist friend wrote an official letter for me stating that I *was not mentally equipped to deal with the military aspect of adult life... that it would be burdensome to others as well as to myself.* As far as I was concerned a person had to be crazy to be mentally equipped to kill – that was my peacenik view of human nature – you had to be in a state of madness to kill people.

"I was told that that was the primary reason for setting up the commune, to enable draft dodgers a way into Canada without having to deal with the Customs Officers, sort of like a modern day Underground Railroad for American youth. In fact, I heard that the FBI was investigating the community and that they tried sending in an undercover agent, but he was very obvious and they ran him off the land. I met this hippie bro while I was there who gave me a ride all the way to Philly and he's spending the night at my house before moving on. You wanna come over and meet him?"

"Far out. I'll be right over."

Patrick O'Malley lived around the corner, so within minutes I was knocking on his door.

"Hey bro, come on in, it's great to see ya. Come down stairs and meet Randy."

During the several weeks since I last saw Patrick, his wavy, curly golden brown hair had grown slightly, flowing over his shoulders and resting upon his muscular chest. There was a look of excitement in his iridescent greenish-blue eyes. He had on his sleeveless Wildwood lifeguard shirt and cut-off jeans, revealing his tanned muscular athletic physique.

Patrick's basement served as a party room for our group of peers. His mother knew he smoked marijuana and she preferred he do it in the house and not in the neighborhood where he could get arrested. She was a very far out mom, tolerant of teen exploratory behavior – which truly was amazing since she was a devout Catholic. She and Patrick had excellent communication and Patrick was able to convince her that pot wasn't dangerous, except that it was against the law, hence the reason for his mom allowing him to smoke in her basement. It was safer than smoking somewhere in the neighborhood where police walked the beat.

"Randy, this is my friend, Oliver."

"Hey bro, pull up a piece of rug, pleased to meet you." Randy had a soothing, friendly voice. He had very long blond hair, a beard and moustache, a long slender nose supporting John Lennon glasses that enlarged his radiant blue eyes. His face brightened with a big smile as he shook my hand. I sat directly across from him. Sitting on the floor between us was a hand-carved wooden *bong* and next to it was a pile of marijuana. As Randy took a pinch of the marijuana and placed it in the bowl of the *bong*, he said in a reverent tone, "This is Lambs Bread, the most potent ganja grown on the island of Jamaica. No matter how high you feel, one toke of this and your mind is taken to another level."

Marijuana was not an indulgence that suited my brain chemistry, especially since I had gone through an intense transformation when I was sick with hepatitis at the beginning of my senior year of high school, keeping my mind steady and in balance was more important than taking it to another chemically induced level. The truth was, marijuana usually made me feel paranoid, the only exception was getting stoned on the beach. The witnessing of so many lives of young people in my neighborhood, close friends cut down, killed, like weeds in their prime, had taught me the horrors of drug abuse. Although, I did develop an understanding of therapeutic medication for the purpose of healing the heart and mind. I had learned from my college courses that leaders in the mental health community were exploring psychotherapeutic medications that influence brain chemistry to both control and explore the mind and it was having some powerful results. It was expected that using drugs that affect the chemicals in the brain would be a big breakthrough for treating mental illness. A drug called Thorazine was used to treat the mental disease schizophrenia, a severe paranoia mind trip for sure.

There was hope that new drugs could be found to cure the many diseases that plagued the mind. I had worked with schizophrenics, manic-depressives, and all types of personality disorders during my mental health practicum experience in college last year. One of the cultural anthropology courses I took focused on the topic of rites-of-passage among the Southwest Native American People, the Navajo, who used a drug called peyote to induce psychoactive states in the mind that took the young adult on what they called a Vision Quest, which was a journey through the inner mindscape into a dimension of thought that claimed to enhance self-awareness and universal understanding, as well as reveal insights into one's own fate or destiny - a window into the true self.

"Oliver, are you sure you don't want a hit of this? This is really good shit, man!" Patrick was always trying to get me stoned, and occasionally he was successful, but only when we were on the beach at the Jersey shore. Being stoned in closed-in places only added to that claustrophobic paranoia that oftentimes overwhelmed me.

"Man, every time I smoke Lamb's Bread I am transported back to the lovely island of Jamaica. I can hear the lilt of the beautiful voices speaking in my head. Oh, man, I long to be back in Negril!" Randy sounded wistful and his eyes had a faraway glassy look. He continued his reminiscing, "Negril is a lot like Alice in Wonderland. You know, like the Jefferson Airplane song, White Rabbit, particularly the line that goes something like this." Randy broke out in song, *"And you just had some kind of mushroom and your mind is moving along ... remember what the door mouse said, feed your head, feed your head.* There are psilocybin mushrooms growing wherever there is donkey dung, and man, there's a lot of that around. Tripping in paradise is a far out trip, man!"

Randy's words reminded me once again of the essay, *Doors of Perception,* by Aldous Huxley. It was required reading for a college course on mental health. For the same course, I read an article that speculated on the possibility of the U.S. government conducting experiments on mind enhancing drugs for their military and espionage capabilities. I wondered if drugs were being used to control people's minds, the ultimate weapon, which led me to the conclusion that I wanted no chemical influences on my brain whatsoever! It was fascinating that on one end of the cultural spectrum there were those who believed that mind-altering chemicals could be used to free the mind, and on the other end, there were those who wanted to use them as a way to manipulate, control, imprison, and even kill people more effectively.

I was of the opinion that what we learn about chemicals and the human mind and body should be used to heal sickness and enhance the quality of our lives, like vaccines that protect us from disease, antibiotics that kill harmful bacteria, and psychoactive drugs that give the mentally ill relief from debilitating symptoms. We were definitely living in an era of a psycho-bio-pharmaceutical revolution. This was a revolution that young people around the globe had seized upon, and in a sense, they were unknowingly self-administering generational guinea pigs.

Randy spoke, taking my mind away from my train of thought. "One of many really far out things for me living in Jamaica was I felt like I had found my soul. The beauty of the place, along with the lovely people, and copious amounts of ganja and magic mushrooms, had put me in touch with my true self."

Randy's words got me thinking about the concept of the true self. I had personal experience with this concept, although without the influence of chemicals in the brain. I had learned to *mind surf* - or thought exploration - right into what I understood to be the heart of creation. Catholic priests claimed that *receiving the Body and Blood of Jesus Christ* was the actual transformation of bread and wine into a mystical-magical substance believed to be the actual body and blood of God's Son, and that it created an intimate experience with Christ's Spirit. Some of my friends claimed that this was no different than ingesting other substances that caused the mind to become more receptive to their spiritual nature. Lots of people used drugs for recreation, and they claimed to be responsible users, which was not too different from drinking a six-pack of beer on occasion. Then again, just because alcohol was legal didn't mean it was safe. Almost every adult male in my family was an alcoholic, mainly because it was part of their culture to drink massive quantities of alcohol, and that went for smoking cigarettes as well. There were legal drugs that could hurt and kill you and ones that could heal you. And there were illegal drugs that could harm and kill, and they could be used responsibly for healing and recreation as well. From what I witnessed, far too many people were being injured by legal and illegal drugs, so I decided to play it safe and not put anything in my body that did not belong there, with the exception of anti-biotic medicine when I got a sore throat from bacteria, and an occasional toke of marijuana, other than that, I was not willing to risk being poisoned. However, I was a little tempted to take LSD with those Jesus Freak babes Patrick and I met on the beach back in September.

"Come on Oliver, give it a try!" Randy insisted.

"No thanks Randy, it tends to make me feel nervous and sometimes a bit paranoid." I responded.

"That's far out. You don't have to partake the Lamb's Bread, Oliver. If you spent some time in Jamaica, the Rastas would teach you how to handle being high. They're professional users." I was relieved that Randy decided to back off from getting me to smoke ganja.

"What are Rastas?" Patrick asked.

"They're members of a religious group called Rastafarians. It is based on King Haile Selassie of Ethiopia. They consider him to be a prophet of liberation, even the incarnation of King Solomon. The religion is complex. It is primarily a Jamaican cult that teaches the eventual redemption of blacks and their return to Africa. They use marijuana ritualistically and some sects forbid the cutting of hair. Most, if not all of them, are vegetarians, and politically they are extremely radical." I continued to be in awe of Randy's knowledge and worldly experience.

"Wow, a religion that uses marijuana as a sacred ritual! No wonder this pot you have is called Lambs Bread. It is sort of like partaking of communion every time you smoke," added Patrick.

"Yeah! A Rastaman once told me that getting high freed the mind from the chains of Babylon and prevented other men from controlling your thoughts, and that's why politicians want to keep it illegal." Randy possessed a great deal of knowledge and the more he spoke the more fascinated I became by his adventures. He continued, "Jamaica is a beautiful country with beaches, cliffs, mountains, and lovely people. If you're looking for adventure, that's the place to go."

"I'm going to Florida to see my girlfriend, Chrissie," said Patrick excitedly, "she just started college at the University of Miami. Maybe I'll catch a plane to Jamaica and take her with me. Is it expensive?" he asked.

"Not if you know where to go. The country is poor and there are lots of small villages where you can find cheap places to stay, sometimes, if Jamaicans like you, they'll barter with you so you can camp on their land. There is food everywhere and because the climate is tropical, shelter from sun and rain are all you need. If you have a good tent, you can find a Jamaican to let you set up camp on their beach or cliff-front property for free or at the most, less than a dollar a day." Randy really knows his stuff!

"That's it, I'm going to Jamaica after I visit Chrissie," Patrick said.

"When are you leaving?" I asked.

"Tomorrow!"

"Wow, you are serious. Can you wait until Saturday to give me time to get things in order and to raise some cash, and then I'll go with you. How much money will we need?" I too was feeling very excited and full of adventure. Randy was quick to answer my question.

"Well, taking a plane from Miami is the cheapest and they are always running deals. October is off-season so airlines want to fill their seats. If you're lucky you can get a round trip ticket for less than $100 and if you bring a tent you won't need to rent a room, but the more money you have, the better off you'll be." Randy advised.

"We'll hitchhike to Florida, and maybe Chrissie isn't into school and she'll come too." Patrick was being unrealistic about Chrissie.

"We could drive the VW magic bus. It will give us a place to sleep and freedom to explore," I suggested.

"I prefer hitchhiking. It's cheaper. We won't have to buy gas and worry about your magic bus breaking down. Plus, hitchhiking is really cool, there's a sense of freedom that goes with not being tied down to a car, you meet all kinds of interesting characters, and you never know what's coming next. It's very adventurous. Besides, we don't know how long we're going to be in Jamaica and you'd have to leave the magic bus in Florida. I say we go without it." All of our friends referred to my VW van as the magic bus, and it had a reputation for breaking down at the most inconvenient times.

"Okay. I've never hitchhiked. It'll be a new experience. The magic bus does have a lot of miles on it and if it does breakdown, it could soak up all my money, which isn't much. Have you talked with Chrissie since the summer ended?" I asked.

"No. She apparently doesn't have a phone hooked up yet, but I have her address. I'll surprise her."

"Patrick, she isn't going to leave college so don't get your hopes up too high," I warned.

"Yeah, I guess you're right. It'll be great to spend some time in Miami with her on our way to Jamaica and on our way back to the U.S. I can wait until Saturday. I'll ask my dad to drop us off on interstate 95. Don't forget to bring your flute and I'll pack my guitar."

Randy's eyes twinkled as he listened to the excitement in our voices. He offered more advice. "The thing to remember about Jamaica is that you need to know how to say no – politely and persistently – because some Jamaicans are shrewd hustlers and try to talk the money right out of your pockets, and never engage in an argument or respond with violence in any form, and never, I mean absolutely never interfere with a Jamaican's business practices. Go to the western most tip of the island to a fishing village called Negril. Ask for Millie and Charley Constance and when you find them, tell them you are friends of mine and they might let you set up camp on their cliff-front property. Negril is becoming known throughout Europe as one of the best out-of-the-way slices of heaven on earth, albeit in a whisper that will inevitably become a shout, however, it is still relatively unknown. You won't need much money there because they mostly barter and there is very little cash flow so a little money goes a long way. Negril is a fishing village and the people catch and grow their food. They mostly live in small shanties with running water but no electricity. Most Jamaicans in Negril build their homes on the side of the road that is across from the cliffs and beach to protect them from hurricanes. So, the beach and cliffs are undeveloped. The tropical climate makes it so people don't need many clothes, but if you bring extra clothes you can use them for bartering. They love blue jeans, but cash is the best commodity."

Again, Randy's knowledge amazed me and he spoke with a tone of self-assurance. And, he was a real hippie so Patrick believed he could be trusted. The way he spoke of Jamaica made it sound like the island of the beautiful Sirens in Homer's Odyssey.

The next day I took city transportation to the Community College and inquired as to when the strike would end. The administrator told me that the autumn semester was lost and that the school wouldn't open until January. This news was sweet music to my ears. I was already given scholarship money for the semester and I had purchased the textbooks for my courses, so I returned the books for a full refund, which, along with some of the scholarship money, gave me $375.00, which I believed would be sufficient funds for an island adventure. When I boarded the bus to return home, I discovered that Sandy, my Italian-Irish childhood sweetheart, was also on board. Sandy was my first and only lover, whose long auburn hair, chocolate eyes, absolutely beautiful petite body, loving personality and highly intelligent mind had convinced me that one day she would become my wife.

"Sandy, you'll never guess where I'm going."

"Home?"

"Well, yeah, but I mean for a couple of weeks or maybe even longer."

"Back to Wildwood?"

"Good guess, but something far more exotic. I'll give you a hint: Patrick returned from Canada yesterday and he is missing Chrissie."

"Florida! That's totally awesome. When are you going? How are you going?"

"Saturday. But Florida is just one of the places we're visiting. Think tropical."

"Florida is tropical."

"Technically, it's sub-tropical. Think paradise."

"You're going to an island, aren't you?"

"Yes! And not just any island, we are going to Jamaica!"

"Oh, now I get it. Marijuana, adventure, and Chrissie, the three great loves of Patrick O'Malley. I'll add one more love, his best friend – you."

"Are you jealous?"

"Only that I'm not going with you. Making love with you on a Jamaican beach under the stars would be absolute heaven," she said dreamily, "and I'd like to visit my sister in her new home."

"Come with me. You always told me that you wanted to be more spontaneous. This is your opportunity." I made this plea to Sandy hoping that her sense of adventure and romantic nature would prove stronger than her loyalty to family expectations.

"Yeah right. Drop out of college and break the hearts of my parents. I don't think so. This is an adventure you're gonna have without your one true love, just make sure you come home, and don't go fooling around with a Jamaican goddess." Sandy warned.

"There is no other goddess before you, my one and only human-deity, Sandy." I kissed her.

Telling my parents was a little awkward. They never traveled any farther than the Jersey seashore and they were fearful that I would get hurt. I knew that my mother would worry about me obsessively while I was gone. It was her nature to worry about her son as she had throughout my life, and I certainly didn't expect this to be any different. As for my father, he just shook his head, offering no opinion or position. When I decided to not take the management position that was offered by my Jewish friends and enrolled in college instead, my mother was fearful that I was giving up a steady job for some far-reaching dream. She was truly imprisoned by the fear-chains of the poverty mentality.

I was concerned for the welfare of my mother. She had become increasingly melancholic and fragile ever since I made my emotional break from the unhealthy family relationship dynamics that at one time had stifled my personal growth. She never recovered from the family therapeutic process I had put them through, and that fiery determination to protect her children had all but disappeared. There was something vitally missing in my mother. I sensed it, and it worried me.

"Mom, you don't have to worry about me. I know how to take good care of myself. Surely I have proven that over and over again. You need to be more concerned with your own health. I guess it is a mother's nature to worry but not to the point where it's harmful, especially when there is no danger."

"No danger? If you think hitchhiking on the highway, sleeping God knows where, and living on an island in the middle of the ocean is nothing to worry about, then you need your head examined!" My mother was partially right. I wasn't thinking about the possible hazards. After all, the world outside of South Philly seemed very tame in comparison to our racially strife-torn neighborhood.

"Mom, you have seen me survive through very difficult times and you have to admit, I've come a long way. I am a healthy young man and I'm ready to experience the world. I promise I will take good care of myself and I won't do anything stupid."

"A young man? You hardly have hair on your chin. The only time I feel you are safe is when you are here in your home, and this is where you belong." She shot back with an intense look in her eyes.

"Mom, do you really expect me to spend the rest of my life in this house, or even on this street in this neighborhood?"

"Yes! What the hell's wrong with it? You have a girlfriend and they like you at the textile mill. You can work there until school opens again, you don't have to go gallivanting around the world." The city block that we lived on was home to five living generations of our extended family, from my great grandmother to my two-year-old cousin. It was frowned upon for anyone to leave the neighborhood or even the city block, let alone the country.

"Mom, you know I'm going and I prefer to have your blessing."

"Never!" she yelled, with all the force she could muster.

I went upstairs to my bedroom and packed my clothes into my backpack, keeping in mind what Randy told me about Jamaicans loving blue jeans, so I threw in a couple pairs that no longer fit. I went through my schoolbooks and packed a few composition notebooks to keep my journal writing up to date. Patrick told me his father had an army tent, two sleeping bags with mosquito netting, and camping utensils that we could borrow. I focused on the bare essentials, figuring that traveling light was the smart thing to do. I looked around the room to see if I was forgetting anything and spotted the flute that Ellen, my friend and mentor from Stone Harbor, had given me. I quickly placed it in its case and strapped it to the top of my pack. There was no way that I was going to an island without my instrument.

When I finished packing, I sat on the edge of my bed and thought about my mother. She had become even more fragile, and this was largely due, I assumed, to the changes I had gone through and the affect it had on our relationship. She was going through a serious life crisis. The unhealthy relationship she had with my father was wearing heavily on her, and the struggles my brother, Billy, had with learning and developmental disabilities throughout his childhood had contributed to the depletion of her strength. And now I was leaving home. I was her pride and joy, and to my dismay, her main purpose in life. It was a fact that was not healthy for either one of us. If she had things her way I would remain her little boy for the rest of my life. It was time for me to leave the world of my childhood, for I had grown beyond its limitations. I knew that my leaving home would be one of the greatest challenges my mother had ever faced and it could make her or break her. This was a strange and unfair burden placed upon my shoulders, as the decision to leave would force my mother to confront the reality of her life. She had used me as a shield to protect herself from doing so, and now the time had arrived. These thoughts frightened me for I was well aware of the possibility that my mother would become increasingly unhealthy. Yet, I had to go. It was time to move on with my life beyond the redbrick human zoo of my childhood.

Saturday morning arrived and I was about to leave the house. I approached my mother to say goodbye.

"Mom. I'm leaving now." My voice was quivering ever so slightly.

"Take this, maybe it will keep you safe. And you make sure you come back home to me, and soon."

She gave me a set of wooden rosary beads that had once belonged to my Aunt Maria who was a nun and my father's sister. She insisted that I wear them for protection. It was a strange idea coming from her since she abhorred most things Catholic and was distrustful of any religion, although I knew she was deeply spiritual. She had faith in goodness. I gracefully accepted them as I looked into my mother's misty emerald eyes. I lightly brushed the tears on her cheeks with my lips as I kissed her goodbye.

"I love you Oliver, and I'll always worry about you. It's a mother's obligation!"

"Thanks Mom. I'll write to you often and I'll be back before school starts in January. I love you." As we hugged, the strength of our love for each other moved through us, and I was touched by the beauty and power of the mother-child bond. We were deeply connected by the most universal of all relationships. A line from a Beatles' song ran through my head and I changed the pronoun to fit my circumstance, *...he's leaving home after living alone for so many years...* The sentiment of the song was appropriate, even though I lived in a household where my mother loved me, I felt like a stranger in my own home. I had an underlying feeling that somehow I was different and didn't quite belong. It was a disturbing feeling that carried with it a burden of guilt as well as a degree of estrangement, and a profound loneliness.

Patrick's father drove us to the entrance ramp of interstate 95 – we were on our way – and our lives quite possibly would never be the same. We were truly leaving behind all that was familiar.

"Patrick, so what's the trick to hitchhiking?"

"No trick. Just stick out your thumb and hope for a good ride."

"What do you consider a good ride?"

"A car with lots of room. Preferably, a luxury car or maybe even a camping van, especially one with young people that like to party. An eight-track tape player makes the ride considerably more pleasurable. The most important thing, though, is a ride that takes us a long way toward where we're going – Miami or bust!" We walked up the entrance ramp, stood on the shoulder of the road, placed our packs on the side and stuck out our thumbs. After fifteen minutes, a car pulled over, it had Virginia license plates. A young man dressed in a Navy uniform stepped out of the car and opened the trunk as we ran toward him weighted down by our gear. I was feeling excited and apprehensive at the same time. This was my first hitchhiking experience, which was exciting, but the military uniform made me feel uneasy.

"Hey, Patrick, this guys in the military. Do you think it's a good idea to take this ride?" I nervously asked while we were running toward the car.

"No problem. Remember, my brother was in the Army and so was my father. I trust military men." Patrick was a boy scout. His father served during WWII, and his brother was a Green Beret and a Vietnam War hero. He had good reason to trust military men. As for me, I had to deal with the draft and almost found myself headed for a tropical jungle quite different from Jamaica. The military made me very nervous. Since Patrick's brother died in Vietnam, he had an automatic draft deferment. My cousin Butch had died in Vietnam and I went through the arduous process of making my case for being conscientiously opposed to the war when the military tried drafting me. I was scared and it was a fight for my life, and fortunately I won.

I became fearful of the government's power to take control of my life, and for taking the lives of people I loved. Many young guys that I knew throughout my childhood were killed in that horrible war, and many were still there fighting. The United States government had given me some very powerful reasons to distrust them. I had become a political radical all because I didn't want people to kill each other, for any reason.

We jumped in the back seat. The young man was driving and the woman sitting next to him, we soon discovered, was his wife. They were newlyweds. Patrick had a lot to talk about with the Navy man, who was familiar with the Green Beret and was well versed in the heroic acts of this elite fighting force. The man told Patrick that he had received orders to go to Vietnam. Patrick told him about his brother's death and how it caused him to look closely at the reasons for the war, and that it had made him angry with the U.S. government. The Navy man listened intently and sympathetically to Patrick, and his wife was brought to tears and she expressed her fear that she would never see her husband again. It was a very touching exchange. The couple welcomed us to spend the night at their apartment in Norfolk, Virginia and the next day they dropped us off at the nearest highway entrance ramp.

We received several short rides throughout the next two days and all of them were uneventful. We had rides from traveling salesmen as well as some young people who were friendly, and some were curious to know where we were coming from and where we were going. Patrick loved to talk, so he entertained the drivers while I slept, wrote in my journal, or stared out the window, occasionally adding a comment to the conversation.

On the second night of our journey we didn't have a place to sleep, so we rolled out our sleeping bags on a grassy knoll on the side of the highway. We truly were living like vagabonds. The people who gave us rides were very generous and without exception insisted on buying us food so we rarely needed to spend money. They assumed we were very poor since we were hitchhiking. A growing sense of freedom was replacing my initial underlying feeling of general insecurity about leaving behind the familiar and venturing off into the great unknown. We never knew what would happen next, and that's what made it so adventurous. When we crossed the Florida State line, we were exuberant, naively thinking that we were close to our destination. The last ride had dropped us off on a country road because Interstate 95 was not completed on the section around the city of Jacksonville. So, we took an alternate route, and then without explanation, the man told us to get out of his car. We found ourselves standing on a country road lined with orange groves on both sides. We rolled out our sleeping bags and quickly went to sleep.

Patrick woke me the next morning with the sound of laughter. I had multiple little red bumps all over my face caused by small insects that apparently bred in orange groves. Our sleeping bags were equipped with mosquito netting, but I neglected to use it. The trees were filled with ripe oranges and we helped ourselves to a Florida breakfast. There was very little traffic on this road, one car every 10 minutes or so, and most of them were pickup trucks and some of them were equipped with rifles setting on racks in the back windows. As we stood there watching a truck approach, I noticed that it was swerving back and forth across the double yellow lines and as he got closer he veered his wheels onto the very narrow shoulder and started speeding up, heading right for us. Without speaking, we kicked our gear to the side and jumped into the neighboring ditch. The truck sped off, stopped, and then made a U-turn. As he rode past us from the other side of the road, he fired two shots from his rifle into the air and yelled: "Get a hair cut you filthy sissy hippies." Then, he sped off around the curve. We were scared, to say the least. There was another car driving a safe distance behind him and the driver had witnessed what had taken place. He stopped his car and said, " Quick, get in before he returns."

Without hesitation we got in the car. "There are some very crazy locals around here and you two make easy target practice. That guy will be back and he'll probably have a few of his drinking buddies with him. What are you folks doing hitchhiking on a back country road like this?"

"We were dropped off here by our ride late last night. We're trying to get to 95 headed south for Miami." I replied.

"We'll you sure are lucky I just happened along. Hey, here he comes and he's moving fast. Get your heads down while he passes."

As the truck whizzed passed, we could hear him hooting and hollering. We really were fortunate to have this guy rescue us.

"I'll take you to 95 and drive you along it for a few miles to get you safely out of range of these locals. They sometimes race each other on 95, so it's best if I take you several exits down the interstate." I couldn't thank this guy enough. He appeared to be in his late twenties and his hair was shoulder length. He wore a

Grateful Dead tee shirt. I surmised that he was one of us, whatever that meant.

"Thanks for the rescue and the ride." I said as he dropped us off on 95.

"Glad to save a few lives. By the way, have you guys ever been to Disney World?"

"I went to Disney Land in California when my family went out there to receive my brother's coffin. It was awesome," replied Patrick.

"You guys will have to pass that area of Florida so you might consider giving it a visit."

"Thanks, we'll give it some thought, and thanks again for the help," I said, as he sped off down the road.

"Let's do it Oliver. Disney Land was great and it'll be fun. What do you think?" Patrick asked.

"Sure. After spending all those years on Saturday mornings on your sofa watching Mickey Mouse, Goofy, Donald Duck and company while eating Breyers ice cream for breakfast, it's only fitting that we pay those characters a visit. Besides, we're in no hurry."

We stood in the hot sun on the side of the highway for two hours without a ride. Then a police car pulled up with his lights flashing. On the side of his car was written the word *Sheriff.* The sheriff stepped out of the car. He was huge: a few inches over six feet tall and well over 250 pounds, a big fat belly, a red bulbous nose and thin tight lips. The cheeks of his face drooped down like a hound dog's ears and his mouth was crowded with crooked yellow smoke-stained teeth. The man was ugly and scary. He wore high-top leather boots, a police uniform including a gun holster, a sheriff's hat, a shiny badge, and sunglasses. He swaggered toward us with one hand resting on the handle of his gun and the other lightly touching the brim of his hat.

"You girls are breaking the law standing on this here highway. I could take ya'll in for trespassing." He spat out a wade of chewing tobacco and wiped his mouth as he strode toward us.

"We'rrrrre ... tryin' to get to Miami." I nervously stammered.

"Yankees! I hear it in that big city accent. Can't you girls afford bus tickets?"

"Yes, but we're on an adventure and we wanna experience America like..."

"Like Gypsies! Ya'll freaky hippies are polluting our highways with your hobo life style: long hair, dirty clothes and you probably have never known an honest day's work. What if I give you girls some real red-blooded true blue white all American experience of hard work? Ya'll make a pretty sight busting rocks on a road gang. What do you say sweethearts, want a little adventure in Southern hospitality?"

"Please sir, we're not doing anyone harm. We're just a couple of city men with a little money that we worked hard to save and the college my friend goes to is on strike so we're taking a vacation to see our friend in Miami." Patrick spoke too fast for the Sheriff to catch everything he said.

"Damn boy, speak English and slow down. Ya'll ain't no men neither. Ya'll just boys lookin' like girls with greasy long hair. I don't even see stubble on your faces. Ya'll have stumbled into my backyard and that's trespassing! That's a criminal offense."

"I don't mean any disrespect sir but this is a free country. It's what makes it great. We have the right to travel. Highways are public property, so we're not trespassing." I said rather sternly.

"Well smarty pants college boy. There's what your school books tell ya'll, and then there's reality, and the reality is this is my county and ya'll are vagrants with no place to live and vagrancy is trespassing, and that's the law."

"It's not against the law to hitchhike, my father checked into it before we left Philadelphia." Patrick was starting to feel feisty and I was feeling worried that he might be forgetting that you don't argue with a man who has a gun and the power to justify using it no matter what our supposed rights are – he is The Man.

"Standing on the edge of high-speed traffic is a dangerous thing, girls, especially if some cars come along filled with characters out to have a little fun with peace-nicks. It's my duty to protect folks no matter what I think of them." As he spoke his eyes looked over the stickers pasted all over Patrick's guitar case: *No Nukes, Peace,* and *Philadelphia Folk Festival.* "Ya'll got anything illegal in that there protest case or ya'll just slingin' a guitar?" Luckily, for us, we weren't carrying marijuana. Patrick wanted to, but I had persuaded him that the risk was too high to get high. The Sheriff continued flapping his deputy-dog jaws. "My father fought in WWII and I was in Korea putting my body on the line so people like ya'll can disgrace our country by desecratin' the flag, burnin' draft cards, protest marchin', and all this civil rights movement disturbance; it can't be good for our country. I wanna know what your generation is so pissed off about living in America – love it or leave it, is what I say." The Sheriff's face was turning red. I didn't like where this was headed.

"My father was in the Army and fought the Japanese all over the South Pacific and he's a war hero. And my brother was a Green Beret in Vietnam and he made the supreme sacrifice. He died so you can drive around in your police car and give people like us who haven't done any harm trouble we don't deserve just because you don't like the way we look. And you judge how we think and the type of people we are without even knowing what goes on in our heads!" Patrick fired off his words like an M16 rifle. My knees started shaking. I could have chimed in with the losses I had experienced - my cousin Butch and the brothers of many friends from the neighborhood, but Patrick was passionate enough for the both of us.

"Now slow down city slicker, that was a mouthful. Did you just tell me your brother died in 'Nam?"

"Yeah."

"Sorry for your loss, boy. I lost my only son two years ago. He was a Marine; made me right proud. I guess war touches folks from all backgrounds. Pain of loss hurts no matter what your lifestyle, I suppose." The Sheriff had completely dropped his tough-guy-I'm-gonna-grill-your-ass demeanor and sounded a little more human.

Patrick wasn't finished speaking his mind. "My brother was one of the greatest men this world will ever know. He knew how to protect this country and he loved this country and so do I. Patriotism doesn't just come from the end of a rifle. It means standing up for what you believe and telling the truth and practicing fairness and justice. That's what my brother and your son died for and it would be shameful to their memories if our civil liberties are trampled on with prejudice." Patrick was speaking from his heart and he was absolutely right, and if this Sheriff was going to trample on our liberties, well, it was our patriotic duty to take a stand.

"You'd make a good soldier, boy. You got fire in your soul and a quick wit, even if you're blindly courageous." The Sheriff's interest in Patrick was definitely taking a shift toward the positive.

A fire had impassioned Patrick and it came from that part of his soul where his brother lives, and he apparently had no fear for pushing the limit with this lawman. I thought about telling the Sheriff that blind courage was also an attribute the military expertly cultivated and exploited, but again, I thought it best to keep my mouth shut. Patrick had the same thought and was not reluctant to express it.

"Blind courage is what my brother had. He believed everything this country told him. It was his country not just right or wrong, it was his country 100% right. The torch of liberty, truth, justice and freedom for all people, and he was completely convinced that our leaders would never intentionally do anything to deprive people of any culture or race of these rights. And he believed that Communism was an evil threat to our world and he was determined to put his body in its deadly path to prevent its spread." Patrick was going a bit far with the, *or race* comment, but I was feeling proud of the way he was speaking. We had shared quite a bit about his brother, my cousin Butch, and others in our neighborhood that had died in Vietnam, and the memory of them stirred courage in my heart and I no longer felt afraid. After all, we had truth, liberty and justice on our side. We were on the side of the American way, just like Superman taught us.

"Shooeey boy! (I noticed he didn't say girl.) You sound like a preacher and politician, a deadly combination. Like I was trying to say before ya'll went on your soapbox. I know what it feels like to lose family for a cause. It don't make much difference whether ya'll believe in the reasons for war, when a life is gone, it hurts like hell. Boys, I got a call from a traveler who said he dropped off some hitchhikers who were being harassed by some good ole' country boys and it was my intention to investigate the situation and possibly prevent a tragedy. It may be legal to hitchhike but that don't make it safe. I thought ya'll could use a little fear in your hearts to keep more alert to the dangers of being vagabonds. There are some nasty people in this world and ya'll are easy targets. Although I'm finding out that ya'll have clever heads on your shoulders. Perhaps there's something to what Yankees call street smarts."

Wow, was it possible that the Sheriff was actually interested in our welfare and did he say we had street smarts? Well, looks like deputy dog isn't as ignorant and stupid as I thought.

"How old was your brother?" The Sheriff asked Patrick in a slightly whispered and surprisingly gentle tone.

"Just turned twenty-one before he died." Patrick was looking at the drifting cumulus clouds as he spoke, avoiding the Sheriff's eyes.

"My boy was nineteen."

The Sheriff and Patrick stood still in shared silence for a few moments. It was a silence of mutual respect and consolation.

"You boys need to learn how to travel more safely. The best way to get good rides is at truck stops. When a truck driver, who is usually going a long distance, drops you off, have him do it at a truck stop. Why, you can even take a shower and grab meals. No one will bother you if you lay your sleeping bags under a tree and catch some shuteye. Truckers use these stops to rest and freshen up. I don't see why you can't enjoy the amenities of the great American highway system. Ya'll just have to be safe and do it right."

"Wow! That's really clever. Thanks Mr. Sheriff. We'll give that a try." I said enthusiastically, partly because of his idea but mostly because he was basically telling us that he was letting us go. And I was impressed that he knew about us being harassed, and maybe he really was interested in protecting us and not harming us. And, perhaps he was just playing the expected role of the tough southern deputy and we were the fairy peace loving America-hating Yankee smart-ass city boys. He had the smart-ass city boy part right. Something definitely shifted in each of us.

"Come on. I'll give ya'll a ride to the nearest truck stop and put out a message to my deputies that you two have been looked over and they'll keep an eye out for your safety."

This was almost too much to accept. One moment we're about to be on a chain gang busting rocks for Florida highways, and the next thing I know were riding in the back of the Sheriff's car being escorted to a truck stop.

"Wow. Far out man. This is really cool!" I couldn't help expressing my jubilation. Patrick looked at me with a smile on his face but his eyes warned me not to get carried away.

"You boys sure do have your own language but I think we understand each other just the same. Throw your gear in the trunk and hop in the back."

The good Sheriff took us to a truck stop, bought us dinner, and found a truck driver willing to take us as far as Orlando. We could have taken a ride all the way to Miami but we were determined to visit Disney World.

The truck driver was friendly enough even if he was a bit rough around the edges. He particularly enjoyed telling stories of his romantic exploits. He was also fond of guns and proudly showed us the ones he kept with him at all times for protection. So far, the people we met in the south seemed to have a strong liking for guns. The right to bear arms was a civil liberty they cherish dearly. I was thinking about my own prejudice toward people from the south and so far my experiences were a mixed bag: we were almost run down, we were shot at, got rescued by a sympathetic southerner, almost arrested by deputy dog who then turned out to be an alright guy once he realized we didn't fit his stereotype, and now we were in a truck with a man who liked showing off his guns. Once again, Patrick did most of the conversing since he knew a little about firearms because of his Eagle Scout training and his father kept various firearms, including hand grenades, around the house. This suited me just fine, being the silent introverted type was a role I knew how to play very well and it gave me a relative degree of privacy so I could be alone with my thoughts, which were usually about Sandy and occasionally about Mom and her tendency to worry excessively about me. I also wrote about the experiences in my journal. The driver let us out on a county road off of 95 that headed directly into Disney World. It was around 10:00 in the evening and the road looked rather lonely. We walked for a little while to stretch our legs before setting down our gear to resume hitchhiking.

"I think we should get as close as we can to Disney World and find a secluded place to roll out our sleeping bags. In the morning, all we have to do is stash our gear in a safe hiding place and then stroll on through the gates to fantasy land." I, too, had the same idea while Patrick had been yapping away with the previous truck driver.

"Great idea. I see some storm clouds though; we may have to set up the tent. Finding a place to do that where we won't be seen may not be easy." Patrick was always thinking of the elements and what strategies were needed to make the proper adaptation. He liked to refer to himself as the completely adaptable animal, and he was, as are most city boys. But I guess a few merit badges and wearing a fancy uniform throughout your young years makes you just a little more adaptable than your average street kid.

We selected a good spot to wait for a car to come along on this lonesome country road. I wasn't feeling hopeful that we'd catch a ride. Patrick propped himself against the trunk of a huge tree, took out his guitar and started strumming chords and picking notes. Feeling inspired I took out my flute and started playing along, feeling my way around his chord progressions and creating a little melody. We were somewhere in central Florida, two city boys on a country road late at night playing music and basking in the sense of freedom that comes with living under the stars and never knowing what new experience the next moment would bring. It was exciting and daring – it was freedom.

Headlights approached in the distance so I stopped playing and put out my thumb. It was a van and when its lights shone on my body it slowed down and pulled over to the side of the road. Patrick and I approached the van and were amazed by what we saw. Painted on the sides of the van were Disney characters: Mickey and Minnie Mouse, Donald Duck, and Snow White and the Seven Dwarves. I walked over to the driver's window and immediately noticed that he was wearing a security guard uniform. He had long black hair, and sported a hefty beard and mustache.

"Where ya'll going and where ya'll from?" he asked.

"Eventually to the island of Jamaica but tonight we want to get as close to Disney World as possible," I replied.

"This is your lucky night. I'm a night security guard for Disney World and I'm heading for work. Jump in, Yanks." He obviously picked up on our Philly accent.

"My names Oliver and this is my pal Patrick. We're from Philadelphia."

"John's my name. My friends call me Little John 'cause I am a bit short and I once played the part in a Robin Hood play." We all shook hands.

"I ride around the Disney grounds all night long, keeping an eye out for anything suspicious – like you guys. Funny thing though, I've been at this gig for six months now and zilch has happened; it's a very boring job."

"This is our lucky night because tomorrow we're gonna spend the day exploring Disney World. It won't be boring to us. Do you know of a good place within walking distance to the main entrance where we could roll out our sleeping bags for the night?" I asked.

"Yeah, there are lots of places 'cause it's still pretty rural around these parts, although real estate prices are skyrocketing and developments are springing up so it won't stay this way for long. Ya'll won't need to worry about being within walking distance to Disney 'cause I'm gonna take ya'll through the security gates and show where ya'll can sleep for the night. That way ya'll won't have to pay admission." Little John's accent was heavy southern. I had never heard the word "ya'll" used that many times in one sentence.

"Wow! Camping out in Disney World. That's really far out." Patrick was obviously thrilled, and so was I.

As we approached the security entrance, Little John told us to get in the back of the van and cover up with a large canvas tarp. We passed through the gates with ease, of course, because of Little John's security clearance.

"Come on up front guys and enjoy your exclusive midnight red-eye express tour of Disney World." Little John was obviously enjoying being mischievous and playing the role of tour guide. To my surprise and Patrick's delight, Little John took out a pipe filled with hashish and fired it up. "Ya'll don't mind if I animate my head with some Afghani Primo black hash, do ya? Want some?" Patrick eagerly accepted the pipe. He knew not to pass it to me, knowing it would make me feel paranoid, although I enjoyed the very pleasant smell.

Disney World was a fascinating, eerie fantasy world of concrete, glass and steel all molded to represent the creative imagination of Walt Disney. More than a third of the park was still under construction, giving the overall appearance of a beautiful dream world taking place in the mind of the sleeper in the process of unfolding. We were inside the weaving of that dream, outsiders journeying through the mind of one of histories most imaginative personalities. We walked up the steps of Cinderella's castle, drove around the Epcot Center, marveled at the Peter Pan and Pirates of the Caribbean exhibits, and toured Mickey's Star Land, the Haunted Mansion and much, much more. It was a surrealistic experience and I was overwhelmed with feelings of awe. Little John took us to the Twenty-thousand Leagues Under the Sea area, which was under construction, and instructed us to sleep in the submarine, assuring us that we would go unnoticed. He said he would wake us up before the park opened. We rolled out our sleeping bags on the submarine deck underneath a raised canvas tarp that was part of the on-going construction. We were so exhausted from the long day of traveling and the excitement of the nighttime tour that we slept soundly, and all too soon Little John woke us up.

"Hey Yanks, it's time to get going. I brought some oranges and bread for your breakfast."

"Wow, it wasn't a dream. We really are in Disney World." I exclaimed, while stretching my body and easing my way out of the sleeping bag. Patrick was yawning and showed little interest for getting out of his bag.

"I have a four day weekend and my shift is over in less than two hours. My uncle is in charge of security for Disney World and sometimes he lets me take the van for weekends. If you guys are up for it, I can drive you to Miami on my way to visit some friends in Key West." Patrick propped himself up giving his full attention to Little John.

"That's great! When do we have to get going?" Patrick asked.

"Well, I know you guys wanna get on rides and hang out in the park, but if I'm gonna take the van, I can't be hanging around and it won't look good if I drive back later on to pick you guys up, my uncle doesn't want other employees seeing me in the company vehicle."

"So that means we have to leave when you get off duty. Patrick is that alright with you?" I asked.

"Hell, we've already seen the entire park via a grand tour of the magical kingdom stoned on hash without crowds of people and I'm not interested in spending loads of money on rides. I want to save my cash for Jamaica. So it's not a problem for me."

"Me neither. I'm not going to look a gift horse in the mouth and say no thank you. This is an express ride to Miami in Disney style." I said.

After eating the food that Little John gave us, Patrick and I went to the nearest rest room, relieved ourselves, stripped off our clothes and washed our bodies in sinks, which freaked out a few fathers and their children. A few hours later, we left the park and met Little John at the designated rendezvous 100 yards from the entrance gates. We drove to Little John's home in Orlando where he grabbed some clothes and a few other essentials and off we went. It was a long ride to Miami but Little John rigged up an eight track stereo in the van so we had great tunes, including my favorite bands: The Who, Led Zeppelin, Moody Blues, CSNY, and of course The Beatles, especially John Lennon's new solo stuff. Little John let me do most of the driving so he and Patrick could smoke Afghani Primo black hash.

We arrived in Miami late that evening and slept in the van. In the morning, Little John drove us to Chrissie's house and, after exchanging addresses and phone numbers, he departed as we stood on the sidewalk looking at Chrissie's door. Patrick was excited and apprehensive as he approached the door and rang the doorbell. A young man around our age answered.

"Hello, can I help you?" He had a military style haircut, which for some reason caused me to feel slightly uncomfortable.

"My name is Patrick and this is my friend Oliver, we're friends of Chrissie and we've hitch-hiked from Philadelphia." Patrick politely explained.

"She isn't here right now but you're welcome to come in. She's at class and will probably be back sometime later this afternoon. I'm Jim." We shook hands and went inside. It was a Florida bungalow with a spacious living room and kitchen. It had three bedrooms.

"So who else lives here besides you and Chrissie?" Patrick asked and he was totally unprepared for the answer.

"Toby. He's Chrissie's boyfriend and he's the quarterback for the University of Miami football team." Patrick went completely pale and looked as if he would vomit. He got up from his chair and without saying a word went into the bathroom.

"Did I say something wrong?" Jim asked.

"Patrick and Chrissie have known each other for several years and were lovers this past summer. They were both lifeguards on the Wildwood, New Jersey beach, sharing the same lifeguard stand."

"Oops!" was all Jim said as he quickly exited the living room. At that very moment the door opened and in walked Toby. He was a tall, muscular and handsome guy, with short blonde hair and blue eyes, definitely the all American quarterback stereotype.

"Hello," he said with a big smile that showed perfect pearly white teeth, "I'm Toby, you must be a friend of Jim's."

"Hi, I'm Oliver and no, actually we're friends of Chrissie."

"Oh, she never mentioned you. Did you meet in one of her classes?"

"No. We've known each other for a long time. We grew up in the same Philly neighborhood. Her twin sister Sandy and I are very close. My friend Patrick and I are on our way to Jamaica so we thought we'd stop in and say hello to Chrissie."

"Great! I don't think she knows you guys were coming 'cause she never said anything to me. Where's her other friend?"

"He's in the bathroom. His name is Patrick. Did Chrissie mention him to you?"

"No. She did say she had some good friends in Philadelphia and she talks a lot about the lifeguard squad, but I don't recall her mentioning either of you. Maybe she did and the names just didn't stick. She talks about her sister all the time. Anyway, welcome to Miami. How long before you guys head off to Jamaica?" I wondered how Chrissie could talk about Sandy and never mention my name, and especially Patrick's.

"We don't have definite plans. We have to check out airlines and prices and all that."

"I'm sure it will be okay with Chrissie and Jim if you guys crash here for a day or two. In fact, we have three bedrooms and Chrissie and I pretty much share her room, so one of you can sleep in my bed and the other can use the couch." This guy was very friendly and obviously had no idea of the gravity of the situation. I was in disbelief that Chrissie had said nothing about Patrick, after all, it was only the second week of October and they had last seen each other in mid-August, the day of my birthday in fact. It was less than two months later and she was living and sleeping with another bro. Patrick was still in the bathroom dealing with what had to be a very hurt heart and confused mind. Chrissie was his first true love and he had told me on our way to Miami several times that he might stay with her in Florida and get a lifeguard job and take classes part-time. That dream along with all of his other fantasies was suddenly shattered. If Patrick had called Chrissie to tell her we were coming this situation would have been avoided. He's being hit with one of the most shocking surprises of his life. I knocked on the bathroom door. "Hey Patrick, you alright in there?"

"I'll be out in a minute." His tone was rather soft. I could only imagine the anguish he was experiencing. Toby was out on the backyard patio talking with Jim. I noticed him placing his hands on his head and his face had the look of shocking disbelief. Jim had told him about the situation. Patrick came out of the bathroom and I immediately told him we had to take a walk. So we exited the front door and began walking rapidly down the street. "Yo bro, Patrick, I'm really sorry bro, this super sucks! We don't have to stay here. Let's get a paper and look in the travel section for flights leaving today for Jamaica." I didn't know what else to say.

"I just can't believe it. We are so much in love. She must be confused with being so far away from home and all that. I have to talk with her. When she sees me things will become clear for her and she'll forget about Mr. Quarterback." Patrick was talking rapidly and with a tone of panic in his voice. He was clearly in a great deal of emotional pain and mental turmoil. Sparks were flying out of his eyes and he was sweating profusely.

"Patrick, Chrissie isn't expected back until late this afternoon. It's early in the day. Let's just explore the area, go to the beach and spend the day, it'll give you a chance to clear your head. This is too much too fast. You have to give yourself time to adjust before seeing Chrissie."

"I want to see her right now. That's all it will take. Words won't be necessary. We only need to look in each other's eyes. That'll bring all the clarity needed."

"She's on campus attending her classes, or working out with the swim team, or whatever. You have time, so use it wisely. Look Patrick, I'm no sage on romantic heartbreak, but I have some experience, with Chrissie's twin sister in fact. So, I do know this is big and you have to take time to calm down and gain some perspective."

"Let's go back to her house and ask Jim if he knows what she's doing on campus," commanded Patrick.

"Patrick, her boyfriend is back there. He came in while you were in the bathroom. I told him we were friends of Chrissie and he invited us to stay for a night or two. It's obvious he doesn't know anything about you and Chrissie."

"I don't understand why Chrissie didn't say anything about our relationship. We were certain about the strength of our love for each other. We made a commitment to always be together no matter what. How can it change so drastically in such a short period of time? Love as real as ours can't just change in an instant of time. She has to be confused, maybe mesmerized by the image of a big shot college quarterback. I have to talk with her." I thought about the time Sandy broke my heart when she fell for the tall blond dude from North Philly.

"Yes, you definitely have to speak with her but timing is very important. While you were still in the bathroom, Jim told Toby about you and Chrissie and he looked stunned and perplexed. They were outside in the yard so I didn't hear exactly what was said. He needs time to let Chrissie know you are here and she needs time to absorb the impact. You know, in hindsight, you should have called her first."

"Shoulda, woulda, coulda! If my aunt had balls I'd call her uncle. Now I know why she didn't respond to the letters I sent while I was traveling and, mister smarty-pants, I didn't have her phone number. So, what's this Toby guy look like?" I recalled Patrick telling me before we left Philly that Chrissie didn't have a phone hooked up.

"He looks like your typical jock. You know the type."

"It just doesn't figure. From what I know of Chrissie, she just doesn't go for that type."

"Is that so? Mister lifeguard-fastest-butterfly-swimmer in Philadelphia, and All American soccer player, not to mention you wore a letter sweater throughout your junior and senior years in high school. And the mantle in your home is full of trophies from every sport there is, not to mention the Eagle Scout status. You are that type, just a lot more hip than most personalities from that genre."

"Well, we can do the *suppose game* all day and still not know what the hell is going on in Chrissie's head and heart. I'll just have to wait until she gets home to talk with her."

"It's going to be very embarrassing for her Patrick. Perhaps it would be best if we just quietly get our things and head for the airport. You can write her when we're in Jamaica and she could write you back explaining everything."

"That would be a lot easier for her and maybe for me too in some ways, but I just have to see her, Oliver. The love we share is too strong and too real to let it pass like this. No, we have to speak to each other face-to-face. I know her, she'd want to do the same thing." I understood Patrick's position. I reacted exactly the same way when Sandy dropped me back in high school. I desperately needed answers.

"Alright! Let's go explore Miami for a few hours then we'll go back to see Chrissie. I think it would be best if we don't stay at her house. That invitation was given before the quarterback knew the situation." I said.

"You got that right. If I stay in that house it will be in Chrissie's arms and Mr. Jock will have to go elsewhere." Patrick had a tone of anger.

"Whew! Patrick, this is one hell of a situation you're dealing with. You can't realistically expect this dude to not sleep in his own home."

"Then Chrissie and I will go somewhere else."

"What if she doesn't want to go with you?"

"I can't think of that right now. I'm so damn confused! I love her. How could this happen?"

"Patrick, one of the things we learned during our experiences on the beach in Stone Harbor and Wildwood and dealing with the drug scene in the neighborhood – all those kids dying of overdoses, and from serving in Vietnam - is that love never dies, it is the super real aspect of life. Her love for you is there, maybe it's just hiding behind the changes she's going through."

"Well, I'll find out soon enough." Again, I didn't want to remind him how long it took before Sandy and I got back together. That was an excruciating experience and it took a lot of time to pass before we got over our hurt.

We found our way to the ocean and we were amazed at its clear blue color. Swimming certainly helped Patrick burn off some of his adrenalin and he seemed a lot calmer. He spent an hour or more alone walking on the beach and he later told me he was praying and thinking about his deceased brother, Avery. When our hearts are caught in the grip of a new hurt, we tend to revisit our wounds and either draw self-pity or strength from them. Patrick seemed to find strength.

"Oliver, whatever happened to Chrissie must be really important to her otherwise she wouldn't have done what she did. I know her. She has a good heart and she would never intentionally hurt me. I need to listen to what she has to say and no matter what happens, I will always be grateful for the love we shared, especially during our wonderful summers in Wildwood."

"You're in a much better place than you were a few hours ago. I think you're ready to see her. Let's go back to her house."

When we got there we could see Chrissie through the large living room window sitting on the sofa with her head cast slightly downward and her hands placed beneath her knees. As we approached it was obvious that she had been crying. I told Patrick that I would stay outside and that he should go in alone. He didn't even knock on the door. He simply walked in. She stood up as he walked over to her and I watched them embrace. Seeing Chrissie's shiny auburn hair and tall slender body reminded me of Sandy. They looked a lot alike after all they were twins. I turned away and walked down the street back toward the ocean.

I spent three hours at the beach, swimming and walking along the shoreline. This was my first Florida beach sunset and it was quite beautiful. The red-golden sun descended in the west behind a line of buildings, and its brilliant rays painted the eastern sky over the ocean with a panorama of pink, lavender and violet hues decorating the feathery cirrus clouds. I thought of Patrick and Chrissie and recalled images of the times they had spent together during the summer. They were with each other every day and night. They shared the same lifeguard stand and even saved a little girl's life together and received a commendation from the captain of the lifeguard squad. They were inseparable. It seemed unreal to me that she could be in love with another person. I understood how devastating it was to Patrick. I meandered my way back to Chrissie's bungalow hopeful that the situation was in some way resolved and I couldn't imagine what form that would take. As I approached the home, I looked into the living room window and saw Patrick, Chrissie, and Toby sitting around the coffee table peering down at a newspaper. I knocked on the door and Toby let me in.

"Come on in Oliver," Toby said a little too cheerfully.

"Hello Oliver!" Chrissie said as she walked over and gave me a very warm hug and a kiss on the cheek. "It's really good to see you again, and so soon. Patrick told me about Jamaica." Chrissie's hazel eyes were red and swollen from crying. She was wearing a University of Miami football jersey with the sleeves cut off at the shoulders, and she had on a pair of cut-off jean shorts. The clothes revealed her luscious body, again reminding me of Sandy. I felt a tug on my heartstrings.

"We were just looking at the travel section of the paper as you knocked. Come have a seat and let's see if we can find any good deals." Toby was eager to accommodate.

"Hi Patrick."

"Hello Oliver, how was the sunset at the beach?" he asked with a slight melancholy tone in his voice. The atmosphere wasn't tense but it certainly felt awkward. The three of them were trying a little too hard to be pleasant. I appreciated the effort in civility full well knowing that this had to be extremely difficult for the three of them, and there was no way I was going to ask them anything pertaining to this highly unusual predicament.

"Look at this ad! American Airlines is offering a round trip flight to Montego Bay for 50 bucks." Toby said excitedly.

"Excellent! I say we get on the phone right now and see if we can purchase two tickets. What do you say Patrick?" I really wanted to leave ASAP and I sensed that the sooner Patrick got away from this situation, the better he'd feel. And a paradise island was exactly what he needed to mend his broken heart.

"Sure, let's call them." Patrick replied.

Toby picked up the phone as Patrick recited the number to him. As the phone began ringing he handed the receiver to me.

"Hello. I am responding to the special advertised in the paper for round trip flights to Jamaica." The receptionist asked when we'd like to leave and without asking Patrick, I said the next available flight. She took a moment and said the next plane leaves Miami International Airport at 10:30 pm this evening and arrives in Montego Bay at 11:50 pm. She told me the cost would be $53 including taxes. The length of your visas will be issued by Jamaican customs. Then she asked if I would like to book my flight.

"Are there any flights leaving tomorrow morning?"

"Yes sir, but you will be charged the regular rate."

"How much?"

"That would be $160 U.S. dollars not including taxes."

"Just a moment please." I told Patrick the information and he immediately asked Chrissie if she could drive us to the airport. It was already 8:30 and we'd have to get moving real fast. She said she would.

"Let's do it Oliver!" Patrick was sounding excited, probably because we'd be escaping this uncomfortable predicament very quickly and in three hours we would be in Jamaica.

"Miss, please reserve two tickets for tonight's flight." I gave her our names and she said we should have already checked in our bags and that if we couldn't make the flight then there would be no rain check on the price. We got moving very quickly. We loaded our gear in Chrissie's trunk. Toby looked like he was uncertain about accompanying us to the airport and without Chrissie or Patrick within hearing range I said, "Hey Toby, I think it would be best if Chrissie and Patrick had a chance to say goodbye to each other at the airport - alone."

"Yeah, I suppose you're right," and then he announced, "Sorry I can't come along with you guys. I have a meeting with the football coach. Have a great time in paradise!" He smiled as he spoke and I do believe he meant it. I had the sense that he was a really good guy and that he genuinely felt bad for both Patrick and Chrissie. I was glad we were on our way and I knew that I'd have plenty of time to process all of this with Patrick sometime in Jamaica. The airport was only twenty-five minutes away. We quickly made our way to the ticket counter, purchased our tickets and checked in our luggage. Patrick wanted to take his guitar on board but they said it was too big to fit in the overhead. For a brief moment he contemplated leaving the guitar with Chrissie because he said he feared it would get damaged or stolen. I advised him to take the chance and bring it along, reminding him of playing music on moonlit beaches. It didn't take much convincing. He checked in his guitar. However, I slipped my flute out of my pack and said, "This will fit in my lap just fine!" We were told that the plane would begin boarding in thirty minutes and that we should make haste. Patrick and Chrissie went off to the side away from earshot and spoke intimately to each other. I watched as they hugged and passionately kissed. I could see tears rolling down Chrissie's cheeks and Patrick affectionately kissed them, moistening his lips with her salty sadness. The loud speaker announced the final call for boarding our flight. Patrick and Chrissie painfully separated and into the boarding tunnel we scurried, a tunnel that led to a new world and promise of adventure.

BUCCANEER INN

This was my first time on a plane and I was thrilled! I had a window seat a few rows in front of the wing, giving me a clear view of the Miami International Airport runway. A feeling of exhilaration ran through my body as we sped down the long asphalt surface and lifted into the sky. There was a near full moon and huge puffy clouds drifted by. There were lots of stars even with the glow of moonlight. I was amazed that such a big heavy craft could soar through the sky.

Sitting on the plane in the seat between us was Steve Tanz. He introduced himself and gave us a quick bio: twenty-four years old and traveler from Michigan on his way to Jamaica.

"So you say you're from Philadelphia and you used the power of the thumb to get to Florida, eh. Did it take you long to hitch to Miami?" he asked. Steve had a full head of long black curly hair and bright blue eyes peering behind John Lennon style classes that were held up by a long thin nose. There was something about his features that reminded me of the son-in-law of the Jewish factory owner I had worked for in Philly. Maybe he was Jewish.

"A little more than five days. We weren't in a hurry 'cause we were into the experience of the journey," replied Patrick.

"Are the people from the South friendly or mean? I have this image in my head from the movie, Easy Rider, when Peter Fonda and that other guy got blown away by a shotgun," Steve asked.

"Dennis Hopper that was the other guy. We had some Southern boys in a pickup truck with a rifle looking to do us some harm, and another guy rescued us. We were harassed by a Sheriff Deputy Dog type dude who turned out to be an okay guy. Most of the people we met were good people. There are good and bad people in the South, just like anywhere else." I really believed that was true. It doesn't matter so much where you are, but who you encounter that contributes to having a good or bad experience, and a good attitude goes a long way.

"Yeah, we had some scary and really far out experiences. That stereotypical southern man deputy dog policeman was, at first, mean, and he turned out to be one of the most helpful people we met. He actually taught us the secret to safe and successful hitchhiking." Patrick's experience with the Sheriff was a positive influence on him. Neither one of us had much respect for policemen or authority. We grew up experiencing our neighborhood police as authorities who abused their power. There were some helpful police but for the most part they were more afraid of us than we were of them even though they carried guns and nightsticks. We understood their job was not easy, especially in a neighborhood like ours, but there were many times when their behavior far exceeded the limits of fairness and justice.

"Wow, that's far out. So what's the secret to hitchhiking?" Steve asked.

"Truck stops! Plain and simple. Truckers are headed in all directions, traveling long distances, and they love the company because it keeps them entertained and awake." I was grateful for what the Sheriff had instructed us to do.

"That sounds practical. I'll remember that tip if I ever need a ride. So where are you guys headed to on the island?" Steve was genuinely curious about the two of us and his warm smile and twinkling eyes made being in his presence comfortable. Besides, his resemblance to John Lennon was a big plus in my book. I sensed he would become a good friend and that he was experienced at island adventures and his knowledge could be very useful.

"We heard about a fishing village, Negril. Do you know of it?" I asked.

"Yeah, but I've never been there. I heard it's one of the best-kept secrets among the out-of-the-way tourists. The word is that European and American hippies looking for an inexpensive non-tourist-trap experience go to Negril. Jamaica is my favorite of the Caribbean islands and it'll be just a matter of time before I make my way to the western end."

"I suppose we qualify as people looking for a non-tourist-trap experience," I replied.

"Yeah, and you look like hippies too," laughed Steve, stating the obvious.

"How many times have you been to Jamaica and where do you usually go?" I asked.

"This is my eighth time. I have friends who own a hotel, the Buccaneer Inn, in the little seaside town of Runaway Bay. We grew up together in Kalamazoo, Michigan. I indulge in a little pleasure while here but business is my main purpose. It's going to be late when we land in Montego Bay. Do you guys have a place to stay?"

I realized that with all the haste to get on the plane and to leave behind an emotionally uncomfortable situation, I hadn't thought of what we would do once we landed.

"No. We'll just find a place to roll out our sleeping bags for the night and then hitch a ride to Negril tomorrow." Patrick was intent on getting to Negril as soon as possible. He had a faraway look in his eyes and a melancholic tone in his voice. I had no doubt that feelings about Chrissie occupied his mind.

"Montego Bay is not a place where you want to sleep on the beach. There are too many poor people out to hustle tourists, or worst. No need for that, gents. I have a ride waiting to take me to the Buccaneer Inn. Come with me and spend some time at the hotel. It's on the beach and has three levels and is shaped like a horseshoe facing the sea with a huge pool in the middle. There's a dining hall on the second floor that extends out onto a veranda. If you like hanging out on the beach after you eat, there's a thatched hut bar with music playing all the time. It'll be a comfortable introduction to Jamaica. There's an added sightseeing bonus too: the Playboy Club resort is right next door, and the bunnies are a hoppin' and their buns and tops are a poppin'!"

"I'm all for it! How 'bout you Patrick?"

"Hoppin' bunnies? What do you mean?" Patrick asked.

"Haven't you guys ever looked through a Playboy magazine?"

"Yeah!" we simultaneously replied. "Is this the pleasure side of your business?" I asked.

"I don't talk about business. As for the Playboy Club, well, the waitresses and bartenders are all super beautiful young women that only wear bunny ears on their heads and very scanty bikinis, in fact they cover the nipples of their breasts with tiny tassels and the bottom half of their bodies are covered with a thin strip of cloth on their front and back cracks with a tiny furry bunny tail on their butts, and they have no hair down there – they are completely shaven. They're Playboy Bunnies!" Steve had a wide grin on his face as he spoke of the Bunnies. Patrick's eyes were popping out of his head. Perhaps some Hugh Hefner beauties will cure Patrick's heartbreak, or at least ease the pain.

"Have you body surfed with any of them?" I asked.

"Do what?" Steve asked.

"Have sex?"

"Normally those women wouldn't touch us with a ten foot pole. However, money has the potential to pry open any crevice. They're high class and they're not prostitutes, as far as I know. I never propositioned them with money, just tried using my charm and abundant good looks. Just kidding. The security guards keep a keen eye out for them. Nonetheless, they sure are great eye candy.

I'm guessing those Bunnies are between twenty-two and twenty-eight. It is the perfect age range for dudes in their prime. I've had some good times with lovely Jamaican babes my own age, and a little older. I say give the Bunnies a try, and you can always go for the Jamaicans since there are a lot more of them." As the plane was landing I had visions of nearly naked girls dancing in my head. Before the wheels hit the airstrip, Steve asked us once again. "So what's it gonna be, guys?"

"Gonna be what?" I asked, being shaken from my erotic reverie.

"Are you coming to the Buccaneer Inn with me?"

"I don't know. It sounds expensive," Patrick replied shaking his head.

"Trust me on this, guys. We will register as the Tanz party and you guys can charge everything while you're there, and I mean everything: meals, drinks, and room service - all of it. We'll keep one tab."

"Steve, you don't understand. We don't have much money. We're here to camp on a cliff on some Jamaican couples' property. Fancy hotel living isn't our lifestyle. We plan on going native." Patrick was right. Our plan was to live simply so we can stay as long as possible. The winter semester at the college wouldn't start until the third week of January and this was only October.

"Not to worry, mon, you're in Jamaica now. Seriously you have to trust me. You can settle up your bill anytime you're ready to leave and you will not be disappointed." We decided to take Steve up on his offer. I figured if we ran out of money then we'd have a sooner than expected adventure hitchhiking back to Philadelphia, which would be fun. Steve was grinning from ear to ear, pleased that we were going to the Buccaneer Inn.

When we stepped off the plane, I was hit with a wave of culture shock. I had thought that the tremendous transformational education process I went through during my time in the mental health degree program at the Community College of Philadelphia had taught me to transcend racial bias and fear. I was wrong. Nothing had prepared me for the shock of entering into a culture where nearly everyone was a black person. Ninety-five percent of the airport patrons and personnel were black. I was surprised by the fear that gripped me. It was visceral and all the understanding that I had accumulated in my education experiences did not enable me to completely shed the deep-seated biological animal fear rooted in my nature. I continued to be afraid of people who were different, especially black people. As we moved through customs I was fearful that I would be arrested for simply being white, a stupid feeling. Oh well, I guess we can't transcend all of our human weaknesses, at least not completely.

Patrick was in the customs line ahead of me. I wondered if he felt scared. He always got along with people of color. Perhaps, he wasn't completely human. He was the most amiable person I knew, and most people took an instant liking to him. When they saw his guitar, they asked him to open the case for inspection. Then, they asked him if he intended to sell the guitar for money. Patrick replied that he was learning to be a musician and he brought the guitar for personal enjoyment. They demanded that he prove it by playing them a song. This demand made him very nervous and since he had been playing for less than a year, he lacked confidence and I was worried that they would not receive his performance favorably. I could see his hands shaking as he took out the guitar. Since it was late at night, there were not a lot of tourists in the customs line, but everyone's attention turned to Patrick. He had never performed for an unfamiliar audience. He played only with his friends on the beach in Wildwood and the street corners and playground in our neighborhood, as well as the usual jam sessions in the basement of his home.

"Oliver, what song should I play?"

"Whatever you know best. How about the first John Lennon song you learned, *Working Class Hero*?" Patrick started strumming the chords, running through the opening several times until he began to feel more confident as the full sound of his Gibson guitar echoed off the large ceiling of the airport lobby and reached our ears. It made a nice sound that captured everyone's attention. The smiles on the Jamaican faces caused Patrick to visibly relax. A slight smile appeared from the corners of his mouth. He started singing the first verse: *"As soon as you're born they make you feel small, by giving you no time instead of it all."* Patrick voice was distinctive – not one that has the full range from baritone to soprano – but one that carries a tune well, and he makes the octave range of his voice adapt to a song's melody. *"They hurt you at home, and they hit you at school, then they expect you to follow their rules..."* Fortunately, and to my surprise, the custom agents knew this song well and began singing along with him. I was inspired and took my flute out of the case and weaved in melodic improvisations. A Jamaican by-stander with a beautiful voice took up singing the next verse along with Patrick, " *... they torture and scare you for twenty-odd years, then they expect you to pick a career, when you can't hardly function, you're so full of fear ... Yeah a working class hero is something to be. Well if you* *want to be a hero then just follow me ...*" We played the song through several times with long instrumental interludes between versus – we were having a good time. The lyrics weren't sung exactly like they were written, but that didn't matter, we were simply having fun playing what we remembered in a fun piece-meal fashion – it was a gas.

The customs officials were thrilled with the performance as were our tourist audience. Everyone clapped when we finished. "Dat was terrific, mon. Welcome ta Jamaica!" The initially skeptical customs agent suddenly became friendly and my culture shock took on a different emotional hue. Instead of fear, I was feeling surprisingly exhilarated. Steve Tanz had faded into the background, not participating at all in the scene, as though he was making a conscious effort not to be noticed. We still had to move through customs to get our visas, three weeks was all they gave us since we only had a few hundred bucks each. "Hey, Steve, what's with the three week visa thing?" I asked.

"They issue visas based on how much money you have. They aren't used to so many new young people from Europe and the United States coming to their island. Tourism is their main industry and they guard it closely," responded Steve.

"Randy, the guy who told us about Jamaica, said we could live cheaply in the fishing village, Negril, and we planned on staying for months," I said.

"Then I don't see any reason why you can't just lose your visas. Avoid encounters with government officials and you can stay as long as your wits allow. When it's time for you to leave, just tell the custom officials your visas were stolen along with other items. They will let you out of the country." I liked what Steve said.

There was a limousine service waiting for Steve and it turned out that the Jamaican driver knew him well. The driver worked for the people who owned the Buccaneer Inn. We tossed our luggage in the huge trunk and hopped in the back seat. After our musical performance and then getting into a long, black limo, we felt like rock stars. I looked at the moonlight-drenched Caribbean Sea and beaches all along the coastal road. The water was more beautiful than anything I had ever seen. I could see shades of color variations in the sea because of the moonlit surface. I could only imagine what it looked like in direct sunlight. There was one beautiful beach after another strung like white pearls around the neck of the island, bordered by a moonlit glistening turquoise sea. I put down the window and took in the smells. I gazed up at the star-studded sky and then the realization dawned on me that we had arrived in paradise.

The Buccaneer Inn was decorated to look like a pirate ship with a distinctive Caribbean flavor. On the outside front wall of the main entrance there was a mural of a pirate with a parrot on his shoulder. The grounds were landscaped with huge aloe and croton plants and a plethora of colorful and sweet smelling flowers. There were palm, banana, and coconut trees, just like I imagined an island having, although it never occurred to me that I'd be staying at a quasi-classy hotel. We entered the torch-lit entranceway and stepped up to the registration counter. An ebony-indigo skinned Jamaican woman in her twenties greeted us with a big smile. "Welcome back ta de island of Jamaica an' de lovely Buccaneer Inn, Mestah Tanz. I see you 'ave friends wit yah dis time." The woman spoke with a melodic voice, yet it was hard to hear some of her words clearly, and Steve was speaking in the same manner.

"It is good ta see yah lovely Jamaican smile, Rosie. Yeahmon, dis mi frens. Dis is Patrick an' Oliver fram de U.S."

"Please ta meet yah, sirs."

"Hello." We said together.

"I tek mi usual room, Rosie, an' dis gentlemen be needin' a room wit a view facin' de sea."

"Aw de rooms be facin de sea, Mestah Tanz, yah know true dat. I get dem a room on de top floor wit de higher view. Are you wantin' someone ta tek your luggage ta de room, sirs?"

"Dat not necessary, Rosie."

"Awrite den, tek yah keys. Go along now, a waiter come up shortly tendin' ta yah comforts."

"Irie!" was Steve's response. It was interesting how he took on a Jamaican accent while speaking with native people. I asked him what *Irie* meant. "It means everything is cool, mon, no need to worry, you know, every little t'ing gonna be awrite." We went to our room. It was simplistic and lovely with two double beds and white-laced curtains with prints of parrots and palm trees. The windows were large, offering a clear view of the sea. After sleeping on the side of the road for a week, this room was heaven. As we unzipped our packs someone knocked lightly on our door. It was a Jamaican man dressed in a short sleeve white cotton shirt and long, white pleated pants. He was sporting a bright smile and holding a covered silver platter.

"Ganja fer yah tastin', mon! Steve say ta bring ta yah room fer samplin' de finest fram de Blue Mountains, compliments of de 'otel. Mi name is Jacob an' I be servin' yah durin' yah stay." Jacob stood in the entrance and lifted the lid from the silver tray, revealing three distinct mounds of huge ganja flower buds, each colored light green with various degrees of red, browns and gold speckled throughout. Patrick stared at the plate of ganja with a look of wonderment. "Dun' jus' be lookin' aw dumbfounded, mon. Invite mi in."

"Sure, sure, ah, excuse me, sir. Come to the table and have a seat," replied Patrick. Jacob sat at the table and unwrapped a white cloth revealing banana leaves. Jacob was a tall, handsome man with very dark skin, like a very deep purple or indigo. His eyes were big and fixed in a permanent smile with etched lines radiating out from the corners of his eyes to his temples. His lips were big and when parted, revealed perfect bright white teeth with one gold tooth on the top front row that glistened.

"Ave yah ever smoked a spliff, mon?"

"No. Randy told me about them, though," I replied.

"So dis Randy be Jamaican?"

"No, he's an American who spent time in Jamaica and he told us about the island," I said.

"Well, den mon, pic' up de banana leaf an' I be instructin' yah in de fine art of spliff makin'." The banana leaves were rectangular and greenish-yellow. Jacob had us follow what he did, although we quickly saw that it was exactly like rolling loose-leaf paper in a spiral beginning at one corner and rolling to the other, just like paper telescopes, except these had nearly a quarter ounce of ganja buds wrapped inside. Jacob licked the edge of the banana leaf with saliva to hold it in place like weak glue. The spliffs were shaped similar to a cone, with one large end and the other end tapered to a tip.

"Nicely dun, mon. You bwoys git de 'ang of dis well, mon. Time ta fiah de torches." Jacob lit a stick match and touched it to the end of his spliff. A slow orange burn formed around the twisted edge. When the heat hit the ganja, a sweet smell of smoke entered our nostrils. Jacob puffed away, inhaling freely and looking delighted. The green banana leaf stopped burning while the ganja wrapped inside continued burning. Patrick picked up the matches and lit his spliff. I just sat there in what became a room clouded in smoke. I didn't have to light my spliff to smoke. There was more marijuana smoke in the room than oxygen. Patrick's brain became so saturated with ganja that he appeared slightly comatose. He was staring off in space with unfocused eyes as the spliff fell from his hand. I picked it up and set it on the table.

"Oh, me almos' forgettin', mon." Jacob lifted his huge body out of the wicker chair and stepped outside the door and re-entered with a basket of fruit. "Dis be fer yah, compliments of de Buccaneer Inn. Effin yah be needin' more ganja, jus' ask fer me." Jacob set the basket on the table and left our room. The basket had a bunch of bananas, oranges and lemons, two coconuts, and other fruit I had never seen before. I peeled and quickly ate a banana. I offered one to Patrick. He took a banana but just held it as he continued staring out the window. I peeled it and began feeding him. He absent mindedly chewed.

The ganja started making me feel nervous but not quite paranoid like it usually does, perhaps it was because we weren't in South Philly. It occurred to me that we'd been traveling without a full night's sleep for several days. Just a few hours here and there on the side of the road and in other places like the night in Disney World. Then followed the emotional shock wave of Chrissie, the rush to the airport, arriving in Montego Bay, Steve and the limousine ride to the Buccaneer Inn, and now our introduction to ganja hospitality.

I took Patrick by the hand and led him outside like a chimpanzee to get fresh air while feeding him another banana. We found our way onto a rooftop patio that gave us a 360-degree view. Sure enough, right next door to our hotel was the Playboy Club and there were indeed gorgeous Bunnies walking around. They may as well have been naked 'cause they mostly were, excepting for the goofy looking bunny costume nipple covers and crack stuffers. Patrick spoke for the first time since smoking the spliff. "God took a paint brush and drew those women into creation right before my eyes." He then went silent again. I promised myself that we would explore the Playboy Club the next day. What we needed more than anything was a good night's sleep. We made our way back to the room, each of us collapsing on our respective beds. Patrick started snoring instantly, while I lay on the bed with scenes from this amazing day reeling through my head. There appeared an image of a Playboy Bunny hopping on a cloud with me sitting in the middle wishing she'd stop bouncing the cloud and come lay beside me. She did and I drifted off into a blissful dream of ecstasy.

I woke up the next morning feeling disoriented as I looked around the room not knowing where I was. I peered through the large window at the sun drenched clear multi blue-green hued Caribbean Sea and I remembered I was in Jamaica and recollections of the previous day's events flashed through my mind. Patrick was snoring away, obviously in a deep sleep. I made my way to the bathroom and relieved myself, went to the table and proceeded to eat a mango, which was messy, juicy and unbelievably delicious. I decided to take a stroll around the hotel. We were on the third floor. The balcony faced the sea and in the center of the complex at the first level was a kidney shaped swimming pool. The hotel was painted in black and orange, pirate colors, just like those of our high school, Bishop Neumann, and there were blood-red stone tiles covering the floors on every level. The balcony railing was a series of posts and thick rope, mimicking an 18th century clipper ship. At the bottom of the pool there was a painting of a pirate ship and a treasure chest full of jewels. A pirate flag of skull and bones flapped on a pole that rose above the hotel roofline. On the beach there was a thatched-hut bar.

As I walked upon all three levels of the horseshoe shaped balcony, I was struck by the absence of people. I saw no evidence of anyone else staying at the hotel. Perhaps it was too early for people to be up and about. Then again, October is not tourist season for the islands. I had a clear view of the Playboy Club and there were a few people stirring, Jamaicans that looked like hotel workers. When I reached the pool, I couldn't resist the temptation to swim. I took off my shirt and dove in. The water was warm. As I was swimming laps, it occurred to me that it was silly to be swimming in a pool when the Caribbean was fifty yards or so away. I got out of the pool and made my way to the sea, walking past the thatched bar, coconut trees, and beach furniture.

The sand was sugar white and lukewarm. I walked slowly into the calm, wave-less water, marveling at its clarity and unbelievable turquoise color. As I stood in the water I looked up and down the coconut and palm tree lined pristine beach. There were three hotels. The third was about a half mile down the beach on the other side of the Buc. It looked like an original Jamaican mom and pop thatched hut mini village with what appeared to be a beachfront bar and restaurant. The beach stretched in a wide arc from one distant point to another outlining a large cove. This was not exactly the island paradise I had envisioned in my imagination that was inspired by the Earl Flynn pirate movies, but close enough. I thought of Sandy and wished she were here.

When the water was waist deep, I dove in. It was bath water warm and soothing. At first, I swam around slowly, taking in the sights of the coastline and the sea bottom. Then I started to swim vigorously, stretching out my body and breathing deeply. I swam my freestyle stroke for an extended period. It felt good to stretch my body and work the muscles. I glided along swiftly, feeling exhilarated by the intake of oxygen and increased heart rate. I was not giving attention to the direction I was swimming, and I avoided opening my eyes under water to keep the salt from stinging them. Eventually, I slowed my pace and when I stopped and looked around I realized that I swam away from the shore and was too far out for my liking. The smaller appearance of the Buccaneer Inn was a clear indication that I swam out a considerable distance. I figured I swam non-stop for about a half-hour, which meant I was approximately a mile off shore.

I looked through the water's surface towards the sea bottom and was surprised that I could see so deeply. I estimated that I was in forty feet of water. The deeper water was a darker blue-turquoise color. I could see coral and what looked like large rocks on the bottom. I saw a school of light blue fish swimming below me, fish I could not identify. It occurred to me that I knew almost nothing about the sea life in these waters. Then, I thought about sharks. A jolt of fear shot through my body. If there were sharks in the area they would know I was there because they have incredible senses, they are the perfect predators. Then, I remembered hearing or reading somewhere that sharks are attracted to splashing and that they sense fear. I was definitely sending out the fear vibe but I wasn't splashing. My body was frozen still, as the buoyant salt water kept me afloat.

The school of fish below me suddenly took off and that frightened me even more, thinking they were fleeing from a shark. I had to do something. I decided that I should make my way towards shore without splashing. I swam a gentle breast stroke, keeping my eyes open at all times, which was ridiculous since there was nothing I could do if a shark did attack. I experienced life-threatening fear many times when my I was in danger in my neighborhood, but this was surrealistically scary. Unlike other situations, I was out of my element and completely defenseless. I swam for what felt like an eternity before reaching the Buccaneer Inn dock. I pressed my foot on a submerged pole to lift my body out of the water. My foot was immediately set on fire with pain from something that was very sharp, for a moment I stupidly thought a shark bit me.

Heart racing, and hyperventilating, I got out of the water and looked at my foot. There were black things sticking in my skin. I quickly pulled out the ones that I could. I noticed that along the poles in the water were black spiny looking creatures. I sat on the deck holding my foot cursing in pain. A Jamaican boy around ten years old ran up to me from the beach, looked at my foot and said, "Piss on it, mon."

"Say what?"

"Piss on de foot, mon, it tek out de sea urchin sting."

"You gotta be kiddin' me. I'm not as dumb as I look."

"Nuh mon, I nuh mek fun, de piss tek away de pain."

"There's no way I'm gonna piss on my foot just so you can laugh at a stupid American tourist."

"Yeahmon, yah be dumb. Yah mus' trus' Jamaicans, mon." The boy waved me off and left me in my agony. I limped back to the pool area and into a shower stall to rinse off the salt water. My foot was on fire and my heart was still pounding from the shark-swim, but I also felt lucky to have gotten back safely and couldn't wait to tell Patrick what happened. As the water ran over me I started to take a piss, and out of curiosity aimed the stream of yellow on my foot. Within seconds the pain had stopped. Urineaka! The boy was right. The acid in the urine must have neutralized whatever was causing the pain. I returned to the room and a cloud of smoke hit me when I opened the door. Patrick was sitting in a chair staring out the window smoking a spliff.

"Feeding your head I see."

"Jamaican breakfast special. It's good for what ails ya. Just like Jefferson Airplane instructed, we gotta feed our heads." Patrick had a big smile on his face and his eyes were blood-shot red, they were like litmus paper. Whenever he gets stoned the capillaries swell with blood and his glowing iridescent green-blue irises get larger and brighten.

"Sharks!"

"Say what?"

"Sharks. I went swimming and went out too far where there are sharks."

"Glad ta see yah 'ave all yah body parts, mate." Patrick burst out laughing with that marijuana saturated brain cackle.

"It was scary. I could have been eaten. I stepped on a spiny thing and it stung my foot. A Jamaican kid told me to piss on it. I did and it stopped the sting."

"Oliver the shark attack survivor and foot pisser. You're off to a spine-y tingling start with your adventure in paradise." He started cackling again.

"Whatever. I'm hungry. Let's get some breakfast." I said, as I tossed Patrick a piece of fruit from the basket and started peeling a banana.

"Yeah, I'm famished. I wonder if they serve breakfast around here." Patrick mumbled with a mouth full of mango. "How do we open one of those coconuts?"

"They have a dining area so they must serve breakfast. Besides Steve Tanz, I think we're the only guest."

"Steve is an interesting guy. An air of mystery surrounds him. Did you see him this morning while on your wild adventure?" Patrick laughed again. Everything struck him as being funny. It was good to see him in better spirits. I suppose the marijuana was doing him some good. I picked up a coconut and inspected it.

"We need to bust this thing open with a hammer or something. It's shell is as hard as rock."

"Try your Swiss army knife," Patrick suggested. I took out my knife and quickly realized there was no way this knife would slice the shell. One of the knife's blades was very pointy and short with a double sharp edge. I used it as a drill to create two holes. It worked. I put my mouth over a hole and sucked on it. The milk was mildly sweet.

"Give me some of that." I handed Patrick the coconut and he greedily sucked all the milk out. "Maybe if we drop it from the balcony it will open. Let's try it," he suggested.

"Maybe if we knock it on your head it will open," I responded. Patrick laughed. "Let's find someone to show us how to crack this nut." We picked up another coconut and went in search for someone. Jacob was sitting at the end of the third floor balcony with a plate of food in his hand.

"Good morning Jacob. Can you show us how to open these coconuts?" I asked.

"Surely, mon. A mashait is de bes' way. I don' 'ave one wit me presently. I show yah after I eat mi breakfast, mon. Wud yah like ta try Jamaican food?" Jacob extended the plate to me. I declined, not liking the idea of eating off someone else's plate, especially since he was eating with his fingers. Patrick declined as well. I had no idea what a mashait was and looked forward to finding out. It was very difficult to understand Jamaican dialect. They spoke very fast and the words were not English, at least many of them weren't. I had to listen carefully and interpret the best I could.

"Very well den. De 'otel serve breakfast. Go ta de dinin' 'all an' yah be served shortly. After yah eat, I open de coconuts."

"Have you seen Steve?" Patrick asked.

"Mestah Tanz is takin' care of business wit de DeSalvas. I expec' we nuh see im dis day."

"Whose the DeSalvas?" I asked.

"Di owners of de Buccaneer Inn. De sweetest couple yah ever 'ave de pleasure ta meet, mon. Dey 'ave a likkle dawta, Kaitlin. De cutest girl on de island." Jacob got up and walked away.

We headed to the dining area. It turned out that Jacob was the waiter and for all we knew could have been the cook as well because we saw no evidence of anyone else. We were the only people eating. The emptiness of the hotel was a little eerie. Yet, it was far out that we had the entire place to ourselves, an island resort complete with all amenities, legal and otherwise. I ate a typical American breakfast of potatoes and eggs with toast and slices of mango, the best food I've eaten in a long time. Patrick had fried plantain and breadfruit with rice and some kind of egg looking stuff and more bananas. He couldn't get enough bananas. I decided that he must be part monkey. When we finished eating, Jacob came to our table carrying a machete and our coconuts. He placed the coconuts on the ground and with two quick swings of his arm sliced them in half. The coconut meat was sweet and chewy. Jacob cleared the table and left. There was no bill to pay, which worried us a bit. The prices on the menu were reasonable, but still, neither of us was used to keeping a running bill and we never asked how much the room cost. And I wondered how keeping everything on one tab with Steve Tanz was going to work out, especially since we had no idea where he was or when he would show up.

We walked to the beach and without hesitation Patrick plunged into the sea and did the exact same thing I had done earlier. He is a fast swimmer and he has an excellent butterfly stroke. He swam at full speed out to sea. My story about the sharks didn't deter him at all. He just kept moving further and further from shore. I felt nervous for him. Finally, he stopped and waved at me. He stayed out there for a good 45 minutes. When he came back to the beach, he looked like a wild man of the sea, grinning from ear to ear as he shook his curly mane of long hair like a Golden Retriever, spraying me with water droplets.

"This sea is awesome! Never swam in anything like it. Beautiful, beautiful, down right …" He paused for a second as his eyes focused on something down the beach … "drop dead gorgeous. Will you look at that girl? Her body is unbelievable. Those breasts are bare and her legs, wow!" The woman he was looking at was stunningly beautiful. She had short black hair, was tall, and her body, even from this distance, was perfect in every way. Patrick dropped to his knees in reverence and let out a whistle. He looked like he was kneeling before a religious relic about to make an offering of prayer.

"Yo, let's take a stroll down the beach and get a closer look," I whispered.

"That's the best thing I heard you suggest in a long time."

We walked briskly towards the Playboy Club and the goddess. We came upon a sign that said *Guests Only*. From where we came from, signs were to be read, briefly considered for the possible danger, and then usually ignored. We walked right up to the goddess. Patrick stood closer to her than me. He looked like he wanted to say something. She was standing sideways as though she had not noticed us. She turned and looked Patrick directly in the eyes and smiled, revealing perfect rows of ivory white teeth surrounded by rose-red full lips. We stood like statues, completely speechless as we stared at her. She had short jet-black hair, boy like, yet exotically feminine, exposing her cute perfectly shaped ears and elegant neck. Her violet eyes were accentuated by long lashes and not too thin eyebrows, reminding me of Elizabeth Taylor. Her dainty nose and high cheekbones were lightly dusted with dark brown freckles. Her body was long and slender, and graced with elongated full breasts with sand dollar sized pink aureoles. Her nipples were teasingly covered with little red tassels. Her legs were long and slender with good muscle tone in her calves and thighs, supporting the perfect curves of her nicely proportioned derrière. She had a way of standing that looked as though she was continuously posing for a camera. When she moved ever so slightly, her delicious pelvis revealed a single beauty mark. The thong hid only the flesh of her crevices leaving little to my imagination, yet plenty to tease my desires. I had never seen a woman with no pubic hair – it was surprisingly erotic. She had a thin waist and a smooth muscle-toned abdomen topped by a long rib cage that had just the right amount of flesh. I could stare at this woman all day and night and continuously find new facets of beauty. I wanted to explore every part of her body. I wanted her more than I had ever desired anything. Pure lust pulsed through my veins. The goddess super-model released a sweet gentle laugh and asked our names.

"Pa, Pa, Pa …" Patrick was stuttering and just could not form the sound of his own name.

"My name is Oliver and this is my friend Patrick. We are pleased to meet you."

"I am Penelope, pleased to meet you Oliver and Patrick. Is there anything I can do for you?" Wow! What a sweet voice. What a smile, and her eyes twinkled with a violet hue. I wanted to ask her if she would like to body surf but that would be totally rude.

"We're from Philadelphia. This is our first time in Jamaica. Where are you from?" I asked.

"Pacific Grove, California. What brings you to Jamaica and the Playboy Club? Are you two playboys?" Wow! Her question was tantalizing. Finally, Patrick found his voice.

"Yep! We are boys and we love to play." His comment struck me as stupid. But Penelope didn't even flinch.

"From the looks of you handsome fellows, it would be safe to wager that you two are quite experienced and very good at playing." Playing what? Sex? Was she teasing us? Leading us on? Surely she wasn't a high-class prostitute. She was so beautiful she could have anything she wanted. People would pay just to look at her. In fact, she had to be a model or something. Maybe even a Playboy centerfold.

"Are you a Playboy model?" I blurted out.

"Yes. All the women that work here have been featured in the magazine. I was in the August issue. You can purchase a copy in the hotel and I would be happy to sign it for you."

"Yeah. Let's get a copy. Where in the hotel?" Patrick was eager to look at pictures of her completely nude body, which seemed ridiculous to me since she was live in the flesh and 99% naked.

"We can do that anytime. In fact, I can have a complimentary copy sent to your room and you can invite me up at your convenience so we can do a signing ceremony. It is such a relief to have young attractive guests. Most of the guests are retired and like looking at pretty women to get their thrills - you know, to get their juices flowing. I get so bored with gray haired men making advances at me when their wives are not around. The money they give me for tips is nice though. I really do need young male company. All the Play Bunnies are hungry for young males, so you boys best be careful you don't tire yourselves out."

Wow! She just invited herself to our room. I got stiff in my pants and from the tent in Patrick's shorts it was evident that he too was excited. There was one problem – we were not staying at the Club. Before I could figure out a way around this predicament, Patrick blurted out. "You're gonna have to come over to the Buccaneer Inn for the signing ceremony. We are the only guests. The place is ours. Invite your friends. We can have a party."

"You aren't guests of the Playboy Club? You shouldn't be here. I can get fired for even talking to you. You have to leave."

"But, but, but, what about coming to our room and the signing ceremony, and the girls hungry for young men?" pleaded Patrick.

"Boys, you are very cute and it would be fun playing with you. I wanted the two of you to myself – double the pleasure, double the fun. But rules are rules and if I want to be in the elite inner circle of Mr. Hefner, I have to stay within the boundaries. I am afraid I have to tell you to leave and if you do not, I will have to have security escort you out. Goodbye." She turned and walked away. The firm smooth muscles of her ass slightly rippled as she moved. I imagined her long legs wrapped around me with my hands caressing her derrière and my lips kissing her nipples. We stared at her until she disappeared into the hotel.

"Ah, man, we could have been laid by a Playboy Bunny sex goddess. I wonder how much it cost to rent a room at the Club?" Patrick was as disappointed as I was and he still had a tent in his pants.

"Let's go in the hotel and find out, but you're gonna have to get rid of that tent in your shorts before we go inside, and make sure your peter behaves itself while we're in there."

"Bro, I would give my life just to put my mouth on one of those over-ripe milk sacs." Patrick looked like he was about to have an eruption.

"Well, it wouldn't be a bad way to die, but I'd rather have a full body surf for that price. Her breasts don't have milk in them. Just the same, they sure are the nicest pair of peaches I've ever seen. Come on, let's go inside and find out the cost of admission. It may be worth spending every penny we have for one night with Penelope." The way I was feeling at the moment, I really was willing to spend every penny to have an evening with Penelope, and hopefully she would bring along a friend.

"Yeah, even if we had to go back to the U.S. tomorrow, it would be worth it. Let's give it a shot," replied Patrick. We walked across the beach, past the huge thatched hut bar, and rows of beach chairs seated with a few gray haired people sunning their bodies, on past the very large swimming pool, through the glass doors with the bunny logo on them, and into the lobby. It was very eloquent, classy - too classy for my comfort. We strolled up to the main desk. A casually dressed and well-groomed effeminate young man welcomed us with a tone of reluctance and disbelief in his voice. We were wearing cutoff jeans, shirtless and shoeless, and our hair was well below shoulder length. Patrick and I were an anomaly in this very prissy upper class den of hedonism.

"How much for a room?" Patrick asked rather bluntly.

"It depends on the amenities you prefer," the man responded.

"The cheapest you got," said Patrick.

"That would be $575.00, garden view and a king sized bed." Our jaws dropped. We simply didn't have the cash. Our fantasy of body surfing with Penelope just got hit with a dose of reality. Patrick pulled me aside.

"It's always about the money, bro. This sucks. Maybe we should try convincing Penelope to come over to the Buc Inn?" Patrick didn't want to let go of the fantasy.

"We tried that already, and it is about the money for her too. If she is going to have sex for the sheer pleasure of it, she can have any man she wants. To her, we're just two hippie boys with no money. She isn't walking around nearly naked for her health. Like you said, it's all about the money." Patrick nodded his head in sad acquiescence. We left the hotel and headed back to the Buc. We went to our room and Patrick rolled another spliff and started smoking away.

"Penelope is a goddess." Patrick spoke in a dreamy, wispy voice.

"Yeah, and just like all goddesses, she isn't really real."

"You call that gorgeous babe not real! She's as real as it gets." Patrick's blood-shot eyes widened, partly because of what I said, but mostly because of the spliff.

"What I mean is she might as well be a mythology-like goddess since she won't be body surfing with us. Besides, I had no intention of sharing her with you. Sex is a completely private thing. You're my best friend but when it comes to sex, well, that's a bit too close for comfort."

"You red-headed devil. I thought you wouldn't do anything with her because you're so loyal to Sandy. And did you think I would just stand by while you body surfed with Penelope?"

"No. I expected that Penelope would bring along another Bunny. As for Sandy, well, I take the position that this is my time to sow my wild oats before marrying her."

"That's a classic rationalization for cheating on Sandy – and as good as any. I guess you're right about the mythological goddess thing. Oh well, maybe we'll meet some hot Jamaican babes. Rosie at the front desk is a babe." Patrick finally accepted reality and spiced it up with another hopeful fantasy. I didn't like his comment about cheating because it gave me a twinge of guilt. Sandy's statement about sex with other women echoed in my head. Yet, being here on this island made me feel as though the world I left behind was frozen in time and whatever I did here had no bearing on what happened there.

We returned to our room at the Buc. I heard music booming loudly. I stepped on to the balcony to determine its source and discovered that there were two large speakers on each level, six in all. *I Can See Clearly Now*, by Johnny Nash was playing. The music had great quality, as the speakers were most likely the best money could buy. I wasn't too fond of the song, even though the lyrics fit the circumstances perfectly. We decided to hang out by the pool before eating lunch in the dining area and then spent to rest of the day between swimming in he sea, drinking rum at the thatched hut – stationed by Jacob, of course, and then dinner on the veranda. By mid evening we crashed and slept the longest sleep since we had left Philly.

For a few days we alternated activities between swimming in the sea, drinking rum mixed with coconut and fruit juices at the thatched hut bar – of course Patrick kept his mind well saturated in ganja, supplied by Jacob. Voyeurism of the Bunnies was a regular activity, which was as torturous as it was pleasurable. There were no young Jamaican women in sight, which we thought was strange. So, one night after eating dinner we decided to venture out of the hotel grounds and into the surrounding village of Runaway Bay in search of Jamaican babes.

It was very dark with the exception of a lone streetlight, which felt out of place and was a grim reminder of our home neighborhood. There were dogs croaking, not barking, as if they were perpetually trying to dislodge bones from their throats. It was a disturbing, tortuous sound. The houses were not houses, they were shacks made of wood with corrugated tin roofs. People sitting on their oil lamp lit porches stared at us like we were from another planet. I felt a very distinct ambience of fear. It was a familiar feeling, akin to being in South Philly on an evening when the threat of violence hung in the air. "Paradise on the edge of a ghetto. Who would have thought such a thing was possible?" said Patrick. This was not the feeling I had anticipated. Patrick accidentally bumped into a trashcan, knocking it over, causing a loud clanking sound. A dog of skin and bones appeared on the road, croaking and hacking. A big Jamaican man suddenly appeared directly in front of us, causing me to jump and go into a defensive battle stance – an automatic response from my days as a young street warrior.

"Wat business yah bwoys 'ave 'ere?" This guy was big, not in tallness, but in sheer bulk! His breath was so foul it offended my nostrils even with the man standing several feet away. I could see a gaping whole where his teeth should be – they were either all gone or mostly rotten.

"Taking a walk," Patrick said with a strained friendly tone.

"Blood clatt, mon, dis is nuh safe. Der robbers waitin' in de shadows. Where yah stayin'?" His voice sounded like he had a throat full of gravel.

"Buccaneer Inn. We're friends of Jacob." Patrick was hoping that dropping Jacob's name would give us a shield of safety.

"I knoh Jacob, his fambly lives nearby. It bes' yah stay in de 'otel wit Jacob. No one be bot'ering yah der, mon. I will walk ta de 'otel wit yah. Presently der t'eifs eyes on us as we speak."

"Thanks. That'd be great. What's the deal with the croaking dogs?" Patrick asked.

"Chicken bones stuck in de throat. Aw dawgs are fed chicken bones. Come, I mus' get yah safe." I was relieved that we had this man's protection. He began escorting us back to the hotel when an idea struck me.

"When I was swimming the other morning, I noticed another hotel or bar type place up the beach in the other direction. Do you know the place?" I asked the man.

"Yeahmon. Dat is de Blue Parrot. It is own an' operated in partnership between Jamaicans and Europeans. It is where white people an' Jamaicans mix. I nuh approve of de place."

"Can you take us there?" Patrick asked.

"Effin I tek yah der, I nuh tek yah back. Yah be on yah own, mon."

"I say we take the risk. Besides, maybe we'll meet someone who can escort us back to the Buc. What do you think, Patrick?"

"I agree. I want to mix with the locals and meet other people from other countries."

"Awrite den, mon. I tek yah effin yah buy me a Red Stripe an' a few Craven 'A' cigarettes."

"Hell, we'll buy you three Red Stripes, and a whole pack of cigs," chimed Patrick.

"Mek we gawaan den." I had no idea what he just said. We followed him. It didn't take long to reach the Blue Parrot. There was a sign in the shape of a parrot with the hotel's name, and it was outlined with blue Christmas tree lights. I could smell the ganja wafting through the air as we made our way along the torch lit blue slate walkway that meandered through the small thatched hut buildings that were obviously hotel rooms. The path led to the bar-restaurant that was closer to the water than the circular stone and thatched hut guest cottages. The entire place was on the beach. A song from the increasingly popular Jamaican band, The Wailers, *Guava Jelly*, was booming through the speakers that were placed throughout the hotel property, adding to the Jamaican culture ambience. I was surprised to see so many white and black people assembled in one place, and what was more surprising was that almost all the women were white and all the men were black, and everyone looked like they were in their twenties. This was a happening place!

"Oreo cookie haven!" Patrick said as he let out a whistle.

"Yeah, and we're the only male cream," I quipped.

"Are you complaining or bragging?" asked Patrick.

"Neither. Just stating the facts."

"We'll it could be to our advantage," replied Patrick.

"How's that?"

"Not all girls like chocolate ice cream, at least not all of the time, and we're the only vanilla." Patrick ran his tongue around his lips as he made an adjustment in his shorts. We made our way to the bar and ordered three Red Stripes and a pack of Craven 'A' cigs. I handed a bottle and cigs to our Jamaican escort, realizing I didn't know his name.

"Thanks for bringing us here. What's your name?" I asked.

"Kenny, mon. T'anks fer de beer an' cigs. I haffin ta gawaan now." I surmised that he just said he had to leave.

"Hey, we promised you three beers, hell we'll buy you all you can drink. Stick around a while." Patrick said.

"No, mon. I nuh approve of white an' black mixin' der bodies – nuh natural, mon. I 'ave fambly waitin'. Mus' gawaan. Cool runnings, mon. Bes' tek care wen gawaan 'ome, mon, fer de be people wantin' ta put de 'urt on yah fer money, mon."

"We'll be careful. Hell, after all, we are from South Philly," said Patrick. I was impressed that Patrick understood what he said. I did get the care part, though. Kenny just shook his head as he left the bar, not knowing a thing about South Philly. Patrick had a point. We were born and bred street fighting boys, and although we had long since changed our ways, we did know how to take care of ourselves in violent circumstances. The thought of being in a situation where I might have to use violence was extremely unpleasant, and I no longer had confidence in my ability to respond with aggression to aggression. It was so strange to be worried about violence on a paradise island.

"Bro, that was almost as bad as walking in the wrong neighborhood in Philly," said Patrick as he sipped on his Red Stripe.

"Worse. At least in Philly we know how to defend ourselves, get away from danger, and more importantly how to stay away from dangerous places. Out there, we have no idea what the dangers are or how to deal with them. I hope Negril isn't like that. Randy said there would be Jamaicans hustling us for money in Montego Bay, but he said nothing about the fear, and threat of violence. I doubt Negril is anything like Runaway Bay village." I was trying to convince myself as well as ease Patrick's mind.

"Maybe we should leave tomorrow for Negril. The hotel is nice, but I am beginning to feel like we are living in a guarded compound. I want to experience the Jamaica that Randy told us about." I agreed with Patrick. I wanted freedom to explore the island and get to know friendly indigenous people, and in a way the Blue Parrot presented us with a novel opportunity to do just that. Then again, I'm not sure we had a clear idea of what the *real* Jamaica is like. Maybe all of it's the real Jamaica, including tourism with its money and fancy hotels.

"Hey, look around you," I implored. "This is one of the many faces of Jamaica. It may not be the native island of our fantasies, but look at those babes. If this is going to be our last night, then I say let's make it one hell of a big bang." The women were definitely employees of the Playboy Club – judging by the fact that without exception all of them were gorgeous. They were wearing slightly more clothes but that didn't hide their shapely bodies and remarkably beautiful faces.

"Yeah, bro, this is the mother lode of babes. Those Jamaicans are all over them. I wonder if we have a chance competing with these exotic and assertive Jamaican men." Patrick was uncharacteristically worried about competition.

"Like you said, some women prefer vanilla," I reminded him. We sat at the bar watching the scene play out before us. There were spliffs and bongs being passed around. The women were toying with the Jamaican men like cats playing with prey. The men didn't seem to mind being toyed with. I think they were pleased to have the attention of these goddesses.

"Hello boys." A sweet voice came from behind us. Simultaneously we spun our bodies around on the bar stools.

"Penelope!" we exclaimed.

"Oliver and Patrick, I believe I have your names right. This is my friend, Jennifer. I'm glad to see you found your way to the Blue Parrot." I looked Jennifer over. She was definitely a bunny!

"Yeah, so are we. Can we get you a drink?" I asked.

"Rum and coke for me. How about you, Jenny?"

"I'll have a shot of Tequila with a Red Stripe chaser," she replied.

"By the way, call me Penny, all my friends do."

"Penny and Jenny – has a nice ring to it," added Patrick. "Do you mind if I call you Jenny?"

"That would be marvelous darling. All my playboys call me their sweet luscious Jenny." And luscious she was! Just like all of the Playboy models, she was purrrfect in every way. She was tall, had long blonde hair, large brilliant green eyes, high cheekbones, and a smile that made my heart melt. She wore a semi-see through bra-less halter-top that held voluptuous breasts with protruding nipples. Her cutoff jeans revealed her cheek bottoms. Her legs were long and well toned.

"Wow, it's really great meeting you here. Do you come often?" Patrick asked in a surprisingly relaxed tone. I expected that he would be nervous, like me. Perhaps all that ganja streaming through his brain put him in a suspended relaxed state.

"We live here, as do all the Playboy Bunnies. Living at the Blue Parrot is part of the benefit package for working at the Club. We enjoy our little village of girls along with freedom from the watchful eyes of our employer. We're like birds in a cage when working, and the clientele are mostly rich old retired people wanting to stimulate their sex lives by surrounding themselves with gorgeous women. It gets annoying having old men, and women, staring at us all the time. The money's good, though. But, we are free of all that. This is our last night in Jamaica. Jenny and I are going back to the U.S. tomorrow. We have interviews and work to complete for a future Playboy issue on island girls of the Caribbean."

"Both of you will be featured?" Patrick asked. Jenny, obviously interested in Patrick, moved closer to him as she answered.

"Yes. They did photo sessions for most of the girls working at the Club, and they selected four of us for the featured magazine. Jenny and I are two of them. Playboy has clubs on several Caribbean islands and they've selected girls from all of them. It should be a great issue."

The thought of seeing these two women posing naked in a magazine made me hard. I felt a little embarrassed and hoped they wouldn't notice. We continued to chat with them for an hour or more, drinking all the while. I was feeling quite comfortable around them. They were beginning to feel like regular girls and not Playboy pinup sex goddesses, although being in the presence of such beauty made me hornier than I have ever felt in my life. Meaning that I felt purely sexual with no feeling of love involved, unlike what I experience with Sandy. Yep, this was purely sexual!

Penny had made her interest in me explicit by looking at me whenever she spoke, and I was grooving on the attention. "It is such a relief to talk with young American men. Besides the old white folks being annoying, Jamaican men can be quite rude and pushy. This is the first time since coming to Jamaica that I haven't felt like I was on display in a meat market," commented Penny with a sigh. "When I first met you boys, I was relieved, although the both of you never stopped staring at me," she laughed and so did Jenny. "I assumed you were young rock and roll stars, they are the only young men who can afford being at the Club."

"We're accustomed to being stared at, it goes with the territory," Jenny moved her hands along her body as she spoke to illustrate her meaning.

"Beauty's only skin deep, yeah, yeah, yeah," Patrick sang a line from a popular tune.

Jenny was impressed with Patrick's singing. "Nice voice, but I disagree with the message. Beauty is both flesh and personality and when the two are combined, well, just take another look." Jenny placed one hand on her rear and another under her left breast to make her point. I wondered how she was going to demonstrate the personality aspect.

"So, are you guys musicians? You certainly look the part, with your long hair and good looks," Penny asked.

"Well, flattery will get you anywhere!" replied Patrick.

"Promise?" replied Jenny.

"Boys Scouts honor!" quipped Patrick, as he held up two fingers and placed the other hand on his heart.

"We like music. Patrick is a guitar player and has a good voice, and I play the flute."

Penny looked delighted, breaking into a big smile. "Hey, I'm a flute player as well. In fact, they did a photo shoot of me standing at the base of Dunn's River waterfall playing the flute, naked of course, with rainbows dancing all around me, you know, because of the falls mist spreading out those light rays. The photo might make it in the island issue." The image of Penny playing the flute by a waterfall, naked, caused some movement in my jeans – again. "I minored in music at Berkley and played flute for the orchestra."

I remembered reading biographies in Playboy magazines of the naked beauties, and almost all of them were smart and talented with lots of hobbies and interests - sort of like the Miss America contestants. I was getting Jenny's point about the beauty of the flesh combined with personality and talent.

"I love to sing and I play the piano," added Jenny, as if to put an exclamation on the personality plus beauty comment. The alcohol was kicking into high gear, and all of us were feeling less inhibited, causing the conversation to flow easily, allowing us to become more expressive.

"Too bad you girls are leaving tomorrow. We could've formed a rock and roll band," lamented Patrick.

"Oh well, perhaps in another lifetime. The night is warm and the sky is clear. How about the four of us take an evening dip," suggested Jenny.

"Great idea!" Patrick said with extra enthusiasm.

"Alright then, lets go." Penny took me by the hand and led the way towards the sea. Holding her hand sent a wave of sexual energy through my body, keeping the blood supply flowing to my groin. This was the first time we touched and it was electric. Jenny and Patrick walked beside us, holding hands as well. We walked rather briskly along the water's edge. We stopped when we were a good distance away from the Blue Parrot.

"This is a lovely spot. Let's swim here, but before we do I have a little treat." Penny took out a metal case from her jean pocket. She opened it and took out a joint and matches. Lit it up, took a long drag, coughed, and passed it around. I passed on the joint without taking a hit. I didn't want to risk getting paranoid. When the joint was finished, Jenny and Penny looked at each other, nodded their heads and giggled, then they stripped completely naked and stood before us silently, smiling and looking too real to be real. I was mesmerized and Patrick looked like a deer whose eyes were caught in a car's headlights. We hesitated taking our clothes off. The women looked at us quizzically. Jenny's eyes scanned our crotches. She giggled and said, "Why look, Penny, they feel embarrassed to take off their pants."

"Don't be embarrassed boys, our bodies are excited too – just not as noticeable," said Penny. I just stared at them. I was hard as a rock – I had been most of the evening and it was throbbing so much it hurt. There was no way I was going to take my pants off.

"Really, guys, we're just going for a swim. The night is young, there's plenty of time for other pleasures. Besides, having sex in the water is not what it's made out to be," said Jenny. I was stunned to hear these girls talking this way. Their directness about wanting to have sex with us made me both uncomfortable and excited, but not so for Patrick.

"Well, if you girls don't mind looking at me in all my glory, than so be it." Patrick took off his jeans. Jenny let out a whistle when she saw his naked body.

"Whoa, what a lovely big bamboo, as the Jamaicans say!" Jenny giggled as she took Patrick by the hand and off they went into the water.

"I completely understand how you feel, Oliver. When I first interviewed for Playboy, they told me to strip down and show them what I had. I was so nervous that I had a panic attack. The people were very understanding and let me take my time. Eventually, I got so comfortable being naked around people that I would sometimes forget I had no clothes on. You can keep your pants on if it makes you feel better." Penny's words made me relax, but my erection didn't go down.

"I skinny dipped before. I just need a little time to calm things down." I replied.

"I can help with that." She said softly, approaching me cautiously, all the while looking into my eyes with her lovely smile. She placed her hand along the outside of my jeans and rubbed along the bump, then slowly unzipped my pants, looking in my eyes for signs of uneasiness - there wasn't any. I sprung out of my jeans. Penny's eyes widened as she let out a pleasing sigh of approval, saying, "Ooh, light lavender - such a lovely color." She took me in her hands and gently squeezed. She removed one hand and licked it with her tongue, placed it back and stroked up and down. Then, she knelt on her knees and ran her tongue along the rim of the throbbing semen seeping blood-engorged mushroom shaped head. The molten love lava was starting to flow from the magma chamber through the vent, and just as I was about to erupt, she engulfed me with her warm, moist mouth, using her lips, tongue, and edges of her teeth to scintillate the nerve endings of my cone. My mind was transported to an otherworldly place. I was losing all sense of self, completely surrendering my body and mind to Penny's fellatio embrace. I erupted in her mouth. Penny groaned in delight from the warm sweet and salty taste sensations of my cream lava flow.

"There, now you are taken care of. That was quite nice, Oliver, do you agree?" I didn't answer. I took her in my arms and kissed her. She pressed her breasts against me and moaned. I placed my hand between her legs and lightly stroked her warm, wet fold. I gently rubbed her erect and surprisingly large clitoris, causing her moans to reach a higher pitch. Our kisses became more passionate. She opened her mouth inviting my tongue to enter.

“Press against me and put two of your fingers inside me,” she whispered. I did as she instructed. I was getting hard again, although not full. I wanted to enter her and told her so – my passion more eager than my bodies capacity to fully respond – but not for long.

“Not yet. Not here. Keep stroking me with your fingers, and suck my right nipple.” I did as she instructed rubbing my growing member against her hairless pelvis.

“I have to have you. I can’t wait," I said.

"Are you strong enough to hold me if I wrap my legs around you?” I didn’t respond with words. I had sex with Sandy while standing and knew what to do. There was a palm tree near by. I walked her to the tree and leaned my body against it. I placed my hands firmly on her cheeks and lifted as she simultaneously wrapped her legs around my waist. I was fully ready and slowly entered her warm wet flesh, teasing the opening. I was surprised that I didn’t explode instantly. The most recent ejaculation turned out to be the best foreplay. It prevented me from erupting prematurely. I entered her fully and again she cried out in pleasure. We kept our pelvises pressed tightly as she moved her hips ever so slightly. I slowly slid my back along the trunk of the tree, easing our bodies down onto the sand while remaining completely engaged. She was now straddled on top of me. Penny looked down into my eyes and then arched her back causing her breasts to thrust forward.

I reached up and engulfed them in my hands, massaging and rubbing, causing her to gyrate her hips with a slow rhythmic motion that was in sync with the gentle lapping of the sea. She squeezed me with every muscle, pulsing her grip as she slowly moved up and down my shaft, enjoying my explorations of the wet flesh of her cavern walls, massaging me like a strong wet hand. She leaned forward, placing one of her nipples within reach of my probing tongue. I licked, sucked, and took the nipple of one breast in between my teeth, gently biting, while pinching the other nipple with my fingers. Again, she arched her back and then let out a cry as she gushed warm soothing liquid - her love cry and the warmth of her juices brought me closer to a climax. I grabbed both cheeks of her ass, raised my head and once again took one of her nipples in my mouth. I thrust my body upward, pushing with all my strength, muscles tightening and rippling all over my body, all the while she continued in the midst of her climax, causing her to gush even more as she cried, “Yes, yes, yes! Oh sweet Oliver, deeper, harder! Come! In! Me! Yesssss!” I roared as she let out a loud love cry in unison while I exploded with hot molten lava spewing into her ocean of love. Penny collapsed on top of me, meeting my lips, lovingly kissing me as my hands stroked her ass and rubbed her wet juices over her cheeks.

"That was fantastic! I've never gushed like that before. I didn't know it was possible. That was the most amazing orgasm of my entire life, a waterfall orgasm. Oliver, we are amazing!"

"I think I love you, Penny."

"You are so sweet, Oliver." I kissed her all over her body, eventually finding my way to her crevice, as I was licking her clitoris, I was getting erect - yet again.

"Oliver, save it for the bed where we can be more comfortable. Do you want to swim first or go to my thatched hut?"

"I'll do whatever you want. I am your playboy." I replied.

"I like the sound of that, and I am your playgirl. This is the last opportunity I'll have to swim in the Caribbean before going home tomorrow. Come on, let's get in the water." We got up and ran into the sea. The water instantly cooled the sweat from our bodies. We saw no sign of Jenny and Patrick. I assumed they were somewhere on the beach making whoopee.

After swimming and playing in the water for a while, we put on our clothes and went to her hut. The circular cottage was rustic and very comfortable. There was a ceiling fan spinning above her queen size bed, providing ample room for us to glide between the sheets throughout the evening. The first light of dawn filtered through the windows. As I was about to leave, Jenny and Patrick showed up at the door, the two of them glowing from their night together. Obviously they had as much fun as we did. They kissed each other for the last time as Penny and I watched in the doorway with appreciation. Jenny wanted to make sure Penny was awake and preparing to leave. Once they left, we turned to each other for our final loving embrace.

"I truly love you Penny!"

"Oliver, I understand that you think all this wonderful passion is love, but do not confuse exquisite pleasure with love. We don't know each other well enough to be in love. True, we are physically compatible – being in our prime made it possible to make love more times in one night than I had in months. And this is amazingly romantic, more so than anything I experienced while in Jamaica, but that is not to say that our personalities can embrace each other equally as well."

"Don't say that. I love you. There is no way that two people can have sex like we did and there not be love present."

“Well, you have a point,” she said while placing her hands upon me, causing arousal. “Unfortunately, we may never know for sure. Besides, I am older than you and have a career ahead of me. Where my life is going, you cannot follow. It is best that we appreciate our special moment for what it is, a wonderful experience. If our paths should cross again, well, perhaps we will discover that love is guiding us. Let’s leave our relationship up to fate.”

I liked what Penny said. It made the experience feel like an adventure yet to be resumed. I took her in my arms and kissed her for the last time. Penny gracefully slid onto the bed, saying she wanted to plant a remembrance picture in my mind that would endure forever. Her goddess-like naked body stretched out upon the ruffled satin sheets. She placed one hand on her inner thigh and slightly moved her legs apart revealing the full beauty of her womanhood, and the other hand held a breast. She had a loving, sexy, longing expression on her beautiful face. Her violet eyes and luscious lips smiled at me as she blew kisses, sending sensations rippling through my body. I slowly closed the door.

Patrick and I strolled out of the Blue Parrot a little older than when we entered. Indeed, the experience we had with these women did much for our confidence as young men, and I do believe it went a long way towards healing Patrick’s heartache over losing Chrissie. We shared generalities of our love adventures, leaving out the finer elements. Penny and Jenny would forever hold a paramount place in the unfolding of our blossoming manhood - we had a supreme lesson in the erotic art of lovemaking by two of Hugh Hefner’s hand picked goddesses of beauty.

Walking through the town of Runaway Bay during the early morning hours did not have the same fear ambience as during the previous night. It only took twenty minutes to get to the Buccaneer Inn.

We stood on the balcony outside our room looking at the sun hovering above the eastern horizon. I noticed a large yacht anchored several hundred yards off the coast. It must have sailed in during the night. I saw Steve and what may have been the DeSalva couple along with Jacob and another Jamaican with dreadlocks, loading bundles wrapped in what appeared to be burlap on to a boat that was moored at the Buccaneer dock. Patrick wanted to go to the boat and tell Steve we were leaving and to ask him how much we owed. I told him we shouldn’t bother them. I suspected that the bundles were marijuana and mentioned that to Patrick.

"Yeah. You're probably right. Yo, these guys are smugglers. I bet they're taking those bundles to that yacht."

"Gee, you're a genius," I quipped.

"Wow, I bet their gonna sail that marijuana to the U.S."

"Yep. You're getting smarter by the minute. Must be the ganja."

"Seriously, Oliver, this place is probably a front for a smuggling operation."

"No shit Sherlock. Sure looks that way. It explains why there are so few guests and the mysterious absence of Steve Tanz. If you smuggle enough dope you're going to make millions. It's no wonder they can afford a hotel next to the Playboy Club. I always wondered how Jamaican marijuana made it to the streets of South Philly."

"South Philly and all the hippies across the pot-crazed good ol' USA and Europe. I hope they don't get busted, especially this morning. The police will think we're part of the operation," Patrick sounded serious.

"Well, we better get ourselves moving just in case," I added.

"Let's watch a little longer to see what happens," suggested Patrick. We watched the boat take off and sure enough it went straight to the yacht. The boat made its way to the side that was not facing the shoreline. We couldn't see them unloading the boat. After an hour had passed, the boat headed back to the dock. Steve wasn't on it. We assumed he was going to sail across the Atlantic with the merchandise. After the DeSalva couple and the Jamaicans got off the boat, we went to the front desk with our gear.

Rosie smiled as we asked for our bill. She told us that the bill was taken care of by Mr. Tanz, and that we were welcome to stay as long as we like. This caused me to pause for a moment, as the offer was very tempting. We stepped aside and discussed the offer. Free room and board at the Buccaneer Inn for as long as we like was not to be taken lightly. Patrick was slightly more tempted to accept the offer, mentioning that we could score more erotic experiences with other playgirls living in the Blue Parrot village. I told him that Penny and Jenny were very special and a repeat performance with any other Bunnies was improbable. "And do you think what happened to us last night was a dream come true? If you want to talk about probability, man, our chances of a repeat performance are a hell of a lot higher hanging out in a bar with bunnies than any other place on this planet. No offense, bro, but you're talking stupid dribble!"

"Well, when you put it like that, I have to agree. It's just that I want to experience the *real* Jamaica that Randy talked about." I was sincere but Patrick's rather poignant comment was very convincing – I was wavering.

"Hey, man, witnessing the illicit marijuana smuggling trade is surely an integral aspect of Jamaican culture, akin to rum running during the age of piracy. All of this is the *real* Jamaica. You have to admit it Oliver, we are having one hell of an island adventure!"

"That we are, bro! So what's it gonna be, Patrick?"

"Well if all else fails, we could return to the Buc. I think they need a few guests to keep up appearances for their smuggling operation, and I wouldn't mind learning the business trade – it could be our ticket to a brighter future. Then again there is always the possibility of the DeSalva couple getting busted and we don't want to be a part of that scene."

It was a hard decision to make and the fact that we could return and try our luck with the Playboy Bunnies at another time had strongly influenced our decision. As for now, we were well satiated in the sex department and felt ready to move on to another phase of our adventures-in-paradise saga. And the fact that Penny and Jenny had left the island, after sharing an amazing evening with us, was a good capstone to our experience at the Buccaneer Inn. We decided to ride the high into the western side of the island. Adventure on!

We told Rosie we were planning on going to Negril and that we might return. She said that we would always be welcomed as guests of Mr. Tanz, just as I had hoped. She asked how we would be traveling and we told her about hitchhiking. Rosie said that would not be safe and that no Jamaican gave free rides on the island because taxi drivers depend on tourists to make a living. She said she would speak to the DeSalva limousine driver and ask if he was available for our use. He was! I was delightfully surprised and asked to speak to the DeSalva couple and Steve to thank them for everything. Rosie said that would not be possible as the DeSalvas rarely speak to guests and Steve was leaving the island with aboard the yacht. It was apparent that they wanted to remain incognito for self-protection.

NEGRIL
(Lord Joseph)

The limousine pulled up and once again, we felt like rock stars as we climbed in. We told the driver we wanted to go to Negril – he already knew.

"Mi name is Peter, mon. You travel ta a lovely place, mon. Negril is on de western mos' tip of de island, an' is de mos' beautiful village in aw of Jamaica!"

These were facts we had heard from Randy. His comment made us feel like we had made the right decision. Peter said that he saw us at the Blue Parrot with those beautiful girls and asked if we had any luck. We excitedly talked about the virtues of Penny and Jenny. He laughed all the while and then told us that that was not their real names, that none of the bunnies use their real names – another policy of the Playboy Club. It occurred to us that we never asked them their full names. We were stunned. Then I recalled that they were featured in past Playboy issues and that we could easily discover their real names.

I asked Peter to describe Negril. He told us that it was a fishing village undisturbed by tourism, and that the people were very friendly and uninfluenced by the money that tourism had brought to other parts of Jamaica. The people were money poor but self-sufficient. He said the village had seven miles of beach with few houses, and that the western end of the village consisted of many miles of cliffs. The village began at the base of the mountains where horticulture was practiced on the gentler slopes, an area called *Red Ground.* A river flowed into the sea from the mountains and was the division between the beach and cliffs. Peter explained that most tourists went to the bigger cities, like Montego Bay and Kingston where there were all-inclusive resorts and that there were very few tourist accommodations in Negril.

"Hippies, mon, fram aw over de world are findin' out 'bout Negril. Dees hippies 'ave no interest in fancy 'otels, de want ta live like *real* Jamaicans. Der nuh ta many of dem, but each year der more an' more. True dat mon. Negril soon be very popular, mon, aw Jamaicans knoh dat comin', mon."

The ride took several hours on winding poorly constructed roads that hugged the coastline. They were curvy roads, narrow, and paved with crushed chalky stone. Peter drove too fast, and when he came to the many blind curves, he would simply honk his horn to inform drivers coming from the other direction of our presence without slowing down. His driving made us nervous. I wondered how many Jamaicans and tourists had lost their lives in car accidents. There were several small villages along the way that were nestled on harbors and the sides of mountains that sloped to the sea. Finally, several hours later, we arrived in Negril. We saw the South Negril River as we crossed a low-lying bridge. Peter dropped us off on the southwest side of the bridge in what was called the *Roundabout.* It was the center of the Negril village and apparently the commercial hub. We gave Peter a five-dollar tip. He laughed and called us big-time spenders.

"Tek dis package, mon, compliments of Mestah Tanz an' de Buccaneer Inn. Across de riva is weh yah fin' de lovely beach. Up dat way are de cliffs, known as de West End an' de road is called West End Road, some call it Lighthouse Road. De road sloping up dat way is de area known as Red Ground. Be safe, mon. Dees people are very friendly. Respect dem an' dey will respect you. Cool runnings, bruddas!" He drove off smiling. The package was a super mini version of the burlap bundles we saw being loaded on the boat – weighting a few ounces – and its contents was no mystery as it had that sweet smell of ganja buds. We decided to open it once we got settled.

There was a restaurant called the Wharf Club that appeared to be the center of the Negril village. We went inside and the smell of chicken hit our nostrils. I was starving. We took a seat and ordered two plates of chicken and rice. It was spiced with flavors and vegetables unknown to my palate that were quite delicious. I asked the waiter if he knew Millie and Charley. He did, telling us that they lived on the West End of Negril along the cliffs, several miles from the Roundabout along Lighthouse Road – a fact we already learned from Randy. It was good to hear a Jamaican tell us that he knew of them – it increased our excitement. The meal cost $1.75 U.S. currency, a real bargain. So far, the tip we gave to our driver, the modest sum we spent at the Blue Parrot, and now this meal, was the only cash we spent in Jamaica.

Donning our backpacks, and our bellies now full, we started the trek to find Millie and Charlie. The walk was hot although not unpleasant for the sight of the sea, cliffs, and lovely foliage was breathtaking. The cliffs started out low-lying and gradually got higher. We came upon a small beach situated between cliffs, a break between volcanic rock that I didn't expect, forming a tranquil cove where the fishermen kept their dugout canoes, traps and nets. I wondered how they made the canoes because the canoes were wooden and each one was slightly different although all of them had the same basic narrow canoe shape. The irregularity of their size along with distinct carved markings indicated that they were individually hand crafted. We spent some time looking over the canoes and fish traps. We had a special interest because we grew up fishing along the Jersey shore.

A short distance past Fishermen Cove we came upon concrete structures built on the cliffs. There was a sign that read, Yacht Club, which struck me as funny because there were no yachts and no docks to moor them. We decided not to explore this out-of-place tourist looking area in this otherwise very native and pristine village.

This was the real Jamaica for there were apparently no hotels besides the so-called Yacht Club, just shanties dotted along the narrow crushed chalky limestone road. The shacks were mostly situated on the side opposite the cliffs. We continued on, eventually stopping to take a rest. We ventured on to the cliffs to get a better view. It was a good thing that we were wearing Converse sneakers because the cliffs consisted of jagged, sharp gray-blue volcanic rock that had cooled quickly and looked like they were frozen in what was once the shape of their liquid state. I estimated the cliff was at the very least twenty feet high. The water below was deep and clear and turquoise. I could see the sea bottom. Sea swells came in and out, making swooshing sounds as they moved up and down the rocks. There was a tree that had a branch that extended out over the cliff's edge. I climbed the tree and made my way out on to the thick branch and looked down. It was an awesome perspective of the cliff and sea. Patrick snapped a picture.

"Yo, I didn't know you had a camera. How come you didn't use the camera to take pictures of Penny and Jenny?"

"I didn't have it with me at the Blue Parrot. Truth is, I forgot I had it. My father gave it to me and said I should record our little odyssey on film. I just remembered as I saw you climbing out on that branch and thought it would make a great photo. Too bad that it didn't dawn on me when we were at the Buc, and while we were hitchhiking, especially during the Disney World red-eye midnight tour. Man, I would give my two front teeth to have naked pictures of Penny and Jenny!"

"Well, we have a standing invitation to return to the Buc. Maybe, before we leave the island, we can spend a few days there and get some pictures of Playboy Bunnies."

"Great idea. Maybe we can make our own Playboy magazine centerfold. Can you envision me in the raw posing with Jenny?"

"Now that's a scary image! And I can have a full-page nude display of my Penny from heaven with us playing a flute duet by a waterfall with rainbows dancing all around. Yeah, let's dream on, Patrick. Speaking of dreams – I can't believe the color variations of this water – it's fantastic." As I sat on the branch looking around, I got the idea to jump from the tree into the water.

"Yo, I'm gonna strip off my clothes and jump into the sea!"

"And how are you going to get back up?" Patrick asked.

"Climb. It can't be that hard."

"There's no guarantee of that, and besides the rocks are sharp." As we were talking, I took off my high-top sneakers and shirt.

"The cliff doesn't look as sharp closer to the water. The sea has worn the rocks smooth. Where there's a will there's a way, and the quickest way to find out is to ... take the plunge ..." I leapt into the air. The descent was quick and exhilarating, I hit the water with my arms extended over my head and my legs together and straight. It was a perfect entry. The water was refreshing. I swam toward the surface with open eyes, seeing the light filter through the water. I broke the surface and let out a yell.

"Yo bro, you've got to jump. It's great." I shouted up to Patrick who was peering over the cliff edge.

"Not until you find a way back up." I looked around and immediately noticed an opening in the cliff, which could not be seen from above. It was a very large opening and I was treading water in front of one of two entrances to what looked like a sea cave. There was a huge rock that extended all the way down from the top of the cliff and narrowed as it connected to the seabed. It was situated dead center between the two openings. I swam along the cliff peering into both sides of the huge cavern openings. The cliff face was completely vertical. There was no way to climb back up.

"There appears to be a sea cave. The rock face is jagged, filled with fossils, and it is completely vertical. There's no way to safely get hand and foot holds to climb up. I'm going to swim into the cave and have a look around."

"Bro, I think you screwed up big time. You may have to swim all the way back to Fishermen Cove, which is quite a distance," shouted Patrick.

"Maybe there are spots along the cliffs that I can climb up, if not, I can swim to where the cliffs are lower and that is not as far as Fishermen Cove, and there is that Yacht Club place. I'm heading into the cave. See you later, alligator."

"Be safe, bro."

I swam into the cave, which was easy as the rising swells carried me in.

The cave was deep. The colors of the walls were surprisingly varied: gray, blue, green, yellow, and deep reddish-purple. Towards the back of the cave, I could see light filtering in somewhere from above. As I swam in further, it became shallower and I was able to stand with my head above water. The bottom was covered with sand. The rocks were very smooth and there were tiers of ledges that rose all the way to the cave's roof. I climbed out of the water on to a ledge. I stood up and turned my eyes towards the cave openings. The rock in the center that extended from the ceiling was huge and took up much of the cave closest to the two openings. The cave was very wide, about one hundred-fifty feet across. The water flowed in the cave in a giant 'U' shape.

I explored along the walls and noticed hundreds of sea creature fossils embedded in rock. I had the feeling that I was inside a palace built by sea, wind, lava, and decorated by the fossils of sea creatures that were millions of years old. Nature was the architect and artist of this lovely place. The air was warm and moist, a nice reprieve from the heat of direct sunlight. I yelled Patrick's name and the sound echoed off the walls. I realized that this would be an excellent place to play my flute. In fact, it would be an awesome cave to live in, if only there was easier access. I wished we had a canoe to bring in supplies. The rock ledges would be an excellent place to sleep. I liked the idea of waking up each morning and diving in the sea. We could even fish right from the ledges. Surely fish swam into the cave.

I became aware of a continuous light breeze that moved past me and up towards the roof at the back of the cave where the light was coming from. Then it hit me: light! There must be an opening in the top of the cliff since light was coming in. I climbed one ledge after another and surely enough, I came upon a hole in the cave's ceiling. It was over three feet in diameter, just the right size to climb through with ease. I poked my head out and looked around. I was on the other side of the road. Behind me there was a small shanty. I realized I was on someone's land. I called out to Patrick. At first, he looked over the edge of the cliff.

"Yo, behind you, over here on the other side of the road." His head turned my way but he still couldn't see me because he wasn't looking at the ground and only my head was sticking up. I started laughing.

"Where are you? I can't see you. Are you okay?" I climbed the rest of the way out and when he saw me he shouted, "Freaking awesome, totally far out, man. I have to go in."

"It is so freaking cool, bro. But you have to jump. It is the best way to get introduced to the cave."

"Come on, bro, I have to climb down that hole."

"Trust me on this, Patrick. You won't regret it. As the founder of the sea cave, I hereby decree that you shall be initiated by jumping off the cliff and swimming in from the sea opening!"

"You're strange sometimes. Okay, have it your way. After all, it was your discovery." Patrick took off his shoes and shirt and without a moment's hesitation did a swan dive off the cliff. Patrick was an excellent diver. I would have followed after him but I was reluctant to walk on the cliff with bare feet. I climbed back into the cave to watch him swim. Like me, he was awe struck by the magnificent beauty of the sea palace.

"Do you realize, Oliver, how much of a treasure this place is? This is the most amazing place on the planet. Look at the colors in here, and those fossils have to be hundreds of thousands of years old. This place is an ancient tomb of sea creatures that lived a very long time ago."

"Without a doubt, it is one of the wonders of the world!" I added.

"The air is humid in here but the breeze is nice. This is the perfect place to get out of the hot sun, and not only that, the hole makes for easy access and it creates a draft so that smoke from a fire would just drift out like a chimney." The Boy Scout was coming out in Patrick, and I knew what he was going to say next. "This is the perfect place to set up camp. What do you say? Let's live in here. Hell, we can even fish for food."

"My exact thoughts, but there is one problem, the opening is on someone's land, and that person may own this cave. We would have to get permission."

"Well then, Oliver James, let's find the owner. It won't hurt to ask." Just as he said that we heard a booming voice coming from the opening.

"Rhaatid! Who dat in mi cave? Yah go inna mi cave yahso?" It was a husky masculine voice with that distinct Jamaican lilt and patois dialect that was nearly impossible to understand – and he had a slightly angry tone.

"Just us!" I nervously called out. I saw two huge bare feet appear through the cave's roof, than a massive body of pure muscle that looked as though it was chiseled out of ebony followed by a huge head with long dreadlocks that draped his excessively muscular chest. He wore only a loincloth. I could see that the soles of his feet were completely calloused, perhaps a half inch of human leather. I doubt that this man had ever worn shoes. He was the quintessential native Jamaican, completely untouched by the Western world.

The sight of this Rastafarian man was absolutely stunning. He stopped on the ledge a few feet above us. His big penetrating dark eyes held us in their grip. I felt like he was peering into my soul. We stood completely still as he looked us over. I was speechless, held in a trance-like state by the aura of this man's presence. Patrick spoke. "I am Patrick and this is my friend, Oliver. Pleased to meet you sir."

"Blood clatt, mon, how yah inna mi cave yahso?" His booming voice echoed off the cavern walls. His words were hard to decipher, but I think he wanted to know how we got in his cave.

"We jumped off the cliff and discovered it from the seaside. We didn't know it belonged to anyone, we are just exploring. It is quite beautiful," Patrick explained.

"I n I Lord Joseph an' dis cave 'as been in mi fambly back ta de time of de English wen slavery no more. Nuh one cum inna 'ere wit ou' mi blessing." It struck me that although it was hard to understand him, he understood us perfectly well.

"Sorry Lord Joseph, sir. We mean no disrespect. We will leave you in peace," I said, hoping that this man was not violent. He certainly was scary and mysterious. He was a least six feet four inches tall, and there was not an ounce of fat on his body. I quickly thought of an exit plan if he turned violent, and that was simply to dive into the sea and swim.

"Bwoys fram de lan' of Babylon, yah defile mi cave! Yah mus' 'ave purification. Partek of de Lamb's Bread wit I n I, Jah! We mus' gi 'omage ta King Haile Selassie an' clean de mind of de thoughts born of de mud of Babylon. I soon return wit de Lamb's Bread of Jah." Lord Joseph ascended from the cave. Leaving us in a state of shock and awe.

"Wow! That man is from another world." I looked at Patrick's eyes as he spoke - they were lit up like candles, as if he just saw an aberration from the spirit world. "This is a great opportunity. That man is one in a million. A true Rastaman and we get to participate in what I assume is a sacred Rastafarian ritual in a sea cave on a paradise island. This is really far out, man!" Patrick was ecstatic.

"Lamb's Bread? Isn't that what Randy called the marijuana he smoked in your basement? And what does he mean by clean the mind of Babylon? All I know about Babylon is that it was a city of sin and God destroyed it." This Jamaican was the most fascinating person I had ever met and he had a mystical aura that was enticing and a little frightening.

"Lord Joseph is a Rastafarian and marijuana is an integral part of their lifestyle. Lamb's Bread is that special ganja Randy shared with me, and I bet he is going to use it like Christians use communion, you know, to cleanse the soul of all sin with the body and blood of Christ. And Christ is the Lamb of God that took away the sins of the world. Babylon was the most iniquitous city on earth during Biblical times. Perhaps Lord Joseph thinks Babylon still exists and it is where we came from – that it is the world that exist outside the one he lives in. He wants to clean our souls so-to-speak, of the sins of Babylon, you know, like he said, cleanse de mind of de thoughts born of de mud of Babylon." Patrick's explanation was impressive and his imitation was funny.

"Well, I hope the cure doesn't kill us. I expect the ganja will be very potent," I added, "it would be great for you. As for me, well, you know how paranoid I can get from marijuana. Hell, all I have to do is breathe in second hand smoke and I get too high. My thoughts get all disoriented and I become fearful. I don't want to offend Lord Joseph, who knows what else he would do to exorcise the thoughts of Babylon from my mind. Perhaps use a machete to decapitate me. What should I do?" My nervousness over the potential pressure to smoke Lamb's Bread made me feel embarrassed.

"Yeah, I heard your *I get paranoid* rap one time too many. Well, you could give it a try. I think getting high in paradise would be different for you than in Philly. Besides, you should have learned by now that the fear always passes and nothing bad ever happens, so get over it. I am, hell, we lived in a world of fear throughout our childhood and we did more than just escape it, we are doing pretty damn well. What's a little fear from a marijuana buzz compared to having your life threatened?" Patrick was annoyed and rightfully so. "I could tell you got buzzed breathing in second-hand smoke when we were at the Buc and you seemed fine."

"Yeah, I got a little stoned at the Buc and it was manageable. Getting high on the beach in New Jersey was a toss up as to whether I got paranoid or had a good time. The paranoia has nothing to do with real threats, its just a mind chemical thing and extremely uncomfortable." Patrick was well aware of this fact, but it is difficult for him to completely understand since getting high is always a pleasant experience for him.

"Maybe it's the thoughts of Babylon in your head that makes you scared. Perhaps Lord Joseph's ritual will dispel those thoughts and you won't be afraid. I remember Randy saying something about Rastas being able to teach you how to enjoy being high." Patrick went from sounding annoyed to trying to be helpful.

Smoking ganja in a prehistoric sea cave with a Rastafarian and my best friend would be different than my previous experiences, although I was not convinced I would be any less paranoid. Even though there was no basis in reality for the irrational fear, nonetheless it was a paralyzing experience. I felt no need to purify my mind from the influences of Babylon. Hell, growing up in South Philly was a type of Babylonian experience and to survive it, well, breaking the chains of fear that the ghetto world held on us was no simple task, and it definitely involved cleansing the mind and heart of all sorts of crap. My only concern was that I did not want to insult Lord Joseph by refusing to participate fully in his ritual.

Lord Joseph returned carrying a pouch and a bag. "Come an' sit wit mi on dis ledge, mon." His voice was surprisingly soothing. We joined him. He opened the bag and took out a red, green, and gold tablecloth that was embroidered with the figure of a lion at its center. He opened the pouch and took out a banana leaf and marijuana buds that were green, red, gold and speckled white with resin. He kissed each bud as he placed them on the flat, greenish-yellow banana leaf. "Dis is Lamb's Bread, mon. A gift from Jah ta heal de mind of sickness." Whenever Lord Joseph spoke, his voice sounded like he was making a prophetic announcement to the world. It struck me that he truly believed he was a prophet, or a priest of some sort. "Tell mi yah names again, bwoys fram Babylon."

"I am Patrick."

"My name is Oli, Oli, Oli ..." I was stammering and couldn't say the last syllable of my name. I was extremely nervous. Not a very good beginning if I was to follow through with this ritual.

"Ollie! Yah are full of fear. Babylon 'as poisoned yah mind. Yah an' Patrick 'ave been led ta dis cave of Jah ta be cured of yah illness." He must have thought that I said my name was Ollie because that's what his pronunciation sounded like, and I was too nervous to correct him. Throughout my life people tried calling me Ollie, and I would not let them. I thought it ironic that I had taught this man to call me that. "Tell I, Ollie, dees thoughts dat 'old yah prisoner ta fear?"

"I, ah, I, ah, I can't smoke ganja. It makes me very scared. I don't want to offend you."

"No offense, mon. Irie. Nuh ta trouble yah self. No need ta fear de ganja. Lamb's Bread 'as de spirit of truth ta free de mind. De fear is awreddy inna yah head, mon. Wen yah smoke ganja de fear gets stronger 'cause yah fightin' it, mon. Yah mus' embrace de spirit in de ganja. Breathe in de sea air, Ollie, let go of de fear. Relax de body. Tek de spirit of de Lamb's Bread inna yah mind. Wat is it yah wear upon yah neck, Ollie? It is religious?"

"Sort of. My mother gave it to me for protection. It belonged to my Aunt Marie, who was a Catholic Nun. She died."

"Den yah are no stranger ta de world of de unseen – Obeah – de spirit world. Patrick, do yah knoh of dis world?"

"I was an altar boy, serving Catholic Mass with priests."

"Dis is good, mon. Wat we do presently will nuh be strange ta yah."

I highly doubted that. I admit, eating and drinking the body and blood of Christ, even symbolically, seemed cannibalistic, and indeed very strange to me. I just wanted to run the hell out of there. I began to shake. Lord Joseph put his hand on my head. His hand was huge. If he was a basketball player, he could easily grip the ball in one hand. At first, I thought he was going to squeeze my head like a melon, but he applied no pressure. I began to feel silly sitting there with his hand covering the top of my head. I was reminded of the Pentecostal religious ritual of laying hands on the head for receiving the Holy Ghost. Patrick was grinning from ear to ear with a twinkle of amusement in his eyes. I knew he was getting a kick out of this. Patrick had been with me on many occasions when I got stoned and the result was paranoia. No harm came from those experiences, just my extreme uncomfortable wrestling with fear until the chemical wore off, which was aided by the ingestion of mass amounts of sugar that for some reason lessened the effects.

"Serious, Ollie. Do as I tell you. Tek de sea air deep inta yah lungs an' let it out slowly. Do dis over an' over an' yah will feel relaxed, mon."

I did as Lord Joseph had instructed and gradually, I began to feel relaxed.

"Listen to de rhydim of de sea risin' an' fallin' as de watta come in an' out of de cave."

I looked at the sea and observed its movement as I breathed in and out deeply and slowly. My breathing gradually became in sync with the sea's motion. Even the sound of the water seemed to match my breathing and the beating of my heart. I imagined that the blood pulsing through my veins was like the sea and my body a living cavern. A feeling of integration, a lack of separation between my body and my surroundings enveloped me. Indeed, I was feeling more than comfortable - I was slightly euphoric. Lord Joseph, sensing the dissipation of my fear, removed his hand from my head, which caused me to feel lighter, as if a weight had been lifted from me – actually his hand did apply some pressure. I looked at Patrick and he too was breathing with the rhythm of the sea.

Lord Joseph held up the spliff, and said: *"Glory be ta de Fadda of Iration, as it was in de Iginning, is now an ever shall be foriva, world wit out end, Selah!"* He struck a match and lit the Lamb's Bread banana leaf spliff. He took several long smooth drags, inhaling each one deeply, and then slowly releasing the smoke from his lungs. He sat quietly for a long time as the smoke from the ganja spiraled from the spliff and drifted slowly like a ghost towards the ceiling and out through the hole. He sat with his eyes staring into space. We waited in mesmerized anticipation for something stupendous to happen. The spliff kept burning away. I wondered when he was going to pass it. Finally, he handed it to Patrick and said, "Tek de Lamb's Bread inna yah mind an' become free fram de chains dat bind yah." Patrick took the spliff and held it as though he was holding the transubstantiated Body of Christ in his trained Catholic altar boy manner. It was obvious that he was treating this as a sacred religious ritual. He followed Lord Joseph's example, taking several deep drags, inhaling and exhaling slowly in the same rhythmic fashion of the breathing exercise. I was impressed that he did so without coughing.

Patrick handed the spliff to me. I did not feel nervous, to my surprise. I turned the spliff in my hand, now curious instead of fearful as to what affect it would have on me. I thought of the decision I had made during my convalescence with hepatitis that I would never ingest chemicals for other than therapeutic and medical reasons. According to Lord Joseph, this ritual was therapeutic. I had the feeling that the healing of our minds Lord Joseph wanted to achieve may have already taken place through the breathing and relaxation activity. It had relaxed my mind and body and brought about a sense of oneness with my surroundings. I surmised that the increased level of oxygen in my blood had contributed to the way I was feeling.

I recalled something I had read in an Anthropology course I took in college about a young man who lived among an Aboriginal tribe in the Amazon rainforest. He participated in the rituals of the tribe in order to gain an inside perspective of their world, and to be welcomed to live among them. It was this thought that gave me the increased comfort I needed to succumb to the ritual. I told myself that if I got really scared I would dive in the sea and swim to where I could climb the cliffs, or all the way to Fishermen Cove if necessary. I raised the spliff to my mouth and inhaled the smoke. It was a very shallow inhalation to prevent too aggressive of an assault on my somewhat virgin lungs. Still, I coughed excessively. I then gestured to give the spliff to Lord Joseph. He ignored me. I held the spliff for a brief moment and then took another drag. This time I didn't cough. I could feel the marijuana taking effect on my body. A pleasant feeling enhanced my already semi-euphoric state. I was surprised that my body and mind welcomed the feeling. In most of my previous experiences, anxiety was the initial response, followed by disoriented thinking and a prevalent feeling of dread leading to outright paranoia.

Again, I extended the spliff to Lord Joseph, who continued to ignore me as he stared off into space. Then he stood up and walked to the edge of the ledge. He raised his arms in the air as his voice boomed out a chant that reverberated off the cavern walls:

Blood, blood, blood an' fiah,
Kill ta de wolf, throw ta de fiah,
King, Haile Selassie, son of Jah,
Bring lightening bolt down from de sky,
Destroy Babylon,
Remove de fear thoughts fram de minds of dees children of Babylon

He chanted these words over and over again. The silhouette of his huge muscular ebony body standing in front of us facing the turquoise sea and surrounded by the magnificent colors and shape of the cave was the most amazing exotic sight I have ever beheld. He stopped chanting and began shaking his head, swinging his long dreadlocks like a lion's mane. He let out a very loud roar and simultaneously a flash of light burst from a thundercloud far out at sea, and a few seconds later the sound of thunder boomed in the cave with a noise so loud Patrick and I covered our ears. The simultaneity of these events was mind-boggling. The thought came to me that Lord Joseph's petition to Jah caused the lightening and thunder. Rational thought quickly dismissed this event as synchronistic and coincidental.

Nonetheless, it did happen and the affect on Patrick and me was profound. There was no true casting out of Babylon from my mind, so I thought, but there was no doubt that I was experiencing euphoria and I was undoubtedly very stoned. There was no complete discounting the influences of this extraordinary ritual. I felt euphoric before ingesting the Lamb's Bread, and being stoned heightened my sensitivity to the beauty that surrounded me even more. This was another form through which to experience mind surfing, which is traveling on thought-wave energy through new doors of perception. Mind surfing was a technique my friends and I discovered one evening while staying up all night on the beach in Stone Harbor, New Jersey during our virgin hippie days in high school – we had a collective experience of transcendence that propelled us further along our path toward lifting our minds beyond the cultural confines of our inner city world.

I thought of how truth is an experiential reality and since we just experienced something way out of the ordinary, I wondered what truth was gained, if any. I learned in the recent past that chemical substances offer temporary experiences that cause the mind to perceive things in new ways, although I wondered if after a while the chemicals would get in the way of the pursuit of true, lasting insight into the nature of reality. We shared with Lord Joseph a ritual that puts him in contact with super reality, and we touched a part of that entity with him. This common experience was unique and yet akin to other forms of spiritual communion.

Lord Joseph stood completely still as the thunderstorm moved across the sea to the land, releasing a torrent of rain. The lightening and thunder were now overhead and the thunderclaps echoed with ear splitting loudness in the cave. I dropped the spliff as it burned my fingers. Patrick's face revealed that he was in a trance-like state. His litmus paper eyes had an otherworldly look, as though he was peering deep into another dimension of thought reality.

When the thunderstorm had passed, Lord Joseph turned toward us and said, "It is done. De fear of Babylon is removed fram yah minds. Yah are purified by Jah, an' may stay in mi cave as yah wish. Ollie an' Patrick, yah are mi white breddas." Lord Joseph folded his tablecloth and as he was leaving the cave he said, "Irie, Oliver and Patrick! Dis a good day. Jah mek His presence wit I n I. Di time 'as come fer I to tek care of business." As I watched him leaving, I noticed water flowing down a nearby ledge. It was pouring through the hole in the roof. "If we camp in the cave, collecting rain water through the cave's ceiling opening could be our fresh water source," I said.

"Good idea. We need to find something to collect it in," replied Patrick. We went over to the water soaked ledge and put our mouths under trickles of water and drank deeply. My mouth was very dry, a clear indication that I was definitely stoned.

"I still want to meet Millie and Charley. We should find them before setting up camp. This was one hell of an orientation to Negril and I have a feeling there is a lot more to come." I wanted to try living in the cave at some point during our stay in Negril, but I wanted to see what else was in store for us.

"Why are you in a hurry? Lord Joseph gave us an invitation to stay in his sea cave. We can safely assume that he wouldn't mind us sleeping in here. This is the place to live in a hot tropical climate, and we have easy access to the sea." Patrick dove from the ledge into the water, and I followed after him. We swam through the openings of the cave – Patrick took one opening and I the other – making our way around the mammoth rock that was part of the cavern roof and jutted downward, gradually tapering as it reached its base anchored deep under the seabed. We moved out into the cloud-filtered sunlight. Rays of light were streaming through openings in the clouds, and a rainbow suddenly appeared creating an arch across the sky with its two ends reaching the silver shimmering surface of the sea.

We explored along the cliffs swimming into smaller caves and as far as we were able to determine, none of them had openings to the land. Eventually we retuned to Lord Joseph's cave and Patrick found a fresh water spring deep in the back of one of the side tunnels. It was seeping out from a crevice in the wall and flowing between two ledges. The water was cold and tasted clean. It was an excellent steady source of fresh water and much cleaner than rain runoff. We decided to get our equipment that we left setting on the cliff. Lord Joseph was nowhere in sight. I knocked on his shanty door and there was no answer. I wanted to make sure we could set up camp in the cave before moving in our stuff. We assumed that his invitation included sleeping in the cave so we went ahead and moved in our belonging – they were soaked! We had to lay out our clothes and sleeping bags on tree limbs and bushes on Lord Joseph's property for them to dry.

Patrick suggested that we search for dead plant vegetation for bed matting, and find firewood and rocks to create a campfire. Also, we were starving so we filled our canteens with spring water and left the cave in search of food.

FISHERMEN
(Elkannah)

We decided to continue walking southwest. The first shanty we came upon had smoke bellowing out from a small hut next to it. A voice called out, "Come 'ere, mon." I couldn't see anyone. We walked towards the hut and peered inside. There was a tall slender man who appeared to be in his late twenties or early thirties. His chest was bare and he wore polyester iridescent slacks. His feet were without shoes and had the same leather sole appearance as Lord Joseph's feet. He did not have dreadlocks so I assumed he was not Rastafarian. "Welcome. I am Elkannah Walker, de bes' fisherman in aw of Negril. I 'ave 'ere fresh bonito fer yah eatin'." I noticed that his teeth were perfect and bright white. He handed each of us a fully cooked fish on a roughly carved slab of wood. The fish still had their heads and tails but were gutted and scaled.

"Thank you, Mr. Elkannah, the fisherman of Negril. My name is Patrick and this is my friend, Ollie." I gave Patrick an inquisitive look as he pronounced my name the same way as Lord Joseph – and he well knew I was not fond of the rendition of my name.

"How long 'ave yah been in Jamaica, mon?"

"A few days. We plan on staying for as long as we can," I responded. Actually, it was the end of October and I needed to get back to Philly in January in time for the winter-spring semester. I had no idea how long our money would hold out, but surprisingly we had spent a miniscule amount.

"Yah 'ave come ta de right village, mon. Dis be de mos' beautiful part of de island. Beach, cliff, mountain, an' de people are frenly, mon. Eat de fish." I had no idea how to eat whole fish, especially without a fork. I looked at Patrick and he wasted no time. He picked the fish apart, peeling back the skin to get to the white meat. I followed his example. We devoured the fish in little time, leaving the head.

"Eat de head, mon. It is de sweetest part. De head give yah de wisdom of de fish."

"I never ate fish head before. And if the fish was so wise, how come it got caught?" I replied. Elkannah laughed.

"Yah very funny, Ollie. De fish purpose is ta feed people, mon. It gives up life fer our bodies. Irie! Jah give de fish fer us ta live an' de fish knoh dis, mon."

"How do I eat it?" I asked.

"Yah suck out it eyes an' brain, mon, like dis." Elkannah demonstrated, sucking on a fish eye socket, and it looked gross. Patrick sucked on the fish. My stomach felt a bit queasy.

"Wat yah waitin' fer, Ollie. No harm come ta yah. Try it, mon." I did. And to my surprise it was very succulent.

"Dat more like it, Ollie. How yah like it?" Elkannah asked.

"It is very good. I even feel wiser." Elkannah laughed and again said I was very funny. Not a description of my character often said.

"Come visit mi before de sunrise tomorrow, Ollie an' Patrick, I will tek yah fishin' wit mi."

"Definitely. We'd love that," replied Patrick. I nodded in agreement.

"Awrite den. I show yah how we Jamaicans catch de fish wit hand lines, mon, how ta use de traps, an' catch de conch wit divin' poles. I must gawaan now ta ten' ta mi fambly. See yah inna de morrow. Remember ta come long before de sun rises over de mountains."

"We will be there bright and early." I said.

"Where yah stay, mon, so I wake yah effin yah nuh 'ere in time?"

"We're staying in Lord Joseph's cave," I replied.

"Jah! Livin in a cave. American bwoys strange. Mi never 'ear of such a t'ing, mon, yah nuh animals. If I 'ad room, yah stay wit mi fambly, mon. We too many in dis small house. I 'ave three pikny." Elkannah pointed to his shanty. Indeed, it was very small, about twelve feet by ten feet. He gave us a peek inside. It was one room with a queen-sized bed that was elevated with another mattress underneath. He explained that his children slept underneath. I guessed that pikny is the patois word for children. There were shelves with a few garments on them. This was a very poor family.

We left Elkannah and continued down the road. I asked how much we owed him for the fish and he looked insulted, and then said we could treat him to a cigarette and a Red Stripe after we come back from catching fish. I was impressed with the generosity of all the people we have met, from the people of the Buccaneer Inn to Lord Joseph and Elkannah.

"He is really poor and yet very generous," I said to Patrick as we walked along the road.

"He may be poor in material goods and money, but he is rich in lifestyle. Think about it. He gets his food from the sea and he probably has a food garden along with fruit trees. There is no need for electricity and the weather does not require much clothing and his feet adapt to being bare. And, he's rich in 'pickny!' Did you notice that he and Lord Joseph have very wide feet with thick calloused soles?"

"Yeah, I noticed that. You are right about Elkannah being rich in lifestyle and having little need for material goods and money. I expect he gets whatever supplies he needs from selling fish and bartering. He seemed to have little interest in money. I mean, he could have charged us a couple bucks for the fish." I said.

"Jamaican hospitality. There is nothing like it. Bro, I have been stoned since the first day and haven't spent a dime for it. And, we only paid for one meal and that was cheap. If things keep going like this, we might return to the U.S. with enough money to keep us fed as we hitch back to Philly from Florida." Patrick was right, we've been fortunate in many ways.

"Yeah, bro, we received lots of treasures in such a short period of time. The most precious treasure so far was Penny and Jenny - well they were more of a pleasure than a treasure, or a pleasure to treasure," I chuckled.

"Whatever, the sea cave is a treasure chest beyond our wildest dreams!" exclaimed Patrick.

"I'm psyched about going fishing Jamaican style. How to you suppose we are going to catch fish with hand lines?" I asked.

"I noticed that Elkannah's hands were almost as calloused as his feet, and they had scar lines all over them that may have come from fish line cutting into them," replied Patrick.

"Yeah, I noticed that too. I don't intend to cut up my hands with fish line. I'm going to use those pieces of leather I brought along to patch my jeans to protect my hands."

"Great idea. Bring along enough for me too," said Patrick.

The thunderstorm cooled off the land and the sun was lower in the sky. We decided to find a nice spot on the cliff to rest and watch the sunset. We walked for a while before coming upon a cliff area that was partially cemented over. It looked out of place in this otherwise completely natural setting. I welcomed the smoothness of the concrete and stretched out my body on its surface. There were steps carved into the cliff and they too were covered with cement. They descended down to the sea. After sitting for a while we went down the steps and dove into the water for another swim. As we were swimming around and exploring the area, the sun got closer to the horizon and was bright gold. There were streaks of high feathery cirrus clouds left over from the afternoon thunderstorm. These clouds reflected sunlight and with each passing second became adorned in a different hue of red, orange, bluish-purple, and lavender. The color of the sea went through changes as well, at one point appearing silver, like a shimmering glass mirror projecting the continuously changing cinematic sky. We stayed in the water treading as the sun disappeared into the sea. We got out and stood on the concrete pad, allowing the breeze to dry our bodies.

I suggested to Patrick that we head back to the cave and look for bed matting and firewood along the way. He agreed. We picked up palm leaves that were still mostly green that would be suitable for our matting. They weren't soft but would provide a cushion from the cool hard rock ledge. Firewood was scarce. Patrick said that Jamaicans most likely use wood as their primary cooking fuel, perhaps their only fuel. He doubted that propane, charcoal or coal would be widely used in this cash poor village. I saw no evidence of there being electricity in Negril's West End. I noticed that Elkannah had oil lamps. We gathered enough wood for a fire to last a few hours. I was not concerned since we weren't going to cook anything and we didn't need fire for warmth, hell, we were living in the tropics. Most likely our sleeping bags would serve as padding since we wouldn't need to cover our bodies as long as we kept some clothes on.

We reached the cave and I went directly to Lord Joseph's shanty only to discover that he was not home. The door had no lock on it, but I dared not go inside. The cave was darker than above ground, of course, but there was enough moonlight filtering through the mouth of the cave and the hole in the roof to enable us to see well enough as our eyes adjusted. Our sleeping bags and clothes were dry. We set up our beds on our chosen ledges and made a fire. The flames danced and cast shadows on the walls. The ambience of the cave was amazingly exotic. I felt like a real native sea cave dwelling primate – a wonderful feeling. I took out my flute and played the 'A' note for as long as I could sustain it. The reverberation of that one note off the cavern walls was as clear as the sounds I produced in the Catholic Church in my home neighborhood, yet distinctively different. A significant difference being that the sound of one was reflected off the walls of what people had made in reverence of God, and natural processes created the cave, a gift from creation to people.

Patrick sat in silence as I continued to play one note after another, holding each note as long as I could, not forming a melody. I wanted to simply hear the purity of the sound. I could feel each note, and when I began to form a melody by stringing together a few very clearly formed notes, the phrasing took on the quality of reverence. My flute was indeed an instrument of praise and the melody became an expression of gratitude for what I was experiencing on this enchanted island culminating in this moment within this beautiful sea cave. Patrick continued to sit in silence as I played for quite some time. When I stopped, Patrick took out his guitar and played notes in a similar fashion to what I produced on the flute. He has a very good ear and musical memory, playing notes I had played in the same sequence and timing, reproducing the melody with variations. I listened to the sweet sound of his guitar and it too sounded like a melody of thanksgiving. When he finished, neither of us said a word. We sat looking out at the sea from our ledge perches. I laid down on my sleeping bag looking at the shadows dancing on the cavern walls and drifted off to sleep.

"Patrick, Ollie! Time ta wake up, mon. De fish nuh wait. Get up, mon." I opened my eyes. Elkannah stood on the ledge above us. Patrick stirred and mumbled, "Who is that? Where am I?"

"Inna Jamaican sea cave, mon, like a wild animal. Wipe de sleep fram yah eyes."

"Wow! I thought I was dreaming. It's still dark," said Patrick.

"Dis is nuh a dream, mon, an' darkness will soon be gone, Patrick. De sun soon come. Drink dis, mon." Elkannah handed a jar to Patrick. He took a long drink.

"Wow, that's delicious!" He handed it back to Elkannah who then gave it to me. I drank the rest of it.

"This is very sweet. What is it?" I asked.

"Mango, pineapple, papaya, an' arinj juice, mon. 'ere, suck on dis." He handed each of us what looked like green bamboo.

"What is it?" Patrick asked.

"Sugarcane. Fresh fram de fields, mon. It give de energy necessary ta catch de fish. Areddi, mon, we mus' go." I wasn't sure what arinj meant, but the juice tasted like it contained oranges. Areddi sounded like '*are you ready?*' or '*we are ready.*' It wasn't easy deciphering the dialect. I often guessed at the meaning and looked for contextual clues. I sucked on the end of the sugarcane, and wow, it was super sweet. I went to the water's edge and took a piss. Patrick did the same. We put on our shirts and shoes and followed Elkannah out of the cave. I was in a dreamy trance state as we walked in the dark along the cliff-lined road. We were silent until we got to Fishermen Cove. Light began filtering over the mountains in the eastern sky. Elkannah walked up to his canoes. There were two. They were definitely handcrafted out of what looked like cedar wood.

"What type of wood are these canoes made from? I asked.

"Dey mek fram cotton wood, light an' strong. I help Fadda build fiah, burn an' carve dem wit our hands. De firs' time I fish in dees canoes I a small pikny. I give dem ta mi sons wen I ol' an' no longer fish."

The canoes were about seventeen feet long. There were four roughly honed paddles, also out of cottonwood. Elkannah explained that he had made two of them himself, having lost the original ones his father had made.

"Wen mi sons ol' enuff ta catch fish, pull up traps, den I use bot' canoes. Catch more fish fer fambly. Now I use jus' dis one. I tek dis one today an' yah tek de otter one an' watch how I fish. Den anot'er time yah try ta fish. Today yah jus' watch. Yah knoh how ta paddle canoe?"

"Wow, awesome! I have used canoes all my life as a Boy Scout, never in an ocean though. This is totally far out!" Patrick was an expert at canoeing. I recalled the time when I was at camp in the Pocono Mountains of Pennsylvania with my buddies and we came upon a Boy Scout group canoeing on a lake. To our surprise and delight, Patrick was among them. We swam out to him and tipped over his canoe.

"Irie! Now we gawaan ta de fish traps." Elkannah had a large burlap sac that contained his fishing lines and hooks wrapped around wood sticks. He opened the bag to show us his equipment and handed us a box that had wooden sides and a glass bottom and told us it was for placing in the water so we could see more clearly. Then, he went over to a tree and picked up two long poles that had three prongs on one end. He put one in his canoe and gave one to us. Patrick asked what they were for and he said to get conch. I told him we would like to try fishing today and I showed him the leather skins I had to protect our hands. He insisted on having us observe trap and hand-line fishing during the first day, and that he would have us try catching conch. Elkannah launched his canoe into the sea, got on board and began paddling. Patrick and I followed after him. We didn't ask him how far we were going. He was a very strong paddler. It was a challenge keeping pace with him. Our canoe was heavier because there were two of us, still, we had twice the paddle power and should have stayed even with him but we lagged behind even though we were paddling full strength. The canoe did not glide through the water as swiftly as the aluminum canoes we were accustomed to since they were heavier. There were no seats so we had to kneel while paddling, which caused poor blood circulation in our legs. I tried sitting while paddling but it didn't work out too well.

Elkannah stopped paddling, placed his glass bottom box in the water and smiled. He took hold of a rope that had a large hook on the end and lowered it in the water. It was then that I realized he did not have an anchor, and neither did we. We stopped paddling and remained several feet away from Elkannah's canoe.

"Watch wat I do, mon. Yah mus' be careful ta keep de balance or yah spill de canoe." Elkannah instructed. He pulled on the rope and we saw a large metal trap move towards the surface. When it came to the top, Elkannah pulled it out of the water and balanced it on the edge of the canoe as he leaned his body back to counter-balance the weight of the trap so the canoe would remain steady. I noticed that we hadn't drifted away from the canoe's original position, so there must have been no or very little current. We simply bobbed in the water like corks. The trap had a variety of size and types of fish caught within. Some of them I recognized as small bonito. Elkannah identified a few of the others as sunfish, red snapper and grunt fish, but he neglected to name them all, particularly the lovely light blue fish and the smaller yellow ones. The trap had a concave funnel with a one-way flap that opened inward. There were fish heads tied in the center of the trap. I could determine that the fish were able to swim into the funnel by pushing lightly against the flap, or as the movement of the water opened them. Once inside feeding on the bait, they could not get back out. It was quite clever. The trap itself was made out of chicken wire mesh with a wood frame.

Elkannah released wire hooks on the top of the trap and lifted it off the canoe's edge and in a quick agile motion, turned the cage upside down, causing the fish to dump into the bottom of his canoe. Once the fish were out of the trap, and flapping around in the canoe, he balanced the trap on the canoe straddling both sides with the opened end facing him. He took his knife from the sheath that was attached to his belt, grabbed a reddish-yellow fish and cut off its head. He did this to several fish of the same species. He then took fishing line from his burlap sac that was pre-cut to length and efficiently strung the fish heads on the line and attached them to the inside of the trap. He reattached the wire hooks to securely close the trap and lowered it back into the water. The process took approximately ten minutes. No one spoke a word during the entire time. Elkannah looked at us with a big grin on his face.

"Dis is a good catch, mon." Elkannah took a cord with a metal end that looked like a nail and weaved it through the gills of every fish, tying one end to a metal loop that was attached to the inside of the canoe. He lowered the fish in the water. I knew that the fish would stay alive longer in the water, but I wondered about fish dangling on the side of the canoe and the possibility of attracting sharks and barracuda. I decided to ask Elkannah about that later.

"Now we look fer conch. Tek yah glass bottom box an' place in de wata like dis." Elkannah placed his box in the water and looked through it. I did the same thing. "Yah see clearly, now, mon, aw de way ta de bottom. Yah mus' practice spottin' de conch. It is hard at first, mon, den git easy. De conch is on de bottom in de coral. Yes mon, de brain coral jus' beneat' yah canoe."

"I don't know what brain coral is." I replied.

"It big rock dat look like brain, mon. T'ink of a rock wit worms aw over it, 'ave yah ever see brain, mon?"

"Yes, we have." I replied for the both of us. Actually, I saw pictures of human brains, but I wasn't sure about Patrick.

"I see it!" Shouted Patrick.

"Good. Look aroun' de edges on de bottom. Yah see pink color?" I could see the pink, but only faintly. "Yes, I see it," I shouted.

"Patrick, yah see de conch, mon?" Elkannah asked.

"No." he replied.

"Well den. I will show you." Elkannah put down his glass bottom box and took a rope out of his bag. He tied the rope through a hole that was bored on the bow of the canoe. I looked at the bow and stern of our canoe and noted the holes. He tied the other end of the very long rope around his waist, grabbed the twelve-foot long pole and to my surprise, he dove overboard. Elkannah had made himself into a human anchor. If a strong wind or current came along, the canoe would pull him away from what he was trying to do. I made a mental note that I would show him how to make an anchor by using a cinder block, which would be much more practical and effective. We watched as he swam towards the bottom with the pole extended with one arm, stroking with the other, and kicking vigorously. I thought how fins, goggles, and snorkels would be a tremendous help. Patrick put the glass bottom box in the water so we could see what he was doing more clearly. As he got closer to the brain coral, he thrust the pole forward and the prongs grabbed hold of the pink looking object, which we assumed was a conch. He then ascended quickly, the conch breaking the surface first. It was very big and quite beautiful. Elkannah put the pole and conch in the canoe. He pulled himself up on to the canoe with surprisingly little rocking motion.

"Does conch taste good?" Patrick asked.

"Very sweet meat, mon, nuh enough ta feed fambly. I sometime mek soup an' sometime fry. Better ta sell. De tourists in Mo-bay give big money ta eat, an' de shell worth much. Yah mus' try ta catch conch, mon. Yah can eat wat yah catch an' I tek de shell ta sell."

Spurred on by Elkannah's comment, we placed the glass bottom box in the water and searched for conch. After a long search I spotted one and therefore had first dibs on diving for it. I didn't have to tie a rope around me because Patrick would paddle the canoe as needed to keep from drifting away. I slipped in the water and Patrick handed the pole to me. It was difficult seeing without goggles so I had to look through the glass box one more time to get oriented, then I dove. It took several dives before I finally located the conch. Grabbing it with the pronged pole proved much more difficult than I had expected. After failing I resurfaced for air. I wanted to give up but Elkannah encouraged me to continue on.

Patrick was losing patience and suggested that he use Elkannah's pole. I agreed with his idea, thinking it would double our chances. Elkannah said no, that I should learn and that Patrick would get his turn. After multiple exasperating attempts I got lucky and brought up the conch. It was slightly larger than Elkannah's. They applauded. My eyes were blurry and stinging from salt. Elkannah told Patrick that it was his turn and he was very eager. Confident that we knew the process, Elkannah continued to hunt for conch on his own with a great deal of success. Patrick took less time getting his first conch and he was successful in getting three altogether. I was so tired from my attempts that I decided not to go for another conch. Elkannah caught four in all. He said we were very fortunate to find so many in one area. Again, he spoke of the high tourist demand in Montego Bay.

Elkannah had three more traps to check. When we got to the last trap, Patrick asked if he could raise and empty the trap. Elkannah smiled and said: "Patrick brave. Can yah keep yah balance, mon? Yah mus' be careful nuh ta turn over de canoe."

"I think I can do it. I spent a lot of time in canoes and I think I have a good sense of balance. I want to do it, Elkannah."

"Okay, den. Ollie, yah swim ta mi canoe so Patrick nuh 'ave ta balance canoe an' yah toss de conch ta me so we nuh lose dem if

Patrick spill canoe." I tossed the conch to Elkannah, slipped in the water and swam to his canoe. We watched as Patrick pulled up the trap and he successfully balanced it on the rim of the canoe. There were a lot of fish, much more than the other traps. Patrick was obviously struggling to keep his balance.

"Patrick, it is good catch. I nuh wan' ta lose dem. Effin yah can nuh do dis, den put de trap back in de wata an' I tek it up."

"I can do this. Just give me time," shouted Patrick.

"Awrite, den, mon. Irie! Yah brave." The light breeze got slightly stronger, causing larger sea swells. The canoes were bobbing more than when Elkannah had raised the other traps. Patrick continued to struggle with keeping his balance, and he looked like he was waiting until he had full confidence in his ability to maintain stability before proceeding. The fish were flipping around, adding to the challenge. I think Patrick was using his intelligence by waiting until the fish became more lethargic from oxygen depravation. I told this to Elkannah and he smiled saying that was a very smart idea. When the fish stopped moving so vigorously, Patrick made his move. The swiftness and accuracy of his motions in unhooking the cage and raising it to empty the fish in the canoe astounded me and filled me with pride that he was my friend. It seemed like it took an instant for him to accomplish the task. Elkannah and I applauded his success. Elkannah complimented him on doing so well on his first try. He said that it took him several attempts when his father taught him, and that he lost many fish before he had success, although at the time he was ten years old and Patrick is nineteen.

Patrick didn't have a knife to cut off fish heads to attach new bait. I suggested that I swim the knife over to Patrick, but Elkannah decided that Patrick lower the trap back in to the water so he could bait the traps himself. When all was done, Elkannah still insisted that we learn to fish with line and hooks another day. He did demonstrate how it is done, which was simply baiting the hook and lowering it in the water where he spotted schools of fish swimming below the canoe with the glass bottom box. Elkannah caught a red snapper and pulled it in using only his hands. The fish was small so there was not a lot of pressure on his skin. It was a process that could be easily improved upon. The most obvious would be to use poles. I was not going to allow my hands to be cut by fish line.

Elkannah told Patrick not to string his fish because we were heading back to Fishermen Cove. I swam to Patrick's canoe and we paddled back to shore with a canoe full of fish and several conch. It was interesting being on my knees paddling with fish covering the bottom of the canoe. A few sharp fish fins pierced my legs. Elkannah said the conch we caught were ours to keep but we gave them to him to sell in the market. He was grateful. We kept enough fish to feed ourselves for several days.

For the next two weeks, we settled into our sea cave abode and went fishing with Elkannah quite often. I devised an easier method for emptying fish from the traps, which was simply to balance the trap on the sides of the canoe while sitting and not standing. Then, I took a stick and herded the fish out through the opening. Elkannah laughed with delight at my ingenuity and to my surprise he adopted the method. Lord Joseph was still absent and we wondered if he had disappeared and if we would ever see him again. We were so into our sea cave and fishing lifestyle that we postponed our explorations of the far West End of Negril. Elkannah knew Millie and Charley and said that they were spending time with a sick relative in Kingston, and that it might be several weeks before they return.

Elkannah's fishing harvest doubled with our added labor. Patrick and I had spent a lot of time fishing at the Jersey Shore, mostly in the bays, so we adapted very well to the fisherman's lifestyle. We made improvements on the line-hook technique by putting out as many as eight lines at once, attaching four lines on each side of the canoe, allowing the lines to troll along while we paddled. I told Elkannah about using a cinder block anchor. The concept was not new to him, of course, although most fishermen in the village did not use anchors. I learned that this was because they rarely searched for conch when the winds were strong, and the current was consistently mild. The canoes drifted very slowly if at all. His father had used the rope-tied-to-the-waist method when diving for conch and Elkannah was reluctant to do it any other way. Elkannah told us that his father had lost a canoe because an anchor came loose, causing the canoe to drift out to sea due to unexpected high winds and it was lost forever. The father had to swim to shore and could have drowned. Ever since that happened, he tied himself to the canoe. After observing Patrick and I using an anchor, which enabled the two of us to fish for conch at the same time, Elkannah eventually adopted the technique while still tying himself to the canoe. I tried using a fishing pole but it wasn't that useful because the canoe served the same purpose. What we needed were reels to make it easier to haul in the larger fish. If we had the money, we would travel to Montego Bay and buy snorkel equipment and reels. We told Elkannah this and he simply shrugged his shoulders.

With the increase in fish and conch, Elkannah was able to purchase materials to add another room to his shanty. We helped him build what became his children's bedroom. One day Elkannah returned from the market in the town of Savannah La-Mar where he had purchased three pair of goggles and one pair of fins. The fins were too small for his feet but were the right size for Patrick and me, since we had the same size feet. Then he presented us with a more precious gift. He offered full-time use of the canoe as long as we continued to fish with him or for him a few times each week. This made it possible for us to canoe in and out of the sea cave, and to fish whenever we wanted. And we could explore the rest of the Negril cliffs all the way up to and beyond the lighthouse, which was on the western most tip of the island, and we could canoe along the seven mile stretch of beach that began on the other side of the river that divided the cliff and beach areas.

Elkannah gave us an abandoned fish trap that was in disrepair along with chicken wire mesh. We went to work on its restoration. For convenience, we set the trap near the opening of the sea cave, which to our good fortune provided us with a steady supply of fish without too much effort. We made a few improvements to the sea cave, adding oil lanterns and candles, a metal grate over the rock-rimmed fireplace for cooking, and we were able to scrounge up cookware with the aid of Elkannah's wife: an iron skillet and large pot with lid, plates, and a few utensils. Patrick created a tripod out of concrete reinforcement bars he found along the road. We used the tripod to hang the pot over the fire.

The goggles and fins made it much easier to catch conch. While exploring along the cliffs where few people lived, we discovered conch that had never been harvested. We gave all but a few to Elkannah, increasing his wealth considerably. Elkannah kept us supplied in fruits and vegetables that he bartered for in the Savannah La-Mar market and with the people who lived in Red Ground. I asked him if we could barter fish for other things at the market and he told us that Jamaicans do not respond favorably to foreigners participating in their business transactions, especially in Sav-La-Mar. He said that non-Jamaicans would rarely get a favorable deal.

I told Elkannah that another pair of fins and two snorkels would improve our search for conch. Not long after, he provided us with these items and he found diver masks as well. He told us that for the price of ten conch, he could get us a spearfish gun. I wasn't sure I wanted to swim in the water with a sophisticated underwater bow and arrow contraption, but Patrick was an expert archer and the idea thrilled him. Patrick spent a lot of time diving for conch to purchase the spearfish gun. Less than a week later, Elkannah was able to get one for Patrick, which he put to good use catching larger prey, most notably barracuda – a fish that Elkannah particularly enjoyed eating and was quite profitable at the market. Elkannah also bought a large roll of chicken wire mesh and gave it to us to make more traps. He instructed us to use the trap we kept at the opening of the sea cave as a template, copying the design closely. We had to spend some of our precious money to purchase sets of pliers and wire cutters. It took us a while to figure out how to construct the trap and we even made a few improvements that Elkannah later adapted to his traps. The additional traps increased our fish yield considerably.

Our cave soon became decorated with the conch we kept for ourselves and Patrick wanted to rename it conch cave. I told him we could call it whatever he wanted but in reality it was Lord Joseph's sea cave. We occasionally talked of Lord Joseph's generosity and of our concern over his long absence. It was our intention to keep him supplied in fish when he returned. Still, several weeks had passed and he had not returned. Elkannah told us not to worry, that Lord Joseph had relatives in the Cock Pit Country of the Blue Mountains and that he spent a great deal of time there. He said that Lord Joseph grew ganja in the mountains and that the autumn months were harvest season. It was a relief to have an explanation for his long absence.

BOOBY CAY, SEVEN-MILE BEACH, RED GROUND

We finally took time to canoe to the beach, which was exquisitely beautiful. The beach, to our surprise and bewilderment, appeared to have only one major structure along the entire seven-mile stretch. It was a large government building that, at one time, was a sugar company, and it was currently used as a park for Jamaican families to visit the beach area. We noticed what looked like small fishing huts for fisherman to keep their equipment. There may have been more dwellings built on the beach but we did not see them. We assumed that the Jamaicans who owned beach property built their shanties on the other side of the road where they cultivated the soil for horticulture, and they were better protected from hurricanes. Many of them were fishermen who kept their boats on the beach. On occasion, families would come down from the mountains and spend a day at the beach, and they made use of the fresh water made available for public use at the government-sugar company structure, which the Jamaican's referred to as Sandy Park. The beach was the most beautiful my eyes had ever beheld. It was a picture perfect tropical paradise stretch of fine white sand, palm trees, and emerald-turquoise crystal clear water that was shallow for a long distance. The absence of buildings and the presence of few people setting up domiciles, along with the apparent endless stretch of beach made this natural wonder idyllic beyond my wildest imagination.

Having spent our summers at the Jersey shore, Patrick and I were excited about setting up a second camp somewhere on the beach. We explored the area for the perfect location. We soon realized that pitching a tent almost anywhere along the beach among shady palm groves would be perfect, as long as we were not trespassing on anyone's property. Several yards short of the very northern-most tip of the part of Negril beach known to Jamaicans as Long Bay, there was a small island slightly over a half-mile off the coast. We learned from a Jamaican boy we met on the beach that this island was called Booby Cay. He told us that the Arawak Indians, the original inhabitants of Jamaica, named it after the birds that used to occupy the island, they were long ago decimated as a food source. The boy did not know if a person or the government owned the small island, stating that no one lived there and that it wasn't used for any purpose. We decided to canoe to Booby Cay and do some exploring.

It did not take long to canoe to the island. The cay was fairly small. It was basically a large volcanic rock surrounded by a coral reef, and protruding enough above sea level for soil and sand to build up from rock erosion, seashells, and coral. The sea wore most of the volcanic rock smooth, and like the sea cave, the rocks were embedded with fossils and glistened with various colors. Seeds excreted from birds brought the plant life, so the island was full of trees and brush. There were plenty of coarse coral sandy areas consisting of small stretches of coves. The numerous trees were suitable for hammocks and the variety of vegetation contained edible berries. The sea flowed in channels throughout the island, carving its way through volcanic rock and around tree roots. Near the center there was a large pool of water that was continuously replenished with the moving tide. The pool was lined with palm trees providing ample shade, and the bottom was covered in coarse varied color coral sand. This natural pool was a nice place to swim, rest, and simply hang out. The island was a paradise for swimmers. We decided to make Booby Cay our second camp.

We traded fish to the young Jamaican boy we had spoken to on the beach for two hammocks, which were essential for siestas and sleeping at night. We built a lean-to for protection from the sun and rain along the edge of the pool using corrugated metal we found on the beach to form the roof that we covered with palm leaves to block sun-heat absorption, and we made use of a grove of palm trees, rope and long sticks. We were able to hang our hammocks under the lean-to when necessary for rain protection, and easily moved them to other locations depending on our needs. We also created a campfire pit.

The coral reef surrounding this island oasis provided a haven for a plethora of sea creatures – it was especially treasure trove of conch, and there was lots of fish. The abundant supply of seafood enabled us to enhance Elkannah's wealth considerably. The tide-replenished sandy pool near the center of the island was perfect for storing the conch we caught. It trapped them in while keeping them alive, and we could simply take them as needed. This seawater pool became our private saltwater almost Olympic size swimming pool. We spent several days at a time on Booby Cay. Indeed, it had become our second living space and there was no indication of private ownership or that it was used for any government purpose, and the Jamaicans rarely, if ever, boated or swam to the island. For the exercise and sheer challenge of it, Patrick and I took turns canoeing from the cay to the beach while the other swam the distance along side the canoe.

We traveled back and forth between Lord Joseph's cave and Booby Cay, which we now commonly referred to as Conch Island, spending several days at a time at each place because it was a considerable distance between the two. The direction of the wind was one factor in how long we stayed at either camp, using the wind to push us along, staying for several days on the island or in the cave depending on the ease of travel and personal preference. Occasionally, we would spend a night or two sleeping on the seven-mile beach. I loved walking the long stretch of sand at night under the canopy of stars. We had met some other young hippies who were living in tents on the beach.

It was fun partying with other hippies and talking about our adventures, although we were protective of our sea cave and of our camp on Booby Cay, so we never invited any of them to either place. Of course, they were free to swim out to Booby Cay it if they dared and none did. We never offered to take them there in the canoe and no one ever asked. The people we met were either small groups of males, or couples, so there was never an opportunity for romance. We discovered that most of them were transient, rarely staying for more than a few nights in one place so the development of long-lasting friendships did not occur. Still, there weren't a large number of hippies since it was not yet the height of the tourist season.

Patrick said he was working on a sail design for the canoe to make our traveling less strenuous and much faster, although he thought we would have to get permission from Elkannah since the alterations would require structural changes to the canoe. He decided that he would wait until he found a way to add a sail and rudder without making drastic changes to the canoes basic structure. Initially, fresh water was a challenge that also determined how long we stayed on the island since it had no fresh water supply. We had to fill glass gallon jugs at the public water spigot at Sandy Park but we couldn't transport enough to stay more than a few days. Eventually, Patrick created a way to catch water runoff to give us a sufficient supply.

We continued to fish along with Elkannah, although less often, which he was comfortable with because we kept him supplied with an abundant harvest of fish and especially conch. The rich supply of conch on the reef that bordered Booby Cay, and the pool we used to store our catch, and the remarkable beauty and isolation, had tempted us to make it our primary camp. We brought chicken wire mesh to Conch Island and along with rocks and huge pieces of dead coral, we were able to convert the pool into a fish trap. In essence, we had converted Booby Cay into a fish and conch-catching island.

All of our native activities sculpted our bodies into optimal fitness. We were both more muscular from swimming and paddling and we were lean from a diet of fish and fresh fruits and vegetables. Occasionally we ate rice and that, along with the very occasional rum and beer, were the only items we spent money on. Patrick had developed a dark tan and my skin exploded with so many freckles that I believed it was a matter of time before they all blended together. Elkannah's wife, Clara, said that I was not a white man but a spotted man. She provided me with Aloe Vera leaves from her garden, informing me that it would protect my skin from sun damage. I had so many sunburns and peeled off so much skin that at times I felt like a molting snake, especially with the increased muscle mass. Patrick had stopped brushing his long, naturally curly golden-brown hair and it became matted like Jamaican Rastas, developing into dreadlocks. As Lord Joseph said, we are his white breddas, and now we looked the part. I did not like my hair getting knotted and tangled, so I brushed it regularly and never developed dreads.

Patrick suggested that we take a respite from the seafaring lifestyle we had settled into and explore Red Ground to get some supplies, particularly ganja. Elkannah gave us a bamboo bong and hand-carved pipe that was made of Jamaican cedar. He said a woodcarver Rasta friend of his had made them. The bowl of the pipe was carved in the shape of a Rastafarian head, and the stem had the appearance of intertwined dreadlocks. The bong and pipe made our ganja supply last longer, and they made the smoke less harsh on our lungs. Still, our supply of ganja was depleted and Patrick wanted to find Lamb's Bread, because it was by far the sweetest tasting and the most potent ganja. We considered selling fish at the Sav-La-Mar market to enhance our money supply, but we understood this would upset our arrangement with Elkannah. So we decided that if necessary, we would part with some of our cash to actually purchase ganja for the first time since we arrived in Jamaica.

The largest concentration of people in Negril lived in *Red Ground*. This area of the village got its name from the distinctive red clay color of the soil. We learned that most people did not get their sustenance directly from the sea. The people were mostly horticulturalist and kept goats and chickens along the slope of the hills where the land was more fertile. They bartered these items for fish. This explained why so much of the cliff, beach, and Conch

Island, were so pristine and relatively uninhabited. In many respects, Negril had a virgin quality that was largely due to the lack of tourist dollars. I feared that one day Negril would become a tourist hotspot and its virginity would be lost to the penetration of capitalism. Red Ground was one of the areas we had not yet explored, and we believed there were some ganja growers there.

I suggested that we bring along a string of fish to Red Ground to barter for ganja as well as fruit and vegetables and Patrick agreed with some hesitancy, reminding me of what Elkannah had said about getting involved in Jamaican business practices. I made the point that we were not taking the fish to a market, but to individuals who might appreciate fresh fish in exchange for other items.

On a Sunday morning, we loaded our canoe and headed for the Roundabout. As we were canoeing from Conch Island back to the sea cave with our final destination being Red Ground, we heard a Jamaican woman screaming for help from the beach that was fairly close to where the river flowed into the sea, causing a brown wide patch of water that discolored the blue-green sea, especially during times of rainfall. I surmised that this runoff provided nutrients that feed the plethora of sea creatures. Patrick, who had a trained eye as a lifeguard, spotted the reason for the Jamaican woman's distress. There was a boy in the sea that had apparently been pulled out by the current of the river, which was particularly strong due to considerable thunderstorms in the mountains the night before. Patrick had rescued swimmers who had been caught in rip currents and this was a similar situation. The boy, instead of swimming parallel to the beach, was frantically swimming against the river current, and this was wearing him out. We paddled with all our strength to the boy. Patrick reached over and grabbed him by the waist of his shorts and lifted him into the canoe. He appeared to be unconscious and not breathing. Patrick pushed on the boy's diaphragm, successfully causing the water to dislodge from his lungs. The boy continued coughing up water as he desperately gasped for air. He was saved, although in a state of shock and shivering. The mother was screaming and crying hysterically the entire time. I shouted to her repeatedly that her son was okay.

As Patrick continued to minister to the boy, I paddled to the beach towards the mother. By the time we got to the beach there was a crowd of people assembled. When we beached the canoe, we lifted the boy out of the craft and placed him on the beach where the mother took him in her arms, sobbing uncontrollably. We stood with the crowd watching as the boy said: "No worries, momma, dees white men saved mi. I okay." To which the crowd applauded. We looked around and noticed they were applauding us as well. The mother hugged the boy for so long and so tight that I thought she might suffocate him. Someone in the crowd asked our names and Patrick introduced me as Ollie the spotted man. I was resigned to the fact that Ollie was to be my Jamaican name.

During our conversations with the bystanders, we were offered the use of a water spigot from a man who owned beachfront land close to the northern end of Long Bay and he welcomed us to camp there whenever we desired. The news of our act of heroism traveled fast and the people who lived in the beach area became friendlier to us. We were the fishermen hippies who lived on Booby Cay, and the friends of Elkannah the fisherman.

We decided to delay going to the sea cave and instead went directly to Red Ground, leaving our canoe beached with our new Jamaican friends. We carried with us freshly caught fish intending to trade them for ganja. Patrick persuaded me that a simple swap of fish for ganja was not an infraction on Jamaican business practices and I agreed since we were not attempting to set up a regular money transaction for our fish. As we walked up the steep slope of the main street leading away from the Roundabout and into Red Ground, a Jamaican boy with dreadlocks who appeared to be no more than twelve years old approached us. He had a spliff in his hand and said: "Smoke dis spliff wit me, mon." I was amazed that a boy so young was smoking ganja. I stood before him staring in disbelief while Patrick gratefully accepted the spliff. I, too, partook of the spliff and asked the boy his name and how old he was. "Eleven, mon. I am Levi an' I live in de Blue Mountains. Presently I n I visitin' fambly, mon. Never 'ave I seen white men wit dreadlocks, mon. Where yah fram?"

"America," I replied.

"Den yah mus' be rich, mon. Give me money, mon."

"We're not rich, just poor Americans living a simple life in the village of Negril. We fish to live. See, we bring fish to trade."

"Tradin' fer wat, mon. Wat yah be needin'?" the boy asked.

"Ganja. Lamb's Bread." Patrick replied without hesitation.

"Plenty ganja 'round 'ere, mon. Jamaica de land of ganja. Dat no problem, mon. Lamb's Bread is ganja of de Rastas, nuh fer white men, dis yah can nuh 'ave. How much yah be wantin'?"

"How much can you get?" Patrick asked.

"Are yah wantin' ta sell in de U.S., mon?"

"No. We just want a little for our use," I replied.

"Dat a shame, mon. Much money you mek in de ganja trade. Yeahmon, mi uncle an' I ganja farmers in Blue Mountains, mon. De best ganja in aw Jamaica. We lookin' ta sell hundreds of pounds, mon. Yah mus' knoh people in America who be wantin' ta buy I n I ganja."

"No, man. We don't know people who are interested in that much ganja. We just want to trade fish for a small amount of ganja for our use. How much ganja can you give us for these fish?" Patrick asked, holding up the fish.

"Fish easy ta get, mon. I Rasta. Ital is de Rasta way. No eat putrid flesh of dead animals." He spat on the ground in disgust. "Money I be needin'," responded Levi.

"Sorry. No offense meant. I forgot Rastafarians don't eat fish. How much for a pound?" I asked.

"Ten dollars, U.S., mon, de bes' I can do," replied Levi.

"That's too much," I said. Knowing full well that cash is not plentiful in Negril, especially U.S. currency, and that ten bucks would go a long way. Also, bartering is the name of the game in Jamaica as there is no such thing as fixed prices, so he must be asking higher than the going rate, if there was a going rate.

"Blood clatt, mon, ten U.S. is fair price. Seven-fifty an' I gi yah dis bag of mushrooms."

"I don't eat mushrooms, to me they aren't real food," responded Patrick.

"Nuh food, mon. Dees magic mushrooms. Dey open de spirit world fer white men, mon Obeah - an' de bag full, mon, enuff fer ten people. Picked fresh dis mornin'." Levi opened the bag to give us a look. I had some knowledge of hallucinogenic mushrooms. I read about an experiment conducted by two psychologists from Harvard University, doctors Timothy Leary and Richard Allen. They wanted to observe the influence of psilocybin mushrooms on violent criminals. The hallucinogen was expected to enable the prisoners to experience the emotion of love, and it was successful to a limited extent. The limitation being they were in prison cells. Having studied mental health, I had interest in the effects of psychotropic drugs for therapeutic use. Also, magic mushrooms were a popular mind expanding drug among the counter-culture youth of America and Europe.

"Do Rastafarians use mushrooms?" I asked, curious about their religion and possible use of substances other than ganja in their rituals.

"Nuh, mon. We nuh put poison in de temples of Jah. Only de pure herb of ganja ta free de mind ta see de spiritual world an' tek away de chains of Babylon, mon. Mushrooms are wat white people be askin' fer aw de time. It mek dem silly. Are yah wantin' de mushrooms an' de ganja fer de price I askin'?"

"Seven-fifty is fair," I said. I asked if we could see the ganja. Levi led us to a shaded grove of trees and produced a packaged wrapped in brown paper. Patrick opened one end and whistled, stating it was all buds and no sticks or seeds were visible.

"Dis sinsemellia, it 'as nuh seeds, mon. It de virgin female flower dat 'ave more potency fer de mind. Yeahmon, good deal. Nuh better quality an' price in aw Jamaica. I n I grow in de Cock Pit country, mon. I n I of de Maroon people. We never slave of de Spanish an' de English never rule us, mon. We fight Babylon an' win. Irie! We 'ave our own country, free fram government polytricksters."

"We'll take the ganja. We don't need the mushrooms," I said.

"Same price mushrooms or nuh, mon."

"May as well take the mushrooms," replied Patrick as he handed the cash to Levi and took the merchandise, including the bag of magic mushrooms.

"Yah won't be regrettin' de purchase, mon. Irie!" and off Levi strolled, his relatively short dreadlocks bouncing from the spring in his step as he made his way down the road towards the Roundabout.

I was full of curiosity about Eli and the things he said. "What do you think he meant by *I n I*, Lord Joseph used that same phrase, and what is a Maroon? What and where is the Cock Pit country? That kid was almost as mysterious as Lord Joseph."

"I expect that since he mentioned both the Blue Mountains and the Cockpit Country that they may be connected. As for the Maroon people, slavery, and the English, we're gonna have to ask Elkannah about that," replied Patrick, "or Lord Joseph if he ever shows up."

"What are we gonna do with all these mushrooms?" I asked.

"We could eat them and peer into the world of Jah." Patrick laughed as he said it.

"You heard Levi, Rastafarians see mushrooms as poison and only ganja is used as part of their spirituality," I responded.

"Well, to each his own. I never peered into the spirit world while smoking pot, and who is to say mushrooms won't place me on the threshold of the divine? You have to admit that Lord Joseph's Babylon cleansing ceremony was powerful," commented Patrick.

"Yeah, it was powerful, but I don't believe ganja was the source of the mysticism," I replied.

"Maybe not, but nonetheless, you did smoke it and you did not get paranoid and you have been smoking it ever since without ill effects. Besides, we both know that the Hopi Indians and other tribes use psychedelic drugs to induce mystical states, and who is to say that Christians drinking wine and breaking bread isn't really the body and blood of Christ after all. And maybe when the Catholic priests do the transubstantiation of wine and bread into Jesus' blood and body, it becomes a mild hallucinogen." Patrick reiterated what we had discussed many times about drug usage and spirituality.

"Perhaps reality and science are the authority on that topic, and not religion. Every time I had communion, the wine did not taste like blood and the bread wafers were bland crackers and not human flesh. As for being a mind drug, alcohol is as strong as any. Those priests love to drink!"

Our conversation got me thinking once again about the religions and cultures that have some form of ritual that involves ingesting chemicals to create an altered state to increase spiritual receptivity. Aboriginal Indians of the Amazon and other regions of South America use mushrooms and even the lick the skin secretion of toads in religious rituals. I was skeptical, though, about Rastafarian ganja, Christian communion, and the licking of toads. I do accept the premise that through ingesting chemicals new windows of perception could be opened, revealing at least the possibility of other dimensions of reality existing outside the realm of physical senses.

Patrick made a good suggestion, "Whatever we may think, we have the mushrooms and we have freedom of choice. I say we just hold on to them for a while. Who knows, maybe we'll meet folks that'll make use of them and we can barter for something we need," I agreed.

I wanted to resume our exploration of Red Ground. We continued walking up the slope of the main road, taking notice of the many wooden shanties and cinder block homes. The houses were beautifully landscaped with a variety of plants and flowers. Every hundred yards or so there were small roadside stands that sold coca-cola, cigarettes, beer, banana bread, and other items. It was the Jamaican version of corner convenience stores. Some people waved as we passed by while others looked away.

I heard hymnal singing coming from a short distance. As we made our way around a curve, we came upon a small church. Without discussion, we walked up the few creaky steps into the simple white wooden clad building that had a huge wooden cross on the front gable. The church was full of Jamaicans, almost all of them dressed in white. A large charcoal portrait of a black Mary holding a black baby Jesus at her bosom captured my eyes. I wondered how Jesus and his mother could possibly be black since all the Jewish people I had ever met were white. Then again, I honestly didn't really know much about the color of people from two thousand years ago in the Middle East. Maybe it was the whole movement towards black pride and the notion that white people have stripped black culture of so much of their history that brought about a process of reconstructing their heritage. I wondered if the American black pride and civil rights movement had graced Jamaican culture and I decided that this village was too remote for such influence to take hold so rapidly. Then again, maybe Jesus was black and whites rewrote history. I couldn't help but wonder how humans have a tendency to make up so-called facts to suit their perceptions of how they want things to be, which brings into question what is real and what is fantasy. Strange how such thoughts flash through my mind within a brief instant of time, all instigated by a painting. Maybe it was the ganja I had just smoked with Levi.

The congregation finished singing a Christian hymnal song that I did not recognize, followed by a period of prayerful silence. Patrick and I stood unnoticed on each side of the double doors. The minister rose to the pulpit and said, "God has blessed us all, go in peace." The people stood from their pews and began moving towards us. When the first sets of eyes gazed upon Patrick and me, they widened with surprise and puzzlement. I got the sense that seeing young white boys sporting cutoff jeans, dreadlock hair, and a string of fish, was extremely unusual. And there was the fact that Patrick was carrying a pound of ganja buds wrapped in brown paper, and it gave off a strong telltale sweet odor. The congregation froze with a look of horror and disbelief on their faces. We were aliens from another world who had invaded their universe. It couldn't be simply because we were white boys, surely they have seen white people, since some Jamaicans are white and mixed race. Perhaps it was the anomaly of white boys looking like we did, a sight they may have never beheld. There weren't many young white people living in Negril, and if there were, I doubt they possessed our wild nature-boy appearance – well, I take that back, most hippies cultivated that bohemian-gypsy look.

The first group of people briskly walked past us with disagreeable grunts, which was our cue to exit the doors. We stood to the side of the stone walkway, observing the people as they left, none of which showed interest in conversing with us. I wondered if they saw us as incarnations of demons. For the first time in all my experiences in Negril, I felt dirty and unwelcomed. The crowd had dispersed without anyone giving the slightest interest to our presence. "Nothing like good ol' religious hospitality," quipped Patrick. Just as Patrick spoke, the preacher came through the doors.

"You boys are filthy! How dare you enter the house of the Lord! You defile His temple. Repent your sins before the Lord and be reborn in His Spirit!" he commanded.

"We have been cleansed of Babylon by Lord Joseph, and that's good enough for me," replied Patrick.

"Blasphemy! There is no Lord but Jesus Christ. Idolatry! Rasta men are demons. They worship a man, proclaiming King Haile Selassie as the reincarnation of King Solomon. This is the work of Satan. You must repent or be damned to hell for eternity!" The preacher's eyes were bugling out of his head, and sweat beaded on his bald head while his body shook. I was worried he would have a heart attack. I noticed he wasn't talking in the usual Jamaican dialect but he did have that distinct Jamaican lilt. Perhaps he was educated in England or something like that.

"We'll take your warning under consideration, sir. We must be on our way," said Patrick. We turned and walked away as the minister called out over and over, "Repent, repent!" I heard something whiz past my head, then another, and whack – a rock hit me in the ass.

"Run!" I shouted. We bolted down the winding steep lime-chalk paved road. I saw a rock hit Patrick on his left shoulder blade – he let out a yell, "What the fuck!" I risked a look over my shoulder and saw a small group of Jamaican men led by the minister chasing after us as they tossed stones our way. We made it all the way to the Roundabout before the Christians stopped chasing us. We stopped under the shade of a palm tree and collapsed on the ground, panting, sweating and bruised – Patrick on his shoulder and me on my ass.

"Whew – that was freggin' crazy!" I exclaimed.

"Man, I never expected anything like that. That is the first time since we arrived in Jamaica that I was really, really scared!" said Patrick.

"It's interesting that Christians and not Rastafarians gave us the cold shoulder and condemned us to an eternity of hell," I said, "and they tried stoning us to death!"

"Yeah man, we gotta stay away from those Christian folks – ironic eh?" Patrick was still panting. I looked at his shoulder. It was turning black and blue and was beginning to swell, but the skin was only scrapped and there was mild bleeding.

"Ironic is right – love your brother – and '*... you without sin cast the first stone...*' bullshit!" I was pissed.

"You know, Oliver, Lord Joseph had us go through a ritual that was sort of a repenting of our sins of Babylon – although we did no repenting. If we told the Christian minister that we wanted him to perform an exorcism on us it might have given him an erection. To Rastafarians we favor their most sacred ritual substance – marijuana. To these good Christian folks, well, we don't exactly look like clean cut American Christian youth, now do we?" I laughed at Patrick's insightful comment, knowing that his assessment was quite accurate. We were calming down from our escape from almost being stoned to death.

"I'm ready to head back to the cave to cook up these fish for lunch before they start smelling worst than we do." I was hungry and the recent stone cold shoulder we got from the good Christian folks dampened my interest in further social explorations.

"I suppose we should head back, although I was hoping to meet some Jamaican babes," replied Patrick.

"Babes? After getting chased by Christian Crusaders trying to stone us to death. You must be nuts! If we want Jamaican girls from Red Ground, I think we better cut our hair, wash our clothes and bodies, and maybe paint our skin black!"

"Just kiddin, Ollie. Yo, bro, we're 100% natural. Body cleansed by de sea an' sunshine, mon. Irie! I n I Jamaican fishermen, mon, dwellers of a sea cave an' Conch Island. We white breddas of Rasta Lord Joseph who cleansed us of Babylon, an' friends of Elkannah Walker, de greatest fisherman of aw Negril. I am Patrick de brown mon wit' dreads, an' yah be Ollie, de spotted mon," boasted Patrick. We laughed heartily as we assisted each other getting to our feet. I rubbed my butt and took a peek at the damage – it was sore but no blood.

"Yeah, we have come a long way from the South Philly Ghetto Flowers Magnificent Seven," I replied.

"If you recall, I never was an official member of that motley crew, just an innocent participant in many of their charades, and the adventures continue," replied Patrick. We laughed and sang the somewhat silly although precious, *Mind Surfing* song that our South Philly peer group wrote one day in Wildwood, NJ. We entered the

Roundabout and made our way across the bridge that straddles the South Negril River to retrieve the canoe and paddle to the sea cave.

RASTAMEN

We paddled along the cliffs, a Jamaican youth who was hand-line fishing waved as we went by. We were a familiar sight for those who spent time along the cliffs and beach. Word had spread among those who were fishermen that we had increased Elkannah's wealth. There was more than one fisherman who asked us to fish for them, and of course we declined. We were eager to keep our fisherman friend well supplied with conch and fish for the market. He had aspirations of adding yet another room to his home, and we were determined to increase his wealth. He was our friend and mentor. As the saying goes, with a slight alteration, give some boys a fish and you feed them for a day, teach them how to fish and you give him a way to live as a Jamaican native.

As we were getting closer to the sea cave we could hear conga drums and chanting. The music was coming from the cave. "Patrick, stop paddling! We have to approach the cave slowly to determine what's going on."

Patrick spoke in a whisper, "I suspect Lord Joseph has returned and has friends are with him. They sound really good, even though I can't understand what they're chanting other than a few words: Jah, King Haile Selassie, Babylon, Irie – the usual Rasta words."

"Yeah, me too. I hope they're not messing with our stuff, especially the instruments," I replied.

"I don't hear a flute or guitar, so I expect they're safe, unless they're stolen, or they don't know how to play them." Patrick's comment about stolen instruments alarmed me. We never took our instruments to Conch Island because of the high probability of them getting ruined by water, so we left them hidden high up in the recesses of the cave's ceiling along with the rest of our possessions. We always took our money and important papers, though, secured from water damage, contained in plastic.

We maneuvered the canoe to the northern end of the sea cave opening, positioning ourselves so they couldn't see us. This also didn't allow for us to see them, so we anchored the canoe and decided to swim along the cliff wall. It was easy to get closer by swimming. We were able to hide behind cliff rock and remain covered in shadow. We stood on a submerged rock and peered through a crack between two rocks that kept us hidden from sight. We now had a clear view of the people. All of them had dreadlocks so they were definitely Rastafarian. Lord Joseph was there. He was one of three Rastas beating on congas. Altogether, there were eight Rastafarians. Then, one more appeared from the back of the cave holding Patrick's guitar case. It was Levi, the young boy that recently sold us the ganja and mushrooms. Patrick startled when he saw him with his guitar causing him to reveal our presence.

"Excuse me, Levi, that is my guitar you have there!" Patrick's voice boomed and echoed in the cave in shocking discordance to the conga rhythm and chanting. The Rastas stopped and the cave went dead silent. "Rhaatid! Who dat?" Lord Joseph's baritone voice filled every space in the cavern. Patrick swam out from behind the rock and went deeper into the cave. He stood on a different submerged smooth rock with only his knees covered in water.

"Lord Joseph, it is I, Patrick."

"Come 'ere, mon. Yah put de fright inna I n I. Nuh mon 'ave ever enter cave wen I gaterin' wit frens an' fambly. Nuh mon enter cave fram de sea. Where Ollie?"

"Right here!" I said in a rather squeaky voice. I swam close to where Patrick stood, and rose from the water standing on a different submerged rock.

"Des are mi white breddas, Patrick an' Ollie. Dem cleansed of Babylon an' nuh defile our presence. Come join I n I." I was relieved that Lord Joseph announced that we were his brothers.

"Welcome back home, Lord Joseph. We need to bring our canoe into the cave. It'll only take a moment," I replied.

"A canoe! How yah come by dat, mon?" Lord Joseph asked.

"Elkannah the fisherman. We fish for him," replied Patrick.

"Irie! Elkannah a good mon. Yah do well Ollie an' Patrick. Awrite den, come an' join I n I." I could tell by Lord Joseph's words and tone of voice that he was truly pleased to see us, and our taking up residence in his cave did not disturb him. I was a little anxious about meeting his Rasta brethren, mainly because of the suspicion etched in their facial expressions. Levi had a look of amazement on his face, partly because of the coincidence of having just sold us ganja, and by the revelation that we are friends of Lord Joseph.

Patrick paddled the canoe into the cave. I assisted in pulling it on to the partially submerged flat ledge and tied the anchor around a rock to keep the canoe stationary during the sea swells. The Rastamen watched as we unloaded the fish and other items from the canoe. One remarked on the fish: "Eatin' de flesh of animals pollutes de temple of Jah! It putrid in de stomach an' poison de mind. Effin yah wearin' dreads, mon, yah mus' nuh eat flesh. I see many conch in cave. Eatin' shellfish nuh good, mon."

"We are not Rastafarian. Are all Rastas vegetarian?" I asked.

"True dat, mon. Yah nuh Rasta, an' can never be. African blood nuh run inna yah veins. Yah dwell in Babylon. De body is de temple of Jah. Many claim ta be Rastas an' eat fish. Dey nuh Ital, nuh true Rastas!"

"What is your name," Patrick asked.

"I Denny of de Maroon people. Aw mi breddas, I n I, are of de Maroon people fram de Cock Pit country. True independent people I n I, Irie! I n I never under de rule of de English an' polytricksters of corrupt Jamaican government. One day I n I return ta Ethiopia an' fulfill prophesy dat one day I n I live in Zion. First mus' free de Jamaican people fram tyranny an' downpression."

Wow, that was quite a speech. It told us a lot about Rastas, at least this particular group.

"Are you family?" Patrick continued questioning Denny.

"I n I aw bredda in de fambly of Jah. One blood! One heart!" Denny replied. I wondered where we fit in to the family of Jah, given that the Rastas are of one blood and we were just told that we do not have African blood in our veins. As is my penchant in such matters, I addressed this issue. It was risky, but I couldn't hold myself back.

"All people have their origins in Africa, and they diverged across the planet. Africa is the birthplace of all humanity. This means that all people have African blood in their veins, and that we all come from the first parents of creation, and according to biblical teachings that would be Adam and Eve in the Garden of Eden. The color of our skin is a matter of pigmentation, and whatever differences we have between us have to do with culture, ideas, beliefs, and values – creations from our minds. And we have the power to change our minds and create our culture by what we choose to believe." The Rastas stared at me with a variety of looks that included bewilderment, anger, amazement, consternation, and smiles. Lord Joseph was the one who responded to my little speech with a smile.

"Irie! Ollie, yah speak wisdom of de ages, mon. I n I of one blood. De skin color is of material t'ings an' nuh of de heart, mind, an' spirit. Jah aw colors an' aw t'ings. Irie! I n I mus' put such matters of difference aside mi breddas. Ollie an' Patrick are frens an' dey join I n I in our *groundation*."

"What is groundation?" Patrick asked.

"Holy day, mon. I n I celebrate ganja harvest. Sit wit us, white breddas!" commanded Lord Joseph.

We sat in the semi circle facing the sea. Lord Joseph walked to the edge of the ledge and turned towards the sea. He raised his arms in the air, palms facing upward and recited the following prayer:

"Princes an' princesses shall come forth out of Egypt, Ethiopia now stretch forth her hands before Jah. O Thou Jah of Ethiopia, Thou Jah of Thy Divine Majesty, Thy Spirit come inna our hearts, ta dwell in de paths of righteousness. Lead an' help I n I ta forgive, that I n I may be forgiven. Teach I n I Love an' loyalty on earth as it is in Zion, Endow us wit Thy wise mind, knowledge an' overstanding ta do thy will, thy blessings ta us, dat de 'ungry might be fed, de sick nourished, de aged protected, de naked clothed an' de infants cared for. Deliver I n I fram de hands of our enemy, dat I n I may prove fruitful in de Last Days, wen our enemies 'ave passed an' decayed in de depths of de sea, in de depths of de earth, or in de belly of a beast. O give us a place inna Thy Kingdom forever an ever, so I n I hail our Jah, King Haile Selassie I, Jehovah God, Rastafari, Almighty God, Rastafari, great an' powerful God Jah, Rastafari. Who sitteth an' reigneth in de heart of man an' woman, 'ear us an' bless us an' sanctify us, an' cause Thy loving Face ta shine upon us thy children, dat I n I may be saved, SELAH."

Lord Joseph stood serenely and motionless. We were silent as the echo of the last word reverberated off the cavern walls. I was gripped by a feeling of reverence. This prayer sounded like it could be the Rastafarian equivalent of the Christian Lord's prayer. Lord Joseph was similar to a priest, a shaman, and clearly a leader among this group of Rastas. I now understood why he held the title Lord as part of his name. When Lord Joseph took his place among the group, Levi, by far the youngest Rasta present, held a spliff in his outstretched hands and recited a prayer: *"An' God say, Let de earth bring forth grass, de 'erb yielding seed, an' de fruit tree yielding fruit after His kind, whose seed is in itself, upon de earth: an' it was so, SELAH."* He lit the spliff and passed it to his left. It made its way around several times before anyone spoke.

"Ganja cleanse de body an' mind, heal de soul, raise de consciousness, an' bring us closer ta Jah. Ganja is de healing of aw nations. It rejected by de governments of Babylon fer it stings de hearts of downpressers who promote evil an' aw sort of injustice."

I didn't know the name of the person who spoke so highly of ganja. His voice was soft and gentle, speaking as though he was inside a sacred church. The statement was a profound pronouncement of the importance of ganja in the religious and political life of Rastas. No doubt, the smoking of ganja was a sacrament.

Denny continued the homage to ganja. "Yeahmon. Babylon mek ganja illegal so dey can keep de minds of people enslaved. De polytricksters nuh want people ta free der minds. True dat! Bondage is of de mind an' heart. Ganja free de mind ta touch de heart of Jah."

The reverence by which these people were speaking of ganja amazed me. I never heard a Catholic priest speak of communion as a way of freeing the mind from oppression. Communion is supposed to bring the believer closer to Christ, but I never heard of it spoken as liberating the mind from political bondage – the devil, original sin, guilt, forgiveness for being a lowly undeserving good for nothing heathen, yes, but not freedom from mental bondage. I decided to add my thoughts, speaking quickly, "Christians practice the ritual of communion to come closer to God. Smoking ganja is very similar." As I completed my sentence, it occurred to me that it might not be proper for a non-Rasta to speak during this ceremony. Then, Patrick added his thoughts.

"I think it's far out, man. Truly revolutionary! Freeing the mind is the key to true liberation from all forms of oppression. When a person can think freely, gain insight into all things, then no prison walls can contain him." Patrick was very high and grooving on the ganja ceremony.

Another Rasta spoke whose name I did not know. "Yahshua, de Christian messiah, showed de way to eternal life, mon. Rasta Tafari true incarnation of King Solomon, defender of de faith."

"Who is Yahshua?" I asked, not picking up on the fact that the person just said he was the Christian messiah.

"Di Christian God, mon!" replied Lord Joseph. "Yah carry His symbol 'round yah neck, Ollie." He was speaking of Jesus and the cross that was dangling from the wooden rosary beads my mother had given to me for so-called protection. I realized that Rastas believe that King Haile Selassie is the messiah of the current age.

"Whoa, that blows my mind, bro. The King of Ethiopia is the messiah – maybe the second coming of Jesus. Wow, that is really far out." The more stoned Patrick became, the more 'groovy' his language became – and I wondered if he was taking this religion seriously.

Denny spoke. "Yeahmon. Irie! King Haile Selassie will restore Zion an' bring de true teachings of Yahshua ta de people. Rastamen are true descendants of de twelve tribes of Israel. Yahshua was a black mon. Babylon 'ave yah t'ink ot'erwise, dat he was white." His statement could be taken as racist, or at the very least, an expression of white men's conspiracy to oppress black men. But hey, maybe Jesus wasn't a white man. Hmm, I was always taught that he was white with light hair and blue eyes and yet I don't recall ever reading a physical description in the bible. I got that image from the famous painting of the Last Supper. I wanted to know more about this King Selassie.

"So, King Haile Selassie is in Ethiopia?" I asked.

"Yeahmon, an' one day I n I will return ta 'im. First I n I mus' free aw Jamaican breddas fram de chains of Babylon." Levi responded.

"King Haile Selassie visit Jamaica, mon, an' gi ta Michael Manley a walkin' stick, *De Rod of Correction*, ta unite Rastas an' aw Jamaicans ta overthrow corruption." The Rasta who spoke had distinctive green eyes. I assumed that someone in his lineage must be of a different ethnicity than African. I wondered if having blood of an ethnic group other than African would be considered an abomination, but I did not want to ask. I wondered, too, if having such a thought was racist. I decided it was simply curiosity.

Lord Joseph spoke next, "Ollie an' Patrick. Dis talkin I n I 'avin' 'ere, Rastas call *reasoning*. Irie! It is de smoking of ganja an' expressin' de mind an' heart of I n I." I was now gaining a greater understanding that the phrase *I n I* was an all-inclusive term that referred to everyone present and the oneness of creation, which now struck me as obvious causing me to feel somewhat idiotic for not realizing this sooner – language is not my strong suit. I also realized that free thinking stimulated by smoking ganja is central to the Rasta religion. Lord Joseph continued speaking, "*Di river of life proceeded ta flow fram de throne of God, an' on either side of de bank der was de tree of life, an' de leaf from dat tree is for de healing of aw nations*. Dis quote is fram de book of Revelations, mon. Ganja is de tree of life given ta us dat I n I see inta Babylon's veil of deception. Ganja criminalized in every country in dis world, yeahmon. It tis a threat ta de many rulers of Babylon. De tree of knowledge dat reveals de truth dat de polytricksters keep I n I from knowin'. It is de truth dat set I n I free."

"Wasn't the tree of life forbidden by God?" I asked.

"De Old Testament tree of life open de door ta evil world. De ganja tree of life restore de Garden so dat de lies of Babylon be tossed inta de fiah." Lord Joseph's response did not strike me as logical and was sprinkled with interpretations of interpretations of mythologies. I decided not to challenge him as he might take offense. Deeply held beliefs are not easily uprooted no matter how much ganja is consumed to open the mind to seeing the truth. That's just a fact of human psychology. I was reminded that people believe creeds and doctrines because it works for them – whether it makes sense or not. It gives some of us a way of seeing the world that makes sense and brings a feeling of security. It is impossible for me to *not* judge the views and beliefs of others, for I can only perceive the world from the perspective of my own learning and subsequent thought system.

Experiencing this ceremony caused my thoughts to travel down many corridors regarding religion, ritual, belief, and the nature of reality. Interpreting the world based on our inner experiences is the nature of human perception of which there may be no exceptions, although there are varying degrees of open mindedness. Rastas truly believe that ganja opens their minds to true insight into the nature of so-called true perception – the clearing of the mind of the influences of Babylon – the corrupted world that hides truth. I had my doubts that the drug had the affect of loosening one fully from the fetters of self-deception. I wondered if it served to free the mind in some aspects, and crystallize a thought system in other ways, which is a fascinating paradox, and one that I have found in every belief system so far encountered.

I had to speak, "You and your Rasta brothers are fortunate, Lord Joseph, to have the tree of life to free your minds of the wrongful influences of the world. Patrick and I are grateful to be recipients of your knowledge and wisdom." I decided it would not be appropriate to push the philosophical and theological envelope of the importance of ganja smoking and other particulars of their religious practice and views. Acknowledging the value they place on ganja was the respectful thing to do.

Lord Joseph replied, "Irie, Ollie. Dis a wondrous t'ing ta share de 'oly sacrament wit I n I. Rastas mus' embrace aw people of Jah's Iration so Zion manifest upon de earth." I wondered if the other Rastas present shared Lord Joseph's perspective, especially Denny, who said earlier that we couldn't be Rasta since we do not have African blood – actually dark skin. I suppose it is the quest for understanding that matters more than the extent of its actualization. At the very least, these folks were envisioning a better world, even if the lenses being looked through may be culturally myopic, not that my perception was by any means unbiased – such is the human condition.

One of the Rastas, the tall skinny one, began tapping out a rhythm on a conga drum. Rasta Denny joined him on another drum, soon followed by yet another Rasta conga player. The conga's got louder and the beat became faster. I went to the back of the cave and retrieved my flute. I discovered a cache of ganja, piled up in bales wrapped in burlap sacks. The smell was powerful and one of the bales was open, revealing the compressed sacred buds. There was no way to know for sure how much was there, possibly a hundred pounds or more.

The Rasta brothers were pleased to have the melody of the flute weaving its notes through the beat of their drums. Patrick soon followed with his guitar, strumming chords in the same rhythm. This was an organic, spontaneous, Jamaican jam session. The sound was louder than it would have been in the open air because of the cavern walls. I thought of the cave as an instrument that synthesized all the sounds into one. The music was intoxicating. I felt giddy and light headed, as the music influenced my consciousness. The uniqueness of the music exceeded anything I had ever heard. In fact, it didn't feel like we were creating the music, but that the music was expressing itself as its own entity through each one of us. I thought, *'this is what it means to create harmony through music – not just in sound, but in mind and spirit.'* Lord Joseph began chanting, empowered by the awe-inspiring music.

JAH Rastafari, JAH mek I n I
Rastafari Holy King of Zion
King of Kings, Elect of JAH

JAH Rastafari, JAH mek I n I
Conquering Lion, Tribe of Judah
Author of Mankind

JAH Rastafari, JAH mek I n I
Zion Paradise for I n I
Ready ta leave Babylon

JAH Rastafari, JAH mek I n I
Zion on High
JAH Rastafari, JAH mek I n I

When Lord Joseph sang the chant once through, the Rastas joined him, repeating the chant over and over as the music played. At times I stopped playing the flute to join the chanting.

Suddenly, without any of us communicating so much as a nod of the head, the chanting and instruments ceased. The cave went silent. Lord Joseph spoke:

"King Haile Selassie stood before de world, de United Nations an' condemned racism, an' dees are His words:

Racial animosities mus' be set aside dat we may 'ave world peace an' harmony. I n I mus' become members of a new race, overcoming petty prejudice, owing our ultimate allegiance not ta nations but ta our fellow men within de human community. Until de human philosophy which holds one race superior an' another inferior is finally an' permanently discredited an' abandoned; until de color of a man's skin is of no more significance than de color of his eyes; until de basic human rights are equally guaranteed ta all wit'out regard ta race; until dat day, de dream of peace an' world citizenship an' de rule of international morality will remain but a fleeting illusion, ta be pursued an' never attained; all breddas an' sisters mus' stand united, den we shall win, as we are confident in de victory of good over evil.

Di words of His Imperial Majesty, King Haile Selassie, Rastafari!" Lord Joseph, upon reciting these words as though they were the closing of a sacred prayer, lit a spliff and said, "Di herb dat comes fram de Lord ta heal de nations." The spliff passed around the cave, each of us taking our turn smoking the sacred herb.

Throughout the rest of the late afternoon, and long into the evening, we played music, sang more chants, and smoked copious amounts of ganja. During the course of the evening, we had a discussion with Lord Joseph. He told us that his Rasta family would be using the cave for an unspecified amount of time. Stored in the recesses of the cave was the family harvest of ganja and that they would be selling it to people from the U.S. and Europe as well as distributing it to Rastas who lived in the Negril village. The Cockpit Country is where his family grew their ganja without fear of the government because they are Maroon people. The polytricksters have no jurisdiction over the Maroon people, having signed a peace treaty and independence agreement in 1738, and later honored when Jamaica gained independence from England in 1962. Lord Joseph had an uncle who left the Cockpit country and settled in Negril. The land he now lives on once belonged to that uncle. He told us that Levi is his nephew.

I realized that Lord Joseph had placed an enormous amount of trust in Patrick and me. We expressed our gratitude over and over. Too bad he didn't eat fish and conch because it was the only resource we had to give for his hospitality. The amount of money we had was so precious little that we did not want to part with it, and he did not ask for anything. Lord Joseph was a generous man whose wealth was his faith, family, sea cave property, and, of course ganja farming. He freely shared his wealth with us without expectation of anything material in exchange. He never asked us for anything. Still, I wanted to give him something.

Eventually everyone left the cave and Patrick and I went to sleep. When the first light of the new day appeared on the sea, we loaded up the canoe with our belongings. Patrick was already in the canoe and I was preparing to get on board when Lord Joseph entered the cave. As I turned my head towards him I became cognizant of the wooden rosary beads dangling from my neck. Without saying a word I approached Lord Joseph. He smiled at me as I took the rosary bead necklace from around my neck and placed them over his head.

"Dis special ta yah, Ollie. It 'as de cross of Yahshua. King Haile Selassie is de continuation of Yahshua prophecy." He took out a knife and cut off the cross. He took a long piece of leather from the pouch he carried over his shoulder and tied the cross to it. He put the cross necklace around my neck. "Dis cross yah keep, Ollie, fer protection fram Babylon." He extended his huge hands and as I grasped them he said, "Come back, mon, an' live in cave wen Rasta fambly return ta Cockpit Maroon Country."

"We will! Your cave has been our first real home in Jamaica. Thank you so much, Lord Joseph." My eyes watered as I spoke.

"Irie! No problem, mon. Jah be wit Ollie an' Patrick."

I got in the canoe and we paddled out of the sea cave. We headed toward Fishermen Cove, not knowing exactly where we would make our next camp. I thought we should go to Conch Island. Patrick reminded me that the distance from Elkannah and the rest of the population did not make the island the most desirable permanent camp. It was great for several days at a time, but it would be preferable for us to have a home base on the mainland. We discussed living on seven-mile beach, and became excited at the idea of living there for indeed Patrick and I loved sandy beaches, however we were enamored with the cliffs and their stunning beauty, and living close to Elkannah was more convenient for our business arrangement. As we paddled into the cove, we saw Elkannah readying his canoe for a morning of fishing.

MILLIE, CHARLIE, ELIJAH & NORLINA

Elkannah was happy to see us. He assumed we were planning to join him. When we pulled up along side his canoe, he saw our belongings.

"Patrick, Ollie, you leave Lord Joseph's cave. Where you go? Booby Cay?" he asked.

"Booby Cay is a good place to spend a few days fishing and diving for conch, but not to live. It is too far from everything."

"Irie, mon. Yah can tent on mi land. It nuh a problem, mon."

"That would be great," Patrick replied.

"Yeahmon. I soon be buying de materials ta build another room. Yah could help."

"Definitely. If we didn't have all our stuff here we'd go fishing with you this morning," I replied.

"Dat nuh a problem, mon. Put yah t'ings over der an' we cover dem, mon. No one trouble dem. Elkannah de fisherman 'ave de right ta dis area of de cove. Seen!" We did not want to leave our precious belongings unprotected no matter what respect people had for Elkannah and his property. By definition, thieves were no respecters of personal property.

"What do you mean by *seen?*" I asked.

"*Seen* mean understand," Elkannah replied.

"We have very expensive musical instruments and everything we own is in this canoe. For now, we think it best to set up camp on your property. We'd feel a lot safer," I explained.

"It no problem mon. Do wat yah t'ink is best, yah mus' do wat yah say. Place yah tent behind mi home mon, away fram de road, near de garden. Tell mi wife Clara yah 'ave permission. Every t'ing be awrite. I gawaan now, see yah later mon." Elkannah shoved off in his canoe.

We were relieved to have a place to camp. His land was a reasonable distance from Fishermen Cove and we needed to haul all of our gear – we had more possessions than when we had first arrived in Negril. The cooking utensils and canvas tent were by far the heaviest items. We loaded our bodies the best we could. I strapped the tent to the top of my backpack, giving me the heavier load. We decided to leave the cooking items beneath the turned over canoe. It was getting hot very fast and as we walked along West End Road, our bodies began sweating profusely. We came upon a water spigot that was a few feet from the road. I stripped off the backpack and placed my head under the cool water and Patrick did the same. We decided to rest for a while under the shade of a palm tree and smoke some ganja.

Less than an hour had passed. I looked down the road and saw people walking with a donkey in our direction. The donkey had large baskets on its sides. They were walking slowly, stopping on occasion to talk to people who lived along West End Road. It was apparent that they were selling goods from their baskets. We stood up as they approached, noticing there were four of them, two adults and two younger people – they appeared to be teen aged, a boy and a girl.

"Good morning." I said.

"Good mornin'," they replied in unison with the familiar Jamaican lilt. The adult woman said, "Yah like ta buy some fruit an' vegetables? Come, 'ave a look." The baskets on the donkey were overflowing with a variety of food items. We choose a bunch of bananas, two papayas and two mangoes.

"I want U.S. money. Yah 'ave U.S. dollars?" said the woman.

"Yes, how much?" Patrick asked.

"Dat be fifty cents U.S. but I 'ave to give yah change in Jamaican money," she replied. The adult man stood smiling at us. He was wearing a wide rimmed straw hat. He had a broad face that was full of wrinkles forming a perpetual smile. I extended my hand to him. His huge hand swallowed mine as he took it gently.

"Hello sir, my name is Ollie and this is my friend Patrick."

His faced broke into a huge smile, "Hello. I am Charley." After shaking our hands he introduced us to his family. "Dis is mi wife, Millie, an' mi lovely grandchildren, Elijah an' Norlina Evans."

"You are Millie and Charley Constance, we came to Jamaica to meet you. Our friend Randy told us about you," exclaimed Patrick exuberantly.

"Yeahmon, we know Randy. Yah come aw de way fram America jus' ta see us?" said Millie. She, too, had a pleasant smile, even though her front teeth were missing. She was a very petite lady, and she reminded me of the cute Disney character, mini-mouse. Her hair was fashioned into two buns on each side of her head. She had brown eyes, a pointy nose, and large ears. I was struck by the fact that their grandchildren had light colored eyes and light-brown skin. They definitely had ancestors from some lineage other than African racial-ethnicity in their family.

"Randy told us you are very good people and that we would be welcomed by you. He said that you might allow us to stay on your land," said Patrick.

"Randy is a good person. He 'as sent many people ta us. We used ta 'ave a spare room ta rent. Now we mus' use it for our two grandchildren. Dey mus' live wit us now," replied Millie with a hint of sadness in her voice.

"Oh. Well, Elkannah said we can put our tent on his property so we will be okay," said Patrick.

"Elkannah is our good fren. His property is small an' he 'as many children. Since yah 'ave a tent, yah can put it up in our garden. We feed yah one meal a day for one U.S. dollar each." Millie was definitely the business mind of the family. I could tell that she saw us as an opportunity for a steady income. Elkannah said nothing about charging us, then again, he made no offer to feed us either. Although, our fishing provided him with more than ample payment and it gave us the protein we needed but not fruits and vegetables. Still, we had not paid for accommodations since we've been in Jamaica and I was reluctant to start now, especially since I knew we had another option. I decided to try a little negotiating.

"I don't think Elkannah would mind if we stayed on your property. We assist him in fishing. He gave us the use of one of his canoes and we have caught enough fish and conch for him to build a room for his children. If we stayed with you, could we trade fish for the meals instead of paying money?"

"We could work out somet'ing like dat, depending on de fish yah catch. I mek coffee every mornin', an' I mek de best banana bread in aw of Negril. As yah can see, we sell fruits an' vegetables. I go ta Sav-La-Mar market every week. People aw along de West End buy mi produce dey can nuh grow on dem own. Charley tek de donkey up an' down de road each day sellin' t'ings. De money we askin' fram yah be necessary now dat we tek care of our grandson an' grandawta. Are we askin' too much?" Millie was persistent in wanting cash from us. Every time we tried bartering we received a lesson in the shrewd business minds of these lovely people. Jamaicans wanted U.S. dollars!

"No. One U.S. dollar is a fair price," I replied. "What do you think Patrick? Should we camp on Millie and Charley's land or stay with Elkannah?"

Patrick and I stepped aside to discuss the situation privately. Patrick responded to my question, "I am so happy to finally meet Millie and Charley. I think we should spend time with them. Elkannah won't mind, especially since they are his friends, and he made the offer because we had no other place to stay, other than canoeing to Booby Cay, or possibly setting up camp on the beach directly across from the island, you know, where that Jamaican guy offered us the use of his water – living on the beach would be awesome - but I think staying at least for a few days with this family would be cool."

The entire time Patrick was talking he kept looking over at Norlina, and she was staring back. It was obvious that he had other reasons for wanting to stay with this family. Norlina looked like she was seventeen, maybe a year older. She was quite pretty. Her hair was black, thick, straight and cropped short. She was taller than the rest of her family, with long, slender legs, partially covered by a white skirt, which contrasted perfectly next to her smooth caramel skin. She had a lovely smile that exhibited perfect ivory white teeth framed by full lips – but not too full. Long lashes accentuated her large round violet eyes, and her nose and ears were well proportioned and set between high cheekbones. Her white blouse revealed firm and pointy breasts, as the bra she was wearing did not squish them. Indeed, they caused her nipples to protrude quite teasingly.

"Well, I guess that settles it. We're going to stay with Millie and Charley," I exclaimed. We shook hands with everyone as though we had just struck a business bargain. Millie handed each of us a piece of banana-nut bread. It was delicious. We also ate the bananas we purchased before putting on our packs.

The walk to their property went slowly because they stopped to sell their produce to folks along the road. This was good for us because the people saw that we were their friends. We had passed Elkannah's property and I was reminded of how small his property was. Our presence would have made for crowded living circumstances. Perhaps we could increase the number of conch and fish we provide Elkannah so he could purchase land.

I asked for Millie and Charley to wait for a moment while I told Elkannah's wife to inform her husband that we would be camping on the Constance family property.

When we reached Millie and Charley's, I recognized the cliffs. We had visited this area a few weeks ago. It was the place where part of the cliff had been covered with cement and there were concrete steps going down to the sea. There was also a small cave not too far from where the steps led to the sea. We had explored this cave and discovered that it was too small to live in and the swell of the sea frequently covered the ledges.

"Do these cliffs belong to you?" I asked, looking at Millie.

"Yes, Ollie. We poured concrete on dem ta make it easier ta swim an' ta sit an' catch de cool sea breeze an' watch de sun set."

"Can we anchor our canoe in front of your cliffs?" I asked.

"Surely!" Millie replied. I decided we would move our traps closer as well.

Millie explained that their shanties, two of them, were set back on the opposite side of the cliff and not visible from the road. There was a hedgerow of very large croton plants bordering their property all along the road front. There was a stone path that meandered on the property through a grove of coconut, banana, mango, plantain, breadfruit, lemon, orange, ackee, and palm trees. Once we passed through their fruit trees, we came upon a lovely garden with a variety of colorful plants and sweet smelling flowers. On the other side of the garden were the two shanties. Millie and the two grandchildren made their way to the shanties, while Charley led the donkey and us to an open area east of the garden and just out of sight of the shanties.

There were several palm trees that created a nice shaded area where they apparently kept their donkey. The area was quite large, a perfect spot to pitch our tent and set up our hammocks. I wasn't so sure I was going to like sharing our living area with a donkey. While we took off our packs and pitched our tent, Charley unloaded the baskets off the donkey. We helped him carry them to the shanties. Charley told us that we were not to use dried donkey dung for fire because it supplemented their wood as fuel for cooking, and it fertilized their vegetable garden. I wondered about the constant smell of Donkey dong wafting around our camping home. It would have never occurred to me to use shit to cook my food, and yet it made perfect sense. After all, we use dung as fertilizer to feed plants, why not cook with it too? Charlie must have sensed what I was thinking and told us that the Donkey did not stay in this area all of time, only during the heat of the day and that the dung was collected regularly to be placed in the sun to dry out or stored in another place to be used for fertilizer. I was relieved.

Both shanties had porches equipped with chairs, a table, and a hammock. They were approximately fifteen by twenty feet, larger than most shanties we had seen. They were wood framed and sided, roofed with metal, and they had crank open glass windows that were screened. Behind the shanties there was a small cooking shack, very similar to the one that Elkannah's family used, only larger. Millie allowed us to peek inside the shanties. They were quite nicely furnished with a large bed, dressers, table, chairs, washbasin, and oil lamps – reminding me that there was no electricity on the West End.

It would be great to live in one but that was not an option. They showed us their outhouse, which, of course, was crude and smelly. For water, they had a pipe running out of the ground and up a pole. There was a spigot on the bottom that controlled the flow of water, directing it to come out from the bottom spout or from the top for showering. Like many Jamaicans in Negril, they showered outdoors.

Charley took us to the vegetable garden that was behind their shanties. He explained that they were able to grow enough vegetables to feed their family, but not to make money. This is why they went to the Savanna La-Mar market each week to purchase produce. This was the same market where Elkannah sold much of his fish and had bought our snorkel gear.

The grandchildren settled into their shanty. Elijah strung a hammock on the porch for his sleeping space, and Norlina, for the most part, had the inside all to herself. Elijah kept his meager belongings in a few of the dresser drawers.

Patrick and I settled quite comfortably in our new home. The donkey was not a problem since he was only in our camp area during the heat of the day. In fact, we enjoyed his company. Charley was very good about picking up the dung and we offered to help, a chore that we took up willingly to keep the smell from overtaking the sweet smell of flowers. At night, Charley took the Donkey to a grassy field along the slope of the hill that was several yards beyond their vegetable garden. The meal Millie had served each day was well worth the price. She provided us with all the breakfast food we could eat, including superb coffee, and we supplemented the chicken and goat meat with fish. Elkannah was pleased that we had made our new home with Millie and Charley, and he liked the idea of anchoring the canoe in front of their cliff. We used a cinderblock anchor for both the bow and stern of the boat for better stability. Every dawn and dusk we would venture out to fish for Elkannah, occasionally making trips to Conch Island to harvest conch and catch fish.

Patrick spent as much time as he could with Norlina. They were definitely sweet on each other, although Charley frowned every time he saw them together. Elijah liked diving off the cliff and he tried convincing me to dive instead of jumping. I was never a good diver and refused his taunts. Patrick, on the other hand, was an excellent diver and enjoyed showing off his acrobatic aerial displays to Norlina. The four of us became good friends. Elijah liked smoking ganja. Norlina, as was the case with most Jamaican females, did not smoke ganja. One day at sunset time, the four of us were sitting on the concrete pad along the cliff, smoking ganja.

Another Jamaican in his early twenties had joined us, introducing himself as Cricket, and he told us he owned cliff property further down the road within sight of the lighthouse. We noticed a large sailboat anchored a few hundred yards from the cliffs. Cricket had binoculars.

"Dat is a smuggling boat, mon. Dey tek ganja ta de U.S.," pointed out Cricket. We watched them for quite some time and similar to what we had witnessed at the Buccaneer Inn, a motorboat with bales of what we assumed to be ganja was being transported to the sailboat.

"Hey, that boat looks like it is coming from the area of Lord Joseph's sea cave," I said.

"Yeah, it certainly does. It looks like Lord Joseph and his Rasta family found a buyer for their harvest," commented Patrick.

"Yeahmon! It much ta far fer us ta mek out who dees people are, but I knoh dey come fram de area yah speakin of. Dees cliffs are free fer us ta walk up an' down, mon. Ollie an' Patrick, yah come back ta Jamaica in several years, mon, an' dees cliffs be aw bought up by foreigners. De ganja trade will mek some people wealthy, an' dey will buy up our land an' build 'otels." Elijah had a slightly angry tone in his voice. I doubted that many miles of cliff and seven miles of beach could be bought up in a few years, turning Negril into a tourist resort.

"No way, bro. This land is too precious, and there is a lot of it – all undeveloped. Jamaicans will never allow foreigners to buy it up," I replied.

"Money! Jamaicans will git drunk on money, mon, an' dey will sell." Elijah's tone continued to be angry. "I will never sell land ta foreigners, or be owners wit dem. I will grow lots of ganja an' build on mi fambly land. Some Jamaicans will make money wit dem foreigners, but mos' will remain poor an' become even poorer. Nuh I!"

Cricket looked at Elijah with an angry expression and said, "True dat, bredda Elijah. Negril will change. I will nuh sell mi land ta Babylon foreigners. I sell ta nuh mon. I will build a place on mi cliffs fer people ta listen ta music, eat food an' smoke ganja. Irie, mon. Cricket's Café, I will build on de land of I n I ancestors." Cricket pointed to the southwest where he owned land.

"You and Elijah are ambitious. I wish you luck," replied Patrick.

Elijah responded, "It is not luck I need mon. I jus' be needin' hard work an' I use mi head ta mek money. Yeahmon. Mi grandparents own much land. De land you 'ave seen, an' some up in de hills where I will grow de ganja. My fadda was an Englishman. Wen he died he left madda de land he owned past de lighthouse. He met mi madda in Negril when he lived 'ere. Wen I was a baby, we moved to Kingston. Dat land now belongs ta Norlina an' I. Dat is where I will build 'otel fer American an' European tourist, mon. I will become wealthy an' tek care of mi sister an' grandparents wen dey too ole ta work."

Elijah was smart and it appeared that he had inherited Millie's business savvy. It was also obvious that he, and probably Norlina, received some formal education. Although they talked in patois most of the time, which indicated that their father was not around them very much. I wanted to know more about their father and mother. Now I understood where Elijah and Norlina got their eye and caramel skin color. And, I was curious about the land he mentioned, particularly the land past the lighthouse.

We had never traveled to the lighthouse. I had seen it from the canoe. It was positioned on the western most tip of Negril, which was the western most tip of Jamaica. We knew that one day we would travel to there. We were so settled into our sea cave, Conch Island, and fishing lifestyle, that we didn't take time to explore the far western tip of Negril. It was time for us to extend our horizons.

One morning after fishing and delivering our catch to Elkannah, we decided to explore the cliffs further west, with the intention of reaching the lighthouse. The numerous caves fascinated us, and we went into several of them. All of them were beautiful but none as large as Lord Joseph's cave and none had obvious access to the land from the inside. A few were large enough to live in, but the cliff faces were too rugged to climb with ease, making access to the land above difficult, which made living in any of the many caves highly impractical. We took the time to dive for conch, knowing that Elkannah would soon be traveling to Sav-La-Mar. We discovered that the sea bottom along these cliffs was not harvested much for conch – if at all. It was a good distance from Fishermen Cove and the beach area, where there was plenty of conch so there was little need for fishermen to travel this far.

It did not take long to reach the lighthouse. I estimated that the cylindrical cement and steel structure was over sixty feet high. Some of the cliffs were low-lying, while other parts were very high with deep water at the base. We explored them looking for a suitable place to climb on to the land. Several yards south of the lighthouse we came upon a metal ladder where we anchored the canoe and climbed onto the cliff top.

The lighthouse was set back seventy-five yards or so from the cliff edge. We walked around the base of the lighthouse, calling out to let people know we were there, but no one answered. The door to the lighthouse tower was padlocked.

"Well, Oliver, should we bust the lock or be law abiding citizens?"

"It would be great to climb the tower and get a sky-high view of Negril. This is the first lock I have seen in Negril. I just realized something. The people of Negril, that is the ones we have met so far, do not have locks on their doors. I think that is really cool."

"Yeah, that is cool. Let's go for it!" Patrick picked up a large rock and was about to pound the lock.

"No! This is not a good idea. We could get busted and end up in a Jamaican jail, be fined, and deported. We don't want to jeopardize paradise and turn it into a nightmare." Initially I was tempted. The South Philly mischievous boy in me wanted to bust the lock but breaking and entering had a potentially very high cost. The risk was simply not worth it.

"Yeah, you're right. It would be stupid. Let's just explore the area more." I was relieved that Patrick did not push the issue.

We were surprised to see grass growing on the cliff area surrounding the lighthouse. I surmised that they must have landscaped it at one time by covering the cliff with dirt and planting grass.

"Why did they build a lighthouse here?" I asked.

"Got me. The English used it for some purpose. Perhaps Negril was a shipping port at one time. Remember, Jamaica did not gain independence from England until eight years ago," replied Patrick.

"Wow, that's right! Jamaica is a young country. I wonder what the English could have been shipping out of Negril?" I asked.

"Who knows? Maybe the usual: banana, coconut, coffee, and sugar cane. There's a great deal of agricultural land further inland. Perhaps Fishermen Cove was once a trading dock," suggested Patrick.

"There are no docks anywhere in Negril, not even at the so-called Yacht Club, and I haven't seen any evidence of there ever being any. I guess they just beached smaller boats and loaded them up, and ferried out to larger cargo ships anchored off shore. Elkannah told me that Bloody Bay, you know, that stretch of beach beyond Conch Island and Long Bay, is called that because the

English used that beach to slaughter whales. Maybe the lighthouse was used for whaling fleets."

"Strange though. Montego Bay and Kingston are big port towns. I think it would be a lot easier to transport the agricultural goods over land to those ports since there is no real harbor in Negril," added Patrick. "I can't imagine a whaling operation in Negril, but whales do migrate to the Caribbean to mate and give birth to their calves."

"The roads are not very good, and it might be easier to load ships by small boat and then have them move on to either city from here. The lack of a large safe harbor could explain why the British never developed Negril. The beach and cliffs are exquisitely beautiful. I am surprised that the Brits never exploited this area for tourism. Perhaps they did to some extent, which would explain the so-called Yacht Club. A few wealthy English who owned yachts and enjoyed spending time in Negril may have built it as their modest resort. It makes sense since it is situated on low-lying cliffs close to Fishermen Cove. Maybe wealthy Englishmen built the lighthouse for their own purposes."

"Well, it's a good thing the Brits never developed the tourist trade in Negril, otherwise we wouldn't be enjoying our *native* adventures in paradise," added Patrick.

"As you pointed out, eight years is not a long time for independence, and as we heard from many people, the word about the beauty of Jamaica is spreading rapidly. That is especially true among the marijuana loving hippies of the U.S. and Europe."

"Yeah, Oliver, you're probably right. What Elijah told us about Negril becoming bought up by foreigners is not far-fetched. Hell, the Buccaneer Inn can't be that old, unless the DeSalvas bought it from the English. It wouldn't surprise me if the couple built it or bought it with ganja money." Patrick had a point. The ganja trade was booming and Jamaica was ganja paradise. Although I was surprised that we had not seen many tourist in Negril.

"There aren't many tourists in Negril. Just the few hippies we met on the beach. Don't you find that odd given all we just said?" I asked.

"Yeah, it is odd. Then again, this is not tourist season. The tourist amenities are scarce at best and most Jamaicans do not treat us like tourists – we are a novelty to them. In essence we are pioneers of a relatively unexplored area." Patrick had a good point and one that emphasized we were doing something really far out.

"Wow, that's really a cool thought. I wonder if we are the only people from the U.S. to fish and live like we do in Negril? If so, that makes us super far out dudes!" The idea that we were pioneers, two real adventurers on a paradise island, struck me as being totally awesome.

"Hey bro, we should write a book about our adventures," suggested Patrick.

"I've been keeping a journal."

"That's right. You've been writing this entire trip. You have a running record of everything that's happened." I was delighted to see that Patrick valued my daily journal entries. "You've been writing stuff down ever since I could remember."

"Ellen, our friend from Stone Harbor, gave me a journal a very long time ago and told me writing would help me sort out my thoughts and feelings. It's just a habit I developed over time, and it really does help."

"You mean all the way back to high school? You've been keeping journals for that long?" Patrick asked.

"Since freshman year. At first, I wrote just a little, but as time went on, I wrote more and more. I filled many books. This is the third one since we left Philly."

"Wow! That's a lot of writing. Will you let me read them some day?"

"I don't know. Yeah, I suppose. Not sure you'd find them interesting though."

"Interesting! Hell, if you wrote about all that stuff we went through, that would make one hell of a story. Better yet, it would make a really far out movie. That would be so cool! *Ghetto Flowers in Paradise*, staring Patrick O'Malley and Oliver James – ha, we'd be the modern day Errol Flynn!"

"I doubt that. Anyway, writing helps me relax. That's reason enough to keep a journal."

"Hell, I'm gonna use the camera more often and keep a photo story of our experiences. They could go along with the book you write about Jamaica, you know, call it *Island Boys.*"

"You have a wild imagination, Patrick. The pictures would be nice to have. Like I said before, I'm surprised you don't use your camera more often."

"I will from now on! I wish I had photos of Penny and Jenny. Bro, I'd give my left nut to be with Jenny again." I think hanging out with Norlina got Patrick's hormones pumping.

"Yeah, you said that before," I responded.

"Well, yeah, wouldn't you give one of your nuts to be with Penny again?"

"I like my nuts, thank you Mr. Horn Dog."

"Oh, sorry, it's been a while since we …"

"Yeah, yeah, come on, let's explore further along the cliffs," I suggested. The cliffs curved southward. I was struck by the amount of vegetation covering much of the cliffs. We walked a relatively short distance south of the lighthouse when we came upon a very interesting cove, which was simply a concave curve, forming a deep pool of water, and the cliffs were much higher than the cliffs in front of the lighthouse. There was a grove of palm trees set back fifty yards or so from the cliff's edge along this cove. In among these trees was small cinder block, zinc roof structures. We cautiously approached them, not knowing if anyone was living in them. We were definitely trespassing on either private or government property.

The structures had windows and doors and inside each one there were cots and a water sink. They were similar to the single room shanties except for the cinder block walls and concrete floors, and they had running water. There were oil lamps attached to the walls. We stalked around like thieves in the night, which was ridiculous since it was mid afternoon and anyone living in the area could easily hear and see us. There were seven buildings in all, built in a wide arc facing the sea, and all of them were covered in the shade of the palm trees. The doors were not locked, so we explored each one. They were in great shape, except for the canvas cots, which were moldy and rotting. I turned on the water in a few of the cottages. At first, the water was a rusty brown color but soon turned clear.

"This is like a small boy scout camp. It is totally awesome!" said Patrick.

"You would know – Mr. Eagle Scout," I teased.

"Yo, bro, that Eagle Scout line is super worn out – as I said a thousand times, give it a rest. My guess is that the English had a small group of military or some type of government personnel living up here. When Jamaica became independent, it was probably abandoned. Do you realize the potential of this place, Oliver?

"As in tourist rentals?" I asked.

"Hey, I didn't think of that. I was thinking of us living here. You know, another option. But the tourist idea is brilliant. All we need do is fix the cots, or create other bedding. And when we come upon tourist, we could direct them up here and charge them." Patrick's business mind had kicked in gear, and having an entrepreneur mind as well, I jumped right in.

"We could sell them fish, and go to the market in Sav-La-Mar ourselves and buy fruits and vegetables to sell. Wow, bro, we could make a fortune," I contributed to the fantasy.

"Don't forget selling them ganja! That could be the big money maker," chimed Patrick. We rolled spliffs as we continued talking about our capitalist scheme. As our minds became filled with ganja, our imaginative thinking got wilder.

After smoking half our spliffs, Patrick spoke. "We could make so much money that we could buy a yacht and smuggle ganja to the U.S. Hey, I bet that's how the DeSalva couple built the Buccaneer Inn. I wouldn't be surprised if Steve Tanz is part owner of everything."

"You got a point, Patrick. I wonder how they got started, though?"

"Maybe they went to the Runaway Bay area just like we came here and started talking like we are."

"Oops! We're forgetting something. Being stoned sometimes makes me lose touch with the obvious," I said with disappointment in my voice.

"What's that?" Patrick asked.

"We don't own this land!"

"Duh. No shit Sherlock," replied Patrick.

"Duh nothing, all this talking is just a futile exercise in creative bullshitting?" I laughed.

"You have a knack for stating the obvious, and for not seeing the obvious," quipped Patrick. "No, it's not bullshit. It is creative thinking, and quite possibly realistic too."

"How's that?"

"We find out who the owners are and go in business with them. We can generate the contacts in the U.S., that's our ace in the hole. Hell, bro, we could generate enough business just from the people we grew up with in Philly. They would love to come here." Patrick had a great idea going.

"Yeah, bro, think of all those Philly dudes who spent their summers in Wildwood. Now don't get me wrong, Wildwood is pretty far out, but compared to Negril, it's a beachfront amusement park." Patrick laughed at my comment, because the truth is, Wildwood is a big boardwalk amusement park with a beach.

"Imagine building huge hotels on Negril's seven mile beach and adding in all kinds of amusements," Patrick said.

"Whoa, you don't suppose that could actually happen do you?" I asked.

"What happen?"

"Building huge Wildwood type hotels and condos on seven mile beach, and just as bad, hotels along the cliffs? You know, a Jamaican style Wildwood." I repeated.

"Nah. Not in Negril. It's too wild and pristine and it's far away from the big cities and their airports," replied Patrick.

"Elijah thinks Negril will become built up, and he is a young Jamaican. Where do you think he got that idea?" I pointed out.

"Hmm! He did say that. I think he is a really smart kid, and even though he is young, perhaps he's intuitive enough to peer into the future like a true visionary." Patrick surmised.

"Yeah, and he also takes the position that he will not be one of the Jamaicans who is left behind in the commercialization of Negril. He plans on making the best of what he sees as the inevitable," I added.

"So, what about us? If the tourism industry infiltrates Negril, are we going to watch it happen and say goodbye to our native paradise or be like Elijah and Cricket and make the most of it?" I asked.

"Well, we can't stop it from happening, that's for sure. If Negril does become inundated with tourism, I suppose we could move on to another part of the island and continue our native lifestyle," suggested Patrick.

"Yeah, and become pioneers in the creation of yet another tourist boom. Man, it is sad to realize that our living in Negril is part of its initiation into tourism!" I didn't like the idea that our enjoyment of Negril was playing a role in its possible demise, and there was nothing we could do to stop it. Negril was just too beautiful to go unnoticed for long. For now, it was relatively isolated from tourism because of its location. And with the exploding interest in ganja smoking and the hippie simple organic life style, it would be a miracle if this part of Jamaica didn't experience a tourism boom.

"You're right. Reality is what it is. Jamaica is poor and its greatest natural resources are its beauty, climate, people, unique culture, and abundant food and other desirable plant life," replied Patrick. We looked down at our almost burned out spliffs and laughed.

"Desirable plant life! You got that right," I replied.

"Listen to you, Mr. I-Can't-Smoke-Ganja because it makes me paranoid, exclaiming the virtue of ganja," Patrick teased.

"Hey, saturating my brain with ganja on a paradise island is no problem. Our only responsibility is swimming for conch, fishing from a canoe, and exploring the beautiful sea, cliffs, beaches, and body surfing with women – too bad body surfing with women is not a regular occurrence. It's all pleasure and no stress. There's too much fear and stress in Philly. There is no way I could get high like this back home," I responded.

"I think Lord Joseph cleansed your mind of Babylon." We laughed at the thought. We both treasured the ceremony as special, although we regarded the Babylon thing as metaphorical – at least I did. "So what about our idea?" Patrick asked.

"You mean becoming tour guides and all other aspects of being tourist industry entrepreneurs?" I responded.

"Yep!"

"Well, I would feel guilty about making money off a place we've been able to live in dirt-cheap because people aren't trying to squeeze us for cash. The commercialization of Negril would make it impossible for people to live as we do now," I said.

"I don't! We've been living off the sweat of our brow and ingenuity, as well as graciously accepting the generosity of these good people - and we are reciprocating. Fact is, it is going to happen with or without our participation, and as we already established, we are among the original catalyst simply by living here. Besides, we have no idea how much commercialism will come to Negril and how long it will take. What we do know is that it has begun, and Jamaicans are poor in material goods. Money is arriving, and it will change the people of Negril. The change will be both good and bad. I think we can add to the good by working with Jamaicans and tourists so both experience the good. I mean, there will be foreigners that will do all they can to cheat Jamaicans. The Jamaicans should control the tourism industry, utilizing foreigners as a resource to that end, not the other way around." added Patrick.

"Yeah, a reciprocal relationship where the hippies and the native Jamaicans continue to benefit equally would be the best scenario. That appears to be the way it is now. So, we either ride the wave or get out of the sea," I said.

"Yep!"

"I say we ride the wave!" I exclaimed.

"Then, we are in agreement. Now we have to keep using our creative imagination, since we have no money, and move in the right direction," said Patrick.

"Irie! No problem, mon, where der is a will, der is a way!" Patrick laughed at my attempt to speak with a Jamaican accent.

"Well, we got a good start on creative thinking. I suggest we do some investigative work and find out who owns this property and go from there," suggested Patrick.

"And if that doesn't work out?" I asked.

"Then we imagine some more. It's like having our own money printing press. We only need to think of our imagination as our money machine. It certainly has been our greatest asset in living a very comfortable lifestyle with very little money," responded Patrick

"True dat! Yeahmon, Irie! We are white Jamaican natives. De completely adaptable animals." We laughed. It was true. We had learned to live a good simple inexpensive so-called hippie native Jamaican lifestyle.

We continued our exploration of the lighthouse area and found no evidence of people living there. It wasn't clear if the buildings were part of the lighthouse property, since they were close yet far enough away to be either owned by private or public interest. There was no one in the area we could speak to. I recalled that Elijah and Norlina said they own land somewhere in this vicinity.

"Yo, Patrick. I wonder where Elijah's property is?"

"You mean Norlina and Elijah's property."

"Of course I mean both of them. I suppose it is Elijah's ambitious plans that make me call it his land." It was interesting that Patrick felt it necessary to mention Norlina's interest – as if he was protecting her.

"He said it was in the lighthouse area. We'll ask him. I'm sure he'd show us."

The road continued on for a mile or more past the lighthouse before becoming increasingly narrow and turning into a little used footpath. Beyond the road the geography looked the same, with land opposite the cliffs that started out flat before gently rolling upward where there was more vegetation. We decided not to go any further. Time had gone by faster than we had expected. We guessed there was a little more than two hours of sunlight left, so we decided to canoe back. As we paddled we continued to discuss the idea of bringing tourists to Negril. Patrick was convinced that Elijah and Norlina were the keys to making it happen, since they owned land up by the lighthouse that could be converted into rental property. The attraction of the lighthouse area is its remoteness, beautiful cliffs and deep-water coves, and it is still within easy access to the rest of Negril. Tourists could experience the wild natural beauty of Jamaica along the cliffs while having essentials easily provided for them, like water, food, shelter, plenty of ganja and magic mushrooms – everything the counter culture hippies need to live their unique lifestyle. Patrick suggested a donkey and cart shuttle to all points in Negril for those who wanted quick access to the beach or Roundabout. I thought that a canoe taxi service would be better.

It was dark by the time we got to Millie and Charley's land. Patrick climbed on to the concrete steps that were carved into the cliff. I handed him our gear and the conch, then I paddled several feet away and anchored the canoe. I swam to the steps, and when I got to the top, I laid flat on my back on the concrete pad to take a rest. It had been a long day. My muscles were sore. I was tired and hungry. I looked up at the starry sky and listened to the sea rising and falling over the rocks at the base of the cliff. Patrick came back and sat beside me. He brought banana bread, fruit and some dried-cooked fish. We ate and continued talking about our ideas for generating income in the tourist industry. I suggested that we eventually buy cliff-front property, and or beach land in Negril. We were both partial to the cliffs since they were so novel to us and we loved the sea caves. It would be a great lifestyle. I wondered if Sandy would like living here. I decided that she would. I missed her!

Patrick woke me up. I had my sleeping bag over me and I was sore from sleeping on concrete. I was so tired the night before that I fell asleep on the cliff and Patrick covered me in my sleeping bag. He said he tried to wake me but that I was totally zonked out. Patrick cut open a pineapple for our breakfast. Millie was already up and had made us a pot of coffee. I was thankful that Patrick brought the coffee and pineapple. Patrick had already taken care of our main fishing chore for the day. He and Charley loaded the conch in the baskets on the Donkey and Charley took them to Elkannah before he left for Sav-La-Mar.

We swam to the canoe and headed out to sea to check our fish traps. As usual, they were full of fish. We spent a few hours hauling in fish and resetting the traps. There was no need to dive for conch, having provided Elkannah with our harvest from yesterday. When we returned, Norlina was waiting for us with lunch prepared. After eating, Patrick asked if I was okay with taking our fish catch to Elkannah's house. He wanted to spend time alone with Norlina. I agreed.

It was mid-afternoon when I returned. It was hot. Patrick and Norlina were not around. I decided to take a nap in my shaded hammock. The rain from a late afternoon thunderstorm woke me. I ran to the front porch of Elijah and Norlina's shanty. I peeked in the window and saw the naked bodies of Patrick and Norlina embraced on the bed. I quickly looked away. Millie and Charley would definitely not approve, and most likely, Elijah would have objections as well. I remained on the porch, enjoying the sound of the rain and thunder graced by the sounds of love cries. Patrick was teaching the young Norlina the arts of pleasure he had learned from Jenny, then again, maybe she was furthering his education, or both. I was jealous, a rare emotion for me. I wondered if Norlina had any female friends in the village that would take an interest in me.

The rain stopped. Patrick and Norlina came onto the porch. Patrick was smiling ear to ear, and Norlina, having seen me, was shy and would not look me in the eyes. She suspected that I knew what they were doing in the shanty. I pretended that their being in the shanty was not unusual. Elijah appeared on the stone path and waved to us as he approached the porch.

"Irie! De rain cool de land. I was wit Cricket, mon. He will begin buildin' his café soon. He wants Ollie an' Patrick ta help."

"Sure! That would be fun," I replied.

"Yes, mon. He will be pleased ta 'ave your assistance," said Elijah.

"When?" Patrick asked.

"He gaterin' de materials, mon. He has most of de cinder blocks an' is seeking de wood an' more money. Soon, mon. His land is within sight of de lighthouse an' de cliffs are very high. The water below is deep." Elijah had a big smile on his face. "I like diving from Cricket's high cliffs!" He was eager to put his dreams into motion. I wondered what his role would be in Cricket's café, so I asked.

"Are you going in business with Cricket?"

"No mon. His café will attract tourists an' bring business ta me. I will build rooms an' de tourist will rent dem. Cricket's café will provide entertainment an' other t'ings."

"When are you going to build rooms?" I asked.

"I will make de money, mon. I grow ganja. It tek time, mon. I will mek it happen." I admired his confidence.

"Hmm, maybe I can provide some ganja customers for you from the states," Patrick stated while rubbing his chin thoughtfully.

"Dat would be irie, Patrick. We mus' talk about tis an' see if it work out fer de both of us. I n I could mek lots of money!" Patrick smiled as he extended his hand to Elijah. The shook hands as if they had just struck a business bargain. I shrugged it off as another creative thinking scheme.

"Have you been to your father's land by the lighthouse?" Patrck asked.

"Not yet. I will visit soon. I 'ave nuh spent much time in Negril, only visit wit me madda on special occasion. I don't knoh where de land is."

"Oh. Why have you decided to live here for good?" I asked. Elijah's eyes began to water. I looked at Norlina and she too looked sad. Norlina spoke.

"Madda passed away. She got de coughing sickness. Grandmadda an' grandfadda tek care of her during de last weeks of her life. We now live in Negril forever." Norlina was shaking as she spoke.

"Dis is our home now. We mus' look ta de future!" Elijah spoke with resolution. Now I understood that there were other motivations behind his ambitions. He wanted to take care of his sister and grandparents – mature sentiments for one so young. I was tempted to ask about his Englishman father. I was curious about when and how he died, and how much time he had spent with his children while they were growing up, but my intuition prevented me. I was worried that Patrick would ask. He didn't.

"When you check out the land by the lighthouse, we'd like to go with you. We could save time traveling by canoe," offered Patrick.

"Irie. Dat would be good, mon. De lighthouse is nuh ta fer, so traveling by canoe nuh necessary. Tomorrow?" responded Elijah.

"Sure. That would be great. We could go in the morning." I said.

"I asked grandparents where de land. Dey tell me dey 'ave a map." Elijah no longer looked sad.

"How far is the lighthouse from here?" Patrick asked.

"Nuh fer, mon, a few miles. Effin we walk, den we knoh fer certainty," said Elijah.

"We're on then. Tomorrow morning bright and early!" I said.

"Irie!" Elijah was grinning ear to ear. I was glad to see him so excited. He walked off with a spring in his step. Norlina followed behind him.

MUSHROOM TEA
(Harold)

My mind continued to churn with ideas for our tourism venture by the lighthouse. "Yo, Patrick. We could create a campground for tourists who have tents, and if they don't have tents, we could get them somehow. Maybe we could build lean-to shelters out of trees and make thatched roofs."

"Not a bad idea. We'd have to get water to the property, though," replied Patrick. "There are water pipes running to those cinder block shanty structures. We could somehow tap into the main water line and run pipes to Elijah's land. Or, we could collect water the original native Jamaican way. Elkannah told me that before the government ran water pipes up the West End, that the people collected rain water off the tin roofs into large barrels."

"Yeah, I noticed those barrels. They still collect water in them. Well, we have to take this one step at a time. We have no idea how far Elijah's land is from the lighthouse structures. Running pipes could be expensive and we have no idea what government regulations there may be," I cautioned.

"Hey bro, I'm simply getting the fantasy factory in gear. None of what we've been talking about may be possible. Then again, it may all be possible. I think we need to keep engaging our greatest asset – our imaginations – remember!" Patrick implored.

"Yeah. I get it. However, we need to apply some practical reality to the situation, is all I'm saying," I responded.

"Yeah, you're right. One step at a time, and we can dream as wild as we want, as long as we don't let fantasy interfere with reality. I think that's what you're saying," added Patrick.

"I think you and I have a good handle on the difference between the two. After all, we had one hell of an orientation in the harsh realities of life growing up in Philly. If we apply our street smarts to paradise, I think we are bound to come out smelling like roses," I said emphatically.

"Yep! Smelling like Ghetto Flowers in paradise – actually more like ganja buds. That would be us!" said Patrick as he laughed. "We've been applying survival street smarts all along – that's why we've been so successful. Who'd ever thought that growing up in an inner city would be the best preparation for living in paradise?" We rolled spliffs and smoked them while sitting side by side on Elijah's hammock.

"I agree. We've done a good job so far applying our penchant for survival strategies!" I said.

"Yeahmon. We are inner city hippie pioneers in paradise. Life is good, mon, Irie!" Patrick was grinning ear to ear.

"Irie!" I replied.

We decided to check out our tent to see if the rain soaked our gear. The air was nice and cool. The tent did get a little wet, which soaked our bag of mushrooms. I suggested we toss them out. Patrick was about to dump them out on the area where the donkey was hitched hoping they would grow in donkey shit just as Millie came walking up.

"Wat yah got der?" she asked.

"Oh, these are mushrooms a boy gave to us a while ago. We dried them out, but they just got wet in our tent so we are throwing them away."

"Dey magic mushrooms?" she asked. I was taken by surprise that she knew about magic mushrooms.

"Ah, yes, Millie, they are. How do you know about magic mushrooms?" Patrick asked.

"Dat boy, Randy, who told yah 'bout me. He liked de mushrooms. It mek 'im silly. I knoh how ta prepare dem effin yah want ta put dem in yah body."

"How?" Patrick asked.

"Tea. Give dem ta me an' I mek de tea fer yah." Patrick handed her the bag. I never had any intention of eating or drinking the mushrooms and neither did Patrick. We held on to them in case we came upon other tourist who would be interested and maybe make some money. "Follow me!" commanded Millie.

Millie led us to her cooking hut. The inside was similar in design to Elkannah's but larger. Millie handed a large iron kettle to me and instructed that I fill it half way with water. When I returned she had a fire going. She told me to place the kettle on the tripod. Then, she put the entire bag of mushrooms in the water.

"Are you gonna brew all of them at once?" asked Patrick, rhetorically.

"Yes. It be de mos' potent dat way. It is as Randy liked. He drink a few cups an' keep de rest in jars stored in mi ice box ta use as he pleased." As the water got warmer, Millie stirred in a can of Carnation sweet evaporated cream along with honey. The cream and honey swirled in with the mushrooms, creating a bluish-purple brew. She said it is important to only steep the mushrooms and not to let them boil, explaining that the magic in the mushroom would be destroyed if the temperature became too hot. She said that Randy had taught her how to prepare the mushroom tea. She dipped in a ladle and poured it into a large cup and handed it to Patrick.

"Let it cool, den drink it straight away. Be sure ta chew an' swallow de mushrooms – dat is de way Randy did it," Millie instructed. She poured a cup for me. I stared at the strange looking concoction and wondered what I was getting myself into. The idea of ingesting something magical was enticing, intoxicating, yet I remained apprehensive, even slightly fearful. Patrick kept blowing air into his cup while stirring it with a wooden spoon. I decided to do the same.

"It is cool enough. Drink it! An' mek sure yah swallow de pieces of mushrooms," Millie reminded us. I was struck by how directive she was being. It was very odd that she was playing this role. I began to see her as more than a Jamaican grandmother - she had transformed into a sorceress.

Patrick drank first. He stopped after drinking half the cup and said, "Not bad. The cream and honey sort of makes it taste good. Sort of." He downed the rest of it. Millie poured him a second cup.

I was hesitant. I held the warm cup in my hand and stared into the magic potion. Patrick was smiling at me. "Yo, Ollie. De fear of Babylon tek hold of yah mind, mon?" He laughed, "Don't worry, mon, thousands of people 'ave eaten de magic 'shrooms, mon. Irie. Der nuttin ta fear, Ollie. Levi says dat it open de spirit world fer de white mon." Patrick's attempt at speaking with a Jamaican accent sounded slightly less pretentious than mine. His words made me laugh and they eased my apprehension. Millie laughed as well.

I took several small sips. Patrick was right, the sweet flavors of the cream and honey made it palatable. Still, I could taste the mustiness of the mushrooms, especially when I chewed the bits and pieces of the fruit-body and stems, which got lodged between my teeth. Millie refilled the cup and after it cooled, I swiftly drank it, this time swallowing the mushroom pieces without chewing.

"Go an' walk. Yah mus' nuh stand around wit de mushroom circulatin' yer body. It bes' yah be movin'. Go now, areddi. Here, tek dees jars of orinj and mango juice, you will need dem fer your bodies. The air is fresh fram de rainfall. Go!" Millie commanded. "I jar up de rest of de tea an' put in de icebox fer later use." I loved the phrase, icebox. My mother used it when referring to the refrigerator when I was a kid. Mom told me that when she was growing up, they did not have electric refrigerators, that they bought dry ice to preserve their food. Millie let us keep our fish in her icebox. Eventually electricity would come to the West End and refrigeration would change their lives, along with having to pay electric bills.

We walked towards the road. Norlina was coming in our direction along the stone path. Patrick stopped to talk with her. I kept on walking, sensing that they wanted to be alone, and I did not want to stop moving. As I walked along the road, I took in deep breaths. My stomach felt a little queasy but it soon passed. The recent rainfall made the plant life more vibrant with colors. The scent of flowers was exceptionally strong. The sea was fully visible from the road, as it is all along the West End cliffs. The sky was exploding with the full spectrum of colors as the sun filtered through enormous cumulus thunderclouds that were left over from the recent storm. Streams of light poured through openings in the clouds, thick rays spread out like a fan reaching all the way to the sea. I imagined that if angels were real, they would have fun riding down these light beams to visit us lowly mortals.

My diaphragm rhythmically expanded and contracted, filling my lungs to capacity, and with each release of air, sensations rushed through my body – wonderful feelings causing every cell to vibrate with pleasure. I felt light as a feather, as though I was more than the material substance that contained me, yet the physicality of my being was in the forefront of my awareness. I was moving within a body and simultaneously felt unrestrained by my physical form. A wonderful, gentle and yet ecstatic feeling embraced me. Within my mind there appeared images of my self, like photographs. I was smiling, happy, and pleased with who I am and with life as I was now living it.

I was aware that I was looking at myself looking at myself. Not like two different entities, one peering upon the other, but one integrated personality with a super conscious awareness, a state of being that was unrestrained by the history of the past and therefore was able to look upon that aspect of self that was shaped by all past experiences without judgment. I felt free, safe, and loved. Then thoughts occurred to me, *'Loved by what? Myself? A spiritual counterpart? God?'* These questions were not disturbing to me. They served only to stimulate my curiosity, and they were not new questions, nor were these thought-feelings new. I was doing what I have done so many times before – *mind surfing*. The mushrooms were fueling my mind with the energy to ride thought currents. I didn't feel as though I needed to find answers to these questions. All I had to do was ride on the feelings pulsing through my body and allow whatever images and thoughts appearing in my mind to flow freely. The key to mind surfing is to not resist the thought waves, but to ride on them, letting them take me wherever. A verse from a Moody Blues song came to me, *You can fly as high as a kite if you want to, faster than light if you want to, speeding through the universe, thinking is the best way to travel.*

As the sun got closer to the sea, the colors in the sky became evermore spectacular, changing hues with each passing moment. I walked out onto a cliff and stood by its edge to watch the sky and sea explode with color. My eyes feasted on the beauty, and I continued to breathe in the salt air laced with the fresh scent of flowers. It occurred to me that I was feeling *super real*, meaning I was more conscious of the nature of my true self than usual. This feeling was similar to the one I experienced during my epiphany in the Catholic Church when I was seventeen years old when my body and mind were diseased by many things. In that moment, as in this one, I felt deeply loved by something greater than any person in this world. It was a spiritual love – spiritual in the sense that it was much more than human affection, possessing a universal, all encompassing quality.

I wrapped my arms around myself and squeezed, imagining that the arms of creation were embracing me. I closed my eyes and continued to breathe deeply. Then, I saw an image of a spirit like person standing in front of me. The spirit person looked similar to my own physical form yet distinctly different, as he appeared significantly more mature, although ageless. His clothes were luminescent with a soft white glow. Then, within an instant, I was that spirit person. I was inside the spirit person's body looking back at myself looking at the spirit person looking at me. As I stood there gazing upon the image of myself, I beheld a beautiful spiritual being in the likeness of my own flesh, and I became aware of the truth that I am a spiritual being having the experience of being human. Gazing upon my physical form, now inhabited by the spirit person, I saw images of my father and mother, and of their parents, this continued down through the generations all the way back to the dawn of creation to the original parents of all human kind. In that instant, I realized that all human beings are of the same origin, that we are indeed one family, and that the multitude of ethnicity on our planet is simply variations of the original parents of all humanity.

I opened my eyes, expecting the image to disappear, thinking it was all taking place within my mind, that I was ultra mind surfing on stupendous imaginative thought waves.

I was back within my own body and there was no one standing in front of me. I closed my eyes and the image of the person once again fully formed in my mind. Then, I saw myself walk into the body of the spirit person and as we merged into one being, a wondrous feeling of spiritual love flowed through me. This love was accompanied by the thought awareness that what I was experiencing was distinctively supernal, and that the spirit person was that part of me that is eternal – that exists beyond the temporal human body. Then, I started crying, a deep healing cry that was a cleansing of my being.

I remained on the cliff long after the sun had set and the stars came out. I felt calm and at peace. The effects of the mushroom tea were exactly what young Rasta Levi, had said, *'It will open yah mind ta de spirit world.'* I couldn't help to wonder how it happened. Did the chemical provide fuel for my mind to surge into the spiritual realm? Was my mental spiritual receptivity capacity enhanced? Were the layers of my conscious mind peeled away, allowing my mind to surf thought currents emanating from my super conscious mind? Yes, was my answer to these questions. The chemical affected my mind in such a way as to open pathways to seeing the nature of reality, or as Aldous Huxley said in his essay, *The Doors of Perception, 'experiencing the All that Is.'*

The words that my dear friend and mentor, Ellen, had recited from a guru she met while traveling in India came to mind: *... to the sincere seeker of truth, drugs may open windows in the mind, but continued use is mistaking the material for the spiritual ... the seeker becomes the finder once the journey begins ... nothing else is necessary.* Remembering these lines was helpful in my contemplation of my experience with my infinite spiritual self. The material mechanism, mushrooms in this case, was simply a catalyst for bringing my attention to that which was already present within my mind. The experience was unique, but it was not the first time I had been embraced by spiritual love. What stayed with me as the chemical gradually wore off was the feeling of having been in touch with the essence of my reality as a conscious personality in relationship with a spiritual personality entity – beyond normal human fraternal associations.

I wondered if a Rasta would call the personality entity of such an experience King Haile Selassie? If the answer is yes, then the role of culture on the 'hue' or interpretation of spiritual experiences is central. It makes the interpretation relativistic to the culture of the individual. If this is the case, then what is the absolute truth of such spiritual experiences? The answer that popped in my mind with astounding clarity was, love. The essence of the reality of our existence is love.

This was not a new revelation to me. It was an affirmation of what I had experienced on previous occasions, and perhaps the experience brought me one step further along the path in my journey as a spiritual seeker. The use of psychedelic mushrooms was a marvelous experience. Yet, I wondered if I could honestly advocate their use by others. It is a personal choice, and like all choices we make, there is always the possibility of negative as well as positive consequences.

So how should I move forward in my spiritual journey? Would I continue to ingest chemicals to fuel my mind and open pathways to the spiritual dimension of my being? I had touched the reality of my spiritual nature on other occasions without the use of chemicals, although I have to admit, they were not as visual and emotionally ecstatic as the one I just had. Would I become like the merry band of LSD-ingesting Jesus Freaks I had met on the beach of Wildwood, New Jersey, and turn mushrooms into a holy sacrament? An immediate answer to this question was not necessary. I decided I would walk the path one step at a time. I was about to get up when someone approached me from behind saying, "Hello! May I sit with you?"

"Sure. My name is Oliver. Jamaicans call me Ollie."

"I am Harold Thomson the wood carver." The man appeared to be in his late twenties or possibly older and he had dreadlocks. He put down two large cloth bags a short distance from where I was sitting. He then joined me.

"Ah, it feels good to sit down. I have been walking all day. You have chosen a most beautiful place to sit and look at the sea and stars." Harold spoke with an English accent combined with the familiar Jamaican lilt minus the peculiar use and absence of certain vowels and consonants – Jamaican patois.

"You sound more English than Jamaican."

"Yes. I attended English schools in Kingston. My parents worked as house servants for a wealthy English family. I was sent to the same schools and had the same tutors as their children. I was raised with them."

"You wear dreadlocks. You are Rasta?"

"Irie! *I am that and much more, and I am not that, and I am evermore."*

"You speak in riddles."

"I do not desire to confuse you my friend. I mean only to say that I am comfortable with my Rasta brothers, and equally comfortable with other faiths."

"What do you mean by what you just said, *I am evermore*?"

"I do not adhere to all Rastafarian beliefs. I respect them and do not dispute them. I acknowledge the universal truths in their teachings as I do in all religions. I n I forever more – we are all one with creation and have eternal life. See, I do not speak in riddles."

"Wow, it is such a relief to meet someone who is not going to preach to me about the way things are. Some people say that I should believe this or that and if not I am living a life of doom, or something to that affect," I said.

"Ah, you are a philosopher, are you not?" Harold had a very gentle way about him. His voice was soothing and his face kind, with twinkling eyes and a bright smile.

"I don't think of myself that way. I just think about things, and have certain experiences. I am no philosopher, just a person seeking, exploring life's mysteries, I guess."

"Yes. I can see that you think about everything. And what were you thinking, experiencing, or seeking as you say when I came upon you?" His inquiry startled me.

"Why do you ask?"

"You have the look of one who has seen the face of Creation."

"Do I look frightened?"

"Quite to the contrary. Your face is glowing and your eyes possess a light I do not see often enough in my brothers and sisters."

"I was thinking about things of, well, of a meta-physical or spiritual nature and the experience I am having."

"Will you not share these thoughts and experience with me?"

"Why? I do not know you." I said.

"You know that I know you are experiencing something extraordinary. And am I not your brother?"

"Let's just say I had a peak experience."

"Ah. You are a student of Dr. Abraham Maslow." I was surprised by his comment. "You look shocked. Do you not think it possible that a Jamaican who wears dreadlocks can know of such things?"

"But he is a psychologist that I studied in school. I have not met many people who know of his theories."

"I attended Oxford University. *Dominus Illuminati Mea!* Do you know what this Latin motto of Oxford means?"

"No."

"*The Lord is my Light*. Does that phrase resonate with you, Oliver?" That was the first time a Jamaican called me by my actual name. His question caused me to feel that he had some notion of my spiritual experience.

"Yes." I said cautiously.

"Will you tell me how?"

"I saw the image of – no, that's not correct, the body and personality of my infinite self, and I entered into it, or him, I mean me. And that infinite me came into the temporal me, and we became one another. Something to that effect."

"Ho, Ho, Ho! I knew you had looked upon the face of Creation. I felt it when I spotted you from the road, and more so when I looked into your eyes. Be comforted, Oliver, I know the experience well."

"You do? Are you a deeply religious person?"

"Aye, I am that and much more, and I am not that, and I am evermore. Do you understand what I mean?"

"I have an idea - it's just like what you said about Rastafarianism. That you acknowledge the universal truth that we are created out of love, but you do not adhere to any specific religious doctrines and you are not a member of any religion."

"Yes, and what else?"

"And that you have or are a part of eternal life."

"Yes, yes, that is precisely my meaning. So, you have had a peak experience and you are on the threshold of becoming a self-actualized person. Quite a feat for one as young as you."

"The experience was extraordinary. I am far from being self-actualized. I have not lived very long," I replied.

"Ah, but you have walked through many fires in your life, that I can tell. It is not the number of years you have lived, but what takes place during them that shapes the character of a man."

"What makes you think I have walked through many fires?"

"Oliver, we would not be talking of such things had life not demanded that you seek the depths of your soul for answers and comfort."

"What about you?"

"Playing dodge ball with my inquiry, tut, tut. Well, fair enough. My family adopted the religion of the wealthy English estate they worked for, which was the Anglican Church of England. I was raised in that faith, but exposed to many others. I have a large extended family that live all over the island and they adhere to many different Christian sects as well as Rastafarianism. As a little boy I was fascinated by religion and yet I was not like so many others who become blinded by the religious veils they wear. For as long as I could remember, I could tell the true from the false, and I learned early on to refrain from criticism of the beliefs of others. Instead, I recognize the truth in them and respond to that. In this manner I am able to move freely among all religions and learn from them."

"Interesting. So, in all your religious affiliations, what truth have you learned?" I asked.

"You are quick to get directly to the heart of the discussion. That is an admirable trait. There is but one central truth that is the thread that runs through all religions and if each one could acknowledge this, then we would learn to celebrate our religious diversity and cease the infantile religious wars. The central truth is that God is Love, and we are all God's children and therefore it is our primary purpose to love each other as brothers and sisters. However, I do acknowledge that there are brothers and sisters among us who have experienced universal love of a spiritual nature and yet do not associate it with an actual personality deity. They, too, believe in the need for a universal spiritual experience of love. "

"Wow! That's exactly what I think. It is amazing that we have met each other. It is such a simple truth and yet so few see it and even fewer experience or live it."

"Simple truth is always the most difficult to see and far more difficult to live. To love each other, well, my young friend, that is what all the great religious teachers have taught and there is a reason for that - it is the most challenging thing for the human animal to do."

"Yes, I found that to be true, and yet I do not understand why loving each other is so hard."

"Was it easy to love your parents?" Harold's question hit me right between the eyes. He noticed the discomfort on my face and responded. "If it is challenging to love those who brought us into the world, how much more difficult it is to love those who are our enemies, or simply our neighbor, or one who has different color skin, or adheres to specific religious creeds different from our own, or any other 'minor' differences from our selves?"

"What does it mean to love others anyway?" I asked.

"That, too, is simple. It means only the desire to do good to others – expressions of kindness - that is all."

"That is so simple. Why is it so hard to practice?"

"Because we are born of the flesh and must be reborn in the spirit," replied Harold.

"That sounds like Pentecostal thinking."

"Ah. There is truth in being born again in the spirit. Have you not this day experienced your mind basking in spiritual light?" Again, I was struck by his awareness of my experience.

"I suppose it could be described that way - yes, I was."

"There you have it. Your mind has visited the realm of the spiritual. It was reborn." Harold clasped his hands in delight, as does a little child when it feels gleeful.

"You're a trip, Harold." I felt appreciation for his child-like quality. He was gentle, playful and very friendly. "You said you are a wood carver and yet you went to Oxford University. How did that come about?"

"I was a student of Anthropology, Religion, and Psychology. I had no interest in trying to make money in these disciplines. When I returned to Jamaica, I decided to live a simple life. My family owns small tracts of land on many parts of the island, so I travel from village to village, spending time living on each parcel while I carve wood and sell my creations. This is how I choose to live."

"Wow, you decided to go native like me." I felt silly making this statement since he really is a native of Jamaica. His English accent must have thrown me off. "I fish and I have lived in a sea cave, a tent, even on a small island of sorts. My friend Patrick and I live wherever we can with as little cost as possible. I studied the same subjects that you have but not at a big university. I learned a great deal, though."

"What brought you to Jamaica and the simple life of a native, as you call it?" Harold took out a jug of water and drank deeply. I, too, felt thirsty and took a long drink of Millie's juice before answering.

"Adventure. Ever since I was a little boy I dreamed of living on an island."

"And I went to the island of England for similar reasons. So we share many qualities, my young sojourner. When I lived in England, I suppose I went native there by attending their prestigious university, and I played the role of an anthropologist, observing the culture around me. This is what you are doing now living in Jamaica is it not?"

"Hmm, I guess I am since you put it that way. I never thought of myself as an anthropologist, though."

"Ah, but the very best anthropologists are those who immerse themselves in a culture by living among the people as one of them. This is what you are doing."

"Yep. Going native. That's what Patrick and I are doing."

"I would like to meet this friend of yours."

"Certainly. In fact, I am getting hungry and I'd like to see how Patrick is doing with his mushroom trip."

"Mushrooms? What are you speaking of?"

"Oh, I thought you knew, since you sensed so many other things about me. I am tripping on magic mushrooms, or I was. I think it wore off."

"Ah, magic mushrooms are the spiritual food of the cosmos. It has taken off the veil that the world has cast upon the face of Creation so you could see your self clearly."

"I suppose that is true. Although, I am not so sure the mushrooms did that."

"You are indeed wise. The chemical itself is an illusion that removes illusions, meaning it is not reality, but has served to shake you from the dream of who you think you are so that your real self, who is one with the source of all reality, *love*, could be revealed to you. It would be a great hindrance if chemicals were required for people to experience the spiritual world. What you saw and experienced was a projection of your deepest desires, and that is to know truth - that we are all one in love."

"Wow, that's far out, man. That is exactly what I was thinking about when you appeared. I felt, or feel so real at this moment, because of the experience I had, but I wasn't sure to what extent it was the mushrooms, I mean, how much of the experience was a hallucination. It felt so other-worldly – or out of this world, so to speak."

"I ask you this, Oliver: Is the feeling still with you?"

"What do you mean?"

"The feeling of universal love. Do you still feel it now that the chemical is wearing off?"

"Yes. I do still feel it."

"Then, it is real. The false religious experiences that people have under the influence of chemicals do not last. They fade, as do dreams. What you experienced is real for it is lasting. Indeed, you have wakened from a dream."

"What do you mean by I have wakened from a dream?'

"I have said already, that the closer we come to our source – Creation - the more real we are. When we touch divine love, the false ideas of our own incorrect thinking, and the images of ourselves that we have learned from the world disappear, as do dreams when we wake up from sleeping. Come, let us go to your friend and then we shall eat together."

We left the cliff and walked along the road towards Millie and Charley's in silence. I rehearsed our conversation in my mind and reflected upon my experience, and realized that the experience was still unfolding, even though the psychedelic effects wore off. I recalled the many times I touched upon the *super real*, as we called it among my Ghetto Flower friends. What I had just experienced was another facet of *mind surfing*, a reaffirmation of what my friends and I have learned. I suppose it is necessary to have such affirmations, least we forget and fall back to sleep, so to speak. It is challenging to manifest the super reality of supernal love in every moment, in every thought, deed and action. I surmise that this is what a so-called saint and guru is able to do – allegedly. Perhaps it is what each of us is on earth to learn but very few of us, if any, ever master.

"Harold, are you a master teacher?"

"What do you mean?"

"A guru?" Harold laughed at my question.

"I was in England when the Beatles were just starting their career. I saw them perform in Liverpool and followed them ever since. They went to India to learn about meditation and eastern religion. It had a great influence upon them and subsequently the entire world. I believe George Harrison was the only Beatle to take the eastern teachings seriously. As a student of religion, I explored eastern religion and philosophy and learned much. As a student of anthropology, I attended sessions with various gurus who were teaching in England, attracted by the youth who wanted to follow the example set by the Beatles. I must say, it was most fascinating, but I did not develop the devotion that gurus require of their disciples. The role of devotee does not suit me. As for a guru, well, all of us are teaching each other all of the time."

"I have a friend who went to India and she basically had the same experience as you regarding gurus. And she came to the same conclusion." I was referring to Ellen of Stone Harbor, New Jersey.

"Well, then, your friend and I are of one mind." We fell silent once again as we continued our walk. I was surprised by how far I had walked while tripping. It did not seem that long at the time. Many hours had passed since I took the mushrooms.

As we approached Millie and Charley's property, I saw a body lying upon the ground. Harold saw it also and he walked briskly ahead of me, reaching the body first. It was Patrick. He had passed out. Harold held two fingers on his neck, feeling for a pulse. I was scared and started and rushed to his side, "Patrick, Patrick, wake up!"

"His pulse is very rapid, and he is breathing very faintly. You said he had mushrooms too, correct?" Harold asked as he opened his eyelids and shined a light in them.

"Yes, but it wouldn't do this, would it?" I asked.

"Every person's body is different. It is possible he is allergic or that he took other things as well. His eyes do not look good," replied Harold.

"Like what other things, ganja?"

"Perhaps, but most likely something more detrimental to the body's respiratory and cardiac system." Harold put his nose by Patrick's face and sniffed. "Alcohol! I must make him some tea. You try waking him up while I seek leaves from the ackee tree and make a fire. Here, put this under his nose." Harold poured something from a jar into my hand. It had a powerful menthol odor. I placed it under Patrick's nose. He did not respond, which made me nervous. With my other hand, I started shaking him and kept saying his name over and over. I rubbed the stuff on his nostrils. Finally, he moved his head and groaned. This was a good sign. I thought that he might simply be sleeping. Harold had returned and got a fire going. I was impressed with his efficiency in creating a fire and boiling water in a tin can. He added some leaves he had picked from a nearby tree to the boiling water.

"We must get him to be awake enough to drink some of this tea," commanded Harold. The urgency in his voice made me nervous. I kept shaking Patrick. I sat him up, leaning him against the tree. I continued shaking him and applied more of the paste to his nostrils. Finally, he opened his eyes and mumbled in slurred speech, "Leave my body."

"Patrick, wake up. You're not going to leave your body."

"Can't feel my body," he said in slurred speech.

"Drink this!" commanded Harold as he put the cup to his mouth. At first, Patrick resisted, moving his head back and forth, saying, "Feel sick," over and over.

"Drink this tea!" commanded Harold, this time more forcefully.

I pried open Patrick's mouth and tilted back his head as Harold poured in the tea. Patrick spit out the first mouth full, and then managed to swallow a small amount. Harold removed the cup and said, "A small amount is all he will need. Stand back, Oliver." I moved slightly away from Patrick. His body began to heave. He violently vomited. Out came a torrent of stuff, mostly smelling like alcohol. Everything came up, and finally he was heaving out pure green bile. Then, he stopped. His body was shaking and he was sucking in air.

"Patrick is very fortunate, Oliver. He was overdosing. We had to clean out his stomach to stop his body from absorbing more of the poison. He will be okay now."

"Thank you, Harold!" I was relieved and no longer frightened. Harold gave Patrick water to drink, instructing him to sip it slowly.

"What was in the tea?" I asked.

"The leaf of the ackee tree and parts of the fruit induces vomiting. My father was a medicine man and taught me all he knew when I was a boy. He wanted me to be a doctor, but I had other interests."

"Well, I am glad you have this knowledge. You saved my friend's life. Thank you."

"You are welcome, my friend."

"I wanted to leave my body," said Patrick.

"Why?" I asked.

"It was limiting me."

"How?"

"The mushrooms made me feel so good. I felt like I could fly. I wanted to fly, but I had to leave my body to fly."

"So what, you drank alcohol?"

"Yeah, but not at first. I am tired. I want to sleep, not talk."

"No, Patrick. Do not go to sleep. You don't have to talk, but you must stay awake for a while longer," insisted Harold.

"Can I at least lay in a hammock?"

"Do you think you can walk?" I asked.

"Maybe. If I get help." His speech was still slurred. We helped him to his feet. Harold told us that walking would help get his circulation going. We walked him to our camp and helped him into his hammock.

To my surprise, Patrick's energy picked up. His hammock was gently swinging as Harold and I built another campfire. Harold had insisted on making dinner. He helped himself to our cookware and began making a stew from vegetables he had in his bag, and to my surprise, goat meat that was tightly wrapped in paper and cloth.

"Bro, I had the most far out experience today," said Patrick.

"You were certainly far out there when we came upon you, and lucky we did or you could have died. Thanks to Harold, you're alive."

"Thanks, Harold. I really appreciate what you did for me, man. Ah, what did you do, exactly?"

"You are most welcome Mr. Patrick. I merely …"

Patrick interrupted, "Wow, man, you talk like you're an English dude, what's with that?"

"He grew up around an English family and he had a scholarship to Oxford," I answered.

"What's Oxford? Some fancy college?" Patrick was obviously still under the effects of the massive quantities of drugs he had taken. His manner of speech suggested his mind was dazed.

"Oxford University in England. One of the oldest and most prestigious universities in Western civilization," I responded for Harold.

"Indeed. It is considered by many scholars to be the oldest, dating back to the 17th century," added Harold.

"Man, it is so strange to hear you talk. So what did you do to me?" Patrick repeated his question.

"When I checked your vitals and determined that you were on the brink of overdosing and quite possibly could die, I made an herbal tea to dislodge all substances from your stomach. I must say, you were very fortunate to have enough strength for your diaphragm to move, otherwise you would have drowned in your own vomit." Harold had stopped his dinner preparations to look Patrick directly in the eyes as he spoke.

"Wow! Die! All I wanted to do was leave my body."

"And that my dear friend, is precisely what would have happened," replied Harold.

"Yeah, and you would have never got back in 'cause it would have been a corpse!" I added with a strong chiding tone.

"Man that was close. Thanks again, Harold. That tea was nasty. I never puked like that in all my life. That was a lot of crap that came up. I'm just now starting to feel my body. I am tingling all over, you know, like pins and needles when you sleep on an arm for too long."

"Whatever prompted you to want to leave your body in the first place? You said something about flying," I asked.

"Yeah, bro. Those mushrooms were something else. I got so high and felt so light that it was like I was an angel. I wanted to be an angel with wings and fly."

"He was caught up in a hallucination. Quite different from your experience, Oliver," interjected Harold.

"Of course, I wasn't gonna sprout wings so I figured I'd have to have one of those out-of-body experiences. You know, like those mystics from India. Anyway, I tried meditating and imagined myself flying. That sort of worked, but only in my imagination, which was really awesome. When I opened my eyes, I was still on the cliff. I never really left my body so I gave up. I walked along the road and this jeep pulled up along side of me."

"Wait a minute. I thought you said you wanted to leave your body. So why were you disappointed that your body was still on the cliff?" I asked.

"Because I realized that I didn't really leave my body. It was all in my mind. I only imagined that I was outside my body. I was only visualizing flying above the sea, gliding along the cliffs. It was awesome, though. I could see everything. I went all the way to the lighthouse and back. When I opened my eyes, I realized I hadn't seen anything at all and that it was all made up."

I took Patrick by the hand as I spoke, "It sounds to me like your personality-spirit entity did leave your body and that you were soaring along the cliffs. You just didn't realize that it was real because you have such a powerful imagination that you were not able to determine the difference between real and fantasy." I decided that I would wait to tell Patrick about my out-of-the-body experience. I wasn't ready to share my experience with him, not in his condition.

"Hey, you might be right about that. Gee, I could have saved myself a great deal of discomfort if you were with me," Patrick's comment caused me some discomfort. I should have waited for him to finish speaking with Norlina after we drank the tea.

"Anyway, this jeep pulls up beside me. This guy in his early thirties rolls down the window and says, '*Hey, what's happening?*' and I say, 'Nothing much, just tryin' to fly.' I don't think he knew I was serious. Then, he says, '*Far out, man, me too. Hop in and let's cruise.*' So we head on down the road towards the Roundabout. He hands me a brown colored miniature bottle, you know, like one of those medicine bottles. I look it over and ask what's in it. He hands me a small spoon and says, '*Blow, man, straight from Peru. Had it flown in myself.*' I ask, 'What's blow?' and he says, '*Coke, man, snow, you know, cocaine.*' 'Oh! I never had this stuff, what's it do to you?' He stares at me in disbelief and says, '*Man, are you from another planet?*' I laughed. Then, he says, '*You said you wanted to fly, well this will definitely give you lift off. Open the bottle and dip in the spoon. Put it up to one nostril, hold the other nostril closed with one finger, and snort.*' I did exactly as he instructed, only I did it several times over and over again because it felt amazing. It did make me feel like I was flying, but not really."

" Bro, you really have to get a grip on this flying thing," I said.

"Yeah. Definitely. No more trying to fly for me, at least not by numbing my body. Well, so, he says to me, *'Hey, man, slow down, that shit's expensive.'* So, I hand it back to him. Man, I was really high. I felt great. I asked him his name and he says, *'Jester Banger, have you heard of me?'* I say, 'Should I?' And he says, *'Anyone who reads Rolling Stone magazine knows my name. I am a rock and roll critic and a show business promoter for The Who.'* Can you believe that Oliver, The Who?"

"Not sure. The guy could have been feeding you a line of bull."

"Maybe he was, don't know for sure. So, I tell him that the first concert I ever went to was The Who and that they performed the entire Tommy album. You know what I'm talking about, Oliver, you were there with me. Then, I ask him if he knows them, personally, as friends to hang out with. He tells me that he parties with them all the time. He told me that Keith Moon is absolutely crazy and he goes on about the destruction of music equipment and hotel rooms and how it causes all kinds of legal nightmares. He told me that he partied with Janis Joplin and that he wrote an article about her for Rolling Stone."

"Wow, this is an amazing story. The Who, Janis Joplin – wow! It really is too bad Janis is dead. Bro, you shouldn't have touched that cocaine. That stuff is as nasty as heroin and meth, and you know what that stuff did to our brothers in the neighborhood." Harold looked over at me with an eyebrow raised.

"Yeah, I realize that now, but at the time it seemed like a good idea. Anyway, we go into the Roundabout Wharf Club bar and restaurant, and ordered Red Stripe beer. We drank quite a few and then left."

"Beer on top of mushrooms and cocaine? Alcohol was never your drug of choice – strictly a pothead, that's you. You were not in your right mind, Patrick. You never did anything like this before. In fact, you always insisted upon putting nothing in your body that is not organic – remember turning down taking that LSD offered by those Jesus Freaks in Wildwood? What got into you?"

"I don't know, bro, it just sort of snowballed. Ha, snowball, get it? Cocaine is called snow. Ha."

Patrick was really hyper. I've never seen him act and talk this way. I figured it must be a residual effect of the cocaine.

"Yeah, real funny. You're lucky you're not dead," I chided him.

"Okay, enough with the dead stuff already. Let me get on with the story. Hey bro, there's feeling back in all my limbs." Patrick hopped out of the hammock and stretched his body. I was amazed that only an hour ago he was comatose. "So, we get back in the jeep and Jester opens the brown bottle and takes a few snorts and then hands it to me. I take a few, making sure to be a little more moderate this time. He starts the car and says, *'How about we drive along the beach road and look for a place to stop?'* I go along with the idea and after a few miles he pulls over and we get out. Now this is where it gets really strange. We walk on to the beach and stroll for a while. He reaches down and takes my hand and holds it. It felt kind of weird. You know, what would a guy be doing holding another dude's hand? Then I thought, oh, man, he's really high and a rock star type, they do things differently. Duh, what a dumb ass I was."

"You got that right," I interjected, "I see where this is going."

"Alright, no comments from the coconut gallery. Anyway, he stops by this tree that has a fallen branch and says, *'This is a good spot don't you think?'* I say, 'Yeah, it's pretty nice.' And then he pulls me close to his body, puts his hands on my ass and kisses me right on the lips. He even tried putting his tongue in my mouth. I pulled away and spit several times. I looked at him and said, 'Whoa, I get it now, you're gay!' And he says, *'Not gay, I'm bi, aren't you?'* 'No way man! I am straighter than an arrow.' Can you believe this happened?"

I was laughing so hard I couldn't stand up straight. I was hunched over holding my stomach. To my delight, Patrick was laughing right along with me. I said, "Jester Banger likes to bang – guys and dolls!" That really got us laughing. "That can't be his real name, he had to be pulling your leg – ha, he wanted to pull on more than that - too funny!"

"It was really creepy. So this is what happens next. I tell him I understand that he is into guys, being a show business promoter and all. I tell him that he must feel frustrated expecting to have sex with me. So, get this, I say to him that I'll go for a swim so he can jerk off or something to relieve himself. I tell him that when he's done, to come to the water's edge and call my name, then drive me home."

"You are out of your freaking mind! Telling a bisexual dude to jerk off while you went swimming." I busted out laughing again.

"Yeah, right. I was definitely out of my mind. No argument there. Geez, I was really high. It is funny how naïve I was. Hmm, drugs do strange things to the mind."

"That's the understatement of your life," I reply, "so what happened next?"

"I went swimming. He never called my name. I waited a long time. I figure he had enough time to get off, so I get out of the water and he is gone. Vamoose! He's nowhere to be found. I walk to where the jeep was parked and it's gone."

"Wow, you must have been ten miles or so from here. How'd you get home?" I asked.

"That was a trip in and of itself! I started walking south along the beach …" Harold interrupted.

"Dinner is served!"

And a great dinner it was! Rice with a combination of vegetables flavored with many spices, and goat meat with curry. We never had goat meat before. I was surprised by its succulence, although the flavor was a bit unusual and took some getting used to. Patrick was ravenous, practically inhaling his food. No wonder, there was nothing left in his stomach after being flushed out by Harold's tea.

"Patrick, it is good to see you are feeling much better," said Harold.

"Thanks to you. Man, this food is great! Hey, where did you come from anyway? I mean, you came with Oliver but how did you guys meet?"

"I saw Oliver sitting on a cliff and he was flying in the spirit world."

Patrick looked at me. "Huh! So you were trying to leave your body too!"

"No. I wasn't trying to do anything. Stuff just happened," I replied.

"Yeah, just like me. It all just happened."

"I do not agree with your self assessment, Patrick," said Harold.

"No. Why not? Man, I can't get used to you not talking like the other Jamaicans."

"He went to college in England, remember? He doesn't speak in the Jamaican dialect." I reminded Patrick.

"I can effin I wantin' ta be talkin' native, mon. Irie! I am Jamaican. True dat!" responded Harold, causing me to laugh. Harold continued addressing Patrick. "Stuff did not just happen to you, Patrick. You made a series of choices that inevitably led to a most undesirable outcome. It is important that you learn from your errors to prevent such happenings from reoccurring."

"I suppose you're right. But at the time it seemed like I was simply going with the flow, like I wasn't choosing anything and that each moment was choosing me."

Harold edged his body closer to Patrick and looked him directly in the eyes. "You assume that you were not in control. The drugs in your body made it seem so. The effects of these chemicals impaired your judgment. You did not take the time necessary to consider your thoughts and actions. Instead of you directing the experience, you were like a pinball in a machine. Let this be a powerful lesson to you and you will be the wiser for it."

Patrick's face broke into a wide grin. "Wow, you are a really far out dude. A pinball machine, huh, well I guess I had a cosmic tilt! I was no pinball wizard – huh, that's funny, get it? Jester Banger, the promoter for The Who, the band who wrote the song called Pinball Wizard. I think that's the name of it. Hey, wanna smoke a spliff?" Patrick's head was definitely still reeling from the chemical stew. I couldn't believe what he just said.

"What? You want to get high after what you've been through. Shouldn't you take a break?" I thought it insane that Patrick wanted to put more chemicals in his body so soon.

"I think a bit of the hair of the dog that bit me might not be a bad thing. But, perhaps you're right. I'm just trying to be friendly. I've never been with a Rasta without passing around ganja."

"He's not a Rasta," I announced.

Patrick, looking directly at Harold said, "You have dreadlocks. What makes you not a Rasta?"

I responded first, "You have long hair and was kissed by a guy, so does that make you a girl?"

"Huh, real funny. Wait till the day when some dude tries to get into your mouth. You won't think it's so funny then!" Patrick actually sounded angry. I was surprised. Harold responded to Patrick's question.

"I have family and friends who are Rastafarian. I am very familiar with their faith and cultural practices. I have smoked ganja but no longer favor it. I do not oppose its use, unless it makes people sick. I think it is good for some people and not good for others. For me it is neutral, having little affect upon me one way or another. I do find that I breathe much better without it, and as we all know, oxygen is good for the brain, in fact it is essential for life, while ganja, is not. As for my hair, well, the English women prefer the hip look - meaning the ones who are interested in carnal pleasures."

Patrick was shaking his head. "Well, I know quite a few Rastamen who disagree with you on the ganja point. It is how they cross the threshold to Jah. Your reason for the dreads is pretty cool, though, nothing wrong with using hair on your head to get some tail." We all laughed.

"Yes, Patrick, Rastas do believe ganja smoking is a sacrament that brings them in communion with Jah, and they experience it as such because they believe it has this power," replied Harold.

"Well, I believed I could fly if I got high enough and you know how that turned out. No matter. Thanks again for the food, though. Goat meat is awesome. Oliver, we need to buy goat meat, and chicken too. I'm getting tired of eating seafood every day." Patrick continued to talk and move in a hyper manner.

Harold was not finished discussing the mushroom issue. "Patrick you were high enough to have the veil pulled away from the source of Creation, as the flying along the cliff experience demonstrated. The problem was you failed to realize the beauty of what was happening because you were not looking for spiritual truth. Instead, you were seeking thrills, to fly, and even when you did, you did not accept it. My dear fellow, simply having the sensation of soaring in your mind is not enough. You must know what you are seeking in order to find it. Flying in the mind is a way to travel through the psychic circles, and what you find there depends on what you bring there."

"Harold, I dig what you're saying, even though I don't understand it. Maybe someday I will," Patrick replied.

"I think you will know the meaning of my words one day. You are a good young man. Your heart will lead you. I suggest that you correct an error in your thinking, and it is this: you see your body as a limitation, when it truth it is the vehicle by which you journey through life. You need not escape the altar of the Creator in order to experience the Creator, which is what you are truly seeking even if you are not conscious of this fact. You have packaged this urge to find the Creator into the desire of wanting to fly, or leave your body. You are alive and flying all the time on the experience of being alive. What you seek you already have, you already are. You are like a fish who is trying to discover water."

Patrick went completely silent and appeared to withdraw within himself. He did not respond to what Harold had said, at least outwardly. I could tell by the look on his face and his overall demeanor that he was contemplating his words. On some level, they had penetrated his mind.

Everything Harold said was fascinating. I knew exactly what he was talking about. I was seeking to touch some deeper meaning or essence of self, or something like that – this was my primary desire – so that is what I experienced. Patrick was trying to fly, and that was the direction his thoughts took him in, with undesirable results. What Harold had said made perfect sense to me. We find what we are seeking – be it real or fanciful.

His statement about Rasta beliefs was also very interesting. I wondered if he thought that my experience of supernal love – my infinite self - happened because I believed it could happen. I did not want to engage him in a conversation on that topic at this time because it would require too much explanation to include Patrick in the discussion. I intended to fill Patrick in on my experience some other time. I was simply glad he was back to his normal self again, sort of, and more importantly, alive! I was pleasantly full, relaxed, and very tired. Harold was yawning, and Patrick looked deeply introspective.

"Harold, would you prefer sleeping in a hammock or a tent?" I asked.

"That is very kind of you. I am used to sleeping on the ground. I have the proper equipment in my bag. It would be a treat to sleep in a hammock, if you don't mind."

"Please. You are our guest. Patrick, do you prefer the hammock or tent this evening?"

"Hammock."

"Okay, then. I'm going to the tent. I need to sleep. Good night." I said.

"Good night, God bless, and pleasant dreams," replied Patrick.

Harold laughed. "I have not heard that sleep blessing since I was a child. Very good, yes very good indeed. Good night and pleasant dreams, gentlemen." Harold chuckled again as he took out his blanket and got into the hammock. I went to the tent and Patrick sat staring into the fire.

PATRICK'S EXPERIENCE … continued
(Abstinence & Other Musings)

The next morning upon awakening, I discovered that Harold had already gone. He left a note on his hammock that said one day he would come by and take us to his land near somewhere on the other side of Bloody Bay. He thanked us for our hospitality. Patrick was snoring away in his hammock.

I made a trip to the outhouse to relieve myself. I saw Elijah, Norlina, Millie and Charley assembled in front of their shanties.

"Good mornin', Ollie," said Charley.

"Good morning, everyone. You look like you're getting ready to go somewhere." I responded.

"Kingston. We 'ave fambly business dat need tendin'," replied Millie.

"Ollie, we will explore de land we spoke of anot'er time, mon," announced Elijah.

"That's cool. We might go to Booby Cay for a few days. We'll catch you a big bonito for when you come home." I said.

"Save it fer anot'er time, Ollie. We nuh be returnin' fer at least ten days, mos' likely longer," replied Millie.

"Yah an' Patrick can stay in mi shanty, while we be gone, effin yah like," offered Norlina.

"That's very generous of you. Thanks," I responded.

"Ollie, listen carefully, mon. I be needin' a favor fram yah an' Patrick. We need yah an' Patrick ta keep an eye on our property. Feed an' wata de donkey. Are yah comfortable takin' de donkey fer some exercise, an' do yah min' postponing travels ta Booby Cay?" Wow, Millie trusted us with a lot. I wasn't so sure about the donkey part.

"No problem delaying our trip to Conch Island. There's plenty of conch along the cliffs further up the West End. Patrick has experiences with horses. He might be okay with taking the donkey for a walk. I don't mind taking care of his water, food, and dung."

"Nuh matter. Effin Patrick nuh knoh how ta 'andle de donkey, den jus' keep 'em on de long rope in de grazing area behind de 'ouse so he can stretch his legs," said Charley, "and heap his dung in a pile fer wen I return."

"We can handle that," I said with confidence.

"Awrite den, t'ank you, Ollie. We mus' be on our way, de ride comin' soon," said Millie. "Oh, yah need nuh concern yourself wit de ice in de icebox. De iceman mek delivery reg'lar. He knoh wat ta do."

Each of them carried a canvas bag hung on their shoulders. The bags were made from the canvas sacs that once contained flour. They walked down the stone pathway, past the flower garden and our camp. Patrick was still sleeping. I stood with them by the road until the small-bus-van-taxi like vehicle picked them up. I returned to the camp.

I built a fire, boiled water and made coffee. The aroma drifted to Patrick's nostrils, causing him to wake.

"Ah. Blue Mountain coffee. The finest in the world! I'll have a cup of that if you don't mind." Patrick sounded chipper for a guy who was on the threshold of death the previous night. I expected that he'd have a hangover.

"Good morning! How you feeling?" I asked.

"Great. I had the strangest dream though. I dreamt that I almost died and this English Rasta guy saved my life."

"That was no dream," I said, slightly irritated.

"No shit Sherlock. I was kidding. That was a close call last night. I'm surprised I don't have a splitting headache."

"Yeah, me too. You are one lucky bastard. If it wasn't for Harold you wouldn't be talking right now."

"Bro, that dude was amazing. Very unusual, you know, the English accent and being scholarly and all. Hey, where is he?"

"He left before I got up. Here, read the note." I handed Patrick the note along with a cup of coffee. He was still laying in the hammock."

"Far out! He's coming back to take us to his land. Bro, we have all kinds of options for living on this island."

"He did not say we could live on his land, Patrick."

"Nonetheless. It will be good to see him again and thank him properly for saving my life. By the way, thank you Oliver."

"You're most welcome. Please, don't do that again. I've never seen you do anything that endangered your life. What got into you last night?"

"It was like I told you and Harold, I just went with the flow of the mushroom trip."

"Yeah, and like Harold said, tripping or not, you made choices that almost got you killed so don't go blaming the mushrooms." I said.

"You're right. I could have been more careful. I guess everyone gets carried away now and then, or at least once in their life. Hopefully, yesterday will be the only time for me."

"Glad to hear it. That makes me feel better – that sounds more like the Patrick O'Malley that I know. Want some fish and fried plantain for breakfast?"

"How about pancakes with maple syrup, bacon, sausage, and eggs?"

"Yeah, and Penny and Jenny for desert," I added. We laughed. It had been awhile since we had a good ole American breakfast. I got the large iron frying pan going and tossed in the last of our bonito fish along with fresh plantain.

"Where did I leave off last night?" Patrick asked.

"What do you mean? You went to bed after we did."

"No, I mean telling you what happened to me."

"Oh. Jester was grabbing your ass and sticking his tongue in your mouth. You were about to tell us the rest of the details of your homosexual virgin losing experience." I laughed. Patrick gave me a disapproving look.

"I remember now. After discovering …" I interrupted.

"The entire family has gone to Kingston. They left us in charge of their property. We have to take care of the donkey, so there won't be any overnight excursions to Conch Island for a while. Oh, Norlina said we can stay in her shanty if we want."

"Why?"

"Why what? Norlina offering her shanty or …"

"All of it. Why did they go to Kingston?" Patrick asked.

"Family business."

"Maybe it has something to do with the land Elijah and Norlina inherited from their parents," suggested Patrick.

"Could be. We can't pursue our tourism ideas until they return."

"We could write a letter to our friends in Philly and let them know about Negril. That could get the ball rolling," suggested Patrick.

"Great idea. I can write it." I offered.

"Yeah, you can look in your journal for juicy details. I don't think we should tell them about the Buccaneer Inn and Penny and Jenny. That might steer them in the wrong direction," advised Patrick.

"I agree. We don't want to mess up the standing invitation we have at the Buc, which most likely includes all expenses paid - a very nice fallback option." I couldn't stress enough the importance of protecting our Buccaneer connection, and to keep our friends' smuggling operation a secret. Even though they don't know that we know what they're really doing.

"They're gonna love it here – plain and simple. Ghetto Flowers Adventures in Paradise – they need to get their heads out of the asphalt, concrete, redbrick row homes jungle and into a tropical one. They dig Wildwood and Stone Harbor – but man, this is seashore living to the height of paradise. It's gonna rock their socks!"

Patrick was right. Our friends would love it here, and they deserve experiencing what living life in total freedom is like. They have been through fire and brimstone in the previous two years: heavy drug use that had killed many kids in the neighborhood, racial violence, and waking up to the fact that living in our neighborhood was akin to being an animal in a human zoo. I wondered, though, how they would adjust to living where the lifestyle included daily recreational use of ganja?

"If I write the letter today, they should get it within ten days. We'll have to make sure we arrange accommodations that are cheap for their pocketbooks with enough extra to cover our living expenses," I felt like writing the letter that very moment.

"Write it now." Patrick must have read my mind, but I was a little hesitant.

"I think we need to secure accommodations first. If Elijah and Norlina's land is suitable for creating a campground, and if they are amenable to our idea, that would be great, but if that pie-in-the-sky scheme doesn't work, where would they stay?" I responded.

"We can invite them even without knowing about Elijah and Norlina's land. No matter what accommodations we find for them, we will negotiate a finder's fee percentage for bringing them here. Hell, there has to be lots of Jamaicans with land in Negril who need cash from tourist. That will not be a problem, so I say write that letter and send it today. We'll work out the details in due time," implored Patrick.

I had some additional thoughts on what the financial set up should be. "If we get the campground thing going, we could negotiate with Elijah and Norlina to let us stay in the campground as managers free of charge, receive a dollar a day commission, and they could toss in meals as well."

"Yeah, and with the money that Elijah and Norlina make from renting the campground, along with Millie and Charley selling meals, they could invest in building structures. People wouldn't need tents and they could charge more," added Patrick.

"Okay. We have a plan that includes Elijah and Norlina. If that falls through, then it's back to using the creative imagination survival machine," I quipped.

"Not to worry, mon. I n I completely adaptable human animals. Irie! Just consider dis idea, mon: De Ghetto Flowers livin' in Lord Joseph's cave!"

"Patrick! That's a brilliant idea. The cave is large enough for six people, and it has its on water supply, access to the sea, all of it. Perfect! You are a genius survivalist! I like that idea better than the Elijah plan. It is more doable and close to Millie and Charley's and Fishermen Cove. Wow, I wonder why we didn't think of that before? Hey, there really is no problem with our friends coming to Negril and finding accommodations - the issue is we are trying to find ways to benefit financially. When I think of it that way it feels kind of selfish."

"Well, we want to help Elijah and Norlina and we just explored the lighthouse cliff area. Like I said, there are lots of options. Remember, we recently made friends with Jamaicans who own beachfront property, and there is Conch Island. I don't see a problem with us wanting to be Negril entrepreneurs. Hell, why shouldn't we make our world more livable as we share it with others? I see nothing wrong with applying the good ole American entrepreneur spirit to enhance our ability to stay in paradise. So let's get that letter written!" said Patrick enthusiastically.

"Well, you just swept my guilt away. You got it! Hey, after I write the letter, we could stroll to the post office. I remember seeing it just this side of the Roundabout. It is a bit more of an official looking shanty of sorts. We'll take a break from fishing today. Maybe I'll write my mom a letter, and Sandy too." I was excited. Patrick was absolutely right. There was no end to options to explore and there is nothing wrong with benefiting from sharing our good fortune.

"Good idea. It's still morning and not too hot. Maybe we could take a swim in a sea cave during the heat of the day," said Patrick.

"Let's get started!" It took a half hour or so to compose the letter to our friends. Patrick read it and suggested a few changes. I wrote a brief letter to my mother, letting her know I was doing very well. Then I wrote Sandy a letter. I told her all about my adventures, minus the Penny and Jenny love-fest. I informed her that I would most likely not be returning to Philly in time for the winter school semester. I told her to seriously consider coming to Jamaica but I knew she wouldn't drop out of school. I finished the letters and we headed for the post office.

As we were walking, I asked Patrick to continue with the story of his drug-crazed adventure.

"OK. So I was walking along the beach, barefoot at the water's edge, carrying my sneakers of course. I remember feeling like I had a lot of energy…"

"The cocaine most likely," I interjected.

"Possibly. Anyway, these two Jamaican dudes appear from the shadow of palm trees and come walking toward me. We engaged in conversation. The taller of the two said, '*Good evenin', mon, how are yah on dis fine night, mon?*' I could tell they weren't Rastas because they didn't have dreadlocks. Irie, I replied, how about you?

'*Yeahmon, Irie. Do yah wan' ta try some hash oil, mon? We mek it fram de ganja we grow in de mountains.*'

I say sure, but that I don't have money with me. The shorter of the two says, '*Noh problem, mon. We nuh be askin' fer anyt'ing, mon. Come, we sit over der in de trees.*' They were young, maybe slightly older than me. I walked in between them, side-by-side.

'*Mi name is David an' dis is Henry.*'

"My name is Patrick."

'*Dat is a good Christian name, mon. Do yah knoh Patrick was one of de apostles, mon?*'

"No, that's news to me."

'*True dat, mon. Patrick was an apostle an' he wen' aw de way ta Ireland, mon, teaching de good news.*'

I asked David how he knew that the apostle Patrick went to Ireland?

'*Mi madda tol' me dat wen I a pikny. She tol me 'bout aw de apostles.*'

David breaks out in a wide grin of pride. While we where speaking, Henry rolled a huge spliff. He opened a jar and spread what looked like tar all over the leaf.

'*Dis is hash oil, mon. It tek lots of ganja ta mek. Very potent.*' Henry announces as he lit the spliff. I expected the spliff to flame up like a torch. I was surprised when it didn't. Henry handed the spliff to me and cautioned, '*Do nuh tek in deeply, mon. De oil is harsh ta de lungs.*' I smoked it, inhaling a little bit, worried that this hash oil tar-like stuff might actually be tar. It wasn't. It had a strong resin smell and taste. I felt the effects immediately."

I interrupted Patrick with a question. "So was it real hash in the form of oil?"

"I'm not sure. It certainly got me super stoned. It tasted, well, like highly resinous ganja oil. I don't know any other way to describe it."

"And all these guys wanted was to get high with you?" I asked Patrick for clarification.

"No. Let me get on with the story. Anyway, we must have smoked three spliffs. My lungs were feeling full of gunk and my head was definitely in the clouds. This is when my body started feeling a little numb. So, David tells me that he and his friend Henry live in the mountains and that they are ganja growers. They came to Negril for the purpose of finding a tourist interested in buying large quantities. David asked me, and this is where it gets wild, *'Can yah get a submarine, mon?'* A submarine? I respond in disbelief, like a U.S. Navy submarine? Are you joking?

Really, Oliver, these guys were a trip. So David says, *'Me nuh be joking wit yah, mon. I nuh speakin' of a big submarine. I talkin' 'bout small enough fer one person ta carry a cargo of a hundred pounds ganja. Can yah get such a t'ing, mon? Seen?'*

I was astounded by this guy's inquiry. Not because it was totally unrealistic, but that he actually thought that I might be wealthy enough to buy a submarine. They really were very naïve. They possessed little knowledge of the world outside their mountain village. I decided to play along, telling them that it's possible. So David says in a gleeful voice, *'We t'ought so mon. Wen I see yah walkin' de beach I somehow know yah be de one.'*

It'll take some time, I explain, I'll have to go back to the U.S., of course. Henry chimes in with excitement in his voice, *'Tell me, where in de U.S. yah buy submarine, mon?'*

I tell them that the city I live in has a Navy shipyard, where most of the men in my family work. I explain that this is where they build most of the ships for the U.S. Navy, and they build lots of submarines. I say that most of the subs are very big, but they build small ones for spy work. The mini-subs are able to move in and out of harbors without detection. When the submarines become ten years old they no longer use them. These submarines are so well made they can last for thirty years, easily. The submarines are sold to anyone who can afford one. *'How long it tek fer yah ta buy one, mon?'* David asked me.

So I tell him I could call one of my uncles and say I'm interested. If there is one presently available, I could buy it within two weeks.

You have to know, Oliver, I am stunned the whole time that these guys are actually buying into the bullshit I'm telling them. David is so excited he looks like he is going to explode as he stands up and tosses his arms around while speaking, *'Dat be perfect, mon. Den yah transport ta Negril an' we fill it up wit ganja. Yah become richer den yah are now. Irie, dis is good. Very good, Irie. We aw be rich!'* over and over again.

Oliver, I had no idea that my wild story would be taken so seriously. I was amazed that they were so gullible. I became even more aware of how secluded their lives have been. So I ask them if this is the first crop of ganja they have ever grown.

'Di first we grow dis large ta sell, mon. We 'ave grown aw our lives ta use, never ta sell.' responded Henry.

How much do you have? I ask.

'We 'ave no scale, mon. We t'ink it weigh more den one hundred pounds. It could be more. It only de flower, mon. We careful ta tek out de male plants. No seeds, only de female flowers. It pure, mon. You be very satisfied,' said David.

Where is it? I asked, and Henry replies.

'It in our village, mon. We can bring it ta Negril at dis very spot wen you 'ave de submarine. We live in Cane Valley, Westmoreland District, nuh far fram 'ere. You mus' come ta see de ganja, mon?'

I tell them I will need to see the ganja before I buy the submarine.

'Irie. Yah come now.' Henry insisted.

No, I respond, explaining that I have a partner, referring to you, Oliver, of course, and that I must discuss the plan with you. I explain that you and I have some business to attend to, and suggest that in a week or possibly longer we will drive to Cane Valley and make the deal? I stumbled a bit on my words, as I was thrown off guard by their invitation.

'Dat be fine, mon. Yah partner is in Jamaica?' David replied.

Yes, I say, informing him that we are staying in Negril and that I will speak to you in the morning.

'We come wit yah ta meet him, mon. Speak ta him dis evenin.' David offers.

I inform them that you are with a special woman that night, and that I will not see you until tomorrow. I say that I will know where to find them.

Oliver, this is where I started feeling really uncomfortable. It was a game to me, but it was a very serious proposition to these guys. I felt a need to escape. So I announce that I must be going! I stood up and extended my hand to David. He took it and held it firmly and said, *'Dis is very good, Patrick. We mek lots of money together. Soon we see yah an' yah fren in Cane Valley. Jus' ask fer David an' Henry. Everyone knows us. Yah will be told where ta find us.'* We shook hands. Feeling quite relieved, and amused, I continued my way down the beach."

"Wow! That's one hell of a story. A submarine. These guys weren't very bright," I said to Patrick.

"No, they weren't stupid, just naïve. These guys spent their entire lives living in a mountain village. I doubt they have ever been to Montego Bay. Negril is probably the biggest town they've been to and as far as I know, we, Jester Banger, and two Swedes are currently the only tourists" explained Patrick.

"What Swedes? You don't plan on us going to Cane Valley, do you?" I asked.

"Hey, not a bad idea. We could play this thing out and maybe get some free or inexpensive ganja out of it. Plus we'd get to see Jamaican mountain living and a large scale growing operation. I'll tell you about the Swedes later." Patrick was genuinely excited by the idea.

"Continuing your fabrication with people who are serious about making money is potentially very dangerous. No way I'm going to Cane Valley. Besides, we'd have to rent a car and we don't have the money."

"We could take local transportation. One of those little buses we see once in a while. They must go to small villages in the mountains," suggested Patrick.

"No way. You have to get this crazy idea out of your head," I implored.

"Alright, alright. No need to get all huffed up. I was just using the old imagination machine," replied Patrick.

"Yeah, and look at what your imagination machine did to you last night, you almost died."

"Well, I'm still here. Live and in color!"

"Thanks to Harold."

"Yeah, he's a very cool and unusual dude, being Oxford educated and all. I hope we see him again," said Patrick.

"He promised to come back for us some day," I said.

"Island time is very different. *Some day* could be six months from now and we'll probably be back in South Philly." Patrick was right. People in Jamaica, for the most part, did not live by clocks. I have never seen a Jamaican wearing a wristwatch. In fact, I don't recall seeing a clock of any kind since leaving the airport.

We had reached Lord Joseph's property. I went up to his shanty and knocked. There was no answer. Patrick got on his knees and called out his name through the sea cave whole in the ground. Again, there was no answer, just Patrick's voice echoing back. We descended into the sanctuary of the sea cave.

"Ah. The beauty of this cave will never cease to surprise and amaze me," commented Patrick.

"Yeah, bro. This is the best place I have ever lived – a cathedral created by the forces of nature," I added.

"Yeahmon! Hey, maybe we should move back in now that Lord Joseph's Rasta family and friends are gone," suggested Patrick.

"We don't know for sure they are gone. Besides, we got a good thing going with our new Jamaican family. And, are you sure you want to be somewhere that is not a short stroll away from Norlina's sexy body?" I teased.

"Yeah, you're right. Norlina is totally awesome. Did I tell you we had a quick rump in the tent right after I drank the mushroom tea?"

"No. You left that juicy tidbit out of your story, which you have yet to finish, by the way."

"Yeah, I'm almost at the end where you and Harold find me. Hey, when I was having sex with Norlina, I began tripping, and let me tell you, when I erupted, man it was like a super nova explosion!"

"I'm jealous. That would be a good reason to drink mushroom tea again," I added.

"Hey, no entertaining the notion of body surfing with Norlina – off limits, bro. Besides, she won't let you touch her, and neither will I!" Patrick sounded seriously protective.

"Nuh ta worry, mon. Nuh problem. I nuh want ta be touchin' de same flesh where yah be putting yah big bamboo. Nuh problem, mon. Seen?" We laughed. I stripped off my clothes and dove from the ledge into the sea. I seriously needed to wash off the stench from the previous day. A saltwater rinse would do for the moment. Patrick joined me. We swam around until satisfied. I got out first and decided to explore the back of the cave. There was still a cache of ganja bundles, all wrapped up in canvas, plastic and burlap. Ninety percent of the original stash was gone. It was most likely shipped out to that yacht the day we sat with Elijah and Cricket on the cliffs and watched it being loaded.

"Anything back there?" Patrick asked.

"Yep, just a few bundles of ganja. We should go. Lord Joseph may not be comfortable with us being on his property with ganja stored here. He might even have someone keeping guard who doesn't know us," I cautioned.

"Bro, you're being paranoid. I think you need to smoke some ganja to get the fear of Babylon cleansed out of your head again," suggested Patrick.

"I had an awesome cleansing last night while on the tea."

"Oh yeah? Tell me what happened," requested Patrick.

"Not yet. I'm not ready to talk about it. Besides, you have to finish your story."

"Okay then. Let's get back on the road and I'll tell you the rest. There really isn't much left to tell though." We ascended out of the cave and continued our trek along the road toward the Roundabout to mail the letters.

"So, back to my story. I'm walking along the beach thinking about the submarine ganja smuggling scheme, laughing to myself, when a boy comes up to me wanting to sell mushrooms."

"You're kidding? Mushrooms must grow wherever there's animal shit." I said.

"You got that right. Hey, maybe the shit from Charley's donkey sprouts mushrooms," said Patrick.

"Maybe, although they use up that donkey manure really fast for cooking and fertilizer - not enough time for mushrooms to grow."

"Well, anyway, I tell this kid I have no money. He's disappointed, but gives me a handful of dried mushrooms and says his name is Jon and if I like them I can find him every day at the Roundabout at noon with mushrooms to sell. I wonder to whom this boy is selling mushrooms. This place isn't crawling with hippies this time of year."

"Good point. It's a puzzler," I added, "So what happened next?"

"I ate a half dozen mushroom caps and stems."

"No wonder you were so screwed up, bro. What the hell got into you?"

"Mushrooms. Cocaine. Alcohol. More cocaine. Hash oil. More mushrooms. And that's not all," said Patrick somewhat humorously.

"Like what?" I asked.

"Well, as I'm walking along, I feel the new infusion of mushrooms kicking in. I feel like running, but I get this impulse to run naked. I take off all my clothes and wrap them in a single bundle – not much, a tee shirt, cut-off jeans and sneakers – and take off sprinting down the beach. It felt great. The wind blew back my hair and my body was tingling all over. My lungs were expanding and my heart was pumping oxygenated blood and I had these amazing sensations throughout my whole body. I think the running speeded up the delivery of the psychedelic chemicals to my brain …"

"Ya think?" I interjected.

"Yeah, I think. Bro, I was flying …"

"Let me guess. Not enough to leave your body, though?"

"Exactly. But it was the most amazing running I had ever done in my life."

"Just like the amazing super nova explosion, right!"

"Well, not as good as that. Hey, stop interrupting me. So, I'm running along, feeling like I could run forever, when suddenly this person appears in front of me stopping me dead in my tracks. He has a gun pointed in my face and says, *'My woman nuh want ta see yah white dick, mon, put yah clothes on!'* So, there I was, stark naked staring down the barrel of a gun. I could hear my heart racing in my ears. At one moment I am running like the Greek God Hermes, and the next I am staring death in the face. So, I say to the Jamaican, *'I am running along the beach and you are not real!'* He looks at me and grins, clicks back the hammer of his gun, clenches his teeth and seethes, *'I am real enuff mon, yah like ta run, see effin yah can outrun bullets, RUN!'* Again I say, *'you are not real. I cannot outrun bullets, so if you are going to shoot, it doesn't matter if I walk or run.'* And I simply walk around him and I don't run. I just calmly walk away telling myself that that did not happen."

"Wow, you are one lucky son-of-a-bitch. Did you put your clothes on?" I was totally amazed by the incident.

"Hey, don't call my mother a female dog in heat, she wouldn't like that, and no, I didn't take the time to put my clothes on. Anyway, I came to the end of the beach, you know, where the South Negril River enters the sea. I cross the bridge and walk up to the Roundabout – putting my clothes on, of course. I have no idea what time it is. I am very thirsty. By the way, don't chew mushrooms and swallow them without water, they taste nasty, very musty. It's a must to wash them down with something."

"Not to worry. I have no designs for eating mushrooms, at least not in the near future."

"What are you saying, you're not gonna trip again?" Patrick asked.

"Not sure. Gotta think about it. There's a lot to process from last night."

"Like what?" Patrick persisted.

"Later. Like I said, I still have some processing to do."

"Bro, you and that deep cosmic-spiritual thinking thing that you trip out on can be super annoying. You've been doing that shit ever since I've known you."

"Yeah, well, it's just the way I am."

"You got that right," complained Patrick.

"Hey, bro, you have the same quality." I pointed out.

"True dat, but not to the extent that you do."

"I suppose not. Well, I guess it's both a blessing and a curse. A blessing in that it leads me to understanding things better and a curse because I am always trying to understand everything. It's a conundrum." It really did feel like a double-edged psychic sword – at times.

"Like I said, Oliver, you got that right. So, I go in the Roundabout bar and ask for a drink of water, which to my surprise they actually want to charge me for and I don't have money on me."

"You're kidding! Bro, maybe the commercialization of Negril is seeping in sooner than we expected. Damn, charging for water!" I added.

"Hey, it is a bar and they do need to make money, tourist industry or not," Patrick replied, "so, I ignore the bartender wanting money for the water, drink it down and ask for a refill and he refuses. Frustrated, I am about to leave the bar and I hear this voice in what sounded like a German accent. He says, *'Give the man a Red Stripe! It's on me.'* I turn toward the voice and there are these two longhaired dudes sitting in a booth. They motion for me to join them. I take my Red Stripe and go sit with these guys. It turns out they're from Sweden and arrived that day in Negril. They have a car and they are staying at the Yacht Club. Can you believe that they actually rent rooms there? Needless to say, I am very high with a chemical stew zooming round my brain, and now these guys are feeding me alcohol. They have a bottle of White Lightening Rum on the table and they're throwing back shots and chasing them with beer. I join them."

"I can't believe your stupidity, Patrick!" I was disappointed in his reckless behavior. It was extremely uncharacteristic of him.

"Like I said, I had a chemical brew racing through my body, so I am not to be held completely accountable. And that concludes my story of last night's adventure. You know the rest."

"How did you get to our camp? Or I should say, laying on the side of the road?"

"The Swedes gave me a ride. Of course they kept passing around the rum bottle. They let me out of the car and I must have passed out. Finished! End of story. And I lived to tell it!"

"Yeah, and if not for the serendipitous presence of Harold, I'd be finding out how to ship your dead carcass home!" For some reason we both found my morbid comment funny and we had a good laugh.

"Serious, though. You almost died."

"Yeah. I guess it hasn't hit me yet. I'm just so glad I didn't, duh."

"Maybe we should lay off the chemical intake," I suggested.

"Perhaps. It wouldn't hurt us none to clean out our systems. In fact it would probably feel pretty good. All this cheap ganja and mushrooms will make abstinence difficult, though," commented Patrick.

"Yeah, bro, sort of like being celibate and living in the Blue Parrot Village with Playboy Bunnies hoppin' around completely naked."

"Ah, now that is one of the best descriptions of heaven on earth I've ever heard. Can you imagine, hanging out every night at the Blue Parrot Village and taking a vow of celibacy? That wouldn't be heaven – it'd be pure hell! Whew, not *I*, said the blind man!" I laughed at Patrick's comment.

"Well, fortunately, we don't have to abstain from women to be healthy. However, I think it's necessary for us to take a break from ganja, mushrooms, alcohol, and oh yeah, cocaine. What the hell were you thinking, Patrick?"

"Enough with that already, bro. I wasn't thinking, okay. Pure and simple and it won't happen again. Ever! Okay. Does that satisfy you?"

"Thanks Patrick. I'm got really scared, that's all."

"Appreciated!"

"So, for how long do we abstain?" I asked.

"A week? How's that sound?"

"Good." I said.

"Okay, let's shake on it!" Patrick extended his hand and we shook. It made me feel a lot better.

"Now, it's your turn," said Patrick.

"My turn what?"

"What happened to you last night? I stopped to chat with Norlina, and we ended up in the tent, and when I came out, you were nowhere to be found. I went looking for you, calling out your name along the cliffs, but no Oliver."

"I walked pretty far in the direction of the lighthouse."

"So, tell me what happened."

"I had a religious experience."

"And?"

"I felt spiritual love."

"Oh, a Catholic thing, like being in St. Aloysius Church having an epiphany. You're not gonna become a hippie Jesus freak, are you?"

"No Jesus freak fanatical stuff for me. And yeah, it had that epiphany quality, except the scenery was better and I wasn't in a life-crisis."

"Describe it."

"Well, I left my body."

"Damn! I knew it was possible. What was it like?"

"I left my body and entered into my infinite form and visa versa. "

"You mean vice versa. Wow, those mushrooms are fantastic. I say we forget the abstinence thing and drink more of Millie's tea before it goes bad."

"What I realized from the experience is that the reality of spiritual love, communing with the supernal infinite love that lives within our minds, puts us in touch with the essence of who we are. The mushrooms only brought to my attention that this reality lives inside each of us, and it is only the distractions of the world and our lack of paying attention to it that inhibits experiencing spiritual love. I want to learn how to access this love more consistently without using drugs."

"Oliver, if it takes drinking tea to bring about a mystical experience that enhances your well-being, then I say there is nothing wrong with that – it is either a chemically induced illusion or a heightened sense of reality – each of us determines what is real based on our experiences, I suppose. We talked about the Holy Eucharist many times before. You know, how communion is a ritual that millions of Christians participate in to 'cleanse de mind of de fear of Babylon'! There is no difference!"

"I'm not sure about that, Patrick. I think there is a difference, and we have talked about this before, too. One is a big-time psychoactive drug, and the other is a sip of wine and a piece of bread that is a symbolic rendezvous with Christ's Spirit. And for many people, it serves the same purpose as what I experienced last night."

"I doubt that it serves the same purpose, Ollie. I'll wager that none of those Christians experienced the heightened awareness and sensory stimulation that you did. From what you told me, and based on my experience, the so-called magic ingredient in mushrooms is not an illusion inducer, it elevates sensory perception to a degree that people are able to gain insight into the nature of reality that otherwise goes undetected – at least for most people. Maybe saints, shamans, gurus, and priests have experiences like that all the time and the rituals they use put the in a receptive state-of-mind."

"Wow - you have a good point, and it's consistent with the practice of many aboriginal people who use psychoactive drugs as a right-of-passage for their young people transitioning into adulthood." I was impressed with Patrick's comment as it indicated thoughtful contemplation of our discussions and experiences.

"You mean aboriginal as in Jamaican Rastas and their religious ritualistic use of ganja. Well then Ollie, perhaps you and I have made the journey over the developmental threshold into adulthood!" Patrick had a wide grin on his face, appearing proud of his insightful statement.

"Maybe! I do detect a glow of maturity on your face. I mean hell, anyone who stares death in the face as you have has got to be a little older, if not wiser," I teased. "However, I would wager that no Christians receiving the Holy Eucharist were enticed to go-with-the-flow, as you did, and drug themselves into near oblivion."

"Are you kidding? You're forgetting I was an altar boy, and I'm telling you, priest serve Mass almost drunk on their ass!"

"Hmm, valid point." I replied.

We were silent for a few moments. Patrick spoke first. "Like Harold suggested, you must have been in a different state-of-mind than I was at the time of drinking the tea. That's what moved you in a more spiritual direction. What if we drink the tea and treat it as a sacrament, you know, with the intention of communing with God?"

"I suppose that would be a healthy use of mushrooms, and we could test the notion that magic mushrooms enhances sensory perception into the domain of super physical or spiritual realities," I replied with slight hesitation.

"Ollie, I think your experience proved that notion – for you – but not for me, although I'm interested in further explorations."

"Hey, what about the Jesus freak group that used LSD as their sacrament?" I reminded Patrick.

"What about them?" he asked.

"Well, remember that they called themselves *Brothers and Sisters of the Holy Order of Light* and the central sacrament of their faith was taking LSD and baptizing in the ocean during what they called the Son Rise – and they were bare assed naked – I would say that was taking the use of psychedelic heightened sensory perception to the next level. And I recall that I stopped you from partaking."

"Partaking of what, Ollie, LSD or bare naked Jesus Freaks?"

"Both!"

"Well, I recall being in a special place. You know, a blissful summer with Chrissie and having just read that book, *Ocean of Love* – my head was in a far out place."

"I was skeptical of LSD, being a man-made chemical that we know little about. I think it is better to go organic, as in ganja and mushrooms."

"Now that I think about it, we could have had a communal sex spiritual orgy." Patrick mused.

"Screw that, man. I am a one-on-one kind a guy. Aren't you?" I asked.

"Definitely – I was just saying, Ollie."

"Only Jamaicans call me Ollie."

"Touchy – it's just a name – Oliver. Hey, do you recall telling me that if I went skinny dipping with those naked Jesus freak babes that I would be taking advantage of them? How the hell would have accepting an invitation to get naked with beautiful women, possibly having sex with them, and dropping LSD to boot, add up to taking advantage of them? I remember us having a very interesting discussion with the Jesus Freaks about spirituality. We concluded that the best thing to do was to respect their religion. You insisted that if we accepted their offer they would have considered us members of their cult and we knew we couldn't do that. You were very insistent about not wanting to hurt them." Patrick's summary of what took place was impressively accurate.

"Well, I think you would have most likely had a different perspective on the situation and would have dived right in if I wasn't with you. Maybe you could have had cosmic psychedelic sex. Bro, it might have been a missed opportunity for a life-altering experience, I mean based on what you told me about having sex with Norlina while tripping!" I was beginning to entertain the idea of psychedelic sex.

"It was a wonderful moving experience for Norlina and me, that's for sure."

"I may never know." I said a little wistfully.

"What - you are interested in sex with Norlina?"

"No, absolutely not. I mean the tripping sex thing."

"Well, there will be plenty of opportunity for psychedelic spiritual-sex in the future. You know, I have to question your attitude concerning the use of substances. You have been smoking ganja since Lord Joseph's cleansing ceremony and you did enjoy the mushroom tea. For reasons I do not understand, you do this mind game thing with drug use. I think you should accept the fact that you benefit from their use and that you are not an abuser and let go of this mind-screw thing you do."

"True dat! You're right, Patrick, I suppose. I have to admit that it is a mysterious phenomenon well worth further exploration. But we do need to rethink our consumption habits, as your debacle last night clearly indicates. I just want to exercise caution and make sure we aren't screwing up our minds and bodies. Don't forget, we did shake on being abstinent for a week." The more I verbalized the abstinence idea, the more I liked it.

"Perhaps I did walk over that threshold of maturity, Oliver. Okay, one week. After that, I'd like for us to consider taking mushrooms with the intention of having a religious experience. Maybe we can find some women and do the naked psychedelic baptism sex and sunrise thing. Who knows, perhaps we would enter into the Body of Christ, or even Rastafari or Jah or something like that. We might even start our own religion. Hey, we could go back to the Buccaneer Inn and try creating a religion with the Bunnies living in the Blue Parrot village. That would be a trip now wouldn't it? A psychedelic sex religion with an all Playboy Bunny congregation with you and I as priests with exclusive coitus privileges."

"There you go with your imagination fantasy factory again, Patrick."

"Well, Oliver, we do have a standing invitation for a place to stay expense free at the Buc. We could even find a fisherman who has an extra boat and set up an arrangement like we have with Elkannah. And, we could start our tourism thing near the Buc. Hell, if we talk to the DeSalva couple and Steve Tanz, we might make a deal with them to start bringing in clientele from the U.S. to stay at their hotel, starting with our Ghetto Flower friends. There are all kinds of possibilities."

"Whew! When you get that fantasy factory going there's no telling where you'll end up. Remember, it was your fantasy factory that got you in trouble last night because you didn't have me to help give it a reality check. We need to do this one step at a time. Abstinence first and then we consider creating a psychedelic sexual religious cult." The line about creating a cult was meant to be humorous, but I think a part of Patrick may actually be serious about the religion-sex idea – too much ganja on the brain.

"Hey, it was my fantasy factory that got his whole Jamaica adventure started in the first place, so don't knock it. What if we find willing female participants before the week is up, do we stick with abstinence?" Patrick asked.

"I doubt that will happen. The chances of finding Jamaican women who will drink mushroom tea and …"

"Yeah, you're right about that," Patrick interrupted. "I asked Norlina to drink Millie's mushroom tea. She refused. I tried getting her to smoke ganja without success."

"Ah, but she does like having sex with you."

"And how! That women is a sweet lover."

"Better than Jenny?"

"Hey, bro, you can't compare like that. Every woman is special."

"You've got that right. There is no comparison between Sandy and Penny. Different women, different circumstances, different hearts."

"Yeah, and different bodies. We have to admit that supermodel, playboy bunnies have bodies like goddesses – heavenly!"

"Amen to that, brother!" I said.

"Amen to Penny and Jenny, our goddesses. May we meet again!" added Patrick. It was interesting that during this part of our discussion, he mentioned his summer romance with Chrissie. I wondered if it was because his pain was gone, or that he had buried it so deep that it didn't penetrate his consciousness. Then it occurred to me that I rarely talked about Sandy. Hmm, maybe it's a guy thing to explore sexual pleasures and conveniently forget prior commitments. I shook off that thought as it created twinges of guilt, an emotion I had no interest indulging in, which supports the stereotype of guys being horn-dog jerks. Oh well, perhaps it is just the nature of the big bamboo. I wonder if women are much different. Do they justify so-called cheating on romantic partners?

We came upon the Post Office, which was about a mile past Fishermen Cove. It was very small. It cost thirty cents to mail each letter. As I was mailing the letters, the realization hit me that it was December 12th, Sandy's birthday – more guilt swelled up. Time had gone by quickly. Originally, I had planned on returning to South

Philly in early January and going back to school. I wrote in my letter to Sandy that I would have to let go of that plan. The thought occurred to me that I was going to be majoring in chemistry and that now I was being an experimental chemist in a real life laboratory with my mind and body serving as the test tube for psychoactive chemicals.

The idea of inviting our friends to Negril along with our ability to live here with very little expense meant that we were going to be living in Jamaica far longer than I had imagined. In fact, I had the sense that we could stay here indefinitely. I thought about what I did not tell Sandy in the letter. I was harboring guilt over my sexual relations with Penny. I had promised Sandy that I would be faithful. I decided not to tell her about Penny because that would break her heart. What good would it do for me to relieve my guilt at her expense? I had to suck it up, admit to myself that I made the choice to be with another woman, and if the opportunity would arise again, most likely I would do it again. Did this mean I had severed my relationship with Sandy? I certainly did not want to and still felt very connected to her, and I always will. Perhaps the solution to this dilemma would be for her to come to Jamaica.

"Patrick, do you think I did the right thing inviting Sandy to come?"

"Do you want her here?"

"Yeah. That would be perfect!"

"Would it?" he asked.

"Of course. She is my one true love."

"What's that got to do with it?" he asked.

"It would be perfect having her in paradise."

"What about experiencing other women? You know, this being the time to sow your wild oats before marrying Sandy notion of yours." Patrick repeated my own rationalization for infidelity.

"I suppose our time away is a good test for our relationship."

Patrick disagreed. "I am not sure the strength of your relationship needs testing. That happened when she was with that tall blond haired dude and she broke your heart. The strength of your love brought the two of you together again. When this adventure is over, you two will be together. I say enjoy the time you have and give yourself permission to experience other women. If the love you have with Sandy is indeed a love that is meant to last forever, than nothing you do here will hurt that. And, bro, you are not married to Sandy, and she may be involved with someone else, it happened before, and it happened to me." That was a rare admission on Patrick's part regarding Chrissie. I was impressed with his comments, leading me to think that he had learned a great deal from his heartbreak over Chrissie.

"Gee, that's insightful, or it could be just another rationalization for not being faithful," I responded.

"Well, it's up to you how you want to see it and deal with it. But you don't have to decide now." I liked Patrick's suggestion to postpone a definitive judgment on my sexual exploits. I was in a different world living a different life and it felt like the world in Philly and all of my relationships there existed in a separate universe – a very interesting feeling for sure.

"What about you and Chrissie?"

"Don't want to go there!" Patrick's tone of voice was eerie, almost threatening - definitely defensive. I knew better than to pry that subject open any further, if he wanted to talk about it more, he would have to be the one to initiate it.

"Hey, bro, it's December already! Can you believe it?" I said, changing the topic.

"Wow, time sure flies when you're having ..."

"Hey, look at that!" I pointed down the road.

"That's two white chicks surrounded by Jamaicans," said Patrick, "Let's check it out."

We immediately walked in their direction.

JAMIE & JULIE STARR
(Twin Explorations)

As we approached the young women we could see that the Jamaican horde surrounding them consisted of boys in their early teens. They were acting like a pack of hound dogs looking for bitches in heat. The women were walking hurriedly, as if by moving faster they would escape the boys. They were clearly frightened.

When they saw us approaching, one of them called out: "Guys, guys, can you help us, please?" When we got close enough to make out their features, we discovered that these young women were identical twin sisters. Patrick was the first to speak.

"Good afternoon ladies. It is a fine afternoon, don't you think?"

"We are looking for Millie and Charley. They are Jamaican and we are going to rent a place from them," said one of the women. "These boys never heard of them and they want to take us a place called Red Ground. Do you know Millie and Charley?"

"Yes, we know them. They're our friends and we live with them," I said.

One of the young Jamaicans spoke in response to my comment.
"We fin' dees girls at de Roundabout. We will tek care of dem. It is nuh yah business!" The boy who spoke was indeed a boy. I wanted to put him in his place. Patrick responded first.

"These women are looking for Millie and Charley. They found what they are looking for. Thank you for taking them this far!" Patrick can be very diplomatic, although it was not well received by the Jamaicans.

"Blood clatt, mon. Yah no interfere wit Jamaican business. Dees women are ours." I was about to set this dude straight when one of the women beat me to it.

The woman turned towards the boy and with her hands on her hips said with a forceful tone, "We are not your property and we are not business. Leave us alone or we will report you to the police!"

At first, the boy was startled and unsure how to respond. The other three boys laughed and hooted. They thought the woman's confrontation with their friend was comical. The boy did not receive this well. "Rass, woman, yah an abomination ta mankind. White women should nuh talk dis way. I am a man an' mus' 'ave respect!" Again, the boys laughed and hooted at their friend.

"And you are just a little boy who needs to learn his manners. You should go home to your mother. Maybe I should meet your parents and tell them how their son treats women," she was really pissed off.

"Me madda an' fadda nuh approve of yah. A white women who speaks ta men like so is corrupted!" he responded.

"I had enough of you and your group. Leave us! We have found what we're looking for. Be on your way!" She was a very feisty young lady!

The boy was angered by her tone and being ridiculed in front of his friends was more than he could bear. He stepped closer to her and raised his hand ready to strike her. I stepped in between them and stared the boy in the eyes. I was taken over by my protective nature.

The boy stood frozen with his open hand raised in the air. Everyone was silent. The boy looked very nervous, even frightened. I had indeed grown muscular from several weeks of living a native lifestyle, and my six feet frame towered over this young boy who was no more than five and a half feet tall. He was visibly afraid of me. I, on the other hand, was seriously pissed off and had lost all tolerance. Anger was streaming out of my eyes. The boy said, "I nuh afraid of yah grey eyes!

"Leave!" was all I said.

"Blood clatt, mon. It wrong fer yah ta interfere wit Jamaicans, mon." His voice was shaking as he spoke, and he lowered his arm.

"You are interfering with the business of Millie and Charley. These girls are their guests. We protect the interest of our Jamaican friends," I said sternly.

"Come Isaac. We 'ad our fun, mon. Dees girls are better wit dees white people. Dey nuh worth de trouble, mon. Dey wit der own kind an' feel safe wit dem. Let dem be."

I kept my eyes focused like laser beams on the boy's eyes, communicating to him that if he were to try and do anything, he was going to have to deal with me. I knew from past experiences in similar aggressive confrontations with rival gang members in my neighborhood that this was a crucial moment. The small window of time when two animals are giving each other the aggression vibe, and one backs down, or a fight erupts. I had fought my way through many attacks from rival gangs and knew how to disable adversaries quickly when necessary without self-injury. I was once a South

Philly street fighting boy. Although, my spiritual epiphany and the newly adopted hippie counter-culture values of peace and love called into question my ability to follow through with physical violence. Fortunately, the boy looked relieved that his friend gave him a way out of this dilemma.

"Yeahmon. Dees girls nuh worth de trouble!" He spat on the ground at my feet, which I ignored. I knew that once his eyes escaped my grip and looked toward the ground, the confrontation was over. "We go now. Tek dees women, mon an' gawaan 'bout yah business. Dey whores of Babylon anyway."

I ignored his comment and fortunately the women remained silent. The group of boys walked away.

I turned toward the woman and asked, "Are you okay?" To my surprise she threw her arms around me and squeezed me tight. I lightly placed one arm around her petite body and said, "It's okay, it's over, and you're safe now."

She spoke softly in my ear, "Thank you. I was so scared." As I stood there being hugged by this woman, Patrick took the hand of her sister and asked if she was all right. She immediately began sobbing. Patrick gently placed his arm around her shoulder. She collapsed. Patrick was able to protect her from falling to the ground. She had fainted.

We sat in the cool shade of palm trees as the woman who had fainted regained consciousness. The experience of traveling from the Montego Bay airport to Negril and being accosted by young Jamaicans was too much for her to handle. She was also dehydrated and she physically recovered after we gave her water and some juice to drink.

The girl who had not fainted explained their circumstances. "We are so grateful that you came along when you did. I was afraid that those boys were going to try and rape us. They would not take no for an answer. They wanted money and were determined for us to stay with them in some place called Red Ground. They are horrible boys. We were harassed at the airport too. There were lots of people wanting to take us to Negril, mostly in junky looking cars. Luckily, a nice young Jamaican offered us a fair price and drove us to Negril. He dropped us off at the Roundabout. We asked him to stay with us until we found Millie and Charley but he had pressing business in Montego Bay. Then, those nasty boys approached us." Her eyes began welling up with tears.

"Well, you are safe now. My name is Oliver and this is my friend Patrick. You were never in real danger. Those boys would not have hurt you. Yes, they were pushy, but ultimately, I believe they would have left you alone."

"That is doubtful. One even touched me on the ass and I almost smacked him. That happened just as I spotted the two of you or I would have hit him. There is no telling what would have happened, had you not ..." she looked away as she struggled to hold back tears.

"What are your names?" I asked.

"Oh, sorry. I'm Jamie Starr and this is my sister Julie Starr."

"Pleased to meet you. Where are you from?" Patrick asked.

"Bloomington, Indiana."

"Wow, I don't even know where Indiana is. All I know is it somewhere out west," I said.

"It's in the Midwest. Bloomington is the city for the main campus of Indiana University. Students from all over the world go there. It is famous for its school of music. Bloomington is a cultural oasis in the Midwest." Jamie's voice became calmer as she spoke of her hometown.

"What brings you two to Jamaica?" Patrick asked, looking at Julie as he spoke.

"We have a cousin who came here a year ago. He had a great time. He stayed with a Jamaican couple, Millie and Charley. I'm glad you know them," said Julie.

"Yes, they are very friendly people. We are fortunate to be camping on their land," Patrick replied.

"Our cousin told us they have a room for rent," added Jamie.

"They used to, but now they have two grandchildren living with them," responded Patrick.

"Oh. Where will we stay?" said Julie in a nervous voice.

"Well, for the time being you are in luck because the family went to Kingston for a week or so and left us in charge of their property. You can stay in the grandchildren's shanty until they return," I offered.

"Thank you so much. Are there other places we can stay when they return?" Jamie asked.

"Something will work out. We'll help you. There is no need to worry. Consider it as part of your adventure in paradise," said Patrick, "we are quite good at finding ways to live in Negril. Hey, would you like to visit a sea cave we used to live in?"

"Wow, a sea cave. That would be great," replied Jamie.

"I would rather get settled before we do any exploring. I am exhausted. It's been a very long day. I need to rest," said Julie. She impressed me as the more fragile of the two. We agreed to take them directly to the shanty.

Jamie and Julie liked the room. They had to keep their belongings in their backpacks since Norlina's clothes were in one dresser, and Elijah kept his things in one of the drawers. I told them they would be welcome to use our tent if we didn't find a suitable place for them by the time the Constance family returned.

It was past mid-afternoon. The air was hot and humid. The four of us were hanging out on the porch. Julie asked, "So, is it easy to get ganja in Negril?"

"It's as plentiful as sunshine," replied Patrick.

"Can you help me get some?" Julie asked.

"Sure thing. We can share with you what we have. Come on, let's go over to the cliffs where there's a breeze. I'll stop at our camp on the way out and pick up some ganja. Would you prefer to smoke a spliff, use a bong, or a regular pipe?" Patrick asked.

"My uncle told me about spliffs. I'd love to try it!" Exclaimed Julie.

I followed Patrick in the tent because I felt a need to talk. Once inside the tent I started our discussion. "Patrick, what about our agreement to not do drugs for a week?"

"Hey bro, that was right before Jamie and Julie came along. Remember, I asked you if the deal was on if we met women just as you spotted the twins, and you never answered. We have to go with the flow. The universe dropped these babes in our lap and they're into getting high. This is an amazing opportunity."

"Yes it is. I am excited about it too, I have to admit."

"Hey bro, maybe we can do some of that mushroom tea stored in Millie's icebox. We can do a spiritual psychedelic sex ceremony with these chicks."

"Bro, your mind is amazing. Okay, so you're gonna postpone doing the cleaning out thing. I suggest you stay away from the mushrooms for now, though." I had a gnawing feeling concerning the need to keep my head clear. Maybe it was a spiritual prompting going on in me but I wasn't sure. I intended to follow through on not doing drugs. There were more things I had to talk with Patrick about.

"Patrick, what about Norlina?" I asked.

"What about her?"

"Jamie and Julie are really cute and very sexy. They are our age and they're here to have a good time. We are the good guys who rescued them from danger and now we have the potential of becoming their tour guides in the art of pleasures in paradise."

"Far out perspective, Oliver. I like it. Tour guides in the art of pleasures in paradise! Wow! That's a nice phrase. We could start a franchise based on that concept."

"Slow down Mr. Fantasy. What about Norlina? She is very sweet on you and if you break her heart there are all kinds of potential consequences."

"Hmm. Good point. I'm sweet on Norlina too and I don't want to mess that up. Ya know, living in Negril is like being a kid who is in an all you can eat buffet candy store," said Patrick.

"Yeah, and I don't want us to get belly aches that we won't be able to cure."

"Okay, so I need you to make sure I don't succumb to the Sirens of Bloomington. I can have a good time with them without indulging in carnal delights. Looks like you're gonna have to be the body surfing instructor for the twins. Hey, that's another mind blowing circumstance," Patrick pointed out.

"What circumstance?" I asked.

"You and I have, or I should say had, relationships with the Caimi twins, Sandy and Chrissie, and now these twin beauty girls show up just as we were talking about the unlikely possibility of finding girls to get high with. What the hell? Is this a cosmic conspiracy or what?"

"Bro, you're right, that's quite a coincidence. Serendipitous in fact, there's been a lot of that happening lately."

"Maybe were in the Twilight Zone. Do, do, do, do …" We busted out laughing. "Hey, we have to get going. Can you gather some banana leaves, Oliver?"

"Will do!"

When I stepped out of the tent, the girls were swinging in the hammocks with sly smiles on their faces, which struck me as peculiar. I walked over to a banana tree where some leaves had fallen and picked up a few that were still green. We headed down the stone path, crossed the road and walked onto the cliffs.

"Wow! This is spectacular," said Jamie as she let out a whistle, "look Jules, there are steps that go down to the water. Let's go for a swim."

"I want to smoke a spliff first with our pleasure tour guides." Julie looked both of us in the eyes as she spoke. She was obviously amused. Of course they could hear us talking in the tent. We were really stupid. We were whispering, but not low enough.

"You're right Jules. It would be your first lesson in the art of pleasures in paradise from these two handsome, knowledgeable and oh so generous pleasure giving guys." I felt embarrassed, and Patrick was blushing.

"So you overheard our conversation," I said.

"Well, canvas walls don't filter sound very well. I think you guys are too accustomed to being alone. Patrick, tell us about Norlina." Jamie was very direct. She struck me as someone who is used to getting what she wants.

"Norlina Evans. As you already know, is the granddaughter of Millie and Charley. She and I have a thing going on." It was interesting to hear Patrick speak as though he was responding to an inquiry from his mother.

"Busted!" said Julie.

"Busted? I have no reason to hide my relationship with Norlina," said Patrick.

"It's too late for that," replied Julie.

"Alright, enough of this. Look, you heard our conversation. We're guys, you're girls, and the possibility of things happening in this setting is high. I just wanted to caution Patrick not to hurt anyone unintentionally," I explained.

"Understood," said Jamie, "and what's this drug abstinence thing about?" Julie asked.

"Well, we've been in Jamaica for seven weeks and a day hasn't gone by where we weren't high. We took mushrooms and Patrick went a little too far by mixing in a cocktail of other drugs. So, I suggested we take a break for a week to clear our heads."

"Hey, guys, you're in Jamaica. I can understand practicing moderation. Abstinence? That's down right cruel in a land of good 'n' plenty." Julie made a compelling point.

"I have other reasons to practice abstinence," I said.

"Like what?" Jamie asked.

"Spiritual. It's not easy to explain," I replied.

"Things of a spiritual nature are deeply personal and need no explanation. You don't have to smoke ganja with my sister because we are cute, sexy, and the Sirens of Bloomington." Again, Jamie's comment made me feel embarrassed that she heard everything we said.

"Hey, ladies, that was a compliment," said Patrick with a big grin.

Julie was eager to smoke ganja. "Well, I want to smoke a spliff. The air has been cleared, so-to-speak, and it will make it easier hanging out with you guys, you know, it takes away the uncomfortable tension, and we can be guided in island pleasures with our eyes wide open."

Patrick demonstrated how to roll a spliff. Julie did an expert job rolling her own. Jamie didn't roll one and I decided not to roll one, although I was wavering a little about keeping my mind free of the influence of chemicals. Patrick and Julie lit their spliffs.

While the two of them were enjoying the ganja, Jamie talked about their hometown, Bloomington, Indiana. "Bloomington is an awesome town. There are more hippies in Bloomington than in all of Indiana. There are lots of talented musicians and artists. Even though our parents are old, they are very hip. They're friends with the Dali Lama's brother, Thubten Norbu, who is a professor of Tibetan studies at Indiana University. The Dali Lama visits Bloomington once a year to spend time with his brother. Norbu has dinner at our house quite regularly, and the Dali Lama ate dinner with us on two occasions. Our parents are Buddhist and we follow some of the religious practices." Jamie's mention of Buddhism and particularly the Dali Lama aroused my interest. I knew very little about that religion and was ripe for learning. I knew a little bit about the Dali Lama. "Our parents are professors of religious studies at the university. We grew up listening to discussions about religion at the dinner table among our parents' friends and students."

"Wow. Were your parents always Buddhist?" I asked.

"No. They both have doctorate degrees in divinity from the Princeton Theological Seminary. They know the Bible inside out. Their education process and spiritual journey led them to Buddhism," replied Jamie.

I was fascinated by what I was hearing. These girls were our age, their parents are very well educated, and they are obviously very smart and adventurous. I wondered why they weren't in college.

"How come you girls aren't in college?" I asked

"We graduated high school last June and our parents encouraged us to take a year to travel before going to college," replied Jamie.

"Wow. That's really far out. Where else have you traveled?" Patrick asked.

"We've been all over Europe," replied Jamie.

"Hey, I have to get in that turquoise water. Anyone want to join me?" Julie asked.

"Definitely. Let's go!" Jamie stood up as she spoke. She looked around and said, "I don't see anyone around, do you think it would be alright to skinny dip?" she asked looking directly at me for an answer.

I, too, scanned the environs and noticed no one was in sight – there usually wasn't. "I suggest you leave your clothes by the base of the steps closer to the water in case people do come around. Although, I doubt we will have company but you never know."

"That works for me. You guys want to join us?" Jamie asked.

"Sure!" said Patrick a little to eagerly. I, too, felt a need to cool off and stretch my body.

The girls stripped off their clothes before diving in, and so did Patrick. I kept my cutoff jeans on.

It was nice swimming around with these girls. They were very playful and thrilled by the experience of swimming off the cliffs. Julie said this was their first time swimming in the Caribbean, saying that they swam in the Mediterranean off the coast of Portugal, Spain, Italy, and Greece. These girls were definitely world travelers and no strangers to exotic experiences.

I could not tell the girls apart from one another. They were identical in every way, including the sound of their voices, breast size, pubic hair, and even a cute mole they each had on their inner thighs. We did not know their personalities well enough to make a distinction. They were very pretty and exceptionally sexy. Their bodies were petite in every way, including breasts, hips, and overall height and weight. They had brown eyes and auburn curly short hair that reached the base of their necks. They had remarkably cute facial features with perfect noses, lips that were not too thin or big, high cheek bones, and dark chocolate eyes that were sweet and perpetually smiling. These twins knew they were attractive and we soon discovered that they enjoyed using their beauty to tease boys.

I swam into a cave and one of the girls followed me. She called my name. I turned and saw her pull herself onto a ledge, stand up and strike a pose that said, 'look at my beautiful body.'

"Oliver, come join me on the ledge," she requested. I swam to the ledge and stood beside her. "Are you uncomfortable skinny dipping?" she asked.

"Sometimes."

"And sometimes includes the present moment I see."

"I guess so."

"Why?"

"We just met you and your sister and I did not want to appear presumptuous."

"We're the ones who decided to swim naked. So why would you think you would be presumptuous?"

"I don't really know."

"Oliver, I think you are modest. Look, if we wanted to have sex then we'd have sex. If we enjoy each other that way then that would be terrific. If not, it's no big deal. Haven't you heard of free love?"

Wow! Did she really say that? "Yes. Of course, it's what the sexual revolution is all about. It's a hippie thing."

"And it is a women liberation thing. Don't you think it is about time that women take control of their sexuality and enjoy it as much as men?"

"That's only fair."

"Then, you don't think that me being free with my body and swimming naked with guys that I just met is being too forward, or should I say, slutty?"

"Not at all. It is completely natural and beautiful," I replied, and I honestly believed that.

"Good. I like the idea of being friends, and who knows maybe it can become more than that," she said suggestively.

"Maybe." I said somewhat mutedly.

"Do you have something going on with another woman?"

"Not in Jamaica, but I love Sandy, my girl in Philly."

"Is she pretty?"

"Who?"

"Sandy." I was feeling uncomfortable talking with a beautiful naked woman about my sweetheart.

"She is gorgeous, smart, and we are very close."

"Ah, you are fortunate. Why is she not with you in Jamaica?"

"She's in college. I wanted her to come but it wasn't the right time for her."

"It must be difficult being apart from her."

"Yes. I miss her."

"Well, I guess it is best to assume that you and I can be good friends and you do not have to worry. Now that we settled that, we can relax and have fun."

"What do you mean by fun?" I asked. I couldn't keep my eyes from looking at her breast. They were small and round and firm and her nipples were pink and pointy.

"Like I already said, we could have sex or not have sex. Free love, you know, no strings attached. Just enjoying the beauty of sexual intimacy without expectations. In other words, we won't try to make claims on each other as if having sex meant that we own each other."

I had never heard a woman speak like this. Penny was very free with her body and enjoyed sex with no strings attached, but there was another dimension to what she was saying – a new way of having friendship with the opposite sex that included having sex without commitment. I was aroused and felt a strong urge to have sex right there and then, but I also felt twinges of guilt having just talked about Sandy. It dawned on me that I did not know which of the twin sisters I was speaking with. I had assumed it was Jamie, but I honestly did not know.

"Jamie?"

"Yes."

"You are Jamie, aren't you?'

"Yes."

"You wouldn't trick me would you?"

"Yes."

"Come on, are you Jamie or Julie?"

"Does it matter?"

"Of course it matters."

"Kiss me."

"What?"

"You're not deaf. Kiss me!" She did not wait for me to comply. She moved her body closer to mine, pressed her pointy breast against my chest and kissed me softly. "Now, when and if you ever kiss my sister, then you will know how to tell us apart."

"How's that?'

"Do you not have a feeling rushing through your body? I mean the change in the shape of your cut-off jeans clearly indicates that you do."

"Yes." I felt embarrassed.

"Describe the feeling!"

"Well, I feel a golden glow throughout my body and I saw you in my mind illuminated in light."

"Wow, that's very beautiful. Gee, no one has ever described kissing me so eloquently. Well, if my sister Jules kisses you, the feeling will be different. Every person has their own distinct sexual-personality-energy that they transmit whenever they kiss and make love. Now you know what mine feels like, and maybe you will get to know what Jules' feels like."

She was right. Every woman I ever kissed felt distinctly different from all the rest. Sandy was different from Ellen, and Penny was definitely uniquely Penny, and Jamie was, well, a golden glow of illumination – and the ambience of kissing in a Caribbean Sea cave certainly gave the feeling an additional unique quality. I wondered what my sexual-personality-energy felt like to women and if each woman would describe it similarly.

"How would you describe what kissing me feels like?" I asked.

"Like swimming in a refreshingly cool sea cave on a hot summer day. Or standing under a lovely waterfall with cool water cascading over me."

"Wow. Thank you."

"You're most welcome. Hey, do you know what your name means?'

"Oliver means peace."

"Yes it does. You do feel like a peaceful spirit, you know." She replied.

"Thanks."

"What's your last name?" she asked.

"James."

"Far out! That is totally awesome. My first name is the same as your last name. That is so cool, serendipitous in fact." Jamie's eyes were lit up with a look of fascination.

"That is pretty cool. It would be weird though if we were to marry," I replied, feeling stupid as soon as the words left my mouth.

"Marriage, why Oliver James, I hardly know you and here you are proposing." Jamie laughed, "Just kidding. I know what you mean, Jamie James – kinda has a nice ring – even though it is redundant, it has the female-male name gender combo. Very cool. You know Oliver, you really do have a sense of peace about you!"

"You're very nice to me."

"Why shouldn't I be, Oliver James?"

"I bet you treated all the guys you met in Europe the same way."

"Well, I did have my share of handsome men, but none of them could claim to be a free peaceful spirit like you, and you are the first to share my name."

"Flattery will get you everywhere."

"Everywhere? Is that an invitation?" Jamie had a sheepish, enticing look in her eyes.

"Ah, it's just a standard reply I give when someone compliments me."

"Oh. That's a slight disappointment. My, oh my, Oliver James, you are blushing!"

"I didn't mean it like that." I was feeling embarrassed for being so suggestive.

"So, it was an invitation. And I think you did, as you say, *mean it like that*, and I am open to your invitation." I felt as though Jamie was toying with me like a cat plays with a mouse – and I liked it. "I like the idea of being good friends and if ..." Julie and Patrick came swimming into the cave. Julie shouted Jamie's name, confirming that she was indeed Jamie.

As Patrick and Julie swam to us, Jamie said, "We'll continue this conversation later. I do take the 'if' as openness to explore on your part. I am certainly open to you swimming in my sea cave, and taking body surfing lessons from you," she laughed. Again, I felt embarrassed that she overheard the tent conversation, as she made reference to body surfing. What she said about me feeling like a waterfall caused me to remember Penny's description the first time we made love. She said she had a waterfall orgasm. Maybe there's substance to Jamie's assertion that each person has a distinct sexual-personality-energy. A woman's comment on a man's sexuality is amazingly powerful.

Patrick and Julie swam up to the ledge and got out. It was quite a site seeing the two of them emerge from the sea completely naked. They were both glowing. Jamie noticed it too and said as much, "You two have that special glow, as in ..." Julie interrupted, "Yep, Patrick is one hell of a pleasure tour guide." She gazed lovingly into his eyes. Patrick started to blush and immediately dove in the sea to avoid embarrassment. Jamie and Julie laughed. It was funny, but my concern over Norlina and the possible consequences prevented me from laughing.

Julie had picked up on my discomfort. "Don't worry, Oliver, Patrick and I have talked about Norlina. The four of us have to keep a secret, that's all. I understand that Norlina most likely would not understand nor go along with free-love female liberation. Patrick and I will end our pleasure tour when Norlina returns."

"Wow. Do you think you can turn it off like a light switch?" My question was a warning.

"Good point. I know I can. I have experience with this kind of thing. This is an area where I can be the tour guide for Patrick."

"What if you fall in love?" I asked.

"If that happens then so be it? Who are we to think that we can dictate the ways of love? If Norlina and Patrick have the kind of love that results in a commitment, then that will be great. I do not expect that to happen to me, but if it does, well, Que Sera, Sera, as the saying goes."

"Wow, you girls really are free spirits," I said.

"You can say that again," Patrick shouted as he came out of the water.

"See, Oliver, there is no need to worry. We live in a more enlightened age of relationships. The old rules and sexual taboos are crumbling. You can fully become what your name says you are," said Jamie.

"What's that about his name?" Julie asked.

"Jules, I introduce to you, Free Peaceful Spirit."

"Is that what you call yourself?" Julie asked in a tone of amusement.

"No. It appears that Jamie decided that's my real name."

"Yeah, and I am guessing that you two …"

"You guess wrong sister," interrupted Jamie, "we are not carnally acquainted."

"Well, you mean to say not yet." The girls laughed and then dove in the sea along with Patrick and the three of them proceeded to swim around the cave.

I remained on the ledge thinking about the conversation I had with Jamie. Her intelligence and open-minded thinking enthralled me. She seemed far more mature than her age, which I assumed was eighteen, since she graduated from high school last spring. The concept of free love was not unfamiliar to me, although this was the first time I discussed it with a woman so openly. I read a magazine article that explained free love as being part of the counter-culture movement and the burgeoning sexual revolution. It had not been a part of my teen peer group experience. It raised questions for me about morality and relationship ethics. Was it possible for people to share their sexuality with each other as part of friendship and not exclusively in a more serious relationship? The recreational sex experience I had with Penny didn't even involve friendship, since we didn't know each other long enough to establish a friendship. Then again, Patrick and Julie, apparently, just had sex and there's no way a friendship developed in such a short period, or did it? Then again, maybe having sex was simply a part of the process of creating a friendship. Man, this was opening up a new way of thinking about relationships of all varieties, that's for sure. The cultural relationship boundaries, definitions, taboos, values, whatever, were being challenged by the concept of free love.

The three of them were swimming towards the cave opening. I dove in and caught up with them. We swam to the steps. The girls got out first. I enjoyed seeing their wet, sexy bodies glistening in the multi-colored rays of the soon to set sun. They stood on the landing at the base of the steps looking out towards the horizon. I noticed water drops dripping from Jamie's nipples and became aroused. The sunlight brought out the red color in her pubic hair. Her eyes caught my eyes and she smiled, fully aware that I was feasting upon her beauty. She turned and bent over to pick up her clothing, giving me a full view of her lusciousness. The idea of free love was gaining quick acceptance in my mind. I wanted her! She ascended the steps slowly, stretching the muscles in her legs and moving her hips from side to side with each stride. She stopped and looked over her shoulder to let me know that she knew that I was watching. I had to have her! I knew that she knew what I was thinking. I knew she was thinking the same thing.

"I love sunsets," sighed Julie, "it is a perfect time to meditate."

"Yes, and during sun rise too," added Jamie. "I'll bet the stars are amazing at night."

"They are quite beautiful. There are no street lights to obscure them," I added.

"After the sunset, let's make dinner and after eating, come back to the cliffs for star gazing," suggested Patrick. We all agreed that it was a good idea. After the sunset, we made dinner at our campsite. It was the usual for Patrick and me: fish, conch, rice, ackee, and breadfruit, with a variety of spices. For the girls it was a treat in Jamaican cuisine – Philly boy style that is.

We brought our instruments with us to the cliff and played music. The girls' voices were lovely. They were hip to rock and roll music and knew the lyrics to most of the songs we played. When we improvised, the girls joined in with their voices, making sounds without words that were in key with our instruments. The girls informed us that they grew up singing in a choir, and that they were official members of the Indiana University School of Music Choir.

At one point during a brief pause in our music playing, Jamie said, "The magical thing about playing music with people is it brings everyone closer to each other. It's no wonder that all cultures going back to the dawn of time had some form of music as part of their tribal gatherings. Music stirs the collective soul and creates feelings of oneness among many."

What she said was consistent with what we were experiencing. As we made music, I felt a feeling of group intimacy. I thought of how wonderful it would be for us to drink mushroom tea together and play music, and make love. I did not mention this thought to Patrick. Just expressing the idea to him would be all it would take to make it happen, and I was still feeling an inner stirring to spend time chemical-free. Again, I wasn't completely sure why I was listening to this feeling. It just felt like it was something I had to do. Patrick and Julie had rolled spliffs and were smoking them. I was tempted to join them, but the sweet smell of the ganja was enough to satisfy my urges. I realized that Jamie never smoked the spliffs, not during the afternoon or this evening. I asked her why she wasn't smoking ganja. "I have no interest in taking drugs. I used to, and enjoyed them as much as Jules does, maybe even more so. It is best for my well being that I refrain from use. I have nothing against recreational use and use for healing and spiritual awareness. It's simply best that I not indulge."

"Wow! That makes me feel better about my decision to abstain for a while," I replied, "and you understand."

"Certainly." she replied.

After we stopped playing music and the spliffs were used up, Patrick and Julie went to the campground, leaving Jamie and me alone on the cliff.

"The air feels nice," she said as she took in a deep breath. She continued breathing deeply, slowly, and rhythmically. She shifted her body into what I recognized as the classic meditation position that I've seen in pictures. It was apparent that she was concentrating. I decided to try and emulate her. I could not get my body in that position – I lacked the flexibility, so I just sat comfortably and took deep breaths. Unlike Jamie, I kept my eyes open. In a short period of time, my breathing became in sync with hers, which caused a curious feeling of intimacy between us. This experience reminded me of the time I was in Lord Joseph's cave when he had instructed me to take deep breaths, and like that time, I felt as though my breathing and heart pace were harmonizing with the sound of the sea and wind.

Jamie opened her eyes. She looked straight ahead, continuing to breathe in the same manner. After awhile she spoke, "It is peaceful sitting here with you, meditating. Thank you for joining me. Did you feel our spirits touch?" she asked.

"I felt a closeness with you while we were doing the breathing exercise."

"Yes, that's what I mean. I call it spirit touching. It is what most people are trying to do through sex, although most people don't know that is what they are reaching for - and need."

"I understand. It is a feeling of oneness that we all need and there are those of us who are conscious of this need and those who are not," I replied.

"Yes, yes, how wonderful, Oliver, that you know this. Have you ever had a feeling of oneness with all of humanity, all of creation?"

I was astounded by her question. This oneness I experienced while tripping on mushrooms was exactly what she is talking about. "Yes, I have."

"You know, I sensed that about you, Oliver. There is a certain look in your eyes that suggest you have seen or felt something very special. I don't know if others recognize this. I think that in order to see it in others you must first experience it within yourself."

"I guess that means you experience God's Love." I shocked myself by saying that. There are only a few people in my life that I openly speak to about my spiritual life, and here I was opening that part of myself to Jamie, so soon.

"I refer to it as universal love, and not a God in the sense of an intelligent personality being. I experience love for all humanity and I feel at one with all of life. My parents are what I call Buddhist Fundamentalist, meaning they do not believe in God. I think of their beliefs and practices as a philosophy of living rather than a religion."

"What do you think of religion and faith?" I asked.

"There is a relationship between what I believe, what I experience, what I practice, and what I think I know – or have discovered to be truth. My experiences stem from my practice. And my interpretation of my experiences are colored by my beliefs. I try to strip my mind of all beliefs so that I can keep the influences of my cultural socialization separate from the experience of pure knowledge, which I consider to be discovered truth. Although, I am not certain that purely removing one's self from cultural influences is possible. I do try."

I was stunned by her words. She was a real seeker of truth! She was pondering the same thoughts as me. And I told her so.

"You are a truth seeker." I exclaimed.

"Yes, I suppose I am."

"Meditation is your practice."

"Yes it is."

"Oneness with all creation, especially humanity, is your experience." I surmised.

"Yes, and that's what I mean by universal love."

"I think that in our very essence we are love," I said.

"Yes. And the fact that you are stating these truths indicates that we are of one mind, Oliver."

"Yes, we are, Jamie." And I felt something else. It was affection stirring in my heart for her.

"Jamie."

"Yes, Oliver."

"I feel close to you."

"I know."

"How?"

"I feel it too."

"What is this feeling? How can it be?"

"You just said it – our essence is love and we are open to feeling that at this moment. It comes from what my parents call the Infinite It Is. We opened ourselves to this reality by meditating together. We are embracing oneness, which is universal love."

"Yes, yes, and something more. I feel it not only with you, I feel it for you." She turned her head and looked at me. Her eyes were radiant. Suddenly, I felt embraced by that similar feeling I had while tripping on mushrooms, the feeling of divine love. I told her.

"Jamie, looking into your eyes I feel that same love. It is beautiful and beyond human emotion."

"Yes, Oliver. I feel it too, although I do not characterize it as divine love. I know it as universal love being manifested and personalized through, and by, our mutual experience – spirit touching, or personality embracing. May I be so bold as to call it Our Love?"

A beautiful feeling gently pulsed through me! It was a soft, soothing emotion with a healing quality. Jamie is a woman of beauty, a woman who knows and experiences the ultimate realities of goodness and truth.

Jamie's eyes were moist and glistening. I put my arms around her and softly kissed the salty tears that were resting upon her cheeks.

"You are beautiful, Jamie," I whispered.

"Thank you, Oliver. I have had a deep yearning ever since I was a child to share this most intimate part of what I know to be the essence of who I am. You are touching my spirit, Oliver. No one has ever …"

I kissed her. It was a gentle kiss, not one of ecstatic sexual passion but one of purity that went beyond the flesh. We moved our bodies into a horizontal position while our lips continued touching. Then an amazing thing happened. I could not tell the difference between my body and her body, my mind and thoughts and her mind and thoughts, my soul and her soul felt as if we had merged into one being. I did not need to ask her if she was experiencing the same thing because I knew, for I was she and she was I. I n I as the Rastafarians say. I n I one with each other, one with all creation. We were not only *in* love we were within love – we had risin in love.

Throughout the evening under the canopy of stars – our newly discovered universe of love - we shared an orgasmic passionate love embrace of our sexual-spiritual-personality beings – we became One Love.

The next morning, Jamie woke me up with a kiss. I rolled on top of her and we continued our love embrace seamlessly from our rapturous night. After our waterfall orgasms, we reluctantly separated our bodies. I worried that once we let go of our embrace we would leave the new universe we had created – it was a foolish concern.

Patrick and Julie were already out of the tent and had a pot of coffee waiting for us.

"Good morning, Julie and Patrick," I said.

"Good morning," they said simultaneously. "Great night, huh!" said Patrick.

"Yes it was," said Jamie.

"What should we have for breakfast?" Patrick asked.

"Millie left us a couple of loaves of banana bread. They're in the icebox. I'll grab some mangoes and a pineapple, too." Jamie came with me to Millie's cooking shed.

"What's that grey-blue stuff in those jars?" she asked.

"Mushroom tea. Millie made it for us. Patrick and I tripped the other night. I had a spiritual experience. Patrick almost died."

"Died. How?" I told a very shortened version of Patrick's ordeal.

"Wow. Now I understand why you want to abstain from using chemicals."

"That's only part of the reason. The mushroom tea was a catalyst for my spiritual experience. I want to feel that heightened sense of super reality without the use of chemicals – like I did with you last night."

"And I still feel it this morning," responded Jamie.

"Yes. I do too. Of course you already knew that."

"I do. One Love!" she replied.

"Irie! One Love!" I said, and we kissed.

"So now that you know that your spiritual experience was real and not a hallucinogenic illusion, are you willing to ingest mushrooms?" Jamie asked.

"Maybe. But I'm not sure what the purpose would be."

"Fun, recreational chemical use to enhance your senses and receptivity to realms of a cosmic nature – you know, to alter your state of consciousness."

"I suppose I am interested in enhancing spiritual awareness, insight into reality – more so than simply getting high. Actually, love is the highest high."

"That it is and we are living proof of that." Jamie kissed me again.

"What about you?"

"What about me, what?" Jamie asked.

"Are you willing to take mushrooms?"

"No."

"Why not?" I asked, feeling curious.

"It is not for me, Oliver. If you want to take them I would love to be with you, and meditate, swim, talk, and make love, whatever, while you are tripping."

"Don't you think it would be fun to do it together? Imagine utilizing the hallucinogenic qualities of the mushrooms while meditating and making love. It could be awesome." I was excited by the possibilities.

"Would it make our experience of One Love any more real than it is?" she asked.

"I suppose not, but it could make it more colorful – as you just said, heighten the senses."

"Perhaps, Oliver. I prefer to enhance the experience of super reality through purely spiritual practice and our shared intimacy without ingesting chemical substances. They can be fun and maybe even enhance the experience in fun ways, but what is true is true, and what is real is real, and no chemical can alter that. No, Oliver, it is best that I put nothing in my body. I know that I have a better chance of living longer if I do not."

"That's interesting. So you think chemicals age the mind and body."

"Maybe they do and maybe they don't. It's known that some chemicals can help people to live longer. I just know that I am better without them. Please, Oliver, feel free to do as you desire."

"I respect your position and admire it. I want to join you in your spiritual practice. Will you teach me?" I asked.

"On one condition."

"What's that?"

"That you continue to be my tour guide in the art of pleasure."

"The pleasure is all mine."

"No, the pleasure is all ours!" she responded. We laughed, hugged and kissed.

"Jamie, I discovered that people can have sex as a part of becoming friends. And, based on my experience with you, find a soul mate in an instant of time. Wow, it is really amazing that we became so close so quickly."

"Yes it is. In the realm of soul mate experiences, I was a virgin until I met you, Oliver. Yep! Friendship and Love – that's my religion," replied Jamie.

"Amen, sister!"

"A-woman, brother!"

"A-man, friend!"

"A-woman, lover!"

"A-woman, soul mate!"

"A-man, soul mate!"

"One Love!" We said simultaneously, causing us to laugh in delight and amazement at how in tune our minds were.

Patrick appeared in the shed doorway. "Soul mates! One Love! Gee, you two have become love birds in paradise rather quickly!"

"And you and Jules?" said Jamie rhetorically.

Patrick simply smiled in response. "Hey, bring a jar of mushroom tea. Julie wants to drink some. I told her I would too, but that I wanted to let you know, Oliver, before I do, since I pledged abstinence, then unpledged, and I know how concerned you are about me doing too many drugs."

"Gee, that's thoughtful of you. Patrick, I don't have a right to impose anything on you. I do have a suggestion though."

"What?"

"Stay with Julie the entire time and don't drink alcohol or ingest anything else other than ganja."

"Agreed, Brother Oliver! Mr. Free Peaceful Spirit!" Patrick laughed at his own comment. "Just kidding. Let's eat."

Patrick and I cooked red snapper, ackee and plantain with coconut and rice, along with a pot of coffee. After eating, Patrick played guitar and Julie added vocals to a song they co-wrote the night before. The lyrics were simple and the guitar chords were similar to the new reggae beat that was coming out of Kingston from a band called The Wailers. We heard some of their music at the Blue Parrot. The Jamaicans were excited about the new sound that was distinctly Jamaican. We hadn't heard much of their music, since we were living in a place where there was no electricity. Elijah had a battery-operated radio and we heard one song by The Wailers called Trench Town Rock. Patrick liked the beat and chords and adapted the style to the song he and Julie had written. They called their song, *Jamaican Nights.* Jamie and I cleaned up the breakfast dishes. I suggested to Patrick and Julie that they not drink the mushroom tea until the food had time to digest, informing them of the queasiness that occurs as the mushrooms start to take affect. So we hung around the campground, talking and playing a little music. I settled in the hammock and wrote in my journal. Jamie, to my delight, took out a sketchpad and did a line drawing of our campground that included the trees, hammocks, tent, and campfire, Patrick playing guitar, and Julie sitting by his side singing. The sketch was impressive.

"Well, my stomach feels quite settled. I think it's time to drink the tea. Are you ready, Julie?" Patrick asked.

"I'm ripe and ready!" she replied.

"Have you ever done psychedelic mushrooms?" I asked.

"Yes, I'm experienced. I know that you and Patrick are and the tea you have, I understand, was made by your friend Millie, so I assume it is safe," said Julie.

"Yes, the tea is safe, and it's quite nice. As long as you don't mix it with anything else." I warned.

"Yeah, Patrick told me about his almost fatal mistake. That won't happen today. I want my sister and you, Oliver, to remain with us the whole time."

"You got it," said Jamie.

"Absolutely!" I added.

Patrick divided the contents of the quart-sized jar into two large cups.

"Ready set go!" said Patrick as he and Julie gulped down the sweet-tasting grayish-blue liquid.

"Wow, that's very sweet, yet it still has a musty after-taste. The mushroom bits are especially distasteful. So, what do we do now?" Julie asked.

"We go for a walk as the tea makes its way into our system. The tea gets the respiratory system going, so it's good to move and breathe deeply. Once the queasiness passes, we can go for a swim," Patrick advised.

"Good idea. I say we take this opportunity to show the girls Lord Joseph's cave. It's just the right distance from here. By the time we get there your bodies should be adjusted. It will be perfect for a mid-morning swim," I suggested. Everyone agreed. I checked in on the donkey, took care of his needs, and grabbed bananas and mangoes and a few jars of water. And, at the last second, I decided to bring my flute, remembering how lovely it sounds in the cave.

The air still had that morning moist coolness – relatively cool, that is, for a tropical island, probably 76 degrees. The scent of flowers was strong. It felt good to get our legs moving. I could hear Patrick and Julie breathing deeply, a sign that the tea was taking affect.

"How's your stomach, Julie?" I asked.

"Just a little queasy but not bad."

"Yeah, mine too," said Patrick, "it'll pass soon, Julie, just breathe slow and deep."

"Yep, I have lots of practice with that as a part of meditating. I feel great. My body is tingling with a really pleasant sensation. This is nice!" Julie described the initial feeling when the mushrooms are ready to kick into full gear.

"I'm having the same feelings. Really, really, nice s-e-n-s-a-t-i-o-n-s ..." Patrick's voice trailed off.

"Wow! This is really far out. The colors of the plants and the sky are vibrant," Julie took in a deep breath and let it out slowly, "the flowers smell great. I have to see the sea! I've got to feel the water on my body!"

"We're almost at Lord Joseph's cave. You'll be in the water soon enough, Julie, and you're gonna love the cave." I said.

"Is the cave like the one at Millie and Charley's cliffs?" Jamie asked.

"Nicer! Bigger, and more colorful with lots of fossils, and smooth tiered ledges. You're gonna love it." Patrick spoke enthusiastically with a tone of reverence and mystery – the mushrooms were definitely stimulating their brains. "Hey, how come you aren't tripping with us, Jamie?"

"Oh, I like to think that I'm tripping on life each and every moment. I think it's cool that people can enhance the experience of beauty, within and without, by using a chemical. I am fine without it, though. See, I brought along my sketchpad to draw the cave. I have my colored pencils too, so I can capture the colorful vibrancy as my sister put it."

Every time Jamie spoke, I fell deeper in love with her. She was exactly where I was striving to be. She wanted to appreciate every moment to its fullest. I was discovering that she knew how to live in the here and now better than anyone I knew. I felt so fortunate to have met her at this time in my life. It was as if the angels knew exactly what I needed and they placed her directly in my path. I thought angels were real and sometimes they took on human form. Jamie, to me, was an earth angel. I was like a puppy in love. Whew, what a high!

Lord Joseph was not at home. Upon exploring the back of the cave, we discovered that his cache of ganja was gone. We assumed he was in the Blue Mountains with his family and Rasta friends. Jamie and Julie were enamored with the cave. They explored along the cave walls, noting the color variations and sea creature fossils. As they were exploring, I played flute music. The girls were impressed by the sound quality produced by the cavern walls, inspiring them to sing. We stayed in the cave throughout the hottest part of the afternoon, including the daily mid afternoon thunderstorm. The sound of thunder was amplified in the cave, and seeing the lightening flash over the sea from the wide cave entrance was a thrilling spectacle.

Jamie produced numerous sketches of the cave, including one with the thunderclouds hovering over the sea with lightening bolts flashing radiance across the sky. She proved herself a gifted artist, expertly reproducing the colors, shapes and fossils of the cavern walls, the predominately turquoise sea with its blue-green hues determined by water depth and undersea topography, and the ever changing sky from clear bright sunny to stormy and ominous.

Patrick and Julie were thoroughly enjoying their recreational mushroom pleasure ride. At one point they disappeared into the recesses of the cave and the sounds of love cries prompted Jamie and I to take a swim outside of the cave. We entered another cave several yards away that was very small but had a ledge that had accumulated a thick layer of sand. This cave accommodated our own production of love embraces. A few hours or so after the thunderstorm subsided we headed back to our campground. Jamie and Julie were excited by the possibility of taking up residence in the sea cave. I informed them that they would have to be purified of Babylon by Lord Joseph if they were to receive his permission to live there. The thought of living in the cave with the twins was exciting on many levels, but there were other things to consider.

When we returned, Julie asked if she could help take care of the donkey. He hadn't had exercise for a few days and it was when I mentioned this as a concern that she offered to take the donkey for a ride. I told her I wasn't aware of anyone ever riding the donkey, and that he may have only been used for transporting baskets of goods and not people.

"I've been riding ponies and horses all my life. I will be able to tell if the donkey is comfortable with me on his back or not," she said.

"What if the donkey kicks its feet up and throws you off? You will get hurt and the donkey could take off down the road and we may never catch it. That would be a disaster," I warned.

"Well, let's put on its bit and bridle and take him for a walk and go from there," she offered.

"Okay. But promise me you won't do anything daring. Are you still feeling the mushrooms?" I asked.

"Yes. I am still cruising on the shrooms. They are long lasting and quite pleasant. Not overwhelming like LSD," she replied.

"Whoa! You've taken LSD?" I asked sounding surprised and incredulous.

"Hey, it's all over Europe. It's part of the international hip scene. You haven't?" she asked.

"No. Well I think I may have. I drank some wine that may have been laced with it when I went to a rock concert, but there were so many other things going on at the same time that I am not certain." I replied.

"Man, if you took LSD, there would be no question in your mind – you would know if you had tripped or not. Acid is a super hallucinogenic, far more potent than mushrooms and a lot less manageable."

"I'll take your word for it. It makes no difference to me one way or another. Having listened to The Who perform Tommy was a transformational experience that was a milestone for my psychic journey. It's possible that it was a very low dose." I replied.

"Hmm. Maybe. I never took a low dose. I won't take it again – it gets me too far out there. I see no value in it for me. It felt wonderful at times, and generated amazing thoughts about life and the universe and all that, but it also produced a sense of psychosis, like artificially manufactured insanity," she added.

"What about you Jamie, have you ever tripped?"

"Yes," was all she said and I wanted to know more.

"I haven't seen you smoke ganja or drink alcohol. Is this new behavior?" I asked.

"I did my share of partying. I smoked pot, drank, and did an occasional acid trip now and then, but no longer. I learned that it is best for my health to put in my body only what I need and nothing more," she explained.

"Wow. That's cool. I was like that for a while until I came to Jamaica. A lot of teens and some older kids from my neighborhood abused drugs and some even died. Patrick and I, along with other friends, did all that we could to reach out to our peers in our school and neighborhood. We worked with priests and mental health professionals and got a really good education on drug abuse and mental health. We were not told bullshit either. It was recognized that recreational drug use was a fact of life and that people of all ages from all cultures had a variety of ways to alter their consciousness. I am not opposed to recreational use, and I have participated extensively in assisting those who were drug abusers to change their habits. I even know mental health professionals who used psychedelics for their own therapy to enhance self-awareness and heal emotional hurts."

"Wow. That's a lot of information about drugs. What made you get so involved in the whole drug thing in your community?" Jamie asked.

"It's a long story. The experience led me to make the choice to attend college to pursue an associate degree in mental health. I went through an extensive therapeutic process for my own healing. It really is a very long story, exhausting, actually."

"Not to me. I want to know everything about you!" Jamie was genuinely interested in every aspect of my life and I of hers.

"I suggest you read his journals," chimed in Patrick, "he's been keeping an on-going record of everything in his life ever since I can remember. He has volumes of journal books filled with everything important that's ever happened."

"Really! Do you have them with you?" Jamie asked.

"I started a new journal shortly before we decided to leave Philly and travel to Jamaica," I replied.

"Yeah, and he's filled several already. He likes to sit up late at night and write, and I noticed if he wakes up in the middle of the night he writes, and in the lazy part of the afternoon, and early morning too. He is a writing fool," piped in Patrick.

"Fool is not the appropriate word," chided Jamie, "it takes a great deal of discipline. I tried keeping a journal but couldn't stay with it."

"You are disciplined with your meditation and you do a lot of sketching," I added, "a practice I could definitely use."

"Well, that's easy enough. Just keep meditating with me. There are some techniques I haven't yet shared with you. Of course, you will develop your own," offered Jamie.

"That's cool! I welcome you as my teacher and co-pleasure explorer. I need to purchase more journal books. Perhaps you can try journal writing again," I suggested.

"I prefer to keep a journal through my sketches. You're welcome to look at my sketchbooks, they do tell a story. Can I read your journals?" I hesitated. I wrote about my experiences with Penny, and I was quite graphic. And I wrote about Sandy that included my conflicting emotions. The thought of Jamie reading them made me feel embarrassed and uncomfortable. "Oliver, you're blushing. I suppose there are things you wrote that you are not comfortable sharing. That is quite understandable. Journals are meant to be personal. You do not have to share them."

"I did not write them with the intention of sharing them. They are a way for me to keep my mind clear, you know, to process things that happen, and to work out difficulties. I am concerned that if you read them you may get wrong impressions."

"Oliver, you don't need to explain. I understand. It would be like inviting people inside your head, exposing every thought and feeling. Now that would truly be going naked to a degree of vulnerability that may not be healthy," said Jamie.

Julie picked up on the naked metaphor, "Wow, imagine that. People are freaked out by seeing other naked people, and by allowing others to see them naked. It is unfathomable that people would expose their every thought and feeling. That would be way too vulnerable. Not me. I like the privacy of my thoughts. This mind is my mind and I only allow others to know what I want them to know!"

Patrick added his thoughts, "I suppose no person is an open book. Nor could anyone be that vulnerable even if they wanted too. Pure honesty about what goes on inside our heads would create social madness. Man, I have so many thoughts and feelings buzzing around in my mind that I can't keep up with them all. I have all kinds of crazy thoughts that I can't believe they are coming from me. Sometimes it seems as if someone else is inside my head."

"Sounds like mushroom talk to me," added Jamie. We all laughed. "Seriously though, we all have bizarre thoughts. After all, we are creatures with multiple natures," asserted Jamie. "We are animals with sexual appetites for pro-creation and aggression to ensure personal survival and we are human in that we think, reason, make tools and create culture, and we are spiritual in that we seek for purpose, meaning and values. And these different aspects of the self are not innately harmonious. So it is perfectly normal to have so-called bizarre thoughts. We need to harmonize these differing natures through mental discipline, which is the purpose of meditation and other spiritual practices. I think it is a good thing that we can't listen to each other's every thought, like you said, Patrick, it would create social madness."

Patrick was impressed with what Jamie said about our multi-faceted nature, "Wow! Awesome! There's a lot of light behind those dark chocolate eyes. Hmm, there's more to this meditation thing than breathing and sitting quiet. I'd like to jump on the meditation band wagon."

"Jules meditates, we were both taught by our Buddhist parents, although neither of us are strictly devotees," explained Jamie.

"Oliver and I once had an encounter with a religious group that used LSD as a sacrament and they were into Jesus Christ – hippie Jesus Freaks. Maybe we can incorporate mushrooms into our meditation practice, and we can use ganja like the Rastafarians. We're going to create our own religion!" Patrick was in his fantasy factory mode and he was speaking in that excited hallucinogenic voice that was somewhat comical and a little disturbing.

Jamie replied to Patrick's fantastical suggestion. "I think it is best if each person creates their own method that enhances their ability to walk the spiritual path. Each person must discover purpose and meaning in life, and truth can only be discovered through personal experience. All else is indoctrination of prescribed doctrine. If you want to use chemicals along with meditation or whatever, that is for you to choose. Whatever works best for you, Patrick, is uniquely for you, and others may find your methods helpful. However, beyond meditation as a group practice, I am not in favor of creating sacraments."

"Amen to that!" I said, emphatically.

Julie was quick to add her thoughts to the conversation. "Well, I took a little detour from my meditation routine in the last few days. It has been one hell of a whirlwind pleasure ride since arriving in Negril. To me, meditation is as ritualistic as brushing my teeth. Our parents had us doing it throughout our childhood. I never really thought of it as a spiritual practice, but it does have a calming affect." Julie glanced at Patrick, and he beamed a wide self-satisfied grin right back at her. "I suppose it is time to return to the discipline. Mom and Dad sure would be pleased. Hey, Jamie, maybe if I meditate while on mushrooms I'll merge in the great Buddha Atman with our parents."

"You can certainly give it a try," Jamie responded.

Patrick made an announcement. "So, are we all agreed that we are going to meditate together, following the practice of Jamie and Julie, and perhaps we could add new techniques or rituals as we progress, of course allowing for some individualized explorations to enhance the pathways to discovery?" I suspected that Patrick's so-called additional techniques would contain an element of spiritual carnalism. I chuckled to myself, thinking of our experiences with the hippie nude holy LSD Jesus Freaks. It appeared that another one of Patrick's fantasies had become a reality.

"Agreed!" We said simultaneously.

Julie was visibly impressed with Patrick's pronouncement as indicated by the pleasantly surprised look on her face. "That was very well put, Patrick. I repeat myself - you are a very good paradise pleasure guide, and I am certain you will make a more than suitable meditation partner. So, now that we are settled on our collective endeavor to pursue the harmonizing of our multi-faceted animal, human, spiritual natures – can we please take care of the donkey?"

We all laughed at Julie's statement. Jamie added, "There is a legend that when the Buddha became enlightened, he simply got up from meditating under the famous Bodhi tree and collected fire wood. I suppose taking a Jack Ass for a walk is comparable." We laughed.

"I wouldn't consider us enlightened. We haven't started meditating yet," said Patrick.

"Well, Patrick, at the very least we can say that your mind and my mind are lit up at the moment," added Julie.

"Whew, you can say that again. We have light bulb brains," Patrick's comment was intended to sound humorous but it struck my ears as being quite goofy. No one laughed.

We went to the shed to get the bridle. Julie noticed a bit, and she said the fact that they had one was a positive sign that the donkey was used for riding. I grabbed the brush, figuring the donkey would appreciate being groomed. We went to where the donkey was grazing. Julie brushed the donkey, talking to him the entire time.

"What's his name?" she asked.

"Charley just calls him Donkey," I replied. Julie placed her hands on the sides of the donkey's head and said, "Sweet Mr. Donkey, you are my friend." She kissed him on the nose several times. The donkey apparently liked the affection. He showed his teeth and made a comical 'he-haw' sound. After making his acquaintance, Julie put the bit and bridles on him. The donkey was complacent. She led him around the periphery of the grazing area as we watched. Julie was a natural with this donkey and I assumed with most if not all animals. Jamie confirmed my assessment.

"Jules is an animal magnet. Since we were little children, animals always liked her. Don't get me wrong, they like me too, but not like Jules. She has a gift when it comes to animals. We were both in 4H, and we took riding lessons. When Jules was eight, she convinced our parents to buy her a pony. We had a small barn on our forty-acre property on Bottom Road – ah, that's where we live, it's actually not in the town of Bloomington but close enough – our parents liked living in the country. They built a small building designed specifically for meditation and they held weekend meditation retreats on our property. Anyway, when she was ten she graduated to riding and owning a horse. An Appaloosa stud named Thorn, and boy he was one ornery horse. He wouldn't let anyone other than Jules ride him. My parents thought Jules should have chosen a gelding or a mare. But not Jules, she wanted a 100% fired up super energetic stallion, and she sure did get one. Thorn was two years old when Jules got him. We had to enlarge the barn. I am sure they miss each other."

"Well then, I feel a lot more at ease if Jules decides to ride Donkey." Jamie's story really did make me feel a lot more comfortable with Julie's intended purpose.

We walked along side Donkey as Julie led him down the road. Children came out to greet us, most likely having never seen a group of white people with a donkey. It wasn't long before we had a crowd of ten children. I was impressed by the fact that Donkey never seemed the slightest bit perturbed by all the people.

Julie stopped walking, handed the reins to Jamie and said, "I am going to try something." She whispered something inaudible into Donkey's ear, and scratched behind the top of his head as she moved to his side. She then leaned the front of her body against him with her arms stretched across his back. She padded him over and over again. Julie moved around Donkey to the opposite side and repeated the same procedure. Then she applied pressure with the palms of her arms and lifted herself off the ground, allowing Donkey to support her weight – he did not move. Julie, encouraged by Donkey's receptivity to her weight, gracefully pulled herself onto his back, her body stretched across him like a large sack of goods. Donkey continued to remain motionless. She then instructed Jamie to walk Donkey. She did. The children thought it was funny to see a girl lying across a donkey.

They laughed and chattered to each other in excitedly inaudible Jamaican patois. Then, in one graceful swift motion, Julie twirled her legs parallel to Donkey's body and then sat up straight, with her legs straddling his back. She leaned forward and scratched behind Donkey's ears. Jamie stopped walking and handed the reins to Julie. The children cheered as we all walked along side Julie and Donkey, heading south along West End Road. Then, to everyone's surprise, Julie somehow communicated to Donkey to break into a sort-of trot. The children ran along side them, only the fastest ones were able to keep pace. The rest of us remained behind, watching the spectacle take off down the road.

Julie slowed Donkey down and turned him around. When she reached us, the children clamored for her to give them rides. For more than an hour, Julie took turns giving each child who had the inclination a ride on Donkey. To our delightful surprise, some of the children who were given rides went to their homes and retrieved food to give to us as gifts in exchange for the rides they had received. Donkey appeared to be enjoying every moment. More than one child had brought carrots so Julie allowed them to feed them to Donkey, a treat he thoroughly enjoyed. One child brought a very large straw hat that was somewhat tattered. With a knife, he carved two holes and placed it on Donkey's head, guiding the ears through the holes. Everyone cheered. Another child put a wreath of flowers over his head and around his neck. Donkey he-hawed in agreement with this adornment and genuine affection from the children. The children laughed when Donkey took a long pee from his gargantuan penis. It was so big it reached halfway to the ground.

We took Donkey home and placed him in the grazing area. It was wonderful to have such a pleasant interaction with the children in the area. Jamie wondered aloud where their school was and that she would like to visit it and perhaps volunteer to teach an art class. Julie liked the idea and said that she would like to read with them, and suggested that Patrick and I could volunteer as well. We decided to look into it another day.

The following days were filled with a mixture of Patrick and me attending to our fishing responsibilities, which included an overnight trip to Conch Island to harvest conch for Elkannah. During that time, Jamie and Julie made their acquaintance with the Negril Elementary School. The girls told us that the children were adorable and that they love drawing and having stories read to them. Unfortunately, they have very few school supplies, even pencils were in short supply and they have few books and precious little paper. Jamie and Julie decided to write home to their parents encouraging them to ship basic school supplies. Jamie included drawings of the schoolchildren. Patrick and I decided to visit the school sometime in the near future. Currently, our time was consumed by increasing our fishing yield for Elkannah as he was gearing up to purchase building supplies for a new room addition and for purchasing land adjacent to his property.

One day after returning from Conch Island and delivering a very lucrative harvest of conch and fish to Elkannah, I took Jamie for a canoe ride out to one of our fish traps and demonstrated how we catch fish. To our surprise, there was a medium size barracuda inside the trap, a phenomenon I had never seen before. This was the second trap Patrick and I had built. We had made the funnel entrance on this trap much larger than the original. The trap also contained several sunfish, red snapper, and one hefty bonito.

Jamie was impressed with my fishing skills. I had to instruct her on how to assist me in keeping the canoe balanced while unloading and re-baiting the trap. While stringing the barracuda, it wiggled fiercely and its sharp teeth caught the side of my right thigh, cutting into the flesh. I bled profusely, causing concern for the both of us. Jamie took off her halter-top and wrapped my thigh after flushing it with salt water and then rinsing it with fresh water. She tied the halter-top tightly around my thigh, which stopped the bleeding. As Jamie was tying her halter-top around my leg, I enjoyed the view of her lovely breasts glistening in the sunlight.

That evening we cooked the barracuda for dinner. I showed Jamie and Julie how to suck out the brains of the fish by placing my mouth over one eyeball, deeply inhaling its succulent contents. They gagged, but Julie did imitate my actions by sucking on the eye of the bonito.

Two weeks had gone by and our adopted Jamaican family had not returned. This had caused me some concern. I expressed this to Elkannah and he assured me that Millie and Charley were very responsible people and since they were gone for so long, their business must be extremely important. He stressed that it was an honor that they trusted us to take care of their property. Lord Joseph also remained absent from his property. His sea cave was our favorite hangout location during very hot and humid afternoons.

The four of us practiced meditation twice daily. At first, it was difficult for me to sit for long periods of time without talking. Jamie and Julie instructed us on how to still our minds, informing us that a quiet mind is a divine mind. It seemed impossible to stop thinking. Jamie told me that the mind never stops thinking and therefore the key is to not struggle with the thoughts, but to watch them as an observer, and to visualize my mind as a sky and each thought as a cloud drifting by. Adopting the concept of being an observer of my thoughts rather than chasing after them to get them to stop was a giant step for both Patrick and me in learning to meditate. Julie instructed us on the idea that our thoughts generate feelings and that they are simply images that we have made and that thoughts are very powerful because we give them meaning, and hence we attribute meaning and value to everything through our thinking.

This was an amazing concept because it was instrumental in teaching us that we do indeed create much of what we experience in life through our perceptions and interpretations. These ideas gave us the sense that we are indeed in control of much of what takes place in our lives through what takes place in our minds. Up to this point in my life, thoughts just seemed to come and go randomly without me paying much attention to their cause. I was now realizing, as was Patrick, that thoughts don't have to just haphazardly happen, that we are the cause, and that we can give our thoughts conscious direction. Through practice, we become the conscious creators of thoughts, and we give all things whatever meaning they have for us. And we have the power to choose how to respond to the environment, and what ever goes on in our animal and human nature is subject to our willful guidance. Jamie said that the spiritual aspect of our being, the super conscious mind, is what we need to access in order to spiritualize all aspects of our thinking. This was a liberating concept and one that would take a lifetime of practice.

The realization of the importance and capability of the conscious control of thoughts, perception, meaning, purpose, values and subsequent actions did not come to us all at once in an ah-hah moment, nor did Patrick and I fully comprehend it. These were lessons that Jamie and Julie were teaching to us, and they instructed that mastery of these concepts is an unfolding lifelong process. They stressed the importance of daily practice and even though they have been meditating since they were children, they consider themselves novices.

Patrick and Julie occasionally enjoyed ingesting mushrooms before our meditation sessions. There was only one noticeable outward appearance of the influence that mushrooms were having upon them, and that was the perpetual smiles on their faces. After completing our meditation sessions, we would discuss our experiences, sharing challenges and insights. Such sharing consisted of invigorating discussions that in one form or another contained the concepts regarding thoughts and perceptions previously mentioned. Patrick and Julie both said that the mushrooms enhanced their senses and that it aided in their ability to focus their minds. I decided that one day I would give it a try, knowing from experience that mushrooms had indeed enhanced my ability to experience my spiritual nature. The fact that Jamie was not interested in using them, or in smoking ganja, aided my resolve to maintain abstinence.

During some of my meditations, I saw images of people that were important to me. Two people in particular were my mother and Sandy. Thoughts of them brought strong emotions of love, guilt, and fear. I was training my mind to both explore and detach from emotions, and to be an observer of the thoughts and feelings that came with each relationship. What I discovered was that I could ride on the energy of the emotions without feeling overwhelmed by them and to simply allow them to happen without attaching judgmental thoughts. I gained a great deal of insight into the meaning and value and judgments I had placed on my relationships, and more importantly on myself.

I discussed with Jamie some of these meditation experiences, but not all of them. I was not ready to discuss with her my thoughts and feelings about Sandy. I was confused that I could love two women so deeply. It seemed that Sandy existed in a far off land in a different time, and I realized that it seemed this way because that was the physical time-space reality. She existed in a world that had become my past and yet she was still vibrantly alive for me in the world of my super emotions. While contemplating how I could feel such strong love for Sandy while meditating, I received an insightful answer: *love exists beyond the boundaries of time and space.* This thought helped me to feel like I was getting closer to disclosing to Jamie my relationship with Sandy. I had to choose the right moment. There was another person that kept coming up during my meditation that I had to talk to Patrick about, and that was Norlina.

"Patrick, have you talked with Julie about Norlina?" I asked.

"Yeah. Julie and I really like each other, duh, pretty obvious. We're not sure what's going to happen. We don't want to hurt Norlina, not only because we live with her family, it just wouldn't be right."

"It's a tricky situation for sure. If you and Julie decide to keep your romance going, we're going to have to leave this area of the West End, and perhaps the cliffs all together. The backup plan is to live on the beach, even on Conch Island for a while until we get set up." I was surprised by the anxiety I felt as we spoke of this situation. Patrick had taken notice.

"You really don't have to worry, Oliver. Julie and I have talked about this on several occasions. We're just going to have to see what unfolds when Norlina gets back. Julie and I will do the right thing." Patrick was doing his best to ease my concern.

"Well, whatever will be will be. We are on this adventure together, that's the bottom line." I said.

"Really, Ollie, no worries, mon. Everyt'ing gonna be awright. Seen?"

"Yeah, I understand. Well, if the worst that happens is that we live on the beach and Conch Island with Jamie and Julie, hey, that's a sweet alternative."

"Irie!" replied Patrick, as he put his arm around my shoulder.

"Irie!" I said in return.

Patrick and Julie decided to take Donkey to Negril Elementary School, and Jamie and I went with them. Patrick rode Donkey for part of the way, showing off his riding skills to Jamie. When we arrived at the school, I was amazed by the reception Jamie and Julie received from the children. Julie and Jamie got permission from the teachers to give short rides around the school grounds to the children, two at a time were able to sit on Donkey's back. This was a really big thrill to these children.

A child came out of the school building kicking a soccer ball. Patrick played soccer in high school. His eyes lit up when he saw the ball and he ran over to the boy and used fancy footwork to take the ball away and then quickly passed it back to him. Within minutes, the pubescent boys were on the field and Patrick had orchestrated a game. In essence, he was putting on a show of his soccer talent and skills. I was mostly an observer of all this wonderful activity. A few children came up to me, touching my long strawberry-blond hair and freckled skin. I enjoyed talking with them about school and what they were learning. It was surprising that they had few textbooks and scarcely any other printed material to read. In fact, pencil and paper were in short supply. A small group of children had assembled around me and one had asked me to tell them a story from my childhood. I heard the sound of a dog hacking because of a chicken bone caught in its throat, that all too common sound in Jamaica that I found very disturbing. I decided to tell them the story of my dog, White Shepherd.

The children had never seen a shepherd dog, but some of them had seen dogs with all white hair. They loved the story, and I discovered that I quite enjoyed the telling. It was very interesting for them to hear a story about a dog that people loved so much. It seemed to me that most Jamaicans didn't hold dogs in high esteem. I had hoped that hearing my story might begin to change that. I also told the children that feeding chicken bones to dogs is not good for them. They asked for another story but their teachers had called them all inside for a lesson. Before leaving, we decided to peek inside their schoolhouse. It was one large room with only one desk, and that was shared among three teachers. There were approximately forty students ages eight through twelve, and all of them were sitting in rows on the floor. What caught my eye was the artwork on the walls. Some of the sketches I recognized as belonging to Jamie, and the rest were from the children. It was obvious that Jamie had given them an art lesson in drawing. Most of the drawings were on brown paper. This was a material that children had access to from the purchased goods that came wrapped in paper. The drawings depicted scenes from around Negril, including the schoolhouse. It was a wonderful experience for all of us.

On our walk towards home from the school visit, we stopped at Elkannah's house. There were lots of building materials on the front of his property. It was good to see Elkannah, and we took the time to help him move the cinder blocks, wood, and sacs of cement away from the road where the delivery truck had dropped them off.

The twins helped too. Elkannah was delighted to meet them and to have their help. Elkannah's children, and his wife Clara, liked Jamie and Julie. We agreed to return the next day and help them build their room addition. When we got home we went for a sunset swim, and later had dinner, played music, meditated on the cliffs and finally went to sleep.

The next day we were eager to help Elkannah build his room addition. It was a long hard days work and we made great progress. The day before, Elkannah had already poured concrete footers and laid cinder blocks that would hold the beams that would support the floor joists and walls. We were able to complete the floor in one day. After following our usual swim, dinner, music, meditation, and sleep routine, we returned the next day. This was an exciting day because we were able to build and raise the walls. Again, on the third day, we raised the rafters and put on the metal roof, which was not easy in the hot sun! Elkannah told us he could work on the house with his wife and the twins while Patrick and I went fishing. Elkannah needed to continue to make money and we were pleased to help. Plus, it was fun to get back out on the water and to use different muscles. Performing construction work is fun and gratifying, but it is hard work.

When we brought in the morning catch, Elkannah and the twins had the siding attached to one wall. The girls were finding that using a hammer and driving nails was not as easy as it appeared. We ate lunch that was prepared by Clara and then went for a swim with

Jamie and Julie and Elkannah's family. After mid afternoon, Patrick and I went back to fishing. This time, we focused solely on diving for conch, which was our favorite thing to do. Patrick was able to spear a barracuda. I had tried spear fishing and decided it was not for me. Patrick used it on those occasions when we dove for conch and he spotted large fish.

Elkannah and the twins had completed putting the cedar siding on the walls. All that was left was putting in the doors and windows. Clara and the girls volunteered to make dinner while Patrick and I helped Elkannah put in the three windows and one door. The addition was complete! Elkannah announced that he had a contract to purchase the adjacent two acres of land, and the quarter acre of cliff property across the road. He had made a down payment and had a five-year agreement to make monthly payments. Elkannah and Clara thanked us for our help in building and more importantly, fishing. We suggested to Elkannah that he build small cottages on his newly acquired property to rent to tourists. The idea of utilizing these cottages to possibly accommodate our own designs for the inevitable tourist industry had not escaped us.

We were now in our third week of taking care of Millie and Charley's property. I expressed my concern over their long absence. We made more visits to the school. I was now known as the storyteller with hair of fire and spotted skin. The children did not call me Ollie, as did all other Jamaicans, they called me Mr. Oliver. Jamie continued giving art lessons, Patrick taught soccer, and Julie led them in singing and creative dance, all of which were big hits! We were at the school during the week before Christmas. The kids were into Christmas decorations, and they even had a simple gift exchange. Jamie and Julie led them in singing Christmas carols accompanied with guitar and flute, of course. This experience caused me to entertain the idea of one day becoming a schoolteacher. And my work with Elkannah on building got me interested in becoming a carpenter. Then again, I liked fishing. I mentioned these thoughts to Jamie and she simply said, "You already are all of those things and much more." Ah, my teacher lover is oh so wise, and quite affirming.

Millie, Charley, Norlina and Elijah were not back for Christmas. The four of us decided not to exchange gifts. It was a fact that none of us really liked celebrating Christmas. The school thing was as far as we were willing to go. Patrick and I entertained the idea of going to church on Christmas morning and decided not to. We simply were not into the practice of traditional Christian religion.

I got the idea for the four of us to spend several days on Booby Cay. We asked Elkannah if he would peek in on Donkey during our absence and he agreed. The canoe would have to be weighted down beyond capacity, since we had to bring our tent, sleeping bags, clothes, fishing gear, food, and cooking utensils, and we brought a bow saw to cut firewood. Patrick got the idea of building a small raft out of bamboo to haul most of our gear. It was fun to make and it worked like a charm. I brought my flute along, and Patrick figured out a way to wrap his guitar in the tent-tarp for water protection.

It took the good part of the day to get to Conch Island as we took our time, stopping at the beach to fill our four gallon sized jugs with water. We were fortunate to have a water supply near the northern tip of Long Bay because it made it easy for us to trek the less than one mile from the island to the beach to refill our water.

Jamie and Julie loved the island! Since we were its only inhabitants, we were naked most of the time. During the course of our Conch Island adventure, the sun browned every inch of our bodies. The girls turned into caramel beauties. Jamie found a large aloe plant. Patrick and I had not discovered it previously because it was in the midst of thickets and thorns that we had no interest in approaching. The girls were searching for dry firewood when Jamie spotted it. The bow saw came in handy cutting away the thickets. The aloe juice felt great on our skin and healed some of the sun burned spots and peeling skin on my ultra sun sensitive body, particularly on my vital parts. Jami had a vested interest in making sure my bamboo would not be taken out of commission – it was untouchable for a full day and that was unacceptable to her. I started wearing a loincloth for protection while in direct sunlight.

Living in the buff super-stimulated everyone's hormones, so there was a great deal of lovemaking going on. Our lifestyle was absolutely idyllic. It was as though we were living in heaven. We discussed the possibility of setting up permanent camp on the island. Jamie and Julie wanted to investigate if it were possible to buy the island and live there forever. When I told Jamie that it was a nice fantasy but the purchase price would probably be way beyond our reach, she simply shrugged her shoulders and said, "Where there's a will, there's a way!" I liked her we-can-do-anything bravado.

Patrick and Julie were so close that I was convinced that Norlina was going to get hurt. Once our Jamaican family returned from Kingston, we were going to arrive at an intersection where major decisions would be made, and the course of our lives could be dramatically affected.

It was tempting to stay longer but we could not expect Elkannah to continue taking care of Donkey and we needed to keep him supplied with seafood. It was time for us to venture back to our West End home. During our weeklong sojourn on the island, we harvested a great deal of conch. It was our primary food source, and everyone's favorite seafood. We had to take an excursion to the beach area in search of more bamboo to enlarge our raft to have room for transporting the large volume of conch. Still, the canoe and raft along with the four of us was too much weight. We realized that we were going to have to make two trips over two days. Julie suggested that we drop them off on the beach so they could walk with some of the gear to the cliffs. Jamie liked the idea, because it would give them the opportunity to explore the beach area. The girls said that they would like to spend a few days with each other on the beach, if they could find suitable shelter. I suggested that they take the tent, hammocks and their sleeping bags. The tent was too heavy and awkward to carry so they declined. If they were lucky and it didn't rain at night, they would be fine. We had learned that it rained almost always during the heat of the day and rarely in the evenings. The biggest concern was the possibility of being harassed by testosterone-raging boys.

Jamie addressed my concern, "Don't worry, Oliver, we are more comfortable with Jamaican people now. The school experience did a great deal in bringing that about. I am confident that if we encounter another group of boys we will be able to handle them quite well." I wasn't convinced. Sure, I believed they could handle aggressive advances from a group of boys, but not if it involved physical violence, and I expressed this fact.

"Take my spear gun." Patrick commanded.

"Do you honestly think I would shoot someone with a spear?" Jamie responded with an alarming tone.

"I would if I had to," announced Julie. "I mean, I am a peaceful soul, but when it comes to physical survival, you know, if it is a true threat, then I have no problem doing whatever it takes to protect myself and my sister. That goes for you guys too. I would never let anyone harm any of us."

"Wow! And I thought I knew everything about you. Huh!" said Patrick. "Reminds me of your mother, Oliver."

"Yeah. She sounds like a Momma Panther."

"Momma who?" replied the twins simultaneously.

"Oliver is speaking of his mother. She was the female protector of the boys in our neighborhood from the police and rival gangs. The boys referred to her as Momma Panther. It also had to do with a cat Oliver had when we were kids. You should ask him to tell you the story someday," explained Patrick.

"I expect you wrote about it in one of your journals," said Jamie.

"Yes, not about the cat, but about my mom," was all I said. The mention of my mother stirred up some uncomfortable feelings. I was worried about my mother's health. Thoughts and feelings would continuously arise concerning her when I meditated. I changed the subject.

"Okay. We have a plan. We will canoe the two of you over to Long Bay beach and meet up sometime in a few days," I said.

"Well, Jules, are you up for a little sister time?" she asked.

"Definitely. It would be good for us to reflect together on the amazing island paradise pleasure tour that our two handsome island boys so graciously bestowed upon us," responded Julie.

"Alright, then. Let's get this plan in motion!" commanded Julie. "First things first, though. Patrick, teach me how to use the spear gun!"

WEST END SUNSET RAINBOW COTTAGES

After Patrick gave both girls a lesson on the safe use of a spear gun, we canoed the girls over to the beach and dropped them off. I was feeling apprehensive about leaving them alone. Jamie reminded me that they had traveled for months all over Europe and were quite capable of taking care of themselves, and that the incident with the group of boys was particularly difficult because they had not expected to be so overwhelmed with culture shock. She reiterated that they were now feeling well adjusted and quite comfortable with Jamaican culture. Her words did comfort me – some.

Patrick and I returned to the island and attached our raft to the canoe and headed for Millie and Charley's cliff. It took much longer than expected to get there because we were paddling in the wind and the raft was heavily laden with conch and our gear. When the cliff was in sight, we spotted Norlina and Elijah waving to us, and there was another, taller person with them. The sight of our Jamaican friends was exhilarating. It occurred to me that it was a good thing that Jamie and Julie were not with us. It would give Patrick a chance to touch base with Norlina.

We pulled the canoe along the base of the steps. I held it steady while Patrick got out. He grabbed one of the cinder blocks and secured the canoe. I handed the gear that was stowed in the canoe to our friends and they carried the items to the top of the cliff. We then proceeded to detach the raft, unload it and anchor the canoe and raft a few yards away from the cliff to prevent waves from pushing the vessels against the cliff, averting possible damage.

"Ollie an' Patrick, it is good ta see yah, mon," said Elijah with a big smile. It struck me that he looked and sounded more mature than when we last saw him. It was not physical changes that impressed us but his general demeanor.

I took Elijah's hand and said, "Welcome home!" Norlina and the tall gentleman were on the top of the cliff waiting for us. Patrick followed behind Elijah and me. I stopped and turned my face toward Patrick. His forehead was furrowed – he was definitely feeling worried and apprehensive.

"Norlina, it is wonderful to see you," I said greeting her by graciously taking her hand.

"Ollie, dis is mi fren, Edward," she said, looking both pleased and nervous. I shook his hand. He was tall, handsome, and wore a white dress shirt and blue slacks with leather shoes. It was unusual to see a young Jamaican so well dressed. I got the impression that he came from a well-off family.

"Patrick. It is good ta see yah, mon," boomed Elijah enthusiastically.

"Elijah, it feels like months since I saw you. How are you?" said Patrick, intentionally averting Norlina's gaze.

"Irie, mon. Kingston was adventurous. Challenging fer sure. But everyt'ing set awrite, now, mon," replied Elijah.

"Hello Patrick," squeaked Norlina, "this is my friend, Edward," she said shyly.

"Norlina. It is wonderful to see you!" Patrick did not touch her. He extended his hand to Edward, and Edward received it enthusiastically, "Pleased to met you, Edward."

"Yeahmon. I 'ear much 'bout yah an' Ollie," responded Edward in a warm baritone voice.

"Ollie an' Patrick, my sister an' Edward are man an' wife. It is a wonderful t'ing, mon! It is one of de reasons we were in Kingston fer so long, mon." Elijah said proudly. I was stunned. Patrick turned his head pretending to look at the canoe in the sea.

"Wonderful! Congratulations!" I said, shaking their hands.

"Excuse me, I need to adjust the anchors on the canoe and raft," Patrick said in an urgent voice. He descended the steep steps and disappeared.

Norlina looked troubled. There was a great deal going on between her and Patrick, for sure. She knew it was a shock for him to hear the news. I was grateful that Elijah did not know of his sister's involvement with Patrick. He suspected that nothing was wrong.

"I will go and help Patrick. We need to make sure the raft will be steady enough to not overturn or come loose. As you have seen, we have lots of conch for Elkannah. We will bring some to share for dinner tonight."

"Dat be wonderful, Ollie. Millie an' Charley will be pleased ta taste de sweetness of conch, mon. We see yah shortly," said Elijah. The three of them left the cliffs. I went to the canoe.

Patrick was the first to speak. "Wow! That was one weird, trip, bro. It's kind of hard to get my head around it. Wow, what a mind blower!"

"Are you alright?" I looked Patrick in the eyes as I spoke.

"Hey, bro. It's just strange, that's all. But, yeah, I am okay. Just a little shocked – and a lot relieved!" Patrick's face broke into a big smile.

"Whoa, what's up with you?" I asked.

"Hey, bro, don't get me wrong. I really dig Norlina, okay. We had a sweet thing going on, but we didn't really talk that much. It was mostly a sex thing. I mean we were really hot on each other. I think she was a virgin and I released the tigress within her. For that, I think she is grateful, but I don't think she ever thought we would become married or anything wild like that. I doubt she will ever tell anyone about our fling, and you are the only other person who knows," said Patrick.

"Well, I am glad to see you are relieved. You are one lucky tigress liberator!" We laughed. "We need to make sure that Jamie and Julie don't let on to Norlina that they know about your fling."

"Bro, this whole situation is gonna work out! You're right, I am one lucky dude!" said Patrick.

"Yep! You are the cats meow! Whew, I am glad that's over." I sighed.

"Tomorrow when we canoe our conch catch to Fishermen Cove for Elkannah, we can head over to the beach and search for the girls. Let's tell our Jamaican family about Jamie and Julie. I think Millie and Charley will appreciate the extra income. Looks like we're going to have to create another shelter in the campground," I said.

"Not a problem. We can build a lean-to shelter, or something. If the girls living at Millie and Charley's don't work out, we can go back to Conch Island, or perhaps live in Lord Joseph's sea cave. Hey, maybe we build a little shanty on Elkannah's new property right on the cliff," replied Patrick in a cheerful voice. He was clearly very happy over the turn of events, and so was I. A potential social-emotional disaster had been avoided.

We grabbed enough conch so that each person could have his or her own for dinner. The family appreciated the seafood. We tossed in a couple fish to add variety. We ate outdoors on a makeshift table, with torches for lighting and a smoky campfire to help keep the mosquito population down. Fortunately, Patrick and I kept a supply of insect repellant, one of the few necessities we were required to spend money on – the Dragon Coil insect repellant incense that most Jamaicans used was minimally effective.

Millie pan-fried the conch, having dipped them in egg and covered with a spicy bread mixture. They were delicious. The conversation was lighthearted and jovial. Charley expressed gratitude for the good care we provided for Donkey. We took his comment as an opportunity to tell them about Jamie and Julie. They listened intently, and they were receptive to the idea of having them live on their property, although they were uncertain as to how that would work out.

"We do nuh 'ave rooms fer dem. Where would dey sleep?" Millie asked.

"They can stay in our campground, sleeping in our tent while we build a small shelter that will protect Patrick and me from the rain. We have mosquito netting as part of our sleeping bags, so we can set up a roof cover and hang our hammocks underneath," I explained.

"Yah can build dis t'ing?" Charley asked.

"Definitely. We helped Elkannah build an addition to his house. We can find the materials. I am confident we can make it work. They can pay you the same amount we are giving you, if that is enough," added Patrick.

"Hmm. Effin yah t'ink yah can build dis t'ing, I will agree. I mus' charge dem more fer food. T'ings are more expensive every day," replied Millie.

"How much more?" I asked.

"One dollar and fifty each, U.S." Millie responded.

"That is very reasonable," I said, "does it include a meal?" I asked.

"One meal," said Millie. "Wen do we meet dees girls?"

"They are exploring the beach area at the moment. It is possible they could arrive tonight, but I doubt it. They want to spend time alone on the beach. If they don't show up in a few days, Patrick and I will go looking for them."

"Ollie, I hopin' dat yah an' Patrick come wit us ta de furthest West End, past de lighthouse. In Kingston, Norlina an' I receive de deed ta our fadda's land. We want ta 'ave a look. Me fadda leased de land ta de government fer many years."

"Wow! Far out. This is exciting. How much land did your father leave you two?" I asked.

"Fifteen acres. We 'ave a map. De land includes de cliffs, an' de road run through it. Some of de land is on de slope of de hill. It is much like my grandparents' land, mon. Norlina an' I very excited," responded Elijah.

"Edward an' I will live on dis land," said Norlina, much to my surprise. I thought she would be worried about offending Patrick, but obviously not. "Edward an' I 'ave known each otter since we were likkle pikny. We always knew one day we'd marry." It puzzled me that she was so vocal about her relationship with Edward, especially since she and Patrick hadn't spoken to each other directly. I suppose it was an indirect way for her to let Patrick know that their liaison was over. But he already understood that.

"Sister an' I live on dis land, an' raise our famblies. We build fer tourist ta come. Ollie an' Patrick, ya help bring de tourist ta our land?" Elijah asked.

"Definitely. We sent a letter to our friends inviting them to come. It won't be long before people from all over will come to Negril. It is very beautiful and peaceful," I said, "our friends, Jamie and Julie could help bring people too."

"An' dey be likin' de Jamaican ganja!" said Millie. Patrick and I laughed in appreciation of Millie's directness.

"True dat!" responded Elijah, "I be cultivatin' ganja ta supply tourist, mon. I will mek lots of money ta raise our famblies. Dis will be good fer many Jamaicans in Negril. Seen!"

As Patrick and I had previously discussed, tourism in Negril was inevitable, and it will have a powerful impact on this lovely small fishing and horticultural village. It was our acknowledgement of this inevitability that caused us to choose to both accept and participate in the tourism industry. We knew that tourism would improve the material wealth of some of our Jamaican friends, and that we could use it to aid our own efforts to continue living in Negril inexpensively for as long as we desired.

There was an element of serendipity in the events that were unfolding that had not escaped my awareness. Patrick and I had already explored parts of the lighthouse cliff area and it was there that we discussed tourism and the role we could play, indeed we were already playing a role in its development. Now, we were engaged in a discussion with our adopted Jamaican family on the possible development of their land that would involve the cultivation of tourism – with our assistance. It felt a bit prophetic, and I hoped that it would not become pathetic – as I had a slight uneasy feeling about capitalizing on our good fortune of living a native lifestyle, one that could be severely compromised by the phenomenon of tourism. But, as we concluded earlier, we can either ride the tide of change or get out of the sea. Actually, there was another option and that was to simply stand on the sidelines and observe the process of change while continuing our native lifestyle. However, meeting Jamie and Julie, and the unfolding events in the lives of our Jamaican friends, had placed us smack on top of the cresting wave.

The next morning, after breakfast, everyone prepared for the morning hike to Norlina and Elijah's land. Charley decided to bring along Donkey to carry food and water supplies. It was decided that we would eat lunch on the family land. We walked slowly, enjoying the relatively cool morning air and the scintillating sight and scent of flowers. Shanties were spread out along the road, although none were built on the cliff side. Millie and Charley knew all of the people, having sold them produce for many years. After a while the road became slightly narrower and there were no more shanties. The lighthouse loomed in the near distant. When we arrived at the lighthouse, Elijah unfolded the map and placed it on the ground beneath the shade of a palm tree. He looked at it carefully. Norlina, Edward, and Elijah spoke in excited voices that were heavily laced in Jamaican Patois, which made their speech indecipherable.

"Ollie an' Patrick, yah 'ave been ta de lighthouse before, yes," said Elijah.

"Yes!" we replied simultaneously.

"Come an' 'ave a look at dis map, mon, an' see effin yah knoh de land," requested Elijah.

We crouched down beside him. On one end of the map there was a cone shaped mark with the word lighthouse written in very small print. The cliff lines were wavy and we assumed they were accurate because we noticed their shape in front of the lighthouse and the curve inward to its south that formed the cove and deep pool of water that Patrick and I had swam in. Further in from this cove-pool cliff area were seven dots placed in an arc with the word, housing, written inside the arc.

"I know those buildings. They are well made and in good shape. Where on this map is your land?" I asked.

"Dis is it, mon. Dees dots an' dis cove are de cliff part of de land. On de other side of dis road behind de dots is land dat go up de hill.

"Whoa! Far out, man. Wow! We do know your land, part of it anyway," exclaimed Patrick.

"Yes, we have been inside those buildings. Man, how did your father get to own them? This is awesome. You can move right in. They even have running water inside, and screened windows. Come on, let's check them out!" I was very excited. It seemed too good to be true. Our friends owned the structures that Patrick and I had fantasized about living in and renting to tourist. This was not only serendipitous – it was surrealistically unbelievable!

Millie and Charley were resting several yards away where Donkey had fresh grass to eat. They did not hear the specifics of what we had discovered, but they could tell we were excited. Norlina called to them.

"Grandfadda, grandmadda, come, Ollie an' Patrick 'ave been ta our land. We mus' see de buildings of our fadda!" Called Norlina.

"Me fadda leased dis land ta de government. Dey mus' 'ave built dees structures fer de government workers," said Elijah, "I want ta see dem!"

We headed in the direction of the structures, which were not too far away. I spotted the grove of trees that hid the buildings from the road and provided them with shade. I turned off from the gravel road into the trees and directly past the backside of the buildings and walked on to the stone covered front courtyard. I stood facing the seven buildings. The family followed me. All of us stood on the stone courtyard facing the buildings. Everyone was smiling.

"Come on, let's look inside," I announced. At first, we went inside one building. Everyone was obviously pleased by the size of the room and the overall condition. The running water in the sink basin particularly excited Millie and Charley, which had a pipe for carrying the grey water out doors and along the ground to some yet to be disclosed location. Millie turned the crank on one of the windows to open the glass slats to let cooler air into the room. She was pleased with the windows and she opened all eight of them, inspecting the condition of the screens. Everyone was talking excitedly about the cottages. We continued on from one cottage to the next. Everyone was in agreement that the cots had to be repaired or replaced with beds, and ideas were exchanged for decorations and furniture.

I had noticed something that escaped my attention the first time I had seen these buildings – there was a pipe running up the outside of each one that must have been used as an outside shower – there were no shower heads on the ends of the pipes. I was hot, so I striped off my shirt and shoes and took a cool rinse. The water was a rusty color at first but cleared up quickly. Edward took notice and went to a shower on the adjacent building and cooled off. Soon, everyone with the exception of Millie had taken a shower. Donkey put his head under Charley's shower and kept sticking out his huge lips and tongue into the water stream.

"Des buildings very good!" exclaimed Millie, "People could live in dem right away. Ollie and Patrick, ya and ya girl frens can stay 'ere. It better den de cloth tent!"

"Yes, Millie, I agree, but we would have to live without your cooking," I added.

“Ya areddi cook fer ya own. Dat nuh be a problem. Effin ya bring de tourist ta rent dees buildings, we provide ya wit de food for ya cookin’,” responded Millie.

Norlina jumped in the discussion. “Edward an’ I will live ‘ere an’ I prepare de food fer de tourist guest. We now ‘ave a ‘otel, de West End Cottages. Elijah, Edward, Patrick, an’ Ollie can build de restaurant over der near on dat part of de cliff. It will tek time, but we can do it,” pronounced Norlina confidently.

“Yeahmon. We will do it. I will plant food an’ ganja on de land up der,” Elijah pointed to the area where the land sloped upward and was covered with vegetation, “It will tek time ta get every t’ing right. We ‘ave some money fram our madda an’ fadda, an’ we will get more money fram de tourist ta buy every t’ing we need.”

“Yes, mi brother, we will produce much of de food for de restaurant,” added Norlina, “an’ we will chisel steps in de cliffs dat go down ta de sea. We will pour concrete on de cliff fer de comfort of de guest while dey soak in de sun an’ watch it set. We will plant flowers an’ plants to mek de land a beautiful garden.” I was amazed by the business minds of Elijah and Norlina. They saw opportunity everywhere they looked. Patrick caught their entrepreneur spirit and chimed in.

“Jamie and Julie will be the first tourist. Ollie and I can send more letters to friends in the U.S., and so can Jamie and Julie. You will have to charge more money, though.” Patrick was right about charging more money but I was not interested in forking over more bucks. I wanted to help our friends, but not at our own expense.

“True dat, mon. We need ta charge more. Ollie an’ Patrick, yah help us wit building an’ gettin’ de land prepared. It cost yah nothin’ ta live ‘ere mon, yah like fambly,” assured Elijah.

His words were a relief. I thought of our financial commitment to Elkannah, and the time involved in fishing. Now we were about to embark on creating the West End Cottages, or whatever it was going to be called, and in reality, we did not need a place to live. We could live on Conch Island as long as we had use of Elkannah’s canoe, which would not be a problem as long as we fished for him and helped him develop his land. I was worried that Patrick and I were about to spread our time too thin and that our relatively leisurely island lifestyle was about to get more complicated. And there really wasn’t much financial gain for us. It was more of a service project provided for our Jamaican friends.

I pulled Patrick aside for a conversation. I told him what I was thinking.

"Yeah, you're right. We could end up working for Elkannah and our friends here, and have little time to ourselves with almost no financial gain. Perhaps we should negotiate a portion of the rentals," suggested Patrick.

"That would be pushing it. Living in one of these buildings with Jamie and Julie would be really cool. It would be nice to live on Booby Cay or anywhere along the beach for that matter. We have lots of choices and few limitations. No problem, bredda, we surf de wave, mon, an' it will tek us safely ta shore!" I responded

"Yeahmon, it is all good! You know, Oliver, this is a really cool opportunity. The far West End of Negril is unpopulated. The land and cliffs around here are awesome. We get to learn to grow food with Elijah. We can set up our fishing operation right off these cliffs – no one fishes up here. It won't take that long to canoe to Elkannah, now that he owns cliff front land and can create easy access to his property from the sea. With all these buildings, everyone has comfort and privacy. And bro, if any of our Ghetto Flower friends come to Negril, this would be an awesome place for them to live. What we can do is negotiate money or more food for additional guest we bring in. There are seven small cottages. Norlina and Edward are taking one, Elijah another and we will be in the third with the twins. That leaves four to rent with lots of land to build even more. If we find the tourist, that will bring in plenty of cash for Norlina's restaurant on the cliffs and whatever other improvements are to be made on the land." Patrick's fantasy factory mind never ceased to amaze me.

"Wow, you really are an entrepreneur! I say we don't engage Norlina and Elijah in conversation about all you just said until we get more settled. As you just heard, they have lots of ideas running around their heads as well. Our contribution is bringing the tourist and providing some labor, and they could get labor from other Jamaicans if necessary. In fact, it won't be long before they won't need us at all. Tourist will eventually find their way up here once the word gets out. So, I say we just go along with the flow and influence things the best we can. The entire process is exciting and could be a lot of fun – it is a lot of fun! We have no idea where it will all lead. Right now, we can bring in the cash from Jamie and Julie. As for the Ghetto Flowers of South Philly, that's a fantasy that we will have to put more work into in order to make it a reality."

"You're right Oliver. I just wish we had some money of our own to buy land instead of putting all this energy into someone else's dream. The bottom line is real estate, and without it, our great ideas only benefit us in the short run – in the long run, we will be just tourist like everyone else," lamented Patrick.

"You're right. Oh well, it is one hell of an experience we are having, though. At least we are making history and we are able to shape the future, a little. That's worth something," I added.

"Yeah, it is an awesome experience, and we are helping poor people in Jamaica. It is ironic that we are actually poorer than our Jamaican friends. Our families back in the states don't have much money, and we live in one of the poorest sections of the city. Hell, these folks own land and have ways of supporting themselves without having to work for anyone. Damn, even we work for them." Patrick just hit me with cold stark reality.

"Wow, I didn't think of it that way. Well, we do have a nice lifestyle. As for the future, after all, it is their country and their land. We are guests and fortunate ones at that. It feels good to help other people. Although, you have a very good point, what do you think about our future?" I asked.

"Unless we come up with lots of cash to buy land, our future may not be in Jamaica," responded Patrick, "not unless we want to keep moving around the island as natives, fishing and squatting on other people's land and exploring ways to make money, but that could get tiring."

"Yeah, but look at the alternative. Creating a future back home in Philly, and there isn't much opportunity there, other than working for slave wages in a factory, or, at best, going to college in hope of getting a good paying job," I said rather bleakly.

"Bro, when you put it that way it sounds like our future is doomed. We are young and the future is ours for the making. We need to lighten up, Oliver, and be grateful for the amazing life we now have. We have two hot babes in paradise and a great place to live with wonderful Jamaican people, and we've spent very little of our money. I say that tomorrow we find Jamie and Julie and bring them to the West End Cottages and get some love making going on! Whadda ya say, Ollie?"

"Irie, mon. Seen!" I responded. We laughed and went in search of Elijah who was exploring the property with his family. We found him on the fertile, vegetated slope on the southern most part of their property.

"Des land is very good fer growing food an' ganja. An' der is land ta keep goats an' chickens. We will spend some of mi parents' money fer animals an' building materials. Here, Ollie an' Patrick, look at dis map. Where ya t'ink de land end?" Elijah asked.

We looked at the map. Without a method of measuring, it was impossible to know exactly where all the boundaries were. The cliff boundary was clearly laid out and easy to discern, and the northern end bordered the government lighthouse property, which was clearly marked by posts. However, whatever markers may have once existed for the southern border that sloped up the hill appeared to be gone, or overgrown by brush. We estimated the approximate boundaries and Elijah decided that he would find out for certain in due time. For now, he had a good sense of the lay of the land and he was able to determine where to grow crops and graze animals.

Millie and Charley prepared lunch and we ate in the shade of the cottage front courtyard. Norlina said she wanted to clear up the stones of overgrown vegetation and grow fruit trees. Millie gave suggestions on where to grow different varieties of plants and flowers. After eating, we offered to show everyone the cliff area, more specifically the unique deep pool of water in the small cove. They were impressed with the deep blue color, noting that it was the depth and sandy bottom that caused the unique hue of blue. I suggested that cliff jumping, diving, and snorkeling would be a big tourist attraction. Patrick and I were eager to explore the cove-pool and the cliffs below. We were hoping the coral rocks along the cliffs bottom were full of conch.

After resting in the shade, discussing how to fix up the cottages with beds, and other furniture, we began our trek back to Millie and Charley's. I mentioned it would be nice to put colored plaster on the cinder block exterior and interior walls. Norlina liked the idea, adding that she would like to create a color theme. She and Elijah could not agree on what color the cottages should be. Norlina wanted conch pink and Elijah wanted green and blues to match the sky and sea. Edward ended the contention by suggesting that each cottage be in a different color, like the rainbow. Norlina liked the idea, "Di West End Rainbow Sunset Cottages! At de entrance ta our land we will 'ave a sign wit a sun an' a rainbow. Our land is on de very west end of Negril, where it is best ta see de sunset. An' de thunderstorms bring colorful rainbows."

"Irie! I like dat. We now 'ave a name an' we know de colors of de cottages!" announced Elijah. Almost everyone liked the name and the decoration idea, including Millie and Charley. The name Sunset Cottages was short and to the point, but I stayed quiet. Millie talked about the importance of fixing the inside of the cottages with paint and curtains, pictures and comfortable beds. She said she could get good deals on mattresses in Sav-La-Mar. Millie pointed out that there were no outhouses, and that they must have deteriorated over time. It didn't occur to me, since I pissed wherever there was a tree, and I would go further into the hills to do my other business. Charley said it would not be difficult to find where the original latrines were, stating that it would be best to use the holes already dug for that purpose, since cutting into rock required the hiring of special workers with special tools. Elijah said that he would rent a generator and jackhammers to shape steps in the cliffs and if necessary, make more or better latrines.

We arrived at Millie and Charley's past mid afternoon, just as the thunderstorms were moving in to cool off the land. Once the storm passed, Patrick and I walked to Elkannah's to see how he was doing. The addition was finished and he was working the soil on his newly acquired land. We told him we would be fishing the next day. He had gone that morning and his traps were full, but he got no conch. We walked on to Lord Joseph's and as usual, he was not there. We visited the cave and went for a swim. It seemed that Lord Joseph spent most of his time away, most likely in the Cock Pit Country with his family. Patrick reminded me that Jamaica has three growing seasons and that he was most likely tending his winter crop.

We returned to Millie and Charley's for the rest of the evening. In the morning, we went fishing, emptying our traps, catching several fish with our lines, and we traveled south along the cliffs to dive the un-harvested reefs for conch. Patrick speared a fifteen-pound King Fish, a wonderful dinner treat for our Jamaican family. We got back from dropping off our fish to Elkannah sometime after the noon hour.

DANISH DELIGHTS
(Michelin, Helena & Karl)

I suggested to Patrick that we canoe to the beach to check on Jamie and Julie. The wind was in our favor. We arrived on the beach in the late afternoon. There were a few Jamaicans along the beach but no white people. We walked along the water's edge uncertain as to which direction to go. After exploring for an hour or more we returned to our canoe and paddled close along the shoreline scanning the beach heading toward north along Long Bay. We traveled almost all the way to the furthest end of Long Bay, near where we dropped off the girls. Patrick noticed a tall blonde-haired woman just beyond the tree line with a younger white boy. We beached the canoe and decided to investigate.

"Oliver, Patrick, what a pleasant surprise!" Jamie came running toward the canoe to greet us. Julie was right behind. Jamie gave me a warm hug and long kiss. Julie did the same for Patrick.

"Come meet our friends. They're from Copenhagen, Denmark. You will like them!" said Jamie. They led us to their camping area nestled in the shady palms. There were two large tents, several hammocks, and set far back along the road was a small shanty.

"Michelin, Karl, Helena, meet Patrick and Oliver, the white fishermen of Negril!" announced Julie. We shook hands with everyone, all of us repeating names. They spoke English very well with a slight Danish accent. Michelin was the mother. She was in her early thirties, tall, slender, short blond hair, and stunningly beautiful in a mature, movie star kind of way. She was definitely as gorgeous as a playboy bunny but slightly older, with telltale stretch marks from childbirth, which made her look even more sexy in a way that is particularly tantalizing to young men – well, to this young man at least – she was hot! She was wearing a scanty bikini and there was not an ounce of excess fat.

Karl was around fifteen or sixteen years old, perhaps older, a boy with long blond hair – all three of them had platinum blond hair and they were exceptionally attractive people. Especially Helena, who appeared close to seventeen, and she was well developed, although it was obvious that there was more blooming yet to unfold. She was a younger version of her mother, and every bit as lovely. She too was wearing a skimpy bikini.

The campground looked very comfortable and well lived in. Besides the tents and hammocks, there was a campfire ring with a metal tripod for holding a cooking pot and a large grill in the center placed on a ring of rocks. There were tree stumps situated around the limestone lined campfire ring. There was a palm leaf privacy enclosure where a water pipe was run up a wooden post for taking showers. The entire area was well shaded and the view of the sea was stunning.

"Oliver and Patrick, we love it here. It is so nice to experience beach living. It is not as exotic as living on our own pleasure island with two handsome pleasure givers, but it is very nice," said Jamie.

"Yes, I can see why you like it so much. Who is the owner of the land?" I asked.

"Conric," answered Michelin. He is a Rasta who used to be a Jamaican soldier. He retired from the government and recently bought this three-acre tract of beachfront land. He has ambitions to create a tourist setup similar to the Sands Club – a place that is a few hundred yards down the beach. I considered staying there but Conric offered me a better deal – along with a business proposition.

"How long have you been in Jamaica?" I asked Michelin.

Helena, who was eager to join the conversation, answered. "We have been here for a few months. At first, we lived in the Kingston area. We got tired of the city and all its problems. Someone told us about Negril. When we arrived in Negril we camped on several places along the beach, but the owners eventually asked us to move on. Most Jamaicans are tolerant of the gypsy lifestyle for a few days, but extended living is not widely accepted. Sooner than later, they will catch on that there is money to be made in charging people rent. We met Conric and he invited us to stay on his property. He and mother have worked out a business arrangement." I was impressed with Helena's maturity, and insight regarding the hippie campers and the inevitability of a burgeoning tourist industry.

"I'd like to meet him. How much does he charge you?" Patrick asked.

"Five dollars U.S., as most Jamaicans prefer U.S. dollars," responded Michelin. "Conric is allowing the twins to stay here as our guest, unless they choose to stay longer, then he will most likely charge them."

"We like the beach, but we never stayed on it overnight, except for the island out there." I pointed to Booby Cay. "The beach seems to be just as secluded here and the sand is much finer."

"Julie and Jamie have told me the cliffs are very beautiful and that it is fun to swim in the caves. My children want to visit the cliffs. You will take us there, yes?" Michelin requested.

"We can do you better than that. We can canoe all of your equipment up to the lighthouse area and for the same price you can stay in a cottage on the cliffs that has running water and screen windows," offered Patrick.

"Oh can we momma? It would be another adventure," said Karl. I was impressed with Karl's muscular body, and like his mother and sister, he was tall. His voice cracked, indicating that he might still be in the throes of puberty.

"We have things we must complete with our friend, Conric, before we make such a big move. Perhaps you and Helena can go with these gentlemen for a few days," suggested Michelin, which was quite surprising that a woman would entrust her children to strangers. "You can only go if Julie and Jamie go too," she added, which made more sense to me, since she had most likely developed a trusting relationship with Jamie and Julie.

"Oliver and Patrick, why don't you spend the night on the beach and we can travel to the cliffs tomorrow. Jules and I can walk and you can give Karl and Helena a ride in the canoe," suggested Jamie.

"Sounds good to me," piped Patrick, "but that's a long walk for you two."

"We can handle it. We'll make a long day of it, pace ourselves. Hey, what's this cottage you've mentioned?" Julie asked.

"Oh man, it is really far out. Norlina and Elijah have returned and they inherited from their English father fifteen acres of beautiful land beyond the lighthouse on the West End. There are seven cottages that the government had built on the land that their father leased to them. The government left the cottages when Jamaica gained its independence eight years ago. They have been sitting empty all this time. The cottages are in great shape and all of them face the sea. There is a cove with deep water off the cliffs. You have to see it to appreciate its beauty and specialness. We told our Jamaican family-friends all about you two and they invited us to stay in one of the cottages," I was talking very enthusiastically.

"Do you mean the four of us will live in the same cottage?" Jamie asked.

Patrick answered. "Yes. It is large enough. We can create a divider between two sides for privacy if we want, or work out some other arrangement. There is a great deal of land, and no one else lives up there. Privacy will not be an issue."

Jamie commented giving her consent to the idea. "It sounds great. I do like the beach, though. Then again, we did have a great time living on Conch Island, which was high quality beach time. I love the cliffs and especially the sea caves. And the cottages sound wonderful. It will be a whole new adventure."

"West End Rainbow Sunset Cottages is the name Norlina gave to the property," announced Patrick.

"How is Norlina?" Julie asked, with a cautious tone that communicated far more than the simple question. I answered her, as Patrick looked a bit stunned by the question.

"She got married when she was in Kingston. That is one of the reasons they were there for almost a month. His name is Edward. He is a really nice guy. They were sweethearts since childhood and it had always been expected that they would be married."

Julie and Jamie smiled at Patrick, having noticed that he was grinning from ear to ear, and obviously pleased by Norlina's marriage.

"Well, that settles the only big concern Jules and I had. I say we do it. You guys can canoe the Danish family's camping gear and supplies, while the rest of us make the long trek to the lighthouse. If we take our time and plan on traveling the entire day, we'll make it before sunset. Right?" Jamie was planning out the big move, but she didn't really know how far and how long it would take."

"The lighthouse is as far from Millie and Charley's property as their land is far from the Roundabout. That's quite a distance. I think it would be more realistic to plan on making it to Millie's property and staying there for the night," I advised. "I can take most of the heavy gear in the canoe. That will make your traveling easier. Patrick, I'll paddle the canoe and perhaps you can escort the group to the cliff property."

Karl made an offer. "I would like to paddle too. It would be fun to see the coastline of Negril from the sea."

"That's a great idea. You are lighter than Patrick and the extra muscle power will make my job easier. What do you think Patrick?" I asked.

"Sounds like a good idea. I paddled along that shoreline one time too many. I like your suggestion Oliver, I would prefer to walk with the ladies."

"Okay, then. It's you and me, Karl." He smiled at me.

"How many days do you think you will need to take care of your business, Michelin?" Jamie asked.

"Three days, maybe a week. That should be sufficient," she replied. While we were talking, Karl and Helena lit up a spliff and were passing it back and forth. Michelin didn't seem to care. Then, I was shocked when she walked over to them, took the spliff from Karl and proceeded to smoke it for a few long hits before giving it back to him. This was a ganja smoking family, and obviously very liberal about its use.

"You look shocked by my permissiveness." Michelin responded to the stunned look on my face.

"Well, yes. I have never seen a mother in America smoke marijuana with her children," I said.

"In Denmark it is not uncommon among the counter-culture community," she said matter-of-factly. Then what happened next shocked me even more.

"It is very hot. I will go for a swim. Anyone care to join me?" Michelin stripped off her bikini and leisurely strolled to the sea. My eyes followed her remarkable lean yet voluptuous naked body all the way into the water, averting them only after she was fully submerged. Jamie observed me staring at her.

"You already have all you need with me, Oliver. Besides, she is too old for you," Jamie laughed as she stripped off her clothes, unzipped my jean shorts and pulled them down my legs and on to the sand. She took my hand and led me to the water. Julie, Patrick and the two Danish children soon followed. It was amazing that we were all skinny dipping together and we had just met. I thought that this must have been what it was like in the Garden of Eden – no inhibition or shame regarding the naked human body. Then again, the time we spent mostly naked on Conch Island was a better fit for that description.

After swimming, Jamie and I took Karl for a canoe ride to Conch Island. Karl was enthralled with the pool area and helped me gather the conch, some for our dinner and some for Elkannah. He snorkeled on the coral reef for a long while, marveling at the plethora of colorful fish and plant life not found in the water close to shore. When we returned to the beach, Patrick had pan-fried bonito fish he had speared for our mid-day meal.

It was just before sunset when Conric returned. He was a tall handsome man, in his mid to late forties. He had dreadlocks that were slightly streaked with strands of gray, and he wore beads around his neck. I was impressed with his acceptance of our presence and he had heard about the white boys who rescued the young boy from drowning. He guessed we were those boys since we had a canoe and Karl was talking excitedly about Booby Cay. We learned from Conric that most Jamaicans who live along the beach road know of the white fisher boys of Booby Cay who rescued the boy. Patrick got all puffy in the head over the idea that we were legendary.

We learned while eating dinner and having conversation around the evening campfire that the business Michelin referred to was a smuggling operation. She and Conric were mailing quarter ounce packages of ganja to Copenhagen. They explained that they compressed completely dried out ganja buds with absolutely no stems or seeds, between boards using clamps. The buds were flattened into thin sheets and then wrapped in saran plastic, scented mildly with perfume, and slipped into 9 x 11 envelopes. Conric travelled to different post offices around small villages in the Westmoreland and Hanover Districts and beyond, mailing one envelope at a time to avoid suspicion. Michelin explained that he never mailed more than one envelope per seven days from a single post office. The packages were going to Michelin's sister in Copenhagen who sold the ganja for a hefty profit. The money was deposited in Michelin's Bank of Jamaica account, giving her access to take care of her needs and to purchase more ganja. It was an ingenious plan.

Jamie told me they were getting quite wealthy in the process and that Michelin had plans to purchase land in Jamaica. This caused Patrick's entrepreneur fantasy factory mind to churn with ideas, suggesting to me that that was how we could get the money needed to buy land in Jamaica. I had to admit that it was a tantalizing idea. I also learned that Michelin's husband died in a Moroccan prison. He was given an eighteen-month sentence for trying to smuggle hashish. Within the first six weeks of his sentence he tried to escape and was killed. This happened just one year ago. Michelin needed a way to make money for her family and the operation she had going in Jamaica was working very well.

Conric was not too keen on the idea of Michelin and her family moving to the West End. Michelin assured him they would keep their operation going and that the move would most likely be temporary. She said she would continue to pay him his camping fee and for assurance, decided to keep one of her tents on Conric's property. This seemed to comfort Conric a little. I sensed that there might be a romantic thing going on, which was later confirmed by the love making noises I heard coming from her tent later that night.

The twins were staying in the large tent with Karl and Helena. Conric gave the four of us permission to stay in his shanty, which was crowded, having enough room for Julie and Patrick to sleep on Conric's bed while Jamie and I were expected to sleep on the floor. In the corner of the room was Conric and Michelin's ganja pressing operation. I thought about the danger of being involved in a smuggling operation, which was to end up in a Jamaican prison, fines, and eventually deportation. This was the value Conric the ex-soldier had provided. He would not arouse suspicion mailing individual packages from post offices scattered throughout the countryside. He showed us his military identification that he presented to postal workers whenever he mailed a package.

Life on the beach may have been nice for our twin goddesses, but sleeping in a crowded tent and not having the pleasures we provided would not have sufficed for long. It was inevitable that they would want to make a change that involved being with us. Just one day and night having their pleasure-guides-in-paradise made that point very clear. Julie and Patrick made no effort to keep their lovemaking silent, causing Jamie and me to leave the shanty to conduct our own love dance on the beach upon our sleeping bags. We listened to the gently lapping waves, and felt the caress of the warm gentle breeze as we moved our bodies in celestial harmony with the planet, solar system, and infinite starry universe. Love making on Negril's seven-mile beach was amazing!

Patrick spent the early part of the morning conversing with Conric and Michelin while I helped Helena and Karl pack their things into the canoe. I suspected that Patrick was seeking more information about their smuggling operation. Conric was convinced that he could find a taxi that would take the travelers all the way to Millie and Charley's land, and he offered to escort Michelin to her children once they completed their business. I felt a little apprehensive leaving Michelin alone without her children. I studied her face just before Karl and I were about to shove off in the canoe. She looked pleased, at ease, and confident that everything was going to be alright. Michelin was a very strong and confident woman. If anyone was to worry, my guess is it would have to be Conric. Michelin was handsomely sexy, intelligent, independent, and I sensed that no man could take advantage of her. Indeed, she struck me as the type of woman that got her way with every one, especially men.

Karl and I paddled away, slowly, as our canoe was laden with no room to spare. I didn't mind and neither did the muscular Karl. Patrick and the women waved. Conric was nowhere in sight. Karl was in the bow and I in the stern. I watched his head move as he scanned the coastline and the sea horizon. It was a lovely panoramic view of paradise: The sandy white beach decorated by palm trees and bordered by the various shades of turquoise sea, the mountains in the distance where the South Negril River gathered rich nutrients to deposit in the sea, the cliffs outlining the land in gray-blue craggy magnificence in the southwest, and the expansive Caribbean that ended where the sky touched the sea, hinting of far off lands and imagined worlds.

The ever-changing sea bottom beneath the canoe thrilled Karl as the water depth changed and the coral and sand continuously shifted its portrait as we glided past its plethora of sea life and varied topography. He chatted on, describing everything he saw with remarkable detail. He asked if I would teach him to fish and dive for conch. I promised I would and welcomed the additional help, especially since Patrick and I were going to be quite busy working on the West End Rainbow Sunset Cottage development.

The wind was coming from the Northeast, which made our task less burdensome. Once we passed the South Negril River and the Roundabout and came upon the first cliffs, Karl became even more excited. He asked if we could canoe closer along the cliffs. I explained that we were canoeing far from shore to avoid the current of the river, and now that we had passed it, we could move closer. The beauty of the cliffs held Karl spellbound. He talked about volcanoes and how they formed islands, lifting the seabed and its entombed fossilized creatures, and how these cliffs were once liquid stone that had cooled instantly and froze in their current position, imprisoned in time, and yet shaped by the unceasing forces of wind and water. I told him about Lord Joseph's cave, giving a full description of the shape, size, colors, and fossils. He asked if we could stop there so he could swim inside. I agreed.

We paddled the canoe into Lord Joseph's cave and secured it along side one of the ledges. Karl wasted no time exploring. He was able to identify many of the fossil creatures embedded in the walls, and he quickly determined the cave's potential as a living space. He borrowed my fins, goggles and snorkel. I was impressed by his swimming ability, and amazed by his knowledge, which revealed to me not only the quality of his academic education, but also the extent of his intelligence. I told him about Lord Joseph and the Rastas and the rituals. Karl knew a great deal about Rastafarianism and he was quite knowledgeable of the new musical genre that was developing in the poor neighborhood of Kingston, called Trench Town. He talked of The Wailers and their lead singer and songwriter Bob Marley, and how he and his mother tried to visit them in Kingston when they had first arrived, but the band was on tour in England with Johnny Nash. He said that Trench Town is very dangerous and that many Jamaicans harassed his mother. The neighborhood had frightened him, but did not cause him to dislike Jamaicans, explaining that poverty is a terrible disease that leads to violence and a multitude of social sicknesses. It was a reality I knew all too well from growing up in South Philly. Karl's knowledge of Jamaican culture was impressive and quite enjoyable to listen to. It was a treat spending time with him, as he was exceptionally entertaining and very mature and worldly for a young teen. We left the cave feeling refreshed and ready to complete the final leg of our journey.

The cliffs of Millie and Charley's property were finally in view. I was tired, and relieved to have finally arrived. To our surprise, the rest of our group was already there. Jamie and Julie were standing on the cliff waving to us as we came in view. We pulled the canoe along side the landing at the base of the carved steps. We secured the canoe and ascended the cliff. Jamie gave me a warm hug and gentle kiss. She explained how they got there so soon. "We were walking along the beach towards the Roundabout while Conric and Michelin walked along the road. Conric waved down an automobile and offered a fee for taking us to Millie and Charley's. Oliver, you are so right about them, they are a wonderful couple and they knew so much about Jules and me already. Millie said she could see in your eyes, Oliver, your affection for me."

"Yes, Jamie, it is not surprising that others see my fondness for you," I replied.

"Yeah, especially if they spot the bulge in your shorts!" she laughed as she rubbed her hand along the front of my pants. Fortunately, Karl had gone with Julie to greet his sister, who was making her acquaintance with Norlina, Edward, and especially Elijah.

Everyone was hanging out in the flower garden area in front of the two shanties. Julie was introducing Millie, Charley, Norlina and Edward to Karl. Elijah and Helena were off to the side from the rest of the group adamantly talking, not even noticing that Karl had arrived. Patrick was swinging in the hammock on Norlina's porch, smoking ganja.

Elijah looked in my direction and called out, "Ollie, good ta see yah, mon. It is wonderful dat yah an' Patrick bring dees people ta live at West End Sunset Cottages. T'ings are movin' fast. Irie, mon, Jah is smiling upon us. An' dis person mus' be Helena's bredda. Welcome!" Elijah walked up to Karl and shook his hand vigorously. "Rest up fram yah travels, mon, den we tek everyone ta de cottages." I was tired, and I wasn't keen on the idea of walking or canoeing several miles to the cottages. Perhaps I would feel differently with a little rest and some food.

There was plenty of food put out by Millie and Norlina, consisting of a variety of fruit and homemade banana bread. I went to the campground and fell asleep in the hammock. Karl was so excited by all that was going on that tiredness from our canoeing had not overtaken him. While I slept, everyone else continued hanging out, getting to know each other. Jamie woke me up after an hour or so as everyone was eager to get going to the cottages. It was late afternoon and would be dark by the time we got there. I mentioned that to Jamie and she reminded me that the moon was almost full and there would be plenty of light.

Donkey was packed up with lots of provisions. Patrick agreed to canoe to the cottages with Karl. I was relieved because I wanted to be with Jamie, plus I needed a break from paddling. Although it would be easier than walking if the canoe was not full of gear. Patrick loaded the bamboo raft with more stuff. The priority was to get the Danish family and Jamie and Julie's stuff to the cottages. Patrick and I would have to travel down this way to transport our fish traps and to continue our work with Elkannah, so we could do the moving of our gear over a period of days.

The walk was pleasant. Since it was approaching sunset, the air was cooling and the breeze off the ocean was picking up. It was a good thing for Patrick and Karl that the wind was still blowing out of the Northeast. There was excitement in the air and no wonder: new people, new land, new place to live, and lots of possibilities. Elijah led the way, walking at a brisker pace than the rest of us, and Helena was by his side. I have never seen Elijah so animated. I knew he was very excited about the land and all of the opportunities that came with it, but it was the beautiful Danish babe that was enlivening his personality. The two of them were talking to each other non-stop! And I was surprised to hear Helena speaking fluently in patois. The Danish family was quite good with languages. I wondered what they could possibly be talking about and what could they possibly have in common, being from two distinctly different worlds. The fact that they were the same age and opposite sex was most likely enough to keep them intensely engaged.

We arrived at the cottages an hour or so after the sun went down. Elijah's fast pace and his occasional word-blast of encouragement kept us moving faster than was necessary. Norlina and Edward walked directly to the center cottage, the fourth one, and no one objected. Elijah took the first one and I led the twins to the last one, cottage number seven. Karl and Helena just stood in the courtyard not knowing what to do. After Elijah dropped off his belongings he went to the Danish siblings and directed them to cottage number two, next to his. Millie and Charlie settled in cottage number three, which would be a temporary arrangement for them. Elijah had packed oil and new wicks for the lamps that were already provided in each cottage. As for what to sleep on, well, there were no mattresses so some of us strung up hammocks inside the cottages while others spread out blankets and sleeping bags on palm leaf matting.

Patrick and Karl soon arrived, although they had to make use of the metal ladder on the cliff in front of the lighthouse. We all pitched in helping unload the canoe and raft, since it was a task made more laborious because of the cliff arrangement. We knew we had to design and construct steps and concrete pads along the cliffs in front of the cottages all in due time.

Charley built a nice campfire and Millie along with Norlina prepared dinner. Patrick was in the mood to play music. I was pleased that he packed his guitar on the raft and I brought my easy to transport flute in my backpack. Just for the hell of it we played the mind surfing song we had written along with our Ghetto Flower friends a few years ago while at the Jersey shore. We had taught the song to Jamie and Julie so they sang along with Patrick while I weaved in and out of the melody. To the pleasant surprise of everyone, Karl took out a set of congas from a canvas bag that he had packed in the canoe, and man he was really, really good.

Elijah said that while he was in Kingston, he heard songs on the radio played by The Wailers. They had released an album called The Best of the Wailers and there was one song he particularly liked, called Cheer Up. He sang it for us so we could learn the lyrics. Karl beat out the timing for the Cheer Up song and told Patrick what the chords were to the original. Everyone learned the song and we played it through many times until we all knew the lyrics by heart. Eventually, we made up our own verse and chanted it over and over in the classic reggae beat:

Cheer up brothers,
Cheer up sisters,
Cheer up madda n fadda too,
Cheer up fer de change has come,
Livin' at de sunset cottages,
Cheer up, Irie, I n I One

We settled in to talking quietly around the fire, and then couples went off for privacy. Jamie and I decided to walk closer to the cliff edge. We startled Elijah and Helena who were leaning against a palm tree kissing. There was such a strong feeling of romance in the air that I wouldn't have been surprised if Millie and Charley were making whoopee. The only creatures left out of the love making energy were Karl and Donkey.

SUNSET VILLAGE CREATION

The next morning the twins, Patrick and I woke up before everyone else. It had become our ritual to rise at the first light of dawn to practice meditation on the cliff. We had missed several days of meditating together. The usual practice was to begin with deep breathing exercises to calm our bodies and still our minds. Jamie began repeating instructions she had given before, suggesting that we visualize our minds as an expansive sky with each thought being a cloud that floats across the sky. She said that all we need do is observe the thought-clouds drifting by, and not attach ourselves to them and to let them go from our consciousness. She said that we can notice the emotions associated with thoughts, and how some have a stronger grip on us than others, and that we need not permit these feelings to overwhelm us and capture our attention.

The practice of this technique and concept was profound because each time I used it I learned something new. This time I thought more about how my thoughts do not control me, that I decide which thoughts to pay attention to. This idea led me to think about the origin of thoughts. It is obvious that thoughts come from my mind. However, it seems like they come and go with little control on my part. I contemplated once again how haphazard my thinking really is. I also wondered why some thoughts have more meaning and feeling than others. Of course, the extent of meaning had to do with how significant the experiences associated with these thoughts, images, and feelings were on impacting my life. Such as the loss of someone I love. Then, I realized that most of my thoughts that have powerful emotions are associated with my past, or anticipation of what may or may not happen in the future. The past and future are not happening in the present moment, so in actuality they aren't happening at all. Can I conclude that that which is real is only what is happening in the present moment? Or is what I determine as being real based upon what I am thinking and interpreting, and therefore is largely created by me?

Then, I wondered about the purpose of meditation. Was it to still my thoughts, to detach me from them? Or was it meant to get me to think about thinking, and to contemplate what is real and what isn't, and how my thoughts determine most of what I experience through interpretation and perception, which are based on previous experiences, values and beliefs, as well as projections into the future? Meditation had caused me to do some serious mind surfing! I was enjoying the process because even though I felt calm and at peace, my mind was free to explore new insights into how the mind works in relation to life circumstances and our ultimate happiness.

When the meditation time had passed, we smiled at each other. I wanted to share my experience and insights. However, I sensed this was not the appropriate time. I decided I would discuss my thoughts later. Patrick stood up and walked to the very edge of the cliff and looked down into the deep pool in the cliff-lined cove below.

"This is a beautiful cliff cove. The water is deep and perfect for high-diving." Without another word, Patrick leaped off the cliff in a graceful swan dive. He entered the water in perfect, almost splashless form. I couldn't resist the temptation. I jumped without hesitation. Diving was not my thing, but I loved cliff jumping. The water was refreshingly lukewarm. I had hoped that Jamie and Julie would join us – they didn't. They hooted and hollered and waved to us and continued to watch as we swam around the cove, looking for a way to climb up the cliff. What we found was an opening in the cliff that was not very large. Once inside, the enormity of the cave was stunning. At first sight, it appeared more than half the size of Lord Joseph's cave in depth, breadth and height, but equal in beauty. The walls were weathered smooth, and although there were few flat ledges, there were many rounded and curved rock formations. Like the other caves we were in, there were some shallow areas formed by sand trapped between rocks. I swam out of the cave to let Jamie and Julie know that we were okay and that we had found a treasure. Patrick explored the entire cave and determined that there was no access to the land. Of all the caves we had found, Lord Joseph's was the only one that had an entrance from the ground above. If we could get our hands on some dynamite, or a jackhammer maybe we could create one.

The cliff walls were mostly steep, with a few areas where it would be possible to climb if the rock was not riddled with razor sharp protrusions. We dove and jumped with our sneakers on, in case we had to walk over cliffs in our attempt to get back to the top.

We had to swim to the metal ladder on the lighthouse cliff, which was a relatively short distance for experienced swimmers. When we returned to the cottages, there was fresh fruit salad and coffee waiting for us.

"How was the swim?" Jamie asked.

"Great!" I said enthusiastically. "The cove-pool is at least forty feet in the deepest area and there's a mini coral reef running through the center. I've never seen anything like it. The cave is not visible from the cliff top because the entrance is very low and hidden by a huge rock. The inside is a lot like Lord Joseph's cave but smaller and of course there's no entrance from the land. It's a great place to keep out of the sun during the hottest part of the day."

"Yeah, Oliver is right," chimed Patrick, "and because of the deep pool and coral, the entrance to the cove will be a great spot for placing our fish traps. The pool should prove to be a good place to spear fish as well. We have to chisel in steps and pour concrete in places for easy access. For now, we could build a bamboo ladder or maybe a rope ladder so people don't have to swim to the lighthouse to get in and out."

Karl jumped up and said, "Let's build a raft and anchor it in the center of the cove. It will be strong enough to hold lots of people and one that we can tie the canoe too. I know how to make rope ladders. Where can we get thick rope?"

"Sav-La-Mar market is a good place ta get rope, mon. Der lots of t'ings we be needin'. Tomorrow I go to Sav-La-Mar an' order every t'ing an 'ave truck deliver quick, mon. We mek de list today," announced Elijah.

Jamie took out her sketchpad and offered to write down everything we would need. It was a long list. We spent most of the morning talking about construction materials, tools, furniture, and most importantly, Jamie used her artistic skills to sketch out everything we planned to do: plastering the cottages and painting them, the cliff sunbathing concrete pads and where the steps and rope ladder would be. Karl drew plans for the raft-dock and Norlina told Jamie how the courtyard plants and furnishings were to be designed, and most importantly, the architecture of the cliff-side restaurant and bar – again, using Karl's engineering talents to design the structure. When we finished, we had the entire West End Rainbow Sunset Cottage Village completely planned and sketched.

"This is going to cost a lot of money," I said.

Elijah responded. "No problem, mon. Fadda an' madda left enuff money fer us ta invest, mon."

"Yes, an' Edward is going ta help," added Norlina, suggesting that he has some inheritance as well.

"We will 'ave enough, mon, ta set everyt'ing up. Den we mus' 'ave de tourist ta support everyt'ing. De tourist will come, mon, I know it. Many are already 'ere." Elijah was confident of his plan and he was a visionary. Patrick and I knew he was right. We also knew that once the village was set up, the days of inexpensively living on the property would be gone. They would have to charge more money in order to support the operation. Currently, the money being paid by the Danish family and Jamie and Julie provided a modest income and more importantly, we were donating our labor and Elijah was well aware of its value.

Elijah said it would take a week or more to get all the supplies we needed, and that there were a lot of things we could do in preparation. I was impressed with his natural leadership ability and his tireless work ethic. He gave instructions on the physical labor that could be done to improve the property before the materials arrived, which was mostly minor maintenance to the cottages, landscaping that involved pulling weeds and transplanting plants, and preparing the soil in the food and ganja gardens along the slope of the hill.

Charley had found the latrine area, and as he suspected, the holes in the ground were still there and they were deep. They had grown over with thick thorny brush. We were lucky that no one had fallen in. I asked Charley if he thought the waste would leech into the sea and he assured me that the rock formation was such that that would not happen. I had to take his word for it. Besides, the latrines were on the other side of the road, a good distance from the sea.

"Hey, where does the water come from? Is there a well?" I asked, as the thought occurred to me that human waste could contaminate the water supply.

"No well, mon. Dere no electricity in de West End ta operate pumps. De wells on de West End were hand pumped, mon, but dey rarely used since de pipe come. Der is a town up in de hills not far fram here, Orange Hill. Dis could be where de government pumps de water. Maybe dey bring de pipe from Negril River aw de way ta de lighthouse, but dat very far, mon," responded Charley.

Millie and Charley stayed only a few days before heading back to their property. They were pleased to see their grandchildren building their dreams. Elijah and Norlina were assured that they could use Donkey whenever they needed him.

For the next two weeks all of us worked hard making improvements on the property. Karl, Patrick, and I constructed a bamboo ladder, a rope ladder, and a large bamboo raft. We also relocated our fish traps, making it easier to provide fresh fish for our community. Karl enjoyed fishing, especially spear fishing and diving for conch. We had no trouble meeting our obligation to Elkannah, especially with Karl's help.

Karl got the idea of making a canoe. He received instruction from Elkannah on how to do it. There was a huge Jamaican cottonwood tree that was up-rooted by a storm long before we settled on the land. Elijah wanted to use it for firewood but Karl persuaded him otherwise. Patrick discussed the plans to adapt Elkannah's canoe for sailing. These plans were modified to make a canoe-sail fishing and transportation craft out of the fallen tree. Elkannah had inherited canoe-making tools from his father and he permitted the ambitious duo to borrow them. Patrick and Karl both had a natural inclination for designing and building. They approached creating their craft with a great deal of zeal. Elkannah offered guidance and some labor during the process, particularly when they burned the center portion of the wood to make it easier to gut out. And later, Harold's wood carving skills and tools became a huge help, especially his artistic talents. This canoe was going to be twice as wide as Elkannah's canoe because the diameter of the tree was greater and the purpose was not for gliding easily through the water under the power of paddling. It was to be moved by the wind and its cargo would primarily be people. Patrick suggested that they make several canoe-sails to create a water taxi service from the Roundabout to Sunset Cottages.

The materials ordered at Sav-La-Mar had arrived! Two five-ton trucks delivered everything in one haul: an assortment of tools – including a gasoline generator and jackhammers, wood, cinder blocks, flagstone, several skid loads of bags of concrete, corrugated metal sheets, paint, and even mattresses. The variety and sheer bulk of items that came off the truck were astounding. These were the materials that we would use to shape our small village. They would make the palette for artists to transform dreams into reality.

On the same day the materials arrived, so did Michelin, and to the pleasant surprise of Patrick and me, Harold the wood carver was with her. She had met him while walking on the road. During their introductions, Harold learned that she was on her way to meet up with her children who were in our care. Harold was on his way to Millie and Charley's to find us. It was on the road in front of their property where Michelin and Harold had met.

For several weeks, we worked ceaselessly constructing the West End Rainbow Sunset Cottage Village – a name we shortened to *Sunset Village*. Michelin was a talented interior decorator and artist. She and Jamie spent some of their leisure time drawing and creating watercolor paintings of nature scenes that were used to decorate the cottages. Elijah enlisted everyone's help in applying concrete to the outside walls of the cottages. He hired an army of young Jamaicans, which accelerated the work progress. These Jamaicans knew how to use the jackhammer to make the steps and other cliff reshaping projects. Paint was mixed into the concrete, with each cottage a different pastel shade, keeping with the rainbow theme. Michelin and Jamie painted a beautiful mural of a rainbow sunset on the front of the center cottage.

Norlina and Edward were the landscape architects, beautifying the grounds with a variety of plants and flowers. They rearranged the flagstone in the courtyard into a sun with pathway rays leading to each cottage and to the cliff. They also put a lot of energy into the construction of the restaurant-bar, doing most of the hard labor, while those of us who had the penchant for carpentry and masonry work performed the skilled tasks. The restaurant-bar was going to take more materials than originally thought, and would most likely be the last project completed. Originally, Norlina envisioned a simple open circular structure, but soon realized she needed it larger than expected to accommodate tables as well as the bar counter. The bar counter sides were to be made of bamboo, but the top needed solid wood. Harold suggested cutting down a cedar tree, so we did. All of the other construction on the buildings and courtyard was largely cosmetic, with the exception of the latrine houses. Harold took on the task of building the latrines, creating outhouse structures there were quite artistic. One looked like the head of a Rasta complete with dreadlocks, another looked like a bong. He used bamboo for the sides and doors and corrugated sheet metal for the roofs.

Patrick, Karl, and I, besides our fishing duties and assisting with the construction whenever necessary, worked tirelessly on the canoe-sail and the cliff-cove area. Harold's wood carving skills and sharp specialized tools enabled us to make significant progress in making the canoe-sail. Karl, with the sewing skills of Norlina, converted a waterproof canvas tarp that he used for his tent into a sail. The burning and digging out of the twenty-six foot cottonwood log took a lot of time. Karl's engineer genius became ever more evident when he kept intact a portion of the wood where the mast was to be placed, unburned. He later used Harold's hand-drill to make a deep hole. Karl inserted steel reinforcement bars inside one of his metal tent poles and then surrounded the pole with long pieces of cotton wood attached with rope wrapped entirely around the outside, creating a mast for the sail.

Karl also used cottonwood and rope to construct outriggers to stabilize the canoe. Harold carved a rudder that Karl attached using a metal pin and peg that enabled it to be easily pivoted. The boom was made of cottonwood as well and designed to fold the sail upright against the mast. The outriggers had cottonwood platforms built across the 'arms' that were attached to the canoe sides by peg and rope. These platforms were designed to hold gear. The canoe-sail was a beauty to behold. Harold carved on its sides a sun with rays along with the name of our village. Karl had to make minor adjustments to his design to make the craft sail steady. Its swift and graceful movement under the power of a full strong wind given its size and weight was a welcomed surprise.

Karl took the canoe-sail out to deeper water to spear fish and to use hand lines. He was able to catch large tuna – too large to put in the canoe, requiring him to attach them to the cottonwood-bamboo platforms as he sailed back to shore.

The hardest and loudest work along the cliffs was made by the jackhammer, which was used for chiseling out steps and other reshaping of the cliff area – it was very, very noisy – so much so that whenever it was being used, Jamie and I would take canoe trips along the coast and explore the cliffs.

We poured large concrete pads on all three sides of the cliff-cove, and each had its own stair access to the water. We chose these areas strategically, keeping in mind the need for easy access from the restaurant as well as one staircase that led directly to the cave. We explored the possibility of using the jackhammer to create a hole on the cliff top as an entrance to the sea cave, but the rock was too thick.

As we worked together on these various projects, a close bond formed among all of us. Individual relationships blossomed along with a strong sense of tribal community. Elijah and Helena moved in together, which to my surprise did not faze Michelin in the least. Harold and Michelin became romantically involved. It turned out that both of them were students of anthropology and religion. Michelin had a doctorate degree in anthropology and the fact that Harold graduated from Oxford had appealed to her intellect. Harold was a near perfect specimen of the Jamaican male, a fact that helped fan the flames of passion between them. They moved in together, which prompted Karl to set up his own makeshift residence in the sea cave, respecting his mother's right to privacy. Karl created level ledges inside the cave using concrete and cinder blocks. The cave became his primary living space and it was a favorite community mid afternoon hangout as a respite from the heat.

On most nights we played music and told stories around the campfire after partaking of our communal meal. Most members of our community soon joined the meditations inspired and occasionally facilitated by Jamie, with Elijah, Norlina, and Edward participating sporadically. The community meditation sessions developed spontaneously on the cliff during sunsets. We were not creating a religion, although we frequently delved into religious and philosophical discussions around the campfire. No one was trying to convince anyone to follow a set of beliefs, and creating a religion with doctrines would be quite contrary to our collective intentions. We simply evolved into a community based on mutual respect and friendship. It was amazing that people from so many different cultures, ethnic and racial heritage were able to get along so well. Work on common goals, healthy friendships and romantic relationships, eating meals in common, openness to sharing ideas, playing music and other artistic expressions, and communal meditation all contributed to the creation of our eclectic tribal community.

Of course there were copious amounts of ganja consumed. The only persons not consuming ganja were Jamie, Harold, Norlina and I. Everyone else were ritualistic consumers, including during our meditation sessions, which were mostly held in complete silence, the only words spoken were usually by Jamie at the beginning to announce the official start of silence and to occasionally offer a focus. Following the meditations, those who felt the need, shared what was on their minds, and these expressions were almost exclusively of a spiritual and deeply personal nature. On one occasion, Jamie spoke of the preciousness of each and every moment in life, and that her time at Sunset Village and more specifically with me was the most treasured period of her life. There was a melancholy tone to her expression, which for reasons I did not understand had caused the deeper part of my being to shudder ever so slightly. I tried to ignore the feeling, but it haunted me from that moment on, particularly when I would awaken in the middle of the night, a time when I loved to observe Jamie sleeping peacefully.

After one of our morning meditations the image of Sandy, my South Philly sweetheart, was overwhelmingly present in my mind. It occurred to me that perhaps the unsettled feeling that kept reoccurring had to do with my concern for her, and the guilt associated with me having found a new love. It was time for me to have a talk with Jamie on this matter.

"Jamie, I need to share something with you."

"Certainly, what is it? You sound so worried!"

"I have a love relationship with a girl in Philly."

"I know."

"How?"

"I heard you mention her to Patrick."

"This doesn't bother you?"

"No. Why should it?"

"Because I love you, and, and, I love her too."

"That is not so strange. She is there and I am here. She is part of your life in another universe, and I am in this one. The only potential conflict would be if the three of us were in the same space and time," replied Jamie in her familiar philosophical tone.

"There is conflict in my heart. I have not told her about you and I am only telling you about her now. A part of me feels like I am betraying the both of you."

"Oliver, you are betraying no one. You feel conflicted because there is no betrayal in you. People who are true betrayers of their trust and love for others rarely, if ever, feel conflicted. You are a good man. Love has chosen us, and it has chosen you and Sandy. There may be a time when you and her are together again." Jamie's words were partially comforting because she was accepting my feelings for Sandy, but I could not bear the thought of ever being without Jamie.

"Jamie, I love you with all my soul. There can never be a single moment that I would be without you." I said emphatically.

"Life is full of surprises, Oliver, and lots of uncertainty. At one time, you could never imagine being without Sandy, I am sure, and yet here you are completely in love with me."

"That's what puzzles me."

"Yes, love is a puzzle, perhaps the greatest challenge and mystery of all."

"The uncertainty doesn't frighten you?" I asked.

"Of course it does, otherwise I wouldn't be human. The Buddha taught that life is constant change and that our suffering is the result of wanting to hold on to things as though they are permanent, resulting in inevitable disappointment and suffering. I have a slightly different perspective than that of the venerable Buddha."

"What's that?"

"That love is eternal. It is constant, and the only change associated with that love is its form of expression. Right now you and I are one form of that expression. In another time and space, it is you and Sandy."

"But don't you want our love expressions to continue forever?"

"Yes I do, and they will. Maybe not as we currently experience them, but the love can never die. I believe that love is the reality-substance of all of creation. It cannot die, Oliver, it only varies its expressions."

"But, I don't want it to vary away from the expression that you and I share."

"Neither do I!" Jamie's affirmation was a deep comfort. "However, Oliver, change is constant, and although it is quite possible that you and I will always be in direct relationship with each other, it is also possible that we will one day separate. You must accept this as a possibility." Jamie's statement that I must accept the possibility of our not being together incited that horrific soul-shudder that was so disturbing to me. I realized that it was not my guilt over Sandy that caused that soul disturbance. It was the fear of losing Jamie.

"I am afraid of losing you, Jamie."

"And I am afraid of losing you, Oliver. But we must train our minds to enjoy the beauty of every moment we share as though it could be our last, and as though it will go on forever – for even though our love is forever, the current form of expression will change! I think it may be time for you to send a letter to Sandy telling her the truth."

"I know you're right. In a way I've been a coward not telling her. I've been telling myself that it would be best to tell her face-to-face. Now I know that that is denial on my part."

"Well, Oliver, it's time to be courageous. It is the right thing to do!"

"Yes, yes, it is. Thank you for understanding and for being honest. I will give it some thought and write a letter to her soon." Jamie and I hugged. I was relieved that I shared this with Jamie and that I now knew what I had to do.

I noticed Karl coming out of his sea cave lair. He dove in the water and swam to the large bamboo raft where our fishing canoe and the canoe-sail were anchored. I watched as he prepared the canoe-sail. I called out to him, "Karl, wait, I want to sail with you."

"Come on, then!" he called back. I put on my shorts and jumped off the cliff into the cove-pool and swam to the canoe-sail. We paddled the craft out of the cove and into the open sea. We unfurled the sail and pointed the bow toward the horizon. The craft glided along smoothly.

"She would move faster if we had only one outrigger," cried Karl above the sound of the wind on the sail, "but she would not be as steady." I was impressed with the design of the canoe-sail. Patrick had shared with me his ideas of converting Elkannah's fishing canoe into a sail boat to make our trips to Conch Island less arduous, and I saw some of his ideas in the design of this craft, but Karl's engineering genius along with the talents of Harold, made this vessel not only versatile, but a work of art.

It was impressive how quickly we were out in very deep water. If we continued toward the horizon, it would not be long before the island was out of sight. Karl turned the boat toward the east and furled the sail.

"I want to try spear fishing. I need you to fasten the rudder so the bow is facing east and the wind doesn't catch the canoe broadside and move it too far from our current position. Our anchor rope is not long enough for this water depth. Paddle to keep up with me if I swim too far from the canoe-sail." Karl put on his fins, mask and snorkel and loaded the spear gun. He slipped into the water. The water was darker blue at this depth, yet still had a turquoise hue. Some time had passed as I watched Karl move through the water, and then suddenly, flying fish surrounded me. I was in the midst of a school of them. They were all around Karl as well. These fish were beautiful! They appeared to have four wings, two longer and two shorter. They soared as high as three feet above the water's surface for distances of at least twelve feet.

There were hundreds of them. They were not very big, perhaps ten to sixteen inches long. They had bluish-green and grey-black scales. I had never seen them before. I had to move my body to keep them from hitting me, and some landed in the canoe and became trapped, while others landed on the outrigger platforms only to flip off again. Karl stopped swimming and looked back at me, waving an arm in an arc in recognition of this amazing aerial display. I knew nothing about these fish, and naively enough, I thought they actually had wings and could really fly. Karl later informed me that they used their fins to glide through the air. They propelled themselves out of the water to avoid predators, gliding on wind currents along the sea's surface. The height and distance of their flight depended upon the wind currents and the speed at which they broke the water's surface. We soon discovered that Mahi-mahi, or Dolphin fish were chasing the flying fish. I could see them beneath the water's surface. Karl had speared one and was having difficulty holding on. It was actually pulling him through the water. I had to paddle hard to keep up with him. Eventually, the Mahi-mahi slowed down and Karl was able to bring it to the canoe-sail. It took at least twenty minutes for the fish to tire out. I was impressed with Karl's strength. I believe if I was the one who had speared the fish, I would have let go of the spear, because it would have worn down my strength.

It was a gorgeous fish, although somewhat odd-looking. Its sides were golden with iridescent greens and blues, and its belly was white and yellow. It had a bulging head with a body that tapered increasingly towards its tail. This fish was three feet long and weighed over twenty-five pounds. Karl tied the fish to one of the bamboo platforms. Karl got in the boat and just sat for a while staring at the fish as he regained his strength. The fish flailed about, causing a loud flapping noise on the water's surface and splashing water in our faces.

"That was a tough fish to haul in! Very strong! I thought I might have to let it go, but I did not want to lose the spear. There were a lot of them. I shot my spear in the school and it was impossible to miss. They were feeding on the flying fish. Wow! What an experience," Karl was ten times more thrilled than I was and I was completely amazed by the experience.

"I have to learn to spear fish. That must have been awesome," I exclaimed.

"True dat!" said Karl. "I would not have the strength to catch another right now. Too bad they have moved on, for once I regain my strength I would catch more." Indeed the scene passed by quickly. Karl had seized the moment. The schools of Dolphin and flying fish had appeared in a sudden burst and were quickly gone, as both species travel very fast. We were lucky to have been directly in their path. This was by far the most thrilling fishing experience I had ever had.

Once Karl gained his strength, he unfurled the sail and we headed back to the cliff. As the Mahi-mahi fish began to die, its colors changed from its original beautiful iridescent blue, green, and yellow to predominately silver with blue spots on its flanks. I was impressed with the size of our fish. It was going to provide Sunset Village with a lot of meat. We were going to have a feast. I decided that taking the time to fish in deep waters would be very profitable as the bigger fish had more meat. One fish would bring as much money as a dozen or more caught in our traps.

As we approached the cliffs, Karl furled the sail and we paddled the rest of the way into the cove, attaching the canoe-sail to the bamboo raft. I took note that the fishing canoe was gone. Patrick was most likely hunting for conch, line fishing, or maybe checking the traps. It turned out that he had done all of those things and that he took Edward with him. Edward was not a fisherman but he had expressed interest in learning. I was pleased that Patrick and Edward were spending time together, and that Patrick was tending to our obligations to Elkannah.

After hoisting the Mahi-mahi up the cliff using a rope and pulley apparatus that Karl designed, I asked if he would teach me to sail. He agreed but wanted to wait until late afternoon when the winds were good and he was well rested. Later that day, I had my first of many sailing lessons. I learned quickly and decided that I would work on creating another canoe-sail.

Jamie and Julie asked if I was interested in visiting the Negril Elementary School, and I was. We decided to wait for Patrick to return, hoping he would want to come along, and he did. Michelin and Helena decided to come as well. We spent the entire afternoon with the school children playing soccer, sharing music, storytelling, and doing art. Helena had inherited her mother's artistic talent and she also had a lovely voice. Michelin had brought a significant supply of paper and colored pencils to share with the children. I told them the story of catching the Mahi-mahi. Most of the children had seen a sailboat, but never a canoe with a sail. They wanted to see the boat and go for a ride. I told them that I had yet to learn to sail the boat and once I did that perhaps something could be arranged.

Again, the thought occurred to me that I would one day become an elementary school teacher. The children complemented me on my storytelling, which made me feel good. I even assisted the classroom teacher in a writing lesson. I encouraged students to write stories of their personal experiences. They became enthusiastic and several told stories of their families, which gave me more insight into Jamaican culture – particularly how removed many fathers were in the rearing of children, and that they had siblings from different mothers. I told them that I write in my journal everyday. Some of them expressed the desire to keep a daily journal, but that paper supplies were limited. I decided that I would start a campaign to ship school supplies from the U.S. to this school. Perhaps I could persuade my Ghetto Flower friends to bring supplies with them, if and when they come to Negril.

I mentioned the idea of school supplies to the Sunset Village community. Harold suggested that purchasing the materials in Jamaica would help the local economy. I said that friends in other countries, meaning Denmark, England, and the United States, could get religious organizations to send supplies, and that they would most likely be more comfortable sending supplies than cash. Harold said he had lots of friends in England that would be glad to help, and Michelin said she would write a request to the university where she had graduated. Jamie and Julie had already written to their parents and were certain that materials would soon be arriving. I wasn't surprised that they had already taken the initiative. We decided to take time out during a hot afternoon to write letters requesting supplies to be sent directly to the school. We created a list and then asked children and teachers what they needed and would like to have. The list was long and varied.

Finally, I wrote to Sandy and told her how much I missed her, and gave a few anecdotes about my adventures in paradise. Then, I told her about Jamie - that I was in love. I knew that this letter would break her heart and that was why I was so afraid to tell her, why I had been such a coward. I was aware that there was a big crack in the center of my heart. I shared my feelings with Harold, giving him a full account of the history. He laid his hand on my shoulder and said, "Cracks are very good, it is how the light comes through." His philosophical comment made me think of the flowers that would spring up between the cracks in the concrete sidewalks in my Philadelphia neighborhood, and how my friends referred to themselves as Ghetto Flowers.

GHETTO FLOWERS IN PARADISE
(Liam, Luke, Jonathan, Donna, Roseann & Shannon)

Time in our little village was an interesting phenomenon. In one sense it stood still, almost as though it did not exist. It was measured by the weather and the positions of the sun and moon. On the other hand, it went by quickly, as if being busy in our daily activities had caused time to accelerate. All of our activities were rewarding and relaxing, whether doing physical labor or leisure activities – they were all healthy and enjoyable. Weeks and then months had gone by as we settled into our island paradise lifestyle. The crops were growing, the cottages were renovated, the landscaping work - although continuously evolving - was well established, the restaurant bar was nearly completed, and our first tourists had arrived. It was our friends from South Philadelphia: Liam, Luke, Jonathan, Roseann, Donna, and Shannon. Patrick and I were both shocked and pleasantly surprised. We were hanging out in the courtyard setting up the campfire for that night's community dinner, music, and storytelling when the Ghetto Flowers walked in.

"Wow! Far out! Man! You're really here. I can't believe it!" shouted Patrick. I just stood there completely stunned by the scene before me. It was surrealistic to suddenly have appear in front of me people from my other world – that strange universe that seemed to exist far, far away and long, long, ago. And yet here they were, live and in color and very white looking. We hugged and laughed and patted each other on the back. There were statements made about how we looked and the beauty of Jamaica. We were eager to show them around but I knew they must be exhausted from their travels so we led them directly to their cottages.

The Ghetto Flowers had received our letter about school supplies and brought two trunks full of stuff. They had to rent two taxis to transport everything they brought with them. There was far more equipment than was necessary, particularly the tents, two large ones which were not needed since they were going to occupy two cottages, three guys in one and three girls in the other. I wondered if any of them had romantic relationships going on. None of them were a couple when I left Philly back in October.

Once they dropped off their stuff in their cottages, we reassembled in the courtyard. We then went to the cliff, and true to their nature, the three boys dove off the cliff. Patrick and I followed after them. We swam to the raft, where they checked out the fishing canoe and the canoe-sail. They had lots of questions about the craft. We filled them in on bits and pieces of how things got built and developed but it was way too much information to share at one time. Roseann and Shannon dove off the cliff to join us and Donna decided to take the stairs that led down to the cave. All of us swam to greet Donna and to explore the cave together. It was a trip hearing them express their amazement at the beauty of everything. It was as though we were listening to ourselves when we had first experienced Jamaica. We were seated on ledges and rocks around the cave, which was an amazing environment to be with my Philly friends.

"Man this cave is really far out. Look at those colors," said Liam.

"Yeah, what's with all those insect looking things in the walls?" Luke asked.

"Fossils," said Jonathan.

"So how's the dope?" Liam asked.

"Fantastic, plentiful and cheap," responded Patrick.

"When do we get to smoke some?" Luke asked.

"As soon as we get up to the top of the cliffs. I am surprised you haven't smoked during your travel from Montego Bay to Negril," said Patrick.

"Didn't want to take any risks. It was my caution or these guys would definitely be stoned by now," said Jonathan. "The taxi driver offered to smoke with us and he tried selling ganja. I told him we weren't interested, much to the dismay of everyone else."

"Oliver is practicing abstinence," announced Patrick.

"No surprise there. He never liked marijuana anyway. Freaked you out, right, Oliver?" said Jonathan.

"Yeah, it used to freak me out. But I did my share of smoking ganja in Jamaica. It's different for me here than in Philly. I don't get paranoid or anxious when I smoke here," I replied.

"A Rastafarian, Lord Joseph, cleansed our minds of Babylon. That made it possible for him to smoke ganja," commented Patrick.

"Babylon? That's a Bible thing, and who is this Lord Rasta person?" Jonathan asked.

"Lord Joseph is a Rastafarian and he is a friend of ours that has a really cool sea cave, similar to this one but bigger and it has an entrance from the land. We lived in it for while. We'll take you there," I said excitedly.

"So how did he cleanse your mind, Oliver?" Donna asked.

"Oh, he did some chanting and we smoked Lambs Bread, that's a super potent ganja. It was part of a ritual, but I honestly don't think it did anything, really. It's the fact that I am in a more pleasant environment that makes it possible for me to get high. Plus, without realizing it, he started me on the path of meditation."

"Wow, meditation? That sounds interesting," replied Donna. I wasn't surprised by Donna's interest in meditation. She had always struck me as a person interested in spiritual things.

"Yeah, we meditate at sunset every day as a community. Patrick, Jamie, Julie, and I meditate every morning," Once I mentioned Jamie's name, I realized that my friends would know about my relationship with her, as all of them were friends with Sandy. My two worlds were merging, and as thrilling as it was, the issue of Sandy and Jamie, the two loves in my heart, made me very, very uneasy.

Shannon continued to press me on my abstinence decision. "Jamie, Julie, community, meditating – wow, that's a lot of information. We're just going to have to learn about all this stuff in due time. What I want to know is why you have chosen to not smoke pot since it no longer makes you afraid. I want to know because I think I am the only one who isn't interested in smoking dope."

"I had an experience while tripping on mushrooms that caused me to rethink the use of chemicals, plus there is the influence of meditation and Jamie." I said.

Everyone looked at me without saying a word. It was obvious that they were thinking about Jamie. The closeness between Sandy and me was well known by everyone in our Philly peer group. I thought that they might disapprove. Liam broke the silence. "Mushrooms. Where did you get mushrooms? And what happened, you had a bad trip or something?" he asked.

"There are mushrooms everywhere. As for my experience, it was spiritual. I felt something beautiful and very real and I want to focus on that without the influence of chemicals," I explained.

"Wait a minute. You had a spiritual experience while on mushrooms and that made you not want to take mushrooms or smoke ganja. That's not logical," said Liam.

"I suppose it isn't," was all I said.

"What was the spiritual experience?" Donna asked.

"I left my body and entered the body of my infinite self, and that self entered my temporal body and I felt an amazing supernal love." I said, matter-of-factly.

"Wow! Cool! I want some mushrooms so I can have that experience," replied Donna.

"I think his point is we can have that experience without drugs," said Shannon.

"Yes, that's what I hear you saying, Oliver. Is that right?" Jonathan asked.

"Yes, that's exactly it," I said.

"And how is that working out for you?" Liam asked.

"Meditation is what is working out for me. I feel no need for ganja or mushrooms." I said.

Liam just looked at me with a smirk on his face and said, "Well, we all had our fill of that religious stuff with the Catholic Church, and I never heard of anyone leaving their body and merging with an imaginary infinite anything, sounds like you have to be super stoned for that to happen. Just the same, knowing how much you like Stone Harbor, New Jersey, I bought a shirt for you the last time I was down the shore." Liam pulled the shirt from his bag, on the front was printed in large letters, *Stoned Harbor*, and there was a lovely green print of a marijuana leaf in the center with the inscription underneath that said, *Department of Higher Education*. I busted out laughing, as did everyone else. I thanked Liam and put on the shirt.

"Wow, this Jamie person must be quite something," Roseann commented. I did not respond. Patrick, fully aware of my discomfort, came to the rescue.

"Jamie and Julie are twins from Indiana. They live here in Sunset Village. Right now they are at the Negril Elementary School. It is a really cool place where we like to spend time with Jamaican kids."

"Yeah, Oliver wrote about that in the letter. I am looking forward to giving them the school supplies," said Shannon.

"Yeah, that's going to be far out, thanks!" Patrick enjoyed playing soccer with the students. "The kids are gonna dig it, and they're gonna get a kick out of all of you," said Patrick.

"Well, I vote for getting stoned, then we can swim some more or do whatever. What do you say folks?" said Liam. Then he dove into the water and swam over to the stairs. Some of us dove in and swam out of the cave, while others walked the bamboo plank Karl built that led from the cave to the steps. Patrick told everyone to meet back on the cliff around the large flagstone sun and campfire ring. Patrick went to retrieve his supply of ganja, all of it, which was a couple of pounds. He wanted to impress our friends and give each person an initiation supply.

While we were waiting, I had a discussion with Elijah about what to charge the Ghetto Flowers for the cottage rentals. He decided to charge them $10 U.S. per night for each cottage, which came to $3.33 per person. It was a very fair price. In addition to the $10 from Michelin and her family, and $2.50 each from the twins, the total Sunset Village income came to $35 per night. This was an excellent income for Negril living. Patrick and I were not paying anything since we provided most of the fish and, so far, all of the tourists.

"The Ghetto Flowers are goggle-eyed over the beauty of Jamaica and totally fascinated by our Sunset Village set-up," I said to Patrick.

"Yeah, and they haven't scratched the surface. And now we will teach them the fine art of spliff rolling. Bro, I can't wait till they smoke this stuff. Getting stoned Jamaican style is going to be a real trip for them," said Patrick. "Hey, how do you want to handle this Jamie and Sandy thing?"

"Hey, thanks, by-the-way, for helping me out with that. It was awkward. It's time for me to face reality. I have to ask them how Sandy responded to my letter."

"Well, it would have been very interesting if Sandy showed up with them, then you would be in a real pickle. You know bro, I think it may be time for you to accept the fact that you have moved on from Sandy and stop feeling guilty about your new life. I think you are over sensitive about all kinds of stuff, bro." Patrick had a valid point. Before I could respond, our friends gathered in the courtyard.

Roseann offered an assessment of our physical appearance. "Patrick and Oliver, I have to say, you two look fantastic. You guys left Philly tall and skinny with little muscle tone, and now you're both carrying six-pack abs, muscular chests, and your arms and legs are totally awesome. Patrick, if your skin was any darker I'd think you were a Jamaican, especially with that wild matted hair. Oliver, you're one big freckle!"

"Roseann, wait till you've been here a few weeks, you too will go through dramatic physical and mental changes," shot back Patrick, "you already have olive skin and a gorgeous body – and your jet-black hair will definitely lighten. You probably got all that beauty from your Italian mother."

"I hope so! Bring it on Jamaica, sculpt my body," she laughed and so did we. "Hey, bros, why didn't you answer our letters?"

"Letters. We didn't get any from you guys. Hmm. Duh, we never put a return address on the envelopes. Damn, how could we have been so stupid?" I said sort-of rhetorically.

"Because we've lived in a cave, a small island, and camped in a flower garden near a cliff without an address!" replied Patrick.

"Elkannah and Millie must have addresses, and hell, we could have used the post office address," I responded.

"Guys, that's where we sent our letters, to the Negril post office. They had a postmark on the envelope that said Westmorland District, Negril, Jamaica. Man, smart people can be really dumb!" said Roseann. "Sandy wrote you several letters, Oliver."

"Man, we need to get to the post office and get those letters," I said, feeling guilty, of course. I wondered what Sandy said in response to my break-up letter.

"Well, we wrote you guys to tell you we were coming and that we were bringing school supplies. We were going to ship the trunks of supplies directly to the school, but we discovered it was cheaper to fly them as part of our luggage," explained Roseann.

"I'm heading to the post office tomorrow first thing in the morning!" I said emphatically. "Hell, there could be a letter or two from my family. That goes for you too Patrick."

"Yeah. I hope the post office didn't send them back or throw them away," he replied.

"There were no letters returned to us, or Sandy," said Roseann as she looked at me - accusingly. "She sent you several letters, Oliver," she repeated.

"I sent her a letter telling her about Jamie," was all I said, a little defensively. Everyone went dead silent. It felt really awkward.

"We know, Oliver. Sandy took it really hard." Roseann said in a gentle voice. My heart sunk.

"Is she okay?" was all I could think to say.

"Well, she didn't have a new boyfriend as of a few days ago when we left Philly, if that's what you mean," Roseann replied.

"Is she angry with me?"

"Yeah, I'd say she was pissed and hurt, damn, what did you expect? She is strong though. It's not like she completely fell apart. She is super into her studies at college and doing quite well. Don't worry, Oliver, she told me to tell you that she is happy for you." Those words just about burst my heart wide open. I wanted to run and hide. Sandy is such a good person, an amazing woman.

Luke broke the tension, “Hey, here comes a few more of the crew.” I was relieved that we were off the topic of Sandy. I withdrew into my feelings – lots of emotions were whirling around in my gut, and yet a part of me felt relieved that everything was out in the open, finally.

“Man, those cottages are pretty cool. Lots of room, but where are the bathrooms?” Shannon asked. I always appreciated Shannon’s beauty. She looked like the classic Irish lassie. She had long wavy strawberry-blond hair, dazzling turquoise eyes, and petite facial features with freckles dusted across her cheeks and nose. I always thought her lips were the most perfect I had ever seen, full but not large. Shannon was the female flower of the Irish people.

“The outhouses are on the other side of the road. You can’t miss them. Harold did some cool carpentry work on them. Shit houses as works of art,” said Patrick. Shannon headed in the direction Patrick had pointed to.

“I just took a piss by a bush,” said Roseann.

“That’s us South Philly kids, we can piss anywhere,” said Patrick.

“That’s mostly true of guys, not gals. All you have to do is whip it out with a little bit of cover. We have to pull down our pants and squat,” complained Roseann. “Where do we shower?”

I laughed at Roseann’s comment. “Not if you wear a skirt without underwear,” She laughed as she lifted her skirt revealing that she wasn’t wearing panties. Everyone cracked up at her crack exposure – a classic Roseann move. “Each cottage has an outdoor shower. They are open air. People around here don’t concern themselves with being naked. It has become so common that we hardly notice,” I explained just as Michelin stepped out of her cottage and headed toward the cliff not looking our way. She was completely nude.

“Wow! Pinch me, bro. Am I dreaming or did I just see the most beautiful woman on the planet stark naked?” said Luke. Patrick pinched him.

“Ouch! What the hell did you do that for?” shouted Luke.

“You told me to pinch you. Is she still there?” Patrick asked rhetorically.

“Well, yeah. She’s stretching over there by the cliff’s edge,” he said, “her body is unbe …"

“Hey, enough of that or I’ll squeeze your nuts till they burst like grapes,” interrupted Roseann, “be like the natives and pretend it’s no big deal, got it?”

"Okay! No need to make threats, Roseann," complained Luke. It became apparent that Roseann and Luke were a couple, and an odd couple at that. Roseann was attractive and very intelligent. Luke was a hunk of a guy but somewhat dim witted. I surmised that Roseann liked having sex with Luke, otherwise there was little to keep them together. Then again, Roseann had a Tomboy quality to her personality that made her one of few females that could handle Luke's crassness.

"*Mind surfin', we're gonna be mind surfin', yeah you and me* ..." Jonathan was heading our way singing the Ghetto Flowers' *Mind Surfing* song. Jonathan had an angelic voice as well as an angelic face with long curly black ringlets and bright lapis lazuli gemstone blue eyes. He was tall and slender with little muscle tone. "*Mind surfin', travelin' inner space* ... hey, you guys see Shannon?" Jonathan asked. I wondered if Jonathan and Shannon were more than a friendship. They shared the classic Irish good looks. Jonathan had somewhat feminine facial features, and he was the pretty boy of the Ghetto Flower garden.

"She went to the outhouses to see a plumber about a leak," said Luke.

"Outhouses? No flush toilets. What is this, a Boy Scout camp?" laughed Jonathan.

"Trust me, you will never see a scout camp as lovely as this place," responded Patrick.

"I got that impression loud and clear the moment we jumped off those cliffs, not to mention looking over the island from the airplane," said Luke. "Hey, here comes Liam and Donna. You better get that ganja out. Those two are serious pot smokers." Shannon arrived at the same time.

"All present and accounted for, the Ghetto Flowers in Paradise. This is quite a site!" said Patrick.

"It's time to christen this special moment with the sacred herb of the Rastafarians," said Patrick. "Okay, take one of these banana leaves and place it in front of you like this," instructed Patrick. We were seated in an arc around the campfire ring.

"Why banana leaves?" Donna asked. "We brought plenty of rolling papers."

"Be patient. You'll see soon enough. This is the native way," replied Patrick as he got up and went to each person placing about an eighth of an ounce of ganja buds on each banana leaf.

"Wow, that's a lot of dope for one joint," said Luke.

"Spliff, mon, not a joint," said Patrick.

"Whatever, it is still a lot of dope. Wasteful." Luke responded.

"Nuh ta worry your self, mon. Ganja as plentiful as sunshine in Jamaica," replied Patrick with a smile as he demonstrated the fine art of spliff rolling. A few of them needed to try several times before getting it right.

"So, are we going to get banana leaf smoke in our lungs?" Donna asked.

"A little, at first, if you inhale right away. The leaves are still green. Once the ends are lit and the ganja burns, the banana leaf will smolder for a short while and then go out while the ganja stays lit. That way all you will get is the ganja smoke, unless you stop puffing, depriving the ganja of oxygen, causing it to go out. Then you have to light it again," explained Patrick.

"Well, let's torch these babies," announced Liam. Patrick had given everyone strike-anywhere stick matches.

"Let's do it at the same time on my cue," instructed Patrick.

"Hell, man, this ain't no Catholic Mass, let's just light the damn things," said Luke. Everyone laughed and ignored Patrick, striking their matches and puffing away.

It was fascinating to observe them smoking spliffs. They coughed and choked and puffed and soon enough, they were laughing and saying silly things, forgetting to puff on their spliffs and having to relight them over and over again. After awhile, everyone went silent and sat like statues puffing on their spliffs and staring out at the cliffs and the sea's horizon. They were now in the ganja twilight zoned-out zone! I found it amusing, and so did Patrick, who was not in the twilight zone because his blood had been saturated with ganja for quite sometime and was used to it. Actually, he was in the ganja zone full-time.

As they were sitting there in relative silence, Jamie, Julie, Helena and Karl came into the courtyard. They had been at the Negril Elementary School all day. They stopped at the courtyard entrance and stared at the new faces surrounding the community campfire ring.

"Wow! It looks like someone found a batch of new island adventurers," said Jamie. Everyone looked at her as she and her companions stepped into the courtyard.

"Meet the Ghetto Flowers newly transplanted in the Sunset Village garden!" announced Patrick rather dramatically.

"We heard a great deal about you folks. Welcome to paradise," said Julie. Helena and Karl just stood smiling and nodding their heads politely. Everyone made cordial introductions.

We sat around in the courtyard for a while sharing stories of travel, adventure and personal biographies. The atmosphere was buzzing with excitement. Soon, Michelin, Harold, Elijah, Norlina and Edward joined the gathering. I introduced each one of them giving very brief essential information, knowing that they would all get to know one another in more depth in due time. I looked around admiring the diversity of people assembled. There were seventeen of us in all. We were a tribe in the making! It was getting near sunset time, which meant it was time for us to assemble on the concrete pad on the cliffs to meditate. Jamie made the announcement, explaining to the Ghetto Flowers what we were about to do and simply stating that we sat in silence for the purpose of stilling our minds and appreciating the presence of the people and the natural beauty of our surroundings. There was a lot more than that to meditating but she understood that the practice may be new to them and further explanation wasn't necessary nor appropriate at this time.

"It's something we enjoy doing as a community. It is a nice way to reflect on the day and other things going on in our minds. Afterwards we sometimes share our thoughts and then we prepare dinner together and spend time singing and telling stories into the night," I explained.

"Can we smoke ganja on the cliff?" Luke asked.

"Certainly. I often do," replied Julie.

"What about those mushrooms you mentioned? Do you ever meditate while tripping?" Donna asked.

"Yes, many of us do from time to time. It would be totally awesome to trip with Philly friends on the Sunset Village cliffs while meditating. What do you think of that Oliver? Does it remind you of those LSD Jesus Freaks you encountered on the Jersey beach back home?" Patrick smiled at me as he asked the question, which I took as a little tease. I didn't respond, but Donna wanted to know more.

"What LSD Jesus Freaks, Oliver?" Donna asked.

"Oh, I'll tell you about it some other time. It happened in Wildwood. It feels like such a long time ago. I didn't take LSD."

We walked over to the cliffs and sat in an arc facing the horizon. Jamie instructed the new village members on breathing and the sky-mind-thought-cloud technique to get them initiated in the practice of meditating.

After we were well settled into a deep silence, Harold spoke up with his soothing voice laced with that unique combination of English and Jamaican accent. "I offer a warm welcome to our new village friends from the City of Brotherly Love, Philadelphia." I was impressed that Harold knew that our hometown was referred to in that way. "It is known to those of us who are scholars of religion that Philadelphia was a Holy Experiment designed by the Quakers, most notably William Penn. You will find that we have created a village of Friends in like manner to those who bear that title as a part of their religious affiliation." There was a look of amazement on the faces of my friends as Harold spoke. I don't think they ever heard anyone speak of our hometown like that, and the fact that they were hearing it here in this place from a man who looked very much the part of a native Jamaican with an English accent must have struck them as super peculiar.

"Wow, man, the way you speak is really far out. How do you know about the Quakers? Do you know they are pissifist?" The Ghetto Flowers laughed at Luke's comment, recalling how he always had difficulty saying the word 'pacifist.' Harold looked at him with a glint of amusement in his eyes. "Hey, man, you guys always laugh at me whenever I say something," complained Luke.

"Luke, we don't mean anything by it. All of us South Philly born and bred people have a tendency to mangle a few words now and then. It's just that the word pissifist is uniquely comical," I explained, and everyone laughed again.

"I assume you mean pacifist," said Harold.

"Yeah, that's the word. Quakers don't fight, man, and I believe the same thing," said Luke.

"As do I, my Friend. Are you a Quaker?" Harold asked.

"Nah, I guess I'm a Catholic, sort of. I don't go for all that mumbo jumbo prayer reciting stuff – it's too fancy and robot like," replied Luke. I appreciated Luke's down-to-earth-no-nonsense way of seeing the world.

"Well, it is a pleasure to have all of you among us. I am certain your stay will be a pleasant one!" Harold finished speaking.

"It's a real pleasure to be here. On behalf of all my friends, I thank you Mr. Harold," said Liam, in a tone uncharacteristically formal for him. He was sincere, but part of me knew that he was ever-so-slightly mocking Harold's English formality. Liam was inherently mischievous, satirical, and over all he had a good heart and a very keen mind.

We settled back into silence as the sun touched the sea and started its very quick descent into relative oblivion. Elijah then stood up and spoke. "Welcome ta de Sunset Village. Norlina, my sister an' I are pleased ta 'ave de friends of Ollie an' Patrick as guests. It is time fer us ta cook dinner. Dere is much food ta prepare an' dere is enough fish fer all."

Karl stood up and said, "Yesterday Ollie and I took the canoe-sail out to the deep waters. I speared a Mahi-mahi fish. There is plenty of meat for everyone. Please, if you have musical instruments, bring them with you. Tonight we celebrate the arrival of our new friends!"

Michelin spoke, saying, "I am pleased to see so many young Americans among us. We have created an intimate community and now we have new members. Enjoy, and may your stay be long and fruitful."

"Wow, you are all really cool people. I am so happy to be here," said Shannon.

"Me too!" added Jonathan.

"Me three, said Luke. "Now, how about cooking that fish, this ganja has got me starving, man!" We all laughed.

"What's so funny?" said Luke a bit defensive.

"We are all laughing in agreement with you Luke, and whether you know it or not, you have a good sense of humor and a delightful personality," I replied.

"That's an over-statement, don't you think?" said Liam.

"Screw you Liam," said Luke angrily.

"Man oh man, you can take the boy out of South Philly, but you can't take the South Philly…"

Luke interrupted Patrick, "Hey, man. Liam and I always talk that way, it's not serious." The Ghetto Flowers all laughed in acknowledgement of Luke's words.

We commenced to our usual roles in preparing the campfire and food for dinner, instructing the Ghetto Flowers in helping out with chores. The food was delicious and the conversation was lively and filled with fascinating stories. After we cleaned up the meal, we played music long into the night. Jonathan amazed the veteran Sunset Village people with his beautiful voice. Michelin commented that he could easily be a professional singer. She said his voice was similar to a rock and roll singer she had heard in England who played for a band called Yes. The singer's name was Jon Anderson.

The Ghetto Flowers wanted to go for a night swim in the pool-cove. Shannon told them it would be best if we entered the water from the bottom of the three stair cases instead of diving and jumping off the cliff, for safety reasons. She was largely ignored, as Luke said, "Hey man, rocks didn't grow over the last few hours and the sea didn't get shallower."

"Well, there is such a thing as tide," responded Shannon.

“Hell, that cove must be at least forty feet deep. The tide won’t change that much. Not along the cliffs,” said Liam, as he stripped off his clothes and dove from the cliff. Within minutes we were all hanging out on the large bamboo raft, with the exception of our Jamaican friends, who were not as fond of swimming as the rest of us, especially at night. They occasionally took a dip to cool off, but never spent extended periods in the water. Elijah once told me that he feared sharks. Elkannah had told me that he was unaware of shark attacks in Negril, although he said he once saw a Tiger shark when he was a kid. He said that Nurse sharks were sighted at different places around the island, but that he never heard of an attack.

Karl and Patrick were showing off the canoe-sail they had designed and built with the help of Harold, Elkannah and myself, although they liked to take most of the credit. After all, it was their design and idea. Luke and Liam wanted to go sailing. Karl said he had not taken the boat out at night and that he was willing to do so, but that he was tired from a long day and not up for it. Besides, he preferred to give them sailing lessons as well and that had to happen during the day.

I learned that Jonathan and Shannon were not a couple, and neither were Liam and Donna, although it looked like that was a possibility. I noticed Karl and Shannon checking each other out. Shannon didn’t know his age and didn’t ask. He was definitely within her dating-mating range and there was romantic energy flowing between them. As people headed off to their respective cottages, Karl and Shannon remained behind sitting and talking on the raft. Jamie and I watched them from the top of the cliff as they disappeared into Karl’s cave. We assumed that they consummated their romantic interest.

Liam and Donna had developed a sexual relationship, causing a change in cottage arrangements. Shannon moved into the cave with Karl. Luke and Roseann took one cottage and Liam and Donna the other. There was still one cottage being unused. Elijah and Norlina offered it to Karl and Shannon but they preferred to live in the cave. So, they offered it to Jamie and me. We accepted because it gave us more privacy. Karl and Shannon were living almost as native as Patrick and I had been. They even sailed to Conch Island and spent several days at a time there, always bringing back copious amounts of conch for the community and for Elkannah.

Jonathan found a shady area with nice sea breezes and a great view to set up a tent. He was the only person without an intimate romantic relationship.

During the next several weeks the Ghetto Flowers became quite settled in the paradise lifestyle. Karl had taught Luke and Liam how to sail the canoe and Patrick and I taught them how to fish. Liam and I approached Elijah and asked his permission to cut down two large Jamaican cottonwood trees to make two more sailboats. We offered him money for the trees to ensure that we would be the owners and he accepted. The making of the canoe sailboats was a creative but arduous process that required considerable help from Karl, Elkannah and Harold. It took several weeks for us to complete making the canoe sailboats. In addition, we began working on making more fish traps. We now had a large fishing operation going on and along with our continued assistance to the economic well being of Elkannah, Millie and Charley began selling our surplus fish at the Sav-La-Mar market, adding significantly to the community's wealth and produce needs. Luke and Liam both purchased spear guns and snorkel equipment. The two of them, along with Karl, were very daring fishermen, going out to deeper waters for both spear fishing and hook and lines. We no longer needed Elkannah's canoe for fishing, so members of the community utilized it for recreational explorations of the cliffs and snorkeling. The economy of our village was booming.

We received periodic school supplies from various international sources. When they arrived we made visits to deliver them and to volunteer our talents. The Ghetto Flowers had visited on a few occasions but they did not take a strong interest as they were consumed in other activities. Jamie, Julie, Patrick and I were the only ones to keep a regular commitment. Michelin's letters to Copenhagen yielded many supplies and the twins' parents came through as well. The school deeply appreciated the contributions. During the last week of the school year, we invited the students to spend a morning at Sunset Village. We had to caution everyone to wear clothes and to not smoke ganja. The braver students went for canoe-sail rides, and others enjoyed swimming in the cove-pool and exploring the cave and hanging out on the raft. Jamie and Michelin conducted an art class on the cliff's concrete pad. The children produced lovely paintings and drawings of Sunset Village environs. I was particularly touched by the interactions my South Philly friends were enjoying with the Jamaican children. Our inner city neighborhood was infamous for its racial violence and it lifted my heart to witness my childhood friends freely sharing affection with Jamaican children.

The Ghetto Flowers had been living in Sunset Village for nearly two months. They were well adapted to their new lifestyle, each making adjustments suited to their unique personalities. I was very pleased that they had this opportunity to live a life very different from the city world that had spawned them.

VILLAGE SHROOMING ALONG

I was surprised by how deeply my Philly cohorts and our Jamaican native friends were involved in meditation. In addition to the sunset meditations, most of the community began meditating with Jamie and me during early morning, and the thoughts that people shared were quite profound. Indeed, we were growing into a spiritual community without a creed. Our spiritual practice was meditation and our other community rituals were dinner, singing, chanting, and storytelling around the campfire on most evenings. And of course, the shared chores of maintaining and improving the Sunset Village property were an integral part of our tribal community life. Everyone appeared happy and healthy. The wonderful food, physical activity, and quality of relationships had enhanced everyone's physical and mental health.

The community garden was producing lots of food and Elijah had his first harvest of ganja, which keep the community well supplied with little expense. Michelin continued her smuggling operation, using Elijah's ganja and Harold as the mail carrier. Also, Patrick had copied Michelin's smuggling model and was mailing ganja to Randy, the person who had turned us on to Jamaica - he ended up staying in South Philly because he developed a romantic relationship with Patrick's sister. Patrick informed me that he was making a lot more money than he had ever dreamed possible. He had plans to purchase land in Negril along with Julie. They had their eye on the property next to Sunset Village, which would be totally awesome if they were to buy it. He asked me if I wanted a part of the smuggling operation but I declined.

I was not comfortable sending ganja to the streets of South Philly, as I had seen too many young people destroy their lives from drug abuse, even though I well understood it was not marijuana that hurt them, but heroin and methamphetamines. I did not accept the premise that smoking pot led to the use of harder drugs. The vast majority of people I knew who smoked marijuana did not use heroin, cocaine, or methamphetamine. Jamaicans were the greatest living proof of that fact. Most people who drink alcohol are not alcoholics, and most people who smoke marijuana are not drug addicts. In fact, it had been proven that marijuana is not physically addictive, however I do believe it is potentially psychologically addictive. And oh yeah, there's tobacco addiction and does that lead to harder drugs? And tobacco is arguably the most addictive and deceptively destructive drug in the world. It is a strange world of legal and illegal chemicals indeed, where governments and powerful greedy individuals get to decide which drugs we can use and become addicted to, and which ones we will be punished for using. Man, so much for freedom and the right to privacy and control over our own bodies.

I had approached Lord Joseph about helping Elijah sell his ganja and he agreed. Apparently there was an increased interest from Lord Joseph's European smugglers for more ganja so the arrangement worked out nicely.

One day Liam and Donna suggested that we all ingest mushrooms as part of a sunset meditation session. Many of the community members were drinking mushroom tea on occasion, and enjoying the experiences. No one had reported having a so-called bad trip. Karl, Shannon, Helena, Michelin, Luke, Roseann, and Jonathan were open to the suggestion. I had not smoked ganja or taken mushrooms since I decided to clean out my body, and simultaneously I fell in love with Jamie who did not use drugs at all, so I had no interest in tripping. Harold, to my surprise agreed to trip, and so did Elijah and Edward. Julie announced that she did not want to take mushrooms and so did Patrick, which was a big surprise to me since that were the most prolific users in the village.

Millie agreed to make a very large pot of psychedelic tea. She harvested psilocybin mushrooms from Donkey's manure. I found it amusing that the community was going to be drinking mushroom tea produced from the shit of Donkey, and brewed by a Jamaican grandmother who was going to serve it to a community of young people on land owned and operated by her grandchildren – only in Jamaica. Approximately two hours before sunset, Millie began making the tea in the campfire ring at the center of the courtyard. We sat around the fire watching her concoct her magical brew, much as she did the first time she made it for Patrick and me. It was discussed that once the tea was consumed that everyone would walk around the courtyard for a half-hour to give the chemical an opportunity to circulate through the bodies and to deal with any initial body and mind adjustments before settling into meditation.

Even though we were not a religious community and did not espouse a spiritual or philosophical set of teachings, at least not overtly, everyone approached the drinking of the tea as though they were engaging in a sacred ceremony. Each person held in his or her hands a half of a coconut shell to be used as a cup. The four of us who were not partaking of the communal hallucinogenic purple-blue liquid, joined in the circle of soon to be shroomers. This scene had the look and feel of a religious ritual complete with a congregation of followers, an altar, Millie as priestess, a sacrament and the spiritual practice of meditation that everyone adhered to on a regular basis. The altar consisted of a courtyard with its flagstones arranged in the form of a sun with seven of its rays streaming out toward seven structures, each one representing a color in the spectrum of light spread out in an arc like a rainbow. The remaining rays fanned out towards the cliffs and the western horizon where the sun would soon be setting.

Millie dipped the large ladle in the magic potion and then gracefully moved from person to person, filling their coconut cups. When the last cup was filled, everyone looked around at each other and without a word they raised their cups in unison and drank the musky smelling sweet tasting mind-altering liquid. True to what they had previously agreed upon, they walked in a circle around the courtyard, and what surprised me is they remained silent, which was not something they had planned. It was fascinating being an observer as well as a participating non-tripper. I could see the shroomers inhaling deeply, filling their lungs, and then slowly exhaling, just as we had learned to do while meditating. I knew the changes their bodies were going through, having been experienced, and so did Jamie and Julie. Norlina had no knowledge of the hallucinogenic experience so she had no way of knowing what was taking place in the participants' minds and bodies. After twenty minutes or more, we walked to the concrete pad on the cliff and sat in an arc facing the sea. Jamie and I sat on one side of the arc and Norlina and Julie sat on the other end. The sun was approximately twelve degrees above the clear horizon line. There were scattered cotton ball clouds drifting across the sky and high in the stratosphere were feather cirrus clouds. The rays of the sun shone on our faces and reflected a burst of colors off the cirrus and cumulus clouds, and caused ever-changing hues of blue-green upon the surface of the rolling sea.

I knew from experience that the chemicals in the brain were producing rushes of pleasant feelings through the shroomers' bodies, causing them to continue to take in deep breaths as their lungs expanded. With each inhale and exhale tingling sensations shot through their bodies like electric currents running through the wires of Christmas tree lights. It was amazing to see smiles spread across their faces, giving the appearance that something wonderful was happening within them and around them.

I had some knowledge of how psychoactive chemicals activate the positive emotional center of the brain. I was able to imagine what they were feeling...the heightened sensations of smell, sound, sight and most of all pleasant physical and emotional feelings, making everything more vibrant, more real, even super real. I also understood what takes place in the mind - the pleasurable feelings and sharpened senses create pleasant thoughts and images. These thought-images often consist of a mixture of joyful memories and experiences of endearing relationships. I could only imagine what was uniquely happening to each person. Being in the presence of twelve good-natured tripping people with whom I had positive relationships gave me the sense that I was sharing fully in their experience. As I contemplated the process that was taking place in their minds, I realized that I was in actuality engaging myself in a similar process. I was having pleasant memories and thoughts and I knew that the next stage would be to move on to the experience of super-emotions. In my previous experience, it was the wonderful feeling of universal love for all of life, the feeling of oneness with all things that was the peak of the trip. This was what had happened to me and it was manifested in my mind as divine love – my supernal infinite self. I accepted that everyone has this universal love experience manifested in a way that is unique to his or her personality and cultural orientation. I also knew that not everyone reaches that spiritual level of experience, for reasons that I do not understand. What I do know is that I wanted that experience as an ongoing phenomenon in my day-to-day life, which is why I made the choice to follow a spiritual practice or path that was integral with my relationship with Jamie. As I was guiding myself through this process during my meditation, the feeling of universal love came over me, and again, it had what I refer to as a supernal divine love quality. I did it! I achieved the same heightened feeling of divine love without ingesting a hallucinogenic substance, just like I had experienced when I was seventeen years old during an epiphany, and during the last time I tripped when I met Harold. I so often come close to having this feeling while making love with Jamie. I felt deeply grateful and wonderfully alive. The sun had slipped below the horizon and the colors blazed across he sky, and the blue-green sea had turned silver-blue.

Again I looked around at the faces of my friends. They were smiling and their eyes were radiant. Only their heads moved as they looked into each other's eyes. I could sense that we were having the same feeling of oneness and somehow we all knew it. And without speaking a word, each of us communicated to one another the same message and that was love. It was a beautiful, wonderful, magnificent love that we shared for each other.

Harold was the first person to speak: *"Creation has reached beyond the limits of time and opened our minds to the realm of eternity. The shadows of this world have faded away in the radiance of light, and the sorrows have fallen from our eyes and we are embraced as children of love. We are lovingly held in creation's arms and our loveliness is revealed to each other. Arise, my brothers and sisters, and let us embrace each other in gratitude for this gift of love. We receive it freely and now we shall give to one another freely. We are children of love and we are held in the arms of the source of creation in blissful peace."*

Harold turned to Michelin and they hugged. Then, he moved to the next person, Jonathan, and extended his hand and lifted him to his feet and they hugged. Then Michelin hugged Jonathan, and so it continued around the arc until everyone had hugged everyone else. Tears of joy and love flowed freely. The words, *I love you,* were repeated, genuinely, over and over again. This was the most amazing communal experience of my life.

As was planned prior to the partaking of the tea, those who had musical instruments had placed them on the cliff where we were meditating. I put my flute to my mouth and played a melody that was an expression of the feeling in my heart. The notes traveled on the wind, across the sea and out into the world. The melody became a prayer for our planet, a prayer of thanksgiving, a prayer of love. When I finished, Patrick played his guitar, strumming sweet, gentle chords that resonated with our commonly shared feeling of oneness. Karl tapped his congas lightly keeping a beat that was synchronized with the strumming of Patrick's chords. The angelic voices of Jonathan, Julie, Jamie, Michelin, and Helena graced our ears with sounds that created a wordless melody. After a long period of voice and instrumental improvisations, Julie and Patrick stood up and asked for our attention.

"We have an announcement to make," said Julie, clearing her voice.

"Everyone brace yourselves," said Patrick, "ready Julie, let's say it together as practiced. *We are going to have a baby!"*

"Oh my god!" Shouted Jamie as she rushed over to her sister and engulfed her in a hug. I wrapped my arms around Patrick while congratulating him. Everyone expressed joy to the couple.

"Now I understand why you stopped smoking ganja and wouldn't take mushrooms," said Jamie.

"At first I wasn't sure," said Julie excitedly. "When the second month went by without having a period I knew there was a possibility so I stopped taking all drugs. I was surprised that no one noticed my abstinence. Patrick and I decided to keep it quiet until we knew for certain. I went to Elkannah's wife, Clara, and spoke with her about it. She examined me and noticed that my breasts were sore and slightly swollen. We also consulted with Millie. She took a sample of my urine and placed it on some crushed leaves and it turned colors – it looked like hocus-pocus to me, but she said I was definitely pregnant. I then spoke with Michelin who gave me a thorough examination and she also determined I was pregnant. Did you know that Michelin is a midwife? Wow, I mean how fortunate is that? The morning sickness and my voracious appetite were the most convincing symptoms!"

"Jules, I am so happy for you and Patrick! Mom and Dad are going to be so pleased. When are you going to tell them?" Jamie asked.

"When they come to our wedding."

"Oh my god! Married!" Jamie shouted. Everyone turned towards her.

"Married, who?" Norlina asked.

"Jules and Patrick!" shouted Jamie. The community erupted in applause. Again, I hugged Patrick and congratulated him.

"When?" I asked Patrick.

"We haven't set a date. All of this has happened rather suddenly," he replied.

"Jamie, we have to contact Mom and Dad and let them know. I have to find out when would be a good time for our parents to come to Jamaica," said Julie.

"Well, they're done teaching until September. I say the sooner the better. We can call them tomorrow if you like and find out if they have travel plans for the summer. Oh, this is so exciting," said Jamie. "What about your family Patrick? Are you going to invite them?"

"You know, I haven' thought about it. I don't think so. My parents are divorced and having them here would be strange. Jamaica is not a culture either of them would be comfortable visiting, and there is no way the two of them could be here at the same time. I think I rather make a visit to Philly some time in the distant future with our baby and surprise them," replied Patrick. Jamie had a puzzled look on her face. Julie looked sympathetic. I knew Patrick's parents. I think his mother could handle coming to Sunset Village but not his father. Patrick is a fair-minded person. He would not choose one parent over the other.

"Di first wedding at Sunset Village an' de first child ta be born! Dis is reason fer celebration!" announced Elijah. We all cheered.

We played music long into the wee hours of the morning. Fruit and beverages were passed around and a copious amount of ganja was smoked. Millie had brought lots of banana bread that had ganja mixed in with the flour. Everyone became super-high as the mushroom tea, ganja smoking, and marijuana-laced banana bread saturated everyone's brains, with the exception of those who were refraining from substance use. I indulged in eating the banana bread and became pleasantly stoned for the first time in a long while. Throughout much of the evening, people shared stories of their mushroom meditation experience with the entire group, and gradually more and more private conversations took place, and eventually couples wondered off to their favorite romantic areas.

"Oliver, do you want children some day?" Jamie asked.

"I've thought about it. I like children. Telling stories at the Negril Elementary School has inspired me to become an elementary school teacher some day. As for having my own children, I am not so sure. The world is so full of hurt and dangers, and it is overpopulated with children who die before they reach five years old. I find that very sad and it makes me think that it is irresponsible to bring more children into the world when we can't take proper care of the ones already here. In all honesty, if you wanted to have children with me, nothing in this world would stop me from creating life with you," I replied.

"I feel exactly the same way, Oliver. The world has too many children who suffer needlessly. And I have to be honest with you, I will never have children."

"Well, we don't have to concern ourselves with that issue now. We are young and have many years ahead of us." I said.

"Jules and Patrick must have consciously decided to have a child. Jules is very careful about birth control. She has said to me on many occasions that she wanted to have children at a young age so she would be young when her kids are teenagers."

"Well, she got what she asked for!" I responded. "Duh, how stupid of me, and typical of most guys I suppose, but I never asked you about birth control. I just assumed you were taking care of it."

"It's taken care of, we don't have to worry about it."

"Taken care of, how?" I asked.

"Trust me on this. It's my body and I am acutely aware of how it functions. You need not concern yourself with us getting pregnant."

"Well, you are the master of your body, and besides, if you do become pregnant, then wow, I would consider it as a meant to be miracle of life – you know, a fate thing! Man, Patrick being a father and he's only nineteen years old. Whew, what a strange trip." I was amazed.

"I hear you. Jules and I will be nineteen next month. Life is full of unexpected twists and turns, isn't it, Oliver?"

"You sound so sad saying that. Look at us, we are an unexpected occurrence."

"Yes we are and a wonderful one at that. I just get frightened sometimes for the future." Jamie said.

"Why? Life couldn't be better!" I replied.

"I suppose you are right. My sister and your best friend are getting married and they are going to have a baby. It's incredible."

"Do you ever think of marriage, Jamie?"

"Oliver, are you asking me to marry you?"

"I think of us as already married. I can't imagine existing without you, ever!" I said. "Hey, are those tears I see? Did I say something wrong?"

"No. I just don't want you to be hurt, Oliver."

"Hurt. I'm not going to be hurt. What are you talking about?"

"Oh, nothing. I am just being silly, that's all. I'm feeling really tired and all the excitement with my sister is wonderful but it is emotionally overwhelming."

"Your face coloring is a bit pale. It's okay, Jamie. I understand. Come here my earth angel." I pulled her close to me and hugged her gently and firmly. We fell asleep in each other's arms.

Everyone slept in late the next morning. It was the first time we had missed morning meditation since the twins spent a few nights on the beach with Michelin and her children. I woke up before Jamie. I was lying by her side admiring the peaceful look upon her face as she breathed softly. I wondered if she and I should join Julie and Patrick in getting married. A double ceremony would be a fitting event since they were twins and all. It was true what I had said to her the night before. In my soul I felt we were joined for all eternity and I knew she felt the same way. We had said as much to each other on several occasions. It would be wonderful to have a public ceremony proclaiming to everyone our love for each other. I decided to explore the possibility of having a double wedding ceremony. It would be so far out!

I decided not to disturb her and instead went to check on what was happening with the canoes. I felt a sense of responsibility to Elkannah and hoped that Karl or Patrick would at least check the fish traps and if not then I would. Luke and Liam had finished making their canoe-sail a few days ago and had taken it on several test runs. The third canoe-sail had a little more work before being completed. We were having difficulty finding the right material for the sail.

No one was in the courtyard so I strolled over to the cliff. All three of the canoe crafts were anchored in the cove-pool. Everything was mysteriously quiet. I decided to jump off the cliff and go for a swim. I swam to the raft and climbed on top. I stretched out my body, feeling the morning breeze tingle the water droplets on my skin. The sun had not risen above the mountains so I did not have its warming rays to dry my body. I looked at the sky and the passing clouds, as images of all that had taken place the night before drifted across my mind. I felt so happy for Patrick. Wow, he was going to be a father. He would make a totally awesome dad and a good husband. I thought of how much things had changed in a very short period of time. A community had formed at Sunset Village, a real tribe of people who cared for each other and lived in mutual respect. I never dreamed that people could live together so harmoniously, especially people of different so-called races and cultural backgrounds. Man, this was a whole different universe from the world of the South Philly neighborhood. Then, I thought of the Ghetto Flowers. They sure were having a great time and going through changes that I was experiencing right along with them. We had been through a lot together going all the way back to our pre-teen years when we were running through the narrow streets and alleys of our neighborhood, getting into all kinds of mischief as city kids are prone to do. Who would have ever imagined that we would be creating an idyllic community on a paradise island? Mind blowing, for sure! I felt grateful, and deeply satisfied. I wanted this lifestyle to go on forever and it felt like there was no reason it wouldn't.

"Yo, Oliver, wanna come sailing and spear fishing with us?" called out Luke. I looked up. Luke and Liam were on the top of the cliff.

"Good morning, guys. Nah, not this morning, maybe later today if you go out again," I replied.

"Suit yourself. We're gonna sail over to Conch Island. We've never been there," called out Liam.

"Yo, guys, you woke us up. Be quiet!" Shannon was standing on the bamboo walkway by the entrance to the sea cave where she and Karl were living. She was completely naked and looking quite lovely with her disheveled strawberry hair and gorgeous well proportioned body – I took particular notice that her pubic hair had that same lovely strawberry color. In many respects, she looked like she could be my twin sister.

"Sorry!" said Luke. The two of them descended the chiseled steps, carrying their equipment in net bags. They slipped into the water and swam over to their canoe sailboat. I swam over to them so we could chat without disturbing Karl and Shannon.

"You guys did a hell of a job making this boat," I said.

"Yeah, she is a real beauty," replied Liam.

"Fast, too. We made the outriggers lighter and the entire canoe structure is much thinner," added Luke.

"Hey, I was just thinking about when we were kids roaming the streets of the neighborhood, and comparing that to the life we live now. Isn't it mind blowing?" I said.

"Yeah mon. This place is paradise. You and Patrick sure did find a cool place. We are Ghetto Flowers transplanted into the Garden of Eden!" said Luke, and we all laughed in appreciation.

"Well, have a safe trip guys, and do me a favor. On the western end of Conch Island, if you go inland a little way and follow the flow of seawater, you will come upon a really nice natural pool. Patrick and I harvested a lot of conch from the surrounding reef and put them there. We also built a fish weir, a sort of large fish trap so fish can get in the pool but not out. Could you guys bring back a dozen or more conch and whatever large fish that may be trapped so I can give them to Elkannah?"

"Wow, an inland seawater pool. That sounds really cool. Sure, we'll get the conch and fish. It sounds like you and Patrick have a nice setup over there." said Liam.

"Yeah, we do. We spent some time there with the twins and it was remarkable. You guys should consider taking Donna and Roseann for a few days. Hey, be careful and don't shoot each other with those spear guns," I said.

"Hey bro, as you remember, Luke and I know how to handle weapons. I know we used to throw a few punches at each other when we were kids and that may concern you, but not anymore. We just hurl words at each other," said Liam, "besides,

Luke has been a pissifist for a few years now!" We all laughed, including Luke.

I helped the guys pull up anchor and watched them paddle out of the cove and hoist the sail, and off they glided. It was a pleasant sight to see my childhood friends sailing on the sea. It was a far cry from when they used to hop trains through the city and run through the alleys hunting feral cats - and people from rival gangs. Life sure is strange how it brings about change - totally awesome.

I boarded Elkannah's canoe and paddled out to our fish traps. They each had a decent number of fish. I unloaded them, cut up more bait and reset the traps. It only took a little more than an hour since I had placed the traps so close to our cliffs. I brought the catch back to the village. Michelin and Harold were making a fire to brew some Blue Mountain coffee. I gave them fish to cook for breakfast. They were grateful.

"Oliver, I would be honored to perform the wedding ceremony for Patrick and Julie. Do you think they would be agreeable to such an offer?" Harold asked.

"That is very kind of you. I think they would love to have you marry them," I said.

"Ah, they marry each other, I simply want to play a small part, you know, to offer a blessing upon their union. The Jamaican authorities have certified me to perform weddings. If they intend to make it legally binding I can make it so." Harold was beaming with delight.

"That's great, although I do not think they care one way or another about the legal stuff, but Julie's parents might." I suggested.

"Ah, yes, I too am of the mind that when you have sex you are engaged, and when you create life, you are married, regardless of legal documentation."

"You are clever, Harold. So that means that you and Michelin are engaged. Do you two plan on ever being married?" Harold looked embarrassed and Michelin laughed.

"I am taking what they call the pill. It tricks the body into thinking you are pregnant. It is a wonderful pharmaceutical breakthrough that has done more to advance the cause of women liberation than any social movement. It has given us control of our bodies and frees us from the sexual tyranny of men – or more of the tyranny of human biology," pronounced Michelin.

"Yes. I heard of the pill. It is better living through chemistry!" I replied. Harold continued to look embarrassed. "Well, enjoy your breakfast. I am going to see if Jamie is awake."

"Bring her back and have breakfast with us. We are making a full pot of coffee," Michelin called after me as I walked towards my cottage.

Jamie was still sleeping, which I found a little surprising. After writing for a while in my journal, I decided to get her a cup of coffee and some food for when she wakes up. Patrick and Julie were eating breakfast with Michelin, Harold, Donna, and Roseann. Jonathan arrived the same time as me. When I returned to the cottage, Jamie was still sleeping. I decided to wake her.

"Jamie, sweetie, I have coffee and fresh fish right out of the pan. The fish was caught fresh this morning. Wake up, honey." She didn't respond. I gently shook her body and she moaned, but did not wake up. I felt alarmed. Something was wrong. I stepped outside and called to Julie who came immediately.

"What's the matter, Oliver?" Julie asked.

"Jamie isn't waking up."

"Jamie, Jamie! Wake up." Julie shook her vigorously.

"Ah, I am so tired, let me sleep."

"Jamie, honey, you've been sleeping for a long time. I have food for you." I said. Her skin was pale and clammy.

"I don't care. Leave me alone. I don't feel good." I looked at Julie. Her eyes were filled with anxiety.

"There is something not right with her, Julie. Maybe she ate some of Millie's ganja laced banana bread. I did and it really got me stoned."

"No, she wouldn't take any form of drug or alcohol," said Julie. Jamie was sound asleep again. "Let her sleep as long as her body needs. It was a long and eventful night."

"Maybe she has a virus or something." I said.

"Yeah, maybe. Come on Oliver join us around the breakfast campfire. We'll check up on her later. She'll be okay." Julie's words did not comfort me.

"You are probably right. For some reason though I sense that something was very wrong." I looked at Julie as I spoke and again I saw a very anxious look in her eyes. The only time I saw Julie look scared was the day I met the twins when they were being harassed by young Jamaican boys and dealing with culture shock.

"Julie, you look frightened," I said.

"No, I had morning sickness earlier, that's what you see." We left the cottage together. I had a feeling that Julie was not being honest with me. I hung out for only a short while as my uneasiness caused me to return to the cottage. Jamie continued sleeping. I resumed writing in my journal. I had a lot of catching up to do. I wrote for two hours when Jamie finally woke up.

"Wow! I really went out. I have a headache." She sat up and then had to brace herself to keep from falling over. "Whew, I feel dizzy." She laughed. "I'll be okay, just give me a minute to adjust." I went to the bed and sat by her side.

"Jamie, you are not well. Your face is pale and you are sweating. My god, your body is shaking."

"It will pass, Oliver. Don't worry. Can you bring me some pineapple juice? That should help."

"Sure. Will you be alright if I leave you alone for a few minutes?"

"Of course, don't be silly." I went to Elijah's cottage and asked him for a pineapple. I brought it back to the room. Jamie was sleeping again. I cut open the pineapple and squeezed the juice from the pulp. I shook Jamie. She woke up, sat up, and sipped on the juice.

"I think you have a bug or something."

"Yes, I think that's it." She said unconvincingly. Julie entered the cottage.

"Jamie," was all she said. She walked over to the bed and placed her arms around her. They both started crying. I was confused. Why would they be crying over Jamie feeling a little ill?

"Girls, what's wrong?" I asked.

"Julie, please leave so I can speak with Oliver alone."

"Why? You're scaring me. Oh, I get it. You're pregnant too, aren't you?" I said feeling slightly relieved. Julie didn't say anything. She placed her hand on my shoulder, gently squeezed and left the cottage.

"Oliver, promise me you won't be angry with anything I tell you."

"Angry. That's crazy. I've never been angry with you about anything. You are scaring me, Jamie." She took my hands into hers and looked me in the eyes with her beautiful soulful look.

"Oliver, there is something about me I have not told you."

"What?"

"The reason I am such a purist when it comes to what I put in my body is because I have a disease."

"A disease? What kind of disease. Are you going to be alright?"

"Please, Oliver, try not to freak out. I know this is going to be hard on you."

"Tell me!" I commanded, in a pleading voice.

"When I was ten years old, I was diagnosed with acute lymphoblastic leukemia."

"What? What's that?"

"It is a form of blood cancer."

"Cancer, oh my god. What's that mean? Are you going to be okay? How can I help you? I'll do anything? What can I do? I'll …"

"Oliver, you can calm down, that's what I need from you right now. I know this must be scary for you and I am deeply sorry for not telling you before."

"Jamie, what's going to happen?"

"When I was ten years old, they treated the cancer with radiation and chemotherapy. It did a lot of nasty things to my body. I lost all my hair and I lost other things as well. It took a while but I got better. When I was fourteen, it returned. Again, I was treated with radiation and chemotherapy. Jules donated her bone marrow to me, a painful procedure for her. It helped put the cancer in remission. For three years, I took many drugs including steroids to insure that all cancerous cells were gone. A year ago, doctors told me I could stop taking them. I have had four good years, and we all hoped it would never return."

"That's terrible. What other things did you lose?"

"I lost my ovaries. I cannot produce eggs. I can never be pregnant." She began crying. I held her close.

"I don't want children anyway. If that's all that is worrying you, hey, cheer up. Even if we did want children, there are plenty to adopt. We could even adopt a Jamaican child. Wouldn't that be cool?"

"Oliver, the cancer has returned."

"No, that can't be. You just have a virus or something."

"It has returned!" she said emphatically.

"Okay, then. Okay, we'll fight it. So what do we have to do? I'll go with you to Bloomington. We can fight this!"

"I love you so much, Oliver!" She cried uncontrollably. Tears streamed down her face and on to my chest, she started wailing loudly, saying she loved me over and over again. I held her and rocked her. Finally, she calmed down and was able to speak. "I can't go through all those nasty treatments again. The doctors told me if it returned that my chances were very slim that I would survive. I want to spend whatever time I have left right here in Sunset Village living with you." Jamie was telling me her dying wish.

"I can't lose you! I refuse to lose you! I will fight God himself to keep you from dying. I won't allow it to happen! Do you hear me God? I will not let you take her from me, not now, not ever. Do you hear me you bastard? You can't have her, she is mine!" This time it was Jamie who held me as I cried until there were no more tears.

"Oliver. Every moment we share together is an eternity. Do you remember me telling you that change is constant, and that love is the only permanence in life?"

"Yes."

"Our love is eternal and by definition cannot die. Even if we were together until old age, death would take these bodies, but it could not take away our love. What a precious gift you and I share! Perhaps it is better that our bodies separate while we are still young. As long as we remain attached to the idea that these frail bodies will go on forever we open ourselves to even deeper suffering. I honestly think that what you and I have few people ever experience. For that, I am grateful and I know you are too."

"I can't lose you, Jamie. I just can't!" I cried again.

"I know, I know, I know ..." she said over and over again as our tears mingled. We cried ourselves to sleep. Several times we woke up, talked, cried, and fell back to sleep. I spent the entire day in the room with her while she slept, writing in my journal. Sometime in the late afternoon, I fell asleep again while holding Jamie. When we woke up, many of our friends were in the room, meditating. It was sunset time and they decided to meditate in our cottage. Jamie and I sat up and looked at them. Apparently, Julie had told everyone about Jamie's cancer.

We said nothing. I could feel the love in the room. Jamie and I meditated with them. I imagined that all the love in the room was pouring into Jamie's body, completely healing her. I wished this thought to be true with all my heart and soul. I had no idea if such a thing is possible, but I hoped, and I prayed. I prayed over and over again for the divine love that I feel so often to enter into Jamie and heal her body. Then, I thought that maybe she wasn't sick after all. That she just had a virus or bacteria and she and Julie only thought that her cancer had come back. I clung to any thread of hope I could muster up in my puny, frightened brain. I refused to accept that Jamie would die.

The meditation ended with Julie leading everyone in singing the song, *Simple Gifts*. Then, without anyone saying a word, they left the cottage.

"What a wonderful group of people. We are so fortunate to have such wonderful friends," said Jamie.

"Yes, we are. Jamie, maybe your cancer hasn't come back. Maybe you have a virus or something." I repeated my hope that it was something less serious.

"I wish that were true, Oliver. I am all too familiar with this disease. I know its symptoms. It will be better for the both of us if you accept reality. Your resistance will only make it more difficult for you, and for me. Let's make the most of our time together."

"We should see a doctor. Maybe they have made new breakthroughs. We have to try."

"Oliver, I know what the medical community can and can't do. This time the cancer will win no matter what I do. I just know it. I am not giving up on life. Instead, I am embracing life by accepting my fate. I need your support in this."

"If you die, then I want to die with you. If there is life after death, then I want to go there with you. If there is nothing but oblivion after life, then I would rather be oblivious than live on this earth without you."

"And I would rather that my sister's baby know you as her uncle," she replied sternly.

"Then, marry me!"

"I will marry you, Oliver, my dear soul-husband."

"Wonderful, wonderful! Let's go and tell everyone that we are going to be married along with Julie and Patrick."

"Terrific. They are preparing dinner now. Let's join them and tell them the good news. There has been enough crying for one day. Let's have another evening of celebration!" Jamie needed to hold on to me while we walked to the campfire. She was very frail.

Everyone was happy that we attended dinner. We announced that we would marry on the same day as Julie and Patrick, much to the delight of everyone. Julie and Patrick were particularly thrilled.

It took eight days for Jamie's strength to return well enough for her and Julie to travel to the Roundabout to make a phone call to Bloomington, Indiana. Norlina had asked Charley if they could use Donkey and he heartily agreed. Charley was fond of Julie and her relationship with Donkey. Jamie rode on the back of Donkey while Julie led him with the reigns. I pleaded that Jamie not make such a long trip so soon after recovering her strength, but she insisted that she needed to speak with her parents.

Initially, the conversation they had with their parents did not go well for obvious reasons. The parents were opposed to the idea of the twins being married so young and to men they had never met. There was concern over their future education, and being married in a foreign country was extremely distasteful. Jamie and Julie told them that the marriage in Jamaica was ceremonial, and that the legal marriage would take place in Bloomington. Of course, they decided this on the spot, assuming that Patrick and I would approve and that we would travel with them to Indiana, and of course we would. The parents were not persuaded by this idea. They were willing to come down to meet us and discuss the situation in person. Jamie and Julie told them that they are always welcome to Sunset Village, and that with or without their presence, they were going to have the wedding ceremony, and sometime after, they would make arrangements for a legal wedding and another public ceremony in Bloomington.

Julie wanted to tell her parents about her pregnancy in person. She was three months pregnant, it was now the beginning of the second week of July, and they suggested that their parents choose a time in July or early August to come to Jamaica. Jamie refused to tell them of her relapse with leukemia over the phone, and she had hoped they would arrive soon, before the disease progressed too rapidly. She tried convincing them to spend the rest of their summer at Sunset Village. The parents said the earliest they could arrive would be the first week of August and that they had to make flight arrangements. Jamie and Julie were not sure when they would make another phone call so they advised their parents to take a taxi from the airport directly to the very end of West End Road. The phone call was relatively successful. Their parents would be in Jamaica sometime in early August, and man, they were in for one hell of a visit! I felt both delighted and sad for them.

RIPPLES IN TRANQUILITY

Luke and Liam were so fascinated with Conch Island that they decided to take Donna and Roseann for an extended vacation. I requested that they hunt conch to increase our supply and they agreed. In turn, we harvested their fish traps. When they returned, they looked even more native than when they had left, which was remarkable. They brought back several dozen fresh conch that they transported on the bamboo platforms attached to their outriggers. Donna and Roseann tanned naturally, and living on a tropical island made them look like Mediterranean women. The fact that they were eating healthy and physically active contributed to their bodies becoming optimally sculpted, and they looked fantastic. This was true of Shannon as well, although like me, she was very fair skinned, causing freckles to explode like a supernova all over her body. Her strawberry hair became more reddish-gold. There was no doubt that living the island life was conducive to holistic health. I only wished it could cure cancer.

Jamie had good days and bad days. Physically, she was losing weight, not that she had much to spare, being a petite woman who was active and ate only what her body needed. She had night sweats and was continually battling fevers. I encouraged her to increase her caloric intake, and she did. We also spent more time together doing moderate swimming in the cove-pool, mostly just treading water to keep her muscles toned and to sustain her energy level. Still, she slept a lot more and I had to keep pushing the increased food intake. The sleeping, balanced with healthy exercise and eating was definitely serving her well. What was noticeable was the coloring in her skin. It would suddenly drain, causing her to look ashen, even with the healthy daily dose of sunrays. She explained to me that all the organs in her body were weakening. It was excruciating to see such a beautiful flower slowly withering during the prime of her life. At times, it was so unbearable that I wished the both of us could leave this world together, now, before her disease overtook her completely. The disease would hit her hard and then subside, permitting Jamie to regain her strength, which caused me to have false hope that her cancer was cured.

What was most impressive was her spirit. Jamie was positive and genuinely upbeat. She spoke openly and honestly about her illness whenever someone inquired about her health. Jamie was not ashamed of her illness, and surprisingly, she was not afraid of it either. Jamie had requested during every sunset meditation ceremony that when her parents arrived, that we were not to discuss with one another and especially to her parents the fact of her disease. Everyone swore a solemn oath. I had many discussions with her concerning her illness and my sadness over the inevitability of her death, and each time she would remind me of the process of life and the reality of change, and how all of us are living on this earth for a relatively short period of time. The fact is, we all die. Some are here longer than others, and there is no good time to die and paradoxically any time is a good time to die. We must live every moment as though we will never die, and we must live every moment as though it is our last.

This is the primary paradox of life. Jamie spoke more frequently at the beginning of our meditations and at the conclusion. Her words expressed after meditations stimulated thoughts that engaged community members in deep philosophical discussions. It was not so much the content of her words but her tone of openness that caused people to express their meditation experiences freely. The contributions of Michelin and Harold, the two more mature members of our community, and the most scholarly regarding religious and philosophical thought, became ever more profound. Jamie was in every sense of the word a teacher, a teacher of life by the way she demonstrated how to deal with the process of death with courage and mental resilience. Her acceptance of the inevitability of her death caused everyone to think more deeply about his or her own life.

Jamie's illness waxed and waned, and we continued to immerse ourselves in our daily living activities that helped occupy our minds as distractions from this grim reality, although we continued a diet, exercise, and rest routine to keep her as healthy as possible.

The Sunset Village community had continued to blossom. Elijah had reinvested the money he was making from the multiple enterprises to build more cottages. After the initial renovation of the seven cottages and grounds, he hired a team of skilled stonemasons to build lovely stone cottages on the cliffs, and they went up quickly. The cliff area was horseshoe shaped, which is what formed our lovely cove-pool. On each side of the horseshoe cliff, he built the stone cottages that were shaped like mini circular castle towers. Each stone cottage was two stories high with the rooftop designed so people could look 360 degrees over the land and seascape.

It was Karl, the natural-born engineer and architect that designed the structures. They had arched windows that took advantage of the sea and land breezes and views of the sunset horizon and mountains. From each castle-cottage the sea could be directly accessed from the chiseled staircases that led directly to the sea. The stone cottage positioned on the cliff-side where the sea cave was located had the added advantage of the staircase that led directly to the cave and sea. Everyone contributed some labor and artistic talent to the building of these lovely structures. However, Elijah and Karl supervised the project, with all of the hard labor performed by the hired skilled Jamaican stonemasons. The shell of the structures consisted of cinder blocks, which went up very quickly. The skilled stonemasons who worked surprisingly fast applied the finer stonework façade – stones that were actually pieces of fossilized coral that were saved from the jackhammer chiseling of the steps and reshaping of the cliff surface, as well as other quarried sources. Jamie, Norlina, Michelin, and Harold contributed their abundant artistic ability to beautifying the interior and exterior. The outer shell of the castle-cottages were completed in six weeks, all that remained was completing the interior. Even though they were not finished, they were habitable. The project began in late April and was nearly completed by mid June, a remarkable feat of construction.

Patrick came up with the idea of building a large King and Queen chair carved out of the cliff directly in the center of the 'U' of the horseshoe at sea level with the best view and perspective of the cove and the sunset horizon. When the wind was high and the tide swells rolled in, the sea would rise high enough to reach several inches below the seat of the chair. The chair was smoothed out with concrete and painted royal purple with a sun in the center. There were iron hand holds anchored in the sides of the majestic chair so couples sitting in them could hold on when the sea was made rough by the winds of powerful storms, causing the water to rush up over them and recede without pulling them off their majestic perch.

The restaurant-bar building was finally complete. It was a beautiful and simple octagon design, open on all sides with a circular bar in the center where the food was also prepared. It was the pride and joy of Norlina and Edward. The bar was stocked with alcohol, and on the occasion of rain storms the community meals were prepared in the new cooking area instead of around the campfire ring in the center of the sun-flagstone arrangement in the center of the courtyard. The plan was to make full use of the restaurant bar for the future tourist enterprise. This idea caused me to feel a little uneasy, because it portended the inevitable change in our idyllic community life. For now, we used it to sit and chat, get some shade, drink Red Stripe beer and smoke ganja. In brief, it was another place to socialize along with our campfire meals and singing, as well as the cliff meditations and cove-pool swimming. We had numerous places to gather and to be alone.

There were other improvements made throughout the property, especially the flower and plant gardens designed by Norlina and Edward with the guidance of Millie, and the flagstone paths made it possible to walk anywhere throughout the village with bare feet comfortably. The Sunset Village had the feel and look of a Garden of Eden, with every man having the stature of Adam, and every woman the beauty of Eve.

One day, when we were all swimming and spending time in various arrangements of small groups upon the large raft and in the sea cave, I took notice of Julie's beautiful naked body, the perfect specimen of a woman carrying life in her womb. Her abdomen was slightly swollen, the first time I had noticed a visible representation of her pregnancy. She was standing on the raft beside Jamie, the two of them identical in every way, and now with two very important differences. Julie was subtly showing evidence of new life, and Jamie's slightly gaunt face, thinner extremities and ashen skin showed the presence of impending death. This did not disturb me as much as it would have a few weeks ago. Jamie was teaching me how to deal with the harshest reality of life. The vice grip of grief held me in its grasp less often. It struck me mostly when I was all alone late at night, woken by disturbing dreams that reminded me that soon I would not have Jamie lying by my side. I basked in every moment with her, and we rarely spent time apart, only when she requested to be alone or with her sister.

Jamie had gathered a small group of children who lived on the West End and did art work with them twice each week. She loved children, and for the first time in my life I yearned to have a child, one of our own, a desire that Jamie told me was an attachment that only intensified my suffering, and one I needed to let go of.

So, I did my best to accept the reality of what is and to live each moment as fully as possible. One delightful distraction was observing my Ghetto Flower friends experiencing a lifestyle that I believed to be quite unique and scarce anywhere else upon this earth. They were learning and doing things that were unimaginable as city kids. Their romantic relationships were maturing and it would not be a surprise if more children were to be born at Sunset Village. The only person without a romantic relationship was

Jonathan, and I wondered if he was lonely. There was no other female in our village with whom he could pair with. One morning I asked him about this.

"Jonathan, do you ever feel lonely for a woman." His face blushed and he did not respond.

"Did I offend you? Or remind you of a broken heart?"

"No. Well sort of, maybe."

"What troubles you?"

"I feel confused."

"How, by what?"

"I have always been fond of Shannon. She and I have been friends since we were five. It was I who encouraged her to come to Jamaica."

"So you do have a broken heart."

"Not exactly."

"Then what is it that is bothering you about her?"

"It is not her that is bothering me. Our relationship is wonderful. It has to do with Karl."

"Do you have romantic feelings for her?"

"No, only a great deal of affection, but not in a romantic sense as you think of it."

"I don't understand, Jonathan, you aren't making sense." Jonathan blushed again and we sat in painful silence for several minutes before he spoke.

"Karl," was all he said.

"What about Karl?"

"I am in love with him." His statement shocked me. Jonathan buried his head between his knees and I saw a tear fall on his arm. Jonathan was effeminate in a lot of ways, and his boyish good looks and slender body did resemble that of a beautiful pubescent girl. But it never occurred to me that he was gay. I mean, we used to rumble with rival gangs and he was as aggressive as any of our street fighting comrades.

"I would have never guessed. I am sorry," was all I could come up with to say.

"You are as ignorant as everyone else. No one can possibly understand, except for Karl. You think that all gay men look as I do, and that we are like girls in every way. Just because I got into fights and played sports with the rest of you, does not mean anything. You are an ignorant bigot like everyone else!" I was taken back by Jonathan's anger, and he was right. I most likely had distorted notions of what it is to be gay. It was truly beyond my scope of comprehension.

"I apologize for my ignorance, Jonathan. I have never known anyone who is gay. It is new to me and I have known you since we were children, so the thought never crossed my mind."

"It is because I had to hide it from everyone. I hated myself for my feelings. I couldn't stand being around all of you when you would talk of women and I would pretend to be attracted to them in the same way. But I wasn't, and I felt like all of you were brutes speaking of women as though they were meat to be consumed," he was sobbing as he spewed his anger.

"Again, Jonathan, I apologize. It must have been terrible growing up like this, how long have you known?"

"It was terrible and it still is terrible. I am an actor on a stage, hiding my true identity, pretending to be what I am not. I have always known. I tried to make myself different, but ever since I can remember I liked boys, I even liked you for a while but you wouldn't even notice me." Him saying he liked me in that way kind of freaked me out a little, but I hid that feeling.

"I had no idea," I said, trying to hide my uneasiness.

"I know. You couldn't possibly know. I had crushes on a lot of our friends that I had to hide, and hiding is what I became really good at."

"Well, you need not hide anymore."

"Yes, I do. How do you think everyone will treat me knowing I am gay? You can't tell anyone. You have to promise."

"I promise. But I do think others will understand and be supportive of you."

"Supportive? What, like I have some kind of disease." His words stung me. "I'm sorry, I didn't mean it like that. I love Jamie and ..."

I interrupted. "It's okay. We all have our pain to bear. I am grateful that you have placed your trust in me, Jonathan. You said you are in love with Karl. Does he know this?"

"Yes."

"You told him?"

"Yes."

"How did he respond?"

"I told him because one afternoon when I was alone with him in the sea cave, he took off his clothes and asked me if I wanted to skinny dip with him. He noticed that I blushed. Then, he came over to me and took my hand and said that I need not be embarrassed, that he understood. Then, he kissed me. We made love." I was startled.

"Karl is gay and you have a relationship with him?"

"He is not gay, he is bisexual. He says he loves me and he loves Shannon and that he enjoys having sex with both of us."

"Wow! Wow! That's wild."

"See, you are no different than anyone else!" he yelled.

"No, no, you misunderstand me. I wonder only about Shannon and how she feels about this, and how confusing it may be for you. I respond only with love and concern."

"Shannon knows," he replied.

"Wow! I'm sorry, I don't mean to act so surprised, but you have to understand, this is new to me."

"It is new to me, too. Shannon is my best friend, and she is in love with Karl and she loves me too."

"So you have talked with her about you being in love with Karl?"

"More than that. The three of us make love together." Now, my mind was completely blown. Flashes appeared in my mind of how that would work, and I had to shake these images loose. "I know what you are thinking. See, Shannon loves me too, and she understands what it is like to love Karl. She likes sharing him with me, and she likes being with me in that way too, you know, she likes my body, and I like hers, too. She and I make love to Karl, Shannon and Karl makes love to me, and Karl and I make love to her. We are a three-some."

"Wow, that's really different, and it sounds cool. It also sounds like you are bisexual."

"Yeah, it is cool, but you are just saying that to be kind, Oliver. And maybe I am bisexual, I just always felt more attracted to guys. I was a virgin before Karl and Shannon."

"Wow, a double virgin. Gee, this is really something. Hey, I really do think it's cool - different, I have to admit, but very cool. Why shouldn't three people love each other and express it?"

"Because that is not the way society works. We will always have to be secretive. You can't tell anyone."

"Does anyone else know?"

"Yes."

"Who?"

"Michelin. She discovered it on her own. She said she was able to tell by the way the three of us looked at each other. One day, she came to the cave when the three of us where in there. We weren't doing anything, but what we did not realize was how close we were sitting with each other and how freely we touched each other, you know, in a casual way, but not at all common with most people. She came right out and said she knew the three of us were in love, and that she was happy for us. Michelin told us about an anthropologist, Margaret Mead, who did studies of sexual behavior among people on some island in the South Pacific, and she said that relationships like ours were not uncommon, and would most likely be more natural if our society wasn't so uptight. Michelin even admitted to having once been in love with a woman before she got married. I think she really understands."

"That must be a big relief for you. Michelin is an amazing woman."

"Yeah, she really is. Are you okay with the way I am, and the relationship I have with Shannon and Karl?"

"Jonathan, I hope you mean that as a rhetorical question."

"Yes, I do." Jonathan hugged me, and thanked me for understanding.

"Don't go kissing me on the lips now," I said, and we laughed.

"I had asked Karl and Shannon permission to tell you. They said they thought you would understand. But don't say anything to them unless they speak to you first," he said.

"I promise. Cross my heart and hope to live forever."

"And don't tell anyone else, not even Jamie. I want to tell her myself. She is so special, Oliver, the most amazing person ever!"

"Yes, she is!"

"You know, it is because of what the two of you are going through that made me believe you would understand and accept me, I mean the three of us." I couldn't respond to what Jonathan said, as it stirred feelings in me that I did not want to indulge in at that moment. "You do know, Oliver, that you can talk to me about anything that is going on with you at anytime, don't you?"

"Well, I do now!" we laughed.

There was yet another secret shared with me that day, and a challenging situation to deal with. Michelin approached me and said that Jonathan told her that we had spoken about his love for Karl and Shannon, and that it was very important to him that he had someone else to share his joy with. She then told me that her daughter, Helena, was pregnant, and that Elijah did not know yet. She asked if I would be present when she and Helena told Elijah the news. I asked why that was so important and she simply said that Elijah has a great deal of respect for me and that Helena, for reasons she couldn't explain, was nervous about telling him alone. She went on to say that she was impressed with the way I respected and responded to Jonathan and his relationship with her son and Shannon. I agreed to her request.

Elijah was overjoyed and immediately asked Helena to marry him. To my surprise, she refused. This angered Elijah. He was confused and could not understand. Helena explained that they were very young and that although she loved him very much and wanted to have the child, she was not ready for the commitment of marriage. This was extremely difficult for Elijah to comprehend. On one hand, he was excited by the news of having a child, while dealing simultaneously with rejection.

"Elijah, I love you. Please understand that I am not rejecting you and I am not planning on leaving you. I do not believe in legal marriage as an institution, but I do accept the importance of fatherhood and motherhood and monogamy in relationships."

"I do nuh understand wat yah mean. Yah words trouble mi. I am a man an' yah are a woman an' we 'ave pikny together. We mus' marry. It is de right t'ing ta do, woman!" Elijah was indeed angry. Now I understood why my presence was needed. I felt a need to say something.

"Elijah, Helena loves you very much and she is happy to have your child. In the country where she comes from, women do not get married so young, and many choose not to have children if they become pregnant. Helena is Danish, and now, thanks to you, she is part Jamaican within her heart. She is living in both worlds within her mind, and body, just as you have created a new life here with people who are not Jamaican. You must try to understand. She is not saying she will not raise the child with you, she is saying that she does not want legal marriage."

"Ollie, I do nuh understand. I will gi her aw dis land, mi home, every t'ing. Wat belongs ta me, belong ta her. She belong ta me."

"My sweet Elijah, I am part of you and yet I do not belong to you. I belong only to myself. I am extended from my mother, and you and I are expressing our union in our unborn child. We are also a part of all the people of this community. In my heart I am married to everyone, it is the way that I think. I share my mind and heart with everyone, I share my body only with you, and most importantly, I have chosen to create life with you. Is that not enough?"

"Nuh, it is nuh enuff. Yah mus' marry me," Elijah insisted.

"What if you and Helena get married along with …" Elijah interrupted, "I get married wit Helena an' wit nuh other people. Dat is de way it mus' be!" I could see that Elijah was very much rooted in his traditional views, as was Helena anchored in her perspective. I wasn't sure there was a way to resolve this. Michelin then spoke.

"The two of you love each other so much that you have created life. Do the two of you recall what Harold said about people being engaged when they have sex and that they are married when they have children? That's reality. What we are really discussing here is commitment, long-term commitment. Elijah, I hear you saying you want Helena to commit her life to you forever. My daughter purposely stopped using birth control so she could get pregnant by you. Helena, I do not hear you saying that you will not make that oath, and I do not hear you saying that you will. Can you explain what your view of this is to Elijah?"

"Seeing what Jamie is going through has taught me that life is to be lived here and now. The future is uncertain and cannot be known. To me it is not honest to tell another person that you will be with them forever when it is impossible to know what will happen in the next moment. I can promise that as long as I am alive that I will have a relationship of love with you, Elijah, and that we will raise our child together as long as we are able to do so. That is the only honest commitment that can be made."

"Will yah always be mi woman as long as yah live?" Elijah asked.

"I will be your partner in raising our child for as long as we both live, and I will always love you. But I am not your woman because I am not property to be owned. I am your lover and the mother of your child to be."

"Yah speak nonsense, woman. Nuh man own nuh person, dat is slavery."

"Exactly, and I think of legal marriage as inviting the government to bind us to a contract as though we own each other."

"Hmmm! I see. Mi ancestors were slaves, but marriage is nuh de same t'ing, it is a t'ing of beauty, nuh like de 'orror of slavery."

"Yes, it is not the same, Elijah, but it feels similar to me."

"Wat yah say woman, dat I treat yah like a slave? I do nuh agree wit de way yah see dis. I accept yah are ta be de madda of mi pikny. Dat is wat is mos' important. I 'fraid yah leave Jamaica wit de pikny one day ef yah nuh marry me."

"No, Elijah, you treat me very well and we love each other. I would never deprive our child of its father. Trust is what is important, and our sharing of love. This is how we stay together, not by a legal document that invites the government to interfere with our lives."

"Yah are a strong minded woman. Dis I like 'bout yah, but yah 'ave strange ideas. I see I mus' accept wat yah tell me, even ef I nuh understand."

I decided to say something. "To me it sounds like the two of you just made vows to each other. Elijah, when you asked Helena if she would be your woman as long as she lives, she promised that as long as she is alive she will have a relationship with you and together the child will be raised. That sounds like a solid commitment to me."

"True dat! Now I see. Yah make sense, Ollie."

"So, Elijah," Helena chimed in, "will you agree to a ceremony with me that acknowledges that we have created life together and that we will raise this child together."

"Dis is very strange ta me, an' it will be strange ta mi grandparents. I do nuh agree wit aw yah say, but I will do de ceremony." Elijah and Helena hugged and they thanked Michelin and me and headed off to their cottage, although Elijah continued to look puzzled.

"Thank you, Oliver, for helping us with this. I somehow knew that you being there would make a big difference," said Michelin. "I wanted Harold to speak with Elijah as well, but he wants me to marry him, legally as well, and I refused. It is a very sensitive topic for him."

"Whew, that must be tough ... bridging gaps between cultures, let alone introducing new ideas about marriage relationships and family. That's extremely challenging," I replied.

"Yes it is, and even with all of Harold's education and cultural experiences, he is unable to let go of some old ideas. You are a good anthropologist and counselor, Oliver."

"I don't know about that. I sort of fumbled my way through that one."

"Seriously, you have an open mind and an intuitive understanding of people and culture. I spent a great deal of time in the academic world among anthropologists and trust me, few people have developed such abilities as you have, regardless of how many books they have read. You have an unusual gift."

"Ah shucks, that is very kind of you, Michelin." I laughed.

"You know, I had a romantic relationship with Conric, but the cultural divide was too wide for us to keep the relationship going. He viewed me as his woman, in the sense of actual property, and he was extremely possessive. I could not submit myself to that. I am proud of my daughter in the way that she is handling her relationship with Elijah. Harold, on the other hand, is a rare find. He has all the wonderful qualities of a Jamaican man, and the education of a worldly scholar. Even though he wants to marry me and disagrees with the way I view relationships, he is respectful and accepting of me."

"Yes, Harold is truly a breed of his own. And you are a rarity as well, Michelin."

"Ha, more like an oddball, as you Americans would say." We laughed as we headed to the cliff to join our friends who were swimming. "Do you think Helena and Elijah should have their *creation of life* ceremony before you and Jamie have your ceremony or afterwards?" Michelin asked.

"Hmmm, good question. Since Jamie and Julie's parents are coming sometime within the next week or so, and we don't know the exact date of their arrival, I think it is best that they wait until after our ceremony."

"That makes sense. I will tell my daughter and Elijah."

"That's a cool name by the way."

"What name is that?" Michelin asked.

"*Creation of Life Ceremony*!"

"Yeah, I suppose it is. It just popped out."

"A lot of cool things pop out of you."

"Oh, yeah, like what?"

"Karl and Helena!"

"That's a wonderful compliment, Oliver. Thank you."

"You are welcome."

Harold greeted us on the way to the cliff. We told him how things went with Elijah. He was not surprised by Elijah's initial response, but he was impressed that he agreed to a creation of life ceremony in place of being legally married, and he said as much, "It is an excellent example of the phenomenon of cross-cultural fertilization and yet much more. Our community is in essence a cultural experiment, one worthy of documentation. We have a variety of ethnic, historical, and racial influences that are bringing about new and very interesting ideas and cultural practices. It is quite fascinating, I must say."

"It is fascinating, Harold, and I know that it creates stress for you, and you are much more worldly, mature, and educated than all of these young people. So if it all these new ideas and practices are a challenge for you, imagine the growth difficulties these young people are experiencing," replied Michelin.

Harold added an insightful comment, "I do understand the growth strain that the unusual confluence of forces within our community places upon the youth. However, I must note that the minds of youth are much more resilient, indeed more malleable than those of us who have the deeper impression of time to shape our thinking."

Michelin responded, "That's a poor excuse, Harold, for the pervasiveness of intellectual laziness among so-called mature adults. We both know the importance of keeping an open mind and that cultural progress is better achieved when there is an open and fluid interchange of ideas. This is how new and better cultural practices are born. Think of how women have struggled for eons to gain the most basic of personal freedoms, and I am not simply talking of the right to vote. I am referring to having control over our own bodies. It has taken science to invent a chemical that frees women from the trap of unwanted procreation without jeopardizing their health by barbaric abortion practices. We now, thanks to science, have the means to control procreation, which means we are not at the mercy of men."

"My, my, how you do get worked up over female issues. Please, let us not confuse healthy social institutions with gender concerns. Marriage is an institution that provides a strong foundation for a healthy society. Children need the nurturing of parents, siblings, and other peers and adults within a community in order to actualize their greatest potential."

"I do not disagree with you on that Harold, but you must admit that societies throughout the history of civilizations and within most, if not all current day cultures, are dominated by men. There is no gender equality."

"Hmm, I must admit, you make an excellent point. It makes me wonder if this patriarchic arrangement developed out of survival necessity, and therefore this inequality you speak of is not intentional."

"Well, I suppose if men had mammary glands and nursed babies back in the cave, the women would have done the hunting and they would have developed bigger muscles and more aggressive behavior, including fighting wars. Although I prefer to think that if women ran the world there would be no war."

"Well, my dear Michelin, that is a speculation that can never be tested. We must deal with things as they are. Indeed, we are living in a time when social experimentation of gender roles and the subsequent influences on the structure of society can take place. In fact, they are happening right here in our very own community."

"Exactly! And isn't that wonderful?" replied Michelin emphatically and with pride.

"Well, you certainly are doing a fine job raising your children under very different circumstances, and our little village, unbeknownst to all its members, save you and I, is a cultural experiment in every sense of the concept. We are fortunate, my dear Michelin, to be part of such a unique process."

It was wild listening to these two talk. I could tell that what they were calling a cultural experiment was a big challenge to their relationship. It was also one of the influences that made them so attracted to one another. Their academic training, and years of maturity, made them see things in ways that the rest of us were experiencing without consciously processing.

"The two of you should put on a cultural anthropology seminar for the rest of us so we can be more consciously aware of the part each of us is playing in this experiment you speak of." I said this half joking.

Michelin clasped her hands and said, "That is a wonderful suggestion, Oliver. We can have open discussions about our community and how we are doing things differently from much of the world. It would be real education in real time! Wonderful! Don't you agree, Harold?"

"Indeed, I do, most heartily. It is a marvelous opportunity. May I suggest it become part of our evening discussions, either after meditations or after our community dinner?"

"We will bring it up at our sunset meditation this evening," said Michelin. I had no idea that my comment would generate so much excitement.

From the top of the cliff, I could see Karl and Jonathan sailing one boat and Luke and Liam were sailing the other. They looked as if they were having a racing contest. Patrick was also out in the sea paddling in the canoe. Donna, Shannon, Roseann, Julie and Jamie were on the raft watching the boys sail. Norlina and Edward were relaxing on chairs beneath the shade of the cliff-side restaurant bar along with Elijah and Helena. All members of Sunset Village were enjoying this lovely afternoon. Michelin and Harold decided to get a few Red Stripes from the bar and then went to sit in the Sunset Village royal throne chair at the base of the cliff. I decided to join the ladies on the raft. I jumped off the cliff and swam to them. Jamie was pleased to see me. I commented on the very slight growth of Julie's belly. Julie was a little more than three months pregnant and her abdomen was bulging only slightly. When she wore a pullover loose fitting dress, it was not visible.

I dove off the raft to swim around. Shannon dove in after me. She swam up to me. "Oliver, thank you for speaking to

Jonathan. Your acceptance of our unusual relationship means a lot to him, and to me."

"You're welcome."

"Do you find it shocking?" she asked as we treaded water, a rather unusual situation to have such an important conversation.

"Surprising, and yes, a bit shocking. I have never heard of such an arrangement. It is a social experiment."

"Well, I don't like the idea of being an experiment, but I know what you mean. Do you think I am weird for liking two men?"

"Hmmm. I think you are courageously honest. Are you comfortable with the arrangement?"

"Most of the time. There are moments when I want to be alone with either Karl or Jonathan, and there are times when they want to be alone with each other and I think that is when it is most difficult."

"What makes it so difficult?"

"Jealousy."

"That could be a problem. Are you jealous of Karl and Jonathan's affection for each other?"

"Yes, I am, but only when I think of them having sex when I'm not with them."

"Shannon, this is a very unusual conversation."

"I'm sorry, if you're uncomfortable talking about it, we can ..."

"No, not at all," I interrupted, "I'm just saying. Hey, let's swim to the cave so we can sit and talk." We swam into the cave and sat on a ledge.

"When we have sex together, it is very sweet and exciting. I like the two of them doing it to me at the same time. It is unlike anything I ever experienced, of course. I even enjoy watching them have sex and I help them by kissing and doing other things that they enjoy. Sometimes, I am afraid that they might like each other more than me, and that they might leave me. I know they sometimes have sex when I am not around and I don't like that."

"Do you have sex with either of them when the other isn't present?"

"Only with Karl. Jonathan, I believe, is only interested in sex with me if Karl is there. He likes being with Karl more than being with me."

"Hmmm. Have you spoken about this with them?"

"No. I'm afraid to."

"Shannon, the three of you need to talk. Jealousy is a poison, and if you don't share how you feel, it will destroy the relationships."

"Honestly, Oliver, now that we are talking about it, I am not sure it is possible for three people to have an on-going intimate relationship. I mean, having sex once in a while, maybe, that can be quite enjoyable, but a serious relationship, well, it gets too complicated."

"That's understandable. For one, I have never heard of it being tried before, and two, it may be common in some isolated cultures, but for the majority of cultures, it is not something that is practiced. That is what I mean by a social experiment. The three of you are relationship pioneers."

"I am beginning to think that the human tendency for jealousy along with the need for special intimacy makes a three-way relationship unworkable," said Shannon.

"Well, you have to expect challenges. Perhaps it is an opportunity to learn how to grow beyond jealousy and possessiveness. I am not saying that that is what should happen. On the other hand, there may be a good reason that we have the emotion of jealousy and the desire to be possessive."

"What could be the reasons for such negative emotions?" she asked.

"Well, I don't really know. Maybe it is simply self-protection and to preserve social cohesion among groups, and to insure the propagation of the species and for the proper care of children. But, I honestly don't know.

"I am afraid of being hurt," she proclaimed.

"Shannon, if you could have the relationship exactly the way you want, what would it be?"

"Karl. I would want to just be with Karl. I love Jonathan, but more like a friend that I occasionally enjoy having sex with. But I am truly in love with Karl."

"Shannon, are you in anyway feeling hurt? Because if you are, the sooner you talk with them the better it will be."

"Yes, I am hurt and confused. I am jealous seeing the two of them sailing together. I am afraid to go in the cave and see them being intimate with each other. You are right, Oliver, I need to talk with them right away. Talking with you made me realize that I have been suppressing feelings for a while. Thank you."

"You are welcome, but I really didn't do anything."

"You listened to me and helped me sort out my feelings, and now I know what I need to do. I can't tell you how important that is. Hey, they are bringing the canoe sailboat back into the cove. I have to go." Shannon slipped into the water and swam out of the cave.

I sat for a while and did some thinking. That was the third conversation I had in less than twenty-four hours that had to do with very personal stuff. And perhaps listening and participating in Michelin and Harold's conversation could be considered personal as well – that would make it four conversations, and each person told me about their most personal relationship issues. I didn't mind, I just found it a bit perplexing. Maybe everyone was sharing with each other everything that was personal. Perhaps we had become such an intimate community that our conversations were becoming more real and meaningful. Then again, people did request that I not repeat what they said to me. Oh well, there is no harm in people talking as long as we respect one another's request for confidentiality. However, maybe everyone was telling everyone not to tell anyone and each person thought they were holding a secret when there were no secrets. I felt confused! One thing was certain - we really were a community that was pioneering new frontiers in relationships and in dealing with the challenges of life. Whew! Paradise was getting quite complex: two weddings, two pregnancies, multiple relationships that involved cross ethnic gender identity issues, chronic illness and stuff I didn't even know about. Communities are very dynamic entities, especially ones that are exploring new territory in relationships with a willingness to question all traditional values. Michelin and Harold were right about this community being a social experiment and it was time for us to open up communication to increase everyone's awareness of the process and make some decisions as to what direction we wanted to go in, if that was at all possible. Whew, maybe this is how cultural progress happens, through the exploration of new ideas and social arrangements.

Karl and Jonathan furled the sail and paddled into the cove. Shannon swam to the canoe sailboat.

"Karl, will you take me out for a sail?"

"Sure."

"Can I come?" Jonathan asked.

"I need to talk with Karl, Jon, if that's okay with you?" she asked respectfully.

"Of course, no problem. Have a good time," said Jonathan. He slipped into the water and Shannon climbed into the sailboat.

"Take me along the southern coast toward the village of Little Bay. I heard Liam talking about the nice, small beach there. Do you mind sailing that far?" Shannon asked.

"It is a long way, Shannon, a lot further than we are prepared for. We do not have much water with us. I will take you on a long sail another day and we can explore as much as you want, even spend several days sailing along the coast if you like. But now is not the right time," responded Karl.

"Okay, I understand. Well, how about sailing out to deeper water so I can look back at the shoreline and see the entire coast of Negril."

"That will be easy. The wind is perfect for heading out to sea. It is coming from the northeast, although it will take much longer for us to get back in. Here we go, Shannon!" Karl pointed the sailboat southwest and the sail caught the wind and sped the craft out to sea. After they were several miles off the coast, Karl brought the boat about and furled the sail.

"This is a good place to sit and float. Look, we can see all of the beach and cliffs of Negril. It is quite beautiful, is it not?"

"Yes, Karl, it is lovely. Thank you for bringing me out here."

"What's on your mind, Shannon?" Karl asked.

"I am confused about our relationship."

"Tell me more," replied Karl.

"Jonathan is my friend. You are my love. I am jealous that you have sex with him."

"Do you not enjoy having sex with both of us?" he asked, sounding a little surprised by Shannon's statement.

"Yes. It is nice. But you do know that Jonathan is really only interested in you, and that he has sex with me because you want him to."

"Yes, I do know that, and I do know that you like having two men, yes?"

"Well, sometimes, yes it does feel good. Physically and emotionally, but something about it bothers me."

"What?" Karl asked.

"I told you, Jonathan is only showing interest in me sexually because you want him to. He'd much rather make love to you without me there. Don't you see that?"

"I only know that he wants to be alone with me sometimes, just like you do. What is wrong with that?"

"I have a hard time sharing you like that. Maybe it would be different if Jonathan liked making love to me as much as he does with you, but he doesn't. He is not bisexual like you are, he is gay, Karl. Do you understand? He is 100% gay and you're not!"

"I don't know what I am." Karl said in an almost whisper tone.

"What did you say?" Shannon asked, wanting to make sure she heard him correctly.

"I don't know if I like guys more than girls," Karl repeated, again in a somewhat muffled tone.

"Well, you better find out, because I am not going to wait around to have my heart broken."

"Why can't you understand?" Karl demanded.

"Understand! You are accusing me of not understanding? I have shared my mind, heart, and body with two men who love each other. It is not more understanding that I need. What I need is to wake the hell up!"

"Shannon, you are very angry, you need ..." Shannon interrupted, "You are goddamn right I am angry. I thought I understood all along that you loved me and that you were attracted to Jonathan, and that it was really me that you truly loved. If Jonathan and I were not best friends, I would have never consented to any of this. I am so stupid!"

"No, you are not stupid. You are a very good person. You love me and you love Jonathan, and I love Jonathan," Karl said, very excitedly.

"Well you can love Jonathan all to yourself, because I am no longer going to be the hole that is stuck between two stiff bamboos!"

"Now, that is unfair to speak that way. We did not use you, we love you."

"Bullshit. You may love me, the way a boy loves a toy. If you loved me like a man loves a woman, you would let go of your relationship with Jonathan."

"This I cannot do."

"What? You can let go of me but you can't let go of Jonathan?"

"Jonathan will continue to love the both of us. It is you who wants to love only me. It is you who are demanding that I not share with Jonathan. If you want to be with me, I will be with you. If you say I have to choose, this I cannot do. It is you who is making the choice to not be with me."

"You got that right. That is exactly what I am doing. Take me back to shore. Now!" Shannon turned her body away from Karl, feeling disgusted and angry, no longer able to look at him.

She was visibly shaken. Karl placed his hand on her shoulder, causing her to stand up and spin around. She lost her balance as the boat rocked causing her to fall overboard, and the current pulled her swiftly away from the craft.

"Shannon, tread water, I will come get you." Karl unfurled the sail and turned the sailboat about. The swells were high and Shannon was bobbing up and down. Karl shuddered with fear, feeling responsible for what happened. He soon reached Shannon who had swallowed water and was gasping for air. Karl wasn't sure how to steady the boat and bring Shannon on board. She was having trouble keeping herself afloat, as she was forcing herself to cough in an attempt to dislodge water from her lungs. Out of desperation, Karl tied the rope from one of the two anchors around his waist, let go of the sail, and leapt overboard. He was attached to the sailboat only by the cinderblock anchor that was wedged under the bow. His timing and aim were perfect, landing in the sea a few feet away from Shannon. He tried swimming toward her but the weight of the boat was pulling on him. Karl did not panic, though, he reached down deep in his heart for all the strength nature had endowed and pulled his body through the water, finally reaching Shannon just as she was about to sink beneath the surface for the last time.

Karl wrapped one arm around her chest, keeping her head above water. With the other arm he held the rope taunt. He did not know how he was going to hold on to Shannon and reach the boat. For the first time in his life, Karl did not know what to do and panic gripped his heart. Shannon was no longer conscious, and this added to Karl's dread.

Then, as if nature decided to lend a hand, the wind had shifted and pushed along the side of the canoe-sailboat moving it in the couple's direction. Karl was able to grab hold of one of the outriggers. Supporting his weight against the bamboo platform that straddled the arms of the outrigger, he was able to gain enough leverage to lift Shannon onto the canoe sailboat. Once he was certain she was secure, he made his way around to the port side and got in the canoe. Immediately he started CPR. Fortunately, within moments, Shannon responded, spitting up water and gulping air. She was going to be alright. Once Karl was confident that Shannon was safe, he set out to gain control of the sailboat. He kept a close eye on Shannon as he rode the wind swiftly back to the cliff.

This was a life-altering ordeal for Karl, Shannon, and Jonathan. The three of them stayed separated from each other and kept to themselves for several days, not speaking of the incident to anyone, and they stopped participating in all community activities.

Elijah, noticing Shannon's estrangement, offered her one of the stone castle cottages for temporary accommodation. Jonathan returned to his tent. Karl continued living in the sea cave. He would go sailing for twelve hours at a time, bringing in large tuna that could only be caught in the deep open sea. We were all concerned that he was taking too much of a risk, and no one was more concerned than Michelin.

She tried speaking to her son at every opportunity, but he refused to speak to anyone. There was a dark cloud surrounding him. Jonathan would spend time with Jamie whenever I wasn't around. She told me he didn't speak about anything of importance, that he simply needed her company. Eventually, he began hanging out with Luke, Liam, Roseann and Donna more and more, receiving comfort from childhood friends. Shannon continued to exist within a shell. At night, I watched her sitting alone on the top of the castle tower, like a princess locked deep within the caverns of her soul. Each evening she sang the same *Shaker* hymn, *How Can I Keep From Singing*, over and over, as if it were a prayer for the angels to carry upon their wings to heaven where her petition may be finally heard.

One night, I decided to bring my flute to the cliff and waited for Shannon to appear in the tower. When she sang her hymn, I played along with her. The notes were pure and clear, and Shannon was able to use them to guide her voice to match the perfect pitch of each note. It seemed as though the flute had worked magic, breaking the spell that held Shannon's spirit captive. She came down from her lonely castle tower and sat beside me.

"Oliver, my heart is in a thousand pieces and my mind is full of questions. I placed my faith in love and like the thorns on the stem of a rose, it pierced my heart, and I am bleeding."

"Shannon, love is our greatest teacher. Love has not wounded your heart. Love only requires that it be shared, and that sharing must happen in ways that truly nurture those who are its recipients, as well as the giver. We are all children in love's playground, and it is the choices we make that determine how well we play together. Sometimes, actually more often than we can adequately handle, our choices hinder love's expression, and that is when we become hurt."

"So love isn't the reason we feel pain and loss?" Shannon asked.

"Love is love and cannot be pain! We are the ones who are doing the learning. It is not much different than anything we do that is harmful to our health. We experience pain that tells us we are doing something that is not contributing to our health, and that we need to make an adjustment." I replied.

"So, I made choices that were not allowing love to be expressed, and the result was pain. Is that what you are telling me?"

"You made choices and so did the guys. For a while, love was being expressed, and then there must have been choices made and or lessons to be learned that caused pain in order to get your attention. It is my experience that whenever I think, say, and do something that hinders love's expression, I experience pain, or fear, and other negative emotions that let me know I have chosen wrongly and must choose again."

"I am not sure what choices I made that hindered our loving each other. I don't know what it is I need to learn. I feel pain, fear, and definitely confusion. I tried loving Karl and Jonathan, and I tried supporting them in loving each other, and for a while it was wonderful and I thought it could go on like that forever. I was wrong. I did something wrong. I ruined everything. I want to become celibate. Maybe, I should become a nun."

"It's a little late for that, don't you think?" I said rhetorically. Shannon laughed, which was a relief to hear.

"No, a bride of Christ I can never be. This is one cherry that has been picked many times over!" We laughed again.

"Shannon, you are very hard on yourself, and you expect too much of yourself. It is a challenge for two people to love each other and to consistently make the right choices for how to best nurture one another. What you were trying to do just may not be humanly possible. Think about it, Shannon. You were supporting two men learning to love each other while simultaneously trying to love both of them, all the while expecting them to love you equally in return. It simply may not be possible for human beings to do something that complicated. I think it was inevitable that the flow of love would become hindered. Love can only flow freely when there is nothing blocking its path."

"You make so much sense, Oliver. I do not like hurting and I do like hurting others." Shannon was hanging on to every word I said.

I continued. "Think of light as a metaphor for love. It must have a clear path in order to travel. Light can be reflected, bouncing off many objects making it possible for us to see, and it is refracted into many colors, all of which enhances the variety and beauty of its expression. However, there are some things light cannot penetrate and we are unable to see. Beauty can be hidden in darkness. Your relationships with Karl and Jonathan had lots of beauty, for a while, and then it came upon obstacles that made love's expression blocked."

"What did I do to create blocks? I must have done something wrong?"

"Maybe you did and maybe you didn't. That is for you to discover. It is your unique growth, your learning about love. It is your lesson. As an outside observer, I can only repeat what I have said already. I think you expected too much from yourself. You wanted to be open to loving as much as you possibly could and perhaps you were attempting the impossible. For me, I have learned that love requires continuous expression that constantly seeks deeper intimacy for fulfillment. Attempting to do that between three people is extremely challenging and may not be possible, at least to sustain over time. I honestly do not know. Hell, it's hard enough between two people. I think that you did nothing wrong. You feel pain because you took your love as far as it could go in that circumstance. The pain you encountered was your psyche's way of telling you something needed to change. I congratulate you for being courageous enough to try, and for being honest when it wasn't working for you."

"Wow, you may be right. Maybe I didn't do anything wrong. In fact, I did everything I could to make the two of them happy, even to the point where I began to neglect my own happiness. That's it! I loved as much as I was capable and had reached my limit. I could no longer be a conduit of love for two men. The pain I was feeling was telling me that I could no longer continue expressing love in that way. I had to change, and change is what I am going through. It is so obvious! My god, I think my prayers have been answered. I understand. Thank you, again, Oliver." Shannon threw her arms around me and kissed my cheeks.

"Hey, you're welcome, but really, I am only sharing with you what I think I know about love, which is actually very little. It is your willingness to open up and communicate your feelings that brought you to a place of understanding, not anything I said or did."

"You are much too humble. You know a lot, and more importantly you care and you listen." Shannon threw her arms around me once again and hugged me tightly. The affection poured out of her. I could feel genuine love and appreciation flowing freely from her. Indeed, her blocks to love's expression had been removed.

"I need to talk with Karl and Jonathan!" she said excitedly.

"Hmmm. I'm not so sure that is a good idea. Perhaps you should wait until they work a few things out on their own. Simply seeing that you are doing better will go a long way toward healing everyone."

"Maybe you're right. I think they need space."

"So, what are your thoughts about your romantic involvement with them?"

"Well, my spontaneous response is that it's over. Love went as far as it could between the three of us. I don't think I could ever be that intimate with either of them again. I do think I still love them though, but it is definitely different."

"In what way?" I asked.

"I think I will always love them as friends, or maybe even as brothers, but never again as lovers. In fact, I think it would be a good idea for me to be celibate for a while."

"It sounds like you are giving attention to taking care of yourself. Good for you Shannon!" We hugged again.

"Hey, I love that Shaker hymn you sing. By the way, Shakers were a community of celibate people. I don't think your celibacy will last a lifetime, though. Do you mind singing the hymn again while I play along with the flute?" Shannon sang and I played the flute and we repeated the song several times over. The entire community could hear us playing as we learned the next day, receiving many compliments during breakfast and throughout the day.

Jonathan had told Jamie that he was seriously thinking about becoming a priest and that it was the only way he could deal with his sexuality without hurting anyone. He obviously had a great deal more healing to go through.

Karl gradually came out of his isolationism, spending time almost exclusively with his mother and Helena. He still was not attending community activities, choosing to cook his meals alone, with his mother and sister occasionally joining him. Michelin reminded me that Karl was new to experiencing romance and sex, and that his physicality, independence, abundant skills and talents, made most people think of him as being far more mature than his years. She told me that spending an extended period of time not involved in a relationship would be the very best thing for Karl. "He is very, very immature in the ways of love, Oliver, and extremely resilient. He will move past this as other interests consume his time and energy." I thought of how we are all immature when it comes to love – even someone as worldly as Michelin, but I kept that thought to myself.

Shannon was back to her normal self, cheerful and friendly and she was consistently kind to Jonathan and Karl, but they did not know how to respond to her for they had not yet healed their wounds as she had. Shannon had learned a great deal about herself and about the process of expressing love. Apparently, it would take more time for Jonathan and Karl to learn whatever their lessons were, and time was indeed necessary for healing to be complete, and, I assumed, there would always be scars to remind them of those lessons.

The occurrences of Jamie's illness, the breakup of Shannon and Karl (few people knew about Jonathan's involvement), two pregnancies, and the inevitable complexities of developing relationships, had sent ripples through our relatively tranquil community lifestyle. We learned from them, and somehow their difficulties had strengthened us. As a community, we became more conscientious of our relationships and more philosophical about the realities of life, death, and the process of change. Michelin and Harold introduced topics for discussion that focused on deepening our understanding of social dynamics, values, beliefs, perceptions, and the kind of community we had created and wanted to create. These discussions, although insightful, made me ever more aware that our community was temporary. We were all growing and changing, new life was on the way, and the possibility of death was an ever-present dark cloud, and there was the economic reality that our community was built on land not owned by all of us. Norlina, Edward, and Elijah were generous, and they were prospering from our labor, artistic talents and financial contributions, and the rewards reaped by all members of the community were abundant.

It was *not* a pleasant realization that the community we were building was temporary, while Sunset Village would eventually live on as a tourist resort that supported the families of our Jamaican friends. Patrick and I were never under any illusion regarding this fact. We had discussed it from the very beginning, long before we even knew that Norlina and Elijah were the owners of this particular piece of land. I had brought up the fact that the future of our community would definitely change from its current form and that our idyllic lifestyle would eventually come to an end. We just did not know how or in what timeframe. Jamie said that this was all the more reason for us to appreciate the preciousness of our current circumstances and to make plans for the future... plans that involved two weddings, a creation of life ceremony, and two births – and other changes.

SLICE OF HEAVEN

Patrick and Michelin were prospering quite nicely with their smuggling operations. Elijah grew the ganja and he along with Norlina and Edward did the mailing. Patrick's sister and her new boyfriend, Randy the hippie, were taking care of the business in Philly. The recent letter Patrick received, which was addressed to Sunset Village, informed Patrick that he had made a considerable sum of money. So much so that Patrick entertained the idea of buying land. He asked me to help him look, saying that we would be equal owners. I told him I had nothing to do with the smuggling business and was surprised that he was offering me potential land ownership. He said that the entire Jamaican adventure was a co-creation and everything that came out of it was ours to share.

"Hell, Oliver, we're even getting married to twin sisters. You're going to be the uncle of my child. Come on bro, we are brothers in every way but genes, and what the hell do genes have to do with brotherhood other than it being an accident of birth?" Patrick convinced me and I accepted his offer. We began our search for land.

When I told Jamie that Patrick and I wanted to buy land, she became very excited. "A fantastic idea! It would be wonderful if it happened soon so the land could be blessed with the birth of my sister's child." I knew she was thinking of her own death as well, and so was I.

"Alight, then. We are embarking on a land seeking adventure!" I announced.

"Cliff or beach?" Jamie asked. "That's something we need to decide."

"Hmm. I am partial to cliffs," Patrick said.

"Me too," I replied.

"Jules and I like both equally. I wonder if it's possible to have both."

"That would be ideal. The only area that I know that comes close to that is Fishermen Cove, and the cliffs there are low-lying and the beach is public land designated for the fishermen of Negril. Maybe there's land outside of Negril."

"We can use the canoe sailboats to explore the coast. That would be fantastic!" It was uplifting to see Jamie so thrilled about the future.

"We also have two weddings to plan for. Are you and Julie going to try calling your parents again?" I asked.

"Jules, Patrick, Elijah, and Michelin went to the Roundabout the other day to take care of business and get some supplies. Jules tried calling Mom and Dad but they weren't home. It's possible that they are on their way," Jamie explained.

"Well, we're just going to have to make wedding plans that can be put into motion at a moment's notice," I suggested.

"Oliver, it's not really that big of a deal. I mean it is, but all we need is food and drinks. We can marry on the cliff and Harold offered to marry us but since we aren't going to go through Jamaican or U.S. legalities, we can marry each other with our friends as witnesses. It will be a spiritual wedding. Hell, if we want, we can make up a written contract, and the entire community can sign it."

"That's true. We can write our vows together if you want," I suggested.

"We can give that a try. Or we can surprise each other and write them privately," added Jamie, "I can create a large scroll and everyone can sign it. Michelin would like to contribute her artistic talent and make it a treasured document, I'm sure."

"That's a great idea. I'm confident you will put your artistic touch on the scroll as well," I added.

"Yes, I will, and I will encourage our friends to draw, write poetry, or simply write their signature and a blessing. Oh, Oliver, this is going to be so wonderful!" It was a pleasure to see Jamie so excited.

"Patrick and I will make sure we have food and drink on hand for the community." I was also feeling thrilled.

"I'll speak with Jules and see what she has to say and what she and Patrick want to do. It is going to be so lovely!" Jamie was in very good spirits. I continued to be amazed by her optimism and strength. She was experiencing an extended period of good health. Apparently, the leukemia had stopped or slowed down its progression. Jamie told me this would happen.

Patrick and I made all the necessary arrangements to make sure there would be a cornucopia of food and beverages available for the double wedding. We employed the help of Millie and Charley who had the best access to food items. Norlina and Edward offered to set up the restaurant and bar. We asked Karl, Liam, and Luke to provide the best fresh fish available on a moments notice and they eagerly agreed. As for the ceremony itself, the four of us were going to speak our vows without anyone presiding over the ritual, and anything else that occurred following that would be, as far as we understood, spontaneous.

The four of us sailed up and down the Negril coast, and a little beyond on both the northern and southern ends, searching for an area that combined both elements of cliff and beach. For a week we sailed along the coast, even camping overnight on remote areas that were quite beautiful. The greatest drawback to the pristine uninhabited areas was that we had no idea if any of this land was for sale. There was no one to talk to. We would have to go to a government office for information. Also, since there were no inhabitants, there was no known water supply, and when we ventured inland, we could find no road. These areas were fun to live on as part of a going-native lifestyle, but for building a home and a life they were impractical. We decided that we would have to be close to a village of Jamaicans for this and other reasons – like basic supplies and social interaction.

The four of us were thoroughly enjoying getting reacquainted with the feeling of being free and native. As much as we loved our community life, we had become so involved in the social dramas of our interpersonal relationships that we were slightly out of touch with the free-spirited life that attracted us to the island in the first place. Living the ideal paradise life, after all, is an escape into fantasy, a time-out from the vicissitudes of life. The truth is, such fantasies are exactly that, unreal, and all we can ever really do is spend glorious stretches of time living a carefree life, and these stretches cannot go on forever – life happens! But hey, interludes of heaven on earth are obtainable and I thoroughly enjoyed them while they were happening. Making love with Jamie was an on-going heavenly interlude – the most precious and the most lasting and one I did not ever, ever, want to let go of. Sailing along the coast and exploring beautiful cliffs and beaches with close friends was definitely a heavenly interlude.

The town of Little Bay, which was several miles south and east of Sunset Village, had caught our attention. It was an extremely smaller version of Negril and we believed that the inevitable onslaught of tourism would come much slower to this fishing village. It had a small three-quarter mile long beach that was situated in a cove, hence the name, Little Bay. On both sides of this bay there were cliffs. They were not as high as the cliffs along Negril's coastline, but they were beautiful. We camped on the beach and got to know a few local Jamaicans. We discovered that they rarely see white people, and because of this we quickly became a local entertainment attraction for the villagers, particularly the children, who liked touching our light-colored skin, and especially my long strawberry blond hair and freckled face. We learned from the locals that Bob Marley was becoming well known in Jamaica but was not yet known to the international community. He had cousins in Little Bay, and it was rumored that he bought land and planned on building a home on the cliffs. Of course we knew of Bob Marley and the Wailers, but our relative isolation, living at Sunset Village without electricity, had taken us out of the commercial music loop. We knew that Reggae music had become popular, which would increase the attraction of Jamaica as a destination for young travelers.

Jamie and Julie liked the friendliness of the people in Little Bay, and it definitely had that unique combination of cliff and sandy beach. Most people in Negril and Little Bay did not build their shanties on the cliffs, preferring to be on top of soil than bare rock, and protected from storms. It was our intention to build on a cliff, and to have easy access to the beach and good soil as well. We strolled around the town, meeting people and asking about land for sale. A young woman told us about an old man who owned land and had no family. She told us where to find him. He lived in a thatched hut cottage in a quaint garden of palm trees and flowering plants. He had a head full of snow-white dreadlocks, and he sported a long braided white beard. His eyes were large and bright and had that salty-sea look that comes from decades of staring at the sea's horizon. His name was Andy, and he was a fisherman in his youth as well as a stonemason. He told us that he built most of the cinder block cottages in Little Bay, and that he did the stonework on the post office. Andy owned several parcels of land, some he had purchased and some he inherited from his parents and siblings who had passed away. Andy had no children. He told us he was sixty-seven years old. He didn't look a day over fifty.

Andy asked how we got to Little Bay. "We sailed from Negril," Patrick said.

"Sail? I want ta see yah boat. Is it a yacht?" Andy inquired.

"No, it is a canoe outrigger with a sail. We designed it ourselves," explained Patrick.

"I need ta see it," said Andy. He walked with us to the beach. I was impressed with how limber he was and the brisk pace at which he walked. Andy was fascinated by our boat. Having been a fisherman all his life, he had never seen such a craft. He wanted to understand how it worked.

"The best way is to take you for a sail," offered Patrick. Andy eagerly accepted and off they went, sailing up and down along the coast of Little Bay, while we sat on the beach. After a little more than an hour, they returned.

"Effin ya 'elp mi mek such a boat, I will sell land ta yah."

"Definitely!" Patrick replied.

"I own a couple canoes. I'm willin' ta put a sail on one."

"We'll have to take a look at your canoes and see which one would work out best," offered Patrick.

"How much land yah be wantin'?" Andy asked.

"Depends on what you have," I replied.

"Tell me wat yah lookin' fer, mon."

"We want cliff and beach, if that's possible," replied Jamie.

"Yes, we like being close to the water, and it would be nice to have some land where we can grow food," added Julie.

"I show ya wat I 'ave an' yah see ef it suit wat yah be needin," responded Andy. "Come, mon, follow mi. I t'ink I may 'ave jus' wat yah lookin' fer."

We walked along the beach with Andy, and then up to the dirt road. He took us along the road for about ten minutes then Andy abruptly turned toward the cliffs. He was barefoot and like so many of the older Jamaicans, the soles of his feet were covered in thick human leather. He was not bothered in the least by the jagged cliff rock. He walked to the edge of the cliff and pointed to his right and said, "Look." Below the cliff there was a sandy beach, enshrined on three sides by cliff that were no more than fifteen feet high. The beach was recessed into the cliff, meaning there was part of the cliff overhanging the sand, creating a beach-cave like appearance. The sandy beach looked like it was a hundred feet wide and twenty feet deep. In all our sailing along the coast we never saw a sandy cove beach at the base of a cliff.

"This is it! This is exactly what we want!" shouted Julie as she hugged the old Jamaican, who was both delighted and very surprised to have a young lady throw her arms around him.

"I was t'inkin' yah be likin' dis land. It belonged ta mi fadda. He had no use fer it. He t'ink it worthless since it nuh easy ta get ta de sandy cove," explained Andy. "At one time I t'ink it be useful ef I beach mi boat wen fishin', but I 'ave better land fer dat along de bay. Come. I show yah de rest of de land." Andy pointed out the cliff boundaries of the property. Then he gave us a tour of the full ten acres that included lots of trees and suitable land for growing a modest amount of food. The food bearing trees consisted of numerous breadfruits, four coconuts, three bananas, and one each of mango, orange, lime, lemon, ackee, and papaya. There were four very large Aloe Vera plants. Andy explained that this was the primary use of the property for his parents - a steady supply of fruit. Other than that, they had no use for it. He asked if he could continue to take enough breadfruit for his own needs if we decided to buy the land.

"How much do you want for the land?" I asked.

"I 'ave never sold land ta white people, an' never spoke ta a person who did. Yah be de first white people ta be livin' in Little Bay."

"If you sold it to a Jamaican, how much would it be?" I asked.

"Yah be a wise one, young mon, but yah nuh Jamaican, so de same business rules nuh be applyin' ta dis purchase." Andy stroked his long white braided beard as he spoke. There was a glint in his eyes. Then Patrick shocked all of us.

"We'll give you $2000 U.S.!" he announced proudly. To us, and to our Jamaican friend, that sounded like an impressive amount of money. However, I knew that land such as this was a jewel in paradise and was worth far more.

"Yah t'ink dat a fair price, do yah?" replied Andy, smiling.

"Yes. I do."

"I be needin' three times dat much!"

"Three thousand, U.S. We can get you the cash in two weeks," replied Patrick. I was stunned and felt totally out of the loop. I never asked Patrick how much money he had earned from his smuggling operation, but I was getting the idea that it was a great deal.

"Nuh, mon. I see dis is exactly de land yah be wantin, an' I knoh dere is nuh another like it. Four thousand U.S., dat is wat I be needin'"

"Agreed!" said Julie, to the surprise of Jamie and me, but not to Patrick. Andy looked at Julie, and then at Patrick.

"Is dis lovely lady's acceptance agreeable ta yah, sir?" Andy asked Patrick, completely ignoring Jamie and me.

"Yes!" Patrick reached out his hand and Andy took it. The deal had been made. We agreed, actually Julie and Patrick agreed to buy land in Jamaica. Ten acres for four thousand dollars! Jamie looked at me with those gorgeous light filled rich chocolate eyes and said, "We have found our slice of heaven, my love!"

That night we camped on the land. Andy sat with us around the campfire and told us stories of his life growing up in Little Bay. We told him what he would need to build his canoe sailboat. "I soon 'ave enough money ta buy a bigger boat. I knoh of a boat dat is nuh a canoe an' effin ya 'elp me, I like ta put a sail on 'er. I be gettin' a motor as well."

"Sure, said Patrick. We just need to look the boat over and determine what it needs." Andy was a ganja smoker, and a grower. He and Patrick discussed business arrangements. It was becoming quite clear that money was not going to be a problem, and I was pleased that I didn't have to be involved in Patrick's business enterprises. He decided to keep me informed, however, and I learned that his business had expanded to several college campuses throughout Philadelphia. He was even harvesting mushrooms, drying them out, and shipping them to the states. He said they were very popular on college campuses and although not as lucrative as ganja, he liked the idea of contributing to the spiritual development of young Americans. "Magic mushrooms are the fruit of the Gods!" he became fond of saying.

We spent the next day walking the land and dreaming of what we would build and where. Patrick, feeling empowered by his "mushrooming" financial success, wanted to build a cliff stone castle-like structure, designing it to blend in with the cliff. He said he was going to ask Karl to help with the design, which I thought was an excellent idea. The twins said they would be happier with a simpler structure, but Patrick assured them that although his idea of a stone castle sounded extravagant, in reality it would be simple, elegant, and well suited as a cliff dwelling to deal with storms.

Andy told us it would not be expensive to have a water pipe run to the land. He said with a little bit of money we could have an electric wire run from the town center to the property. The main expense would be the installation of large poles along the road to the property, which, he added, would help some of the local villagers who were without electricity. "Electricity would mek it possible ta use specialty tools, mon, dat would mek carving de cliff an' building much faster an' easier. I knoh many good, young, strong, skilled workers dat be 'appy ta 'ave de work. We build yah stone house quick!" Andy was obviously a man who loved construction work.

Patrick and I discussed the best area of the cliff to build the stone castle. We agreed that it would be positioned directly above the beach cove, so that when we stand on the tower or looked out of the arched windows, or stood on a veranda, we would see the beach below. Of course, we would carve steps going from the castle directly to the beach. Patrick suggested that we have a stone staircase that would wind around the castle going from level to level, with each floor having its own veranda, and the stairway would go all the way to the sandy cove – a fantastic idea!

We went with Andy to the Little Bay post office where we wrote a promissory note and had a government official witness the purchase. The post office is where the land deeds are recorded. All four of us signed the note, and the government official said he would draw up the proper documents for the final sale and transfer of deed once a payment was made. Patrick would have preferred to pay for the land that very day, but there was no bank in Little Bay, the closest being in Savanna La Mar. Patrick and Julie agreed that the land was to be paid for in one cash payment, due within two weeks. Later, Patrick explained that his sister had deposited his smuggling money in the Bank of Jamaica in his name through a wire transfer. I also learned that both Julie and Jamie had inherited money from their grandparents and that the sum we paid for the Little Bay property was a relatively small amount compared to the combined wealth, and that there would be plenty of funds available to build whatever we desired. I couldn't help but think that money is a necessary commodity and even though Patrick and I had learned to live with precious little, we were still engaged in economic activity. I learned that economics is simply the interaction between people that involves meeting needs, and that there is no such thing as living without being engaged in economic activity, whether it involves the exchange of currency or other things of value. It is a fact of existence. Duh! It occurred to me how naïve and stupid I could be.

After taking care of the promissory note, we sailed off. We decided to take a stop at our cliff beach cove. We were pleasantly surprised to discover that the sandy beach was actually a very large cliff ledge that was shaped just right so that sand formed from coral erosion was deposited over centuries. There were several amazing geological features to this sandy cove. The ledge's shape served as a sandbox, keeping the sea swells from pulling the sand off the beach. The ledge extended seaward for seventy-five yards and then there was a big drop off. The ledge was an elevated bowl protruding from the main cliff face and had collected coral-sand deposits from a coral reef that followed the contour of the land. This reef was a few hundred yards off shore, and in between the reef and the cliff there was deep water that was a haven for fish, a perfect place to position our fish traps. Another amazing geological feature was that beneath the sandbox ledge, there was an underwater cave. Sea plants and animals attached to the walls of the undersea cave, providing a plethora of colors and shapes, as well as food for fish, another reason why this was an excellent natural fishing area. Jamie's words were perfectly descriptive – we had definitely found our *slice of heaven!*

After swimming and exploring our cove for a few hours, we made our way back to the community. During our sail, we discussed telling the community of our purchase and decided to wait until after the wedding, thinking it might create emotional upheaval. I was concerned that we would no longer be able to fish for Elkannah. We decided to ask Luke, Liam, and Karl to fully take over this obligation. We were fortunate to have a canoe outrigger sailboat to transport our gear. However, it would not be sufficient for the four of us, so we made the decision to purchase another canoe to convert into a sailboat once we got settled in Little Bay. The wind was in our favor and before the sun had set we were in sight of the Sunset Village cove.

To our delight, we could see the entire community meditating on the cliff. They were clearly visible from our position in the sea. The golden rays of sun reflected off their hair, faces and clothing. The community waved to us as our boat entered the cove. Patrick and I paddled the boat to the steps. Jamie and Julie were sailing naked and as we approached the cove, they put on their one piece loose fitting cotton dresses. We anchored the boat while Julie and Jamie ascended the stairs. We heard them scream out in joy: "Oh my god, you are here, you are here. I love you!" When I got to the top of the cliff, I saw two people hugging Jamie and Julie. It was their parents. We were introduced to Mr. and Mrs. Starr. They were very friendly to Patrick and me, not a single negative vibe was communicated from either of them, just amiable acceptance, much to our relief. It was a good thing that Julie put on her loosely fitting dress, otherwise her mother would have noticed that she was pregnant. Her mother commented on her daughters' appearances, stating how tan they were and how Julie gained some weight while Jamie was slimmer.

We celebrated throughout the night, eating, talking, storytelling, and playing music. Jamie's father, Michael, played the lute, which was a very nice accompaniment to Patrick's guitar, and her mother, Lucinda, played the violin – beautifully. I had learned that the violin and flute are very compatible instruments, and that Lucinda viewed her violin playing in the same manner that I regarded my flute – as an instrument for expressions from the heart. She and I played an improvisational rendition of amazing grace that brought tears to her eyes. As the evening progressed, people gathered in smaller groups or pairs engaging in more intimate conversations. Some people drifted off to be alone with their thoughts. I decided to invite the twins, their parents, and Patrick to the community meditation area on the cliffs. To my surprise, Michael lit up a joint and offered it to me. Out of respect, I shared it with him and to my surprise, and concern, Jamie smoked too. It was the first time I had seen her put any mind enhancing substance into her body. Lucinda and Patrick got stoned as well, but Julie declined. We sat quietly, taking in the beauty of the night sky and the surrounding sea and cliffs. I was delighted by the feeling of comfort I had from being in the presence of Jamie's parents.

"This truly is one of the most beautiful places I have ever been," said Lucinda.

"Yes, honey, I agree, and we have traveled to many islands, my dear," added Michael.

"I see why the four of you want to create a life here," said Lucinda. "I do assume that since you are going to be married in Jamaica that you plan on living here, at least for a while." I was struck by the fact that Lucinda had completely accepted that her daughters were going to be married. I was astonished.

"We are so happy that the two of you have found the men that you love, and in such a beautiful place," added Michael.

It was the father's statement, followed by what the mother had said that made the situation feel ultra surrealistic. It caused me to wonder how parents of nineteen-year-old twins could be so accepting of them getting married and choosing to live away from home on an island, and to men they have just met. And they are professional educators who most likely, I assumed, wanted their children to pursue professional careers as well. Jamie and Julie were suspiciously silent. They simply sat still with smiles upon their faces.

"Tell me, Oliver and Patrick, how did you come to meet our daughters?" Michael asked.

Patrick responded, "They were damsels in distress and we rescued them!"

"Oh my, and what was the distress and the valiant actions you performed?" Lucinda asked.

I answered, "They were surrounded by rude and crude young Jamaican boys who were harassing them. Your daughters were experiencing culture shock and, as I later learned, were simply caught off guard. We intervened."

"What do you mean by your statement, 'as you later learned'?" Michael asked.

"Sir, your daughters are very independent and strong-willed, and they know how to fend for themselves very well. They were in a rare weakened state from traveling. They were lacking rest, and the onslaught of young men who wanted money and other things had overwhelmed them. We later discovered that your daughters are world travelers and very experienced in dealing with ruffians," I replied.

"Yes, we have the utmost confidence in the good judgment of our daughters," Lucinda said, while looking at her daughters lovingly. "Julie, Jamie, tell us what you like about your husbands to be. Who wants to go first?"

Jamie was quick to respond. "Mother, I prefer you get to know Oliver over time without me having to characterize him for you. I will say one thing: he is the most loving person I have ever met and no one on this earth has ever made me feel happier."

Lucinda chuckled delightfully. "There isn't anything else you need to say!"

"Gee, that just about makes anything I could possibly say very pale in comparison," replied Julie, "but how about this: there is no man I have ever known who is more intelligent, insightful, courageous, handsome, and – hold on to your bodhisattvas – sexy!"

Michael and Lucinda burst out laughing so hard that they rolled on to their sides. "That's our Jules! I don't think you have ever said anything that would come close to being insipid," Lucinda said. "Well, I suppose we could now ask these loving, intelligent, courageous, and sexy young men to characterize our daughters but that would not be fair. Besides, we know your qualities all too well."

"Agreed, my love. These young lads have excellent taste in women!" said Michael. "And the two of you are fine musicians. Patrick, you are quite talented on the guitar, and Oliver, I have never heard my wife play with anyone else with so much, ah, so much, well, comfort is the word. Yes, that's it, she usually is quite nervous performing, but not with you. I wonder why that is?"

"It is the way he plays, Michael. Like me, he plays what he feels, which is what makes playing the violin so personal for me, so spiritual. Can you not hear the quality in the tone of his flute? It is not his technique that makes the flute sound so pure, it is because he plays from his heart." Wow, I have never heard anyone speak of my flute playing like that. She completely understood what the instrument means to me - what I express through it.

"Thank you for putting words to what I have never been able to articulate," I said.

"I am able to describe your flute playing because it is exactly what creating music is to me. Tell me, do you have difficulty playing when the focus is upon you and your performance?"

"Yes. I get very nervous and can't get enough air to play well."

"And when you play while others are listening and you are not the center of attention, do you enjoy playing for them?"

"Yes, I do. In fact, it is my favorite way to play for people. I do not like the focus to be on me. That has always puzzled me. I am not as nervous when I play with other people. I have gotten better with that."

"I understand. I am the same way. The truth is, Oliver, you and I are innately shy people." I never thought of myself as being a shy person. I'm not sure I agree with that assessment, at least not to my over all character.

"See, Mother, you are getting to know Oliver through a more natural process other than having me characterize him for you," said Jamie.

"Yes, I am. Actually, I understood that about him when we performed together earlier this evening," she replied, "Did you notice that we did not announce that we would be performing for you, we simply went to the periphery of the group and started playing."

Michael chimed in, "Well, I have no trouble standing in front of people and having them watch me play the lute and sing, and I learned that neither does Patrick. How nice that we have discovered compatibilities with your husbands to be."

"So, my children, when is the wedding?" Lucinda asked.

"We have everything prepared so it can happen at any time, including tomorrow, if you like," replied Julie.

"If we like? My dear child, it is your wedding. The decision is up to the four of you," responded Lucinda.

"Okay then, I say three days from now. That will be a Saturday, and isn't that usually the best day to hold a wedding?"

"Any day to see my daughters married to such wonderful young men is a good day!" replied Michael.

The next morning the twins' parents were on the cliff when Jamie and I arrived for meditation. They were sitting in the classic lotus yoga Buddha meditation position, the one that made me feel like a pretzel every time I gave it a try. We sat next to them without saying a word. Soon, Julie and Patrick arrived. I noticed that Julie continued wearing a dress that hid her belly. She was concealing her pregnancy from her parents quite well. I was surprised they had not noticed the night before. It occurred to me that no one in the community had mentioned her pregnancy to the parents. I was impressed with how well our community was able to keep such a tantalizing secret. I wondered when Jules would tell them. Then a feeling of dread gripped my heart. Jamie's cancer! She had been doing so well these past few weeks that I mostly pushed the reality of her illness out from the forefront of my mind. I understood that I was living in denial of the inevitable, and was secretly hoping for a miracle. The big question was when would Jamie tell her parents, and how would they respond? I imagined them being alarmed, sad, and then angry. They would have every right to demand that she return to Bloomington, Indiana, and receive the best medical treatment available and I would support them in this. I would go with Jamie and support every step in the treatment process.

These thoughts were very disturbing. I could not still my mind and enjoy the peace that often comes with meditation. Jamie must have sensed my uneasiness. She placed her hand on mine and gently squeezed, letting me know that everything was going to be all right. Other members of the community arrived to join the morning meditation. Helena usually arrived with Michelin and Harold, and Elijah always tended to his garden and animal duties first thing each morning. Norlina and Edward never attended the morning meditation, only the evening sessions. Karl, Luke and Liam would sometimes attend, but most mornings they would go fishing very early. Donna and Roseann usually showed up, and they were always the last to arrive.

We watched Karl emerge from his sea cave lair and set sail for what I assumed were the deep waters. It became his daily morning practice to go far out to sea, hunting for the big fish with his spear gun. Karl said he was able to spear tuna from the canoe, and that catching them with hand lines was not possible because they were too big and strong to haul in. He even took to using a spear he designed for throwing into the water. Karl was usually successful, keeping Sunset Village abundantly supplied with succulent fresh meat. It became my early morning ritual to observe Luke and Liam descend the staircase and launch their fishing craft. They sometimes accompanied Karl when they weren't tending to the traps and diving for conch. It was particularly delightful for me to observe my childhood friends sailing out to sea. I was proud of them, and grateful that they were living a life far removed from the concrete jungle that had spawned them. They must have already gone out to sea and returned because their craft was attached to the bamboo raft, and they were not present this morning. In fact, I had not seen them since day before I had left for Little Bay; perhaps they were taking a break from fishing. Thinking of my childhood friends living in Jamaica took my mind away from the thoughts that were disturbing me. As soon as Karl's boat left the cove, my mind returned to thoughts of the twins and their parents, of our wedding, of Jamie's illness, of the Little Bay property, of… too many thoughts racing through my brain. Then, just as I felt like I had to get up and jump off the cliff to plunge my body into the turquoise sea as a way to stop these streaming thoughts, Michael stood up and spoke. "Each of us is the light of the world. We bring to every mind the light of life with our loving thoughts. I am grateful that my daughters have found such a wonderful community of people in such a place of magnificent physical beauty." Michael sat down after he spoke. There was a shift in the way I was feeling because of the words he spoke. I wondered if loving thoughts could heal Jamie, and since she had not shown signs of sickness since many days before her parents had arrived, perhaps the miracle I was hoping for was happening. Then again, I was probably just engaging in wishful thinking.

Lucinda got up and spoke. "I, too, am grateful that my daughters live here among you. And I am filled with even more gratitude that they have found men whom they truly love, and I have learned that they love my daughters equally as much. Soon they will be wed, and into each other's hearts they will ascend." She sat down, and a warm feeling spread through the community. I could see it in their faces and I could feel it in my bones. Then, the most surprising thing of the morning happened. Julie stood up. She was quiet for several minutes. I could hear her taking in deep breaths, seemingly to calm her nerves, although she did not look agitated.

"Mother, Father, I thank you for coming to Sunset Village, and I am fortunate to have such loving, accepting, and understanding parents. It is a wonderful gift to have you here among our community of friends, and more importantly for you to meet my husband to be, Patrick. I have an even greater gift to present to you, my dear mother and father!" Julie pulled the loosely fitting dress she was wearing over her head. She stood before the astonished community in all of her womanly glory. Her pregnant body was one of the most beautiful things my eyes have ever beheld. The sunlight accentuated every lovely curve of her body. The contour of her abdomen revealed that life was forming in her womb. Her parents were speechless, motionless, frozen in disbelief and surprise. Tears rolled down Lucinda's cheeks. Then, as Julie put her dress back on, the parents went to her, embraced and kissed her. The community burst out in cheers. Now, I don't know if anyone else thought about what just happened in the way that I did, but man, if I was a parent, I would not feel comfortable having my nineteen year old daughter strip in front of a group of people, let alone doing it for the purpose of announcing her pregnancy. I looked at Patrick and he too appeared to be in a state of disbelief.

"Oliver," Jamie whispered, "I know you are surprised by Jules' actions ..."

I interrupted, "And you're not?"

"Not at all. It is classic Jules. She has a flare for the dramatic moments. She told me last night that she was going to tell our parents in front of the community."

"Did she tell you she was going to strip off her clothes?"

"No."

"Well, why didn't that shock you?"

"Why should it?"

"She was stark naked!"

"We're naked all the time around here."

"Yeah, but not with your parents. And why weren't they embarrassed?"

"They had no cause to be."

"No cause? Julie was standing in front of your parents and God and everyone completely naked."

"I am shocked that you're shocked. Wasn't it the most beautiful sight you ever beheld?"

"Yes! Definitely! Well almost – nothing compares to your naked beauty."

"Perfect answer! Well, imagine how my parents feel having it revealed to them that their child is with child in such a beautiful way, with the rising sun rays illuminating a mother goddess!"

"Yes, yes, you are right, but she was naked in front of her parents and ..."

Jamie interrupted, "Oliver, my parents were beatniks and they are like, you know, the original hippies of hippies. They are used to nudity. We grew up with nudity. I am surprised they showed up for morning meditation with clothes on. Our home in Bloomington is basically known as the Starr Buddhist nudist colony!"

"Well, then, that explains it. So, the nudity thing was not unusual, in fact, they would view it as a spectacularly beautiful way for Julie to let them know about her pregnancy."

"And that is exactly how they responded. Now you get it!" Patrick was listening to our conversation and now he too was no longer stunned. He looked less puzzled.

"I don't get why she didn't tell me that she was going to do that," said Patrick.

Jamie responded, "She wanted to surprise you. Besides, judging from the way you responded, I assume she thought you would not approve and would try to stop her."

"Well, yeah!"

"Why?" she asked

"Why, what?" Patrick asked.

"Why would you have tried to stop her?"

"Well, for all the things that Oliver just said to you, but now, well now, I think it was really cool!"

"That's the spirit! Come on! Let's invite my parents to some Jamaican Blue Mountain coffee and breakfast. Then, we can all go for a swim – a skinny dip! But you, Oliver, must keep your shorts on." We laughed. As we were preparing breakfast, I kept wondering when Jamie would tell her parents about her leukemia. I needed to speak with her about how she was going to handle that. I wanted to be with her when she told them. I decided to speak with her after breakfast before the mid- morning swim with her parents.

Most of the community had gathered for breakfast. We were leisurely sharing our thoughts and plans for the day when I heard Luke call out, "Yo everybody, we have got a big surprise, check us out!"

On the road that entered our community property, Luke and Liam were sitting on top of a pile of burlap bundles riding in a wagon pulled by a donkey with two Jamaicans sitting at the reigns.

"Holy shit, those are the two Jamaicans I met on the beach who wanted me to supply them with a mini-submarine to smuggle their ganja crop to the States. Unbelievable!" Patrick stood up and headed for the cart. Luke and Liam jumped off their perch upon the bundles. The strong aroma had made it obvious that the bundles were filled with ganja. Patrick ignored Luke and Liam's greeting and spoke directly to the two young Jamaicans. "Irie mon, I am happy to see that you have met my brothers from the U.S. Welcome to Sunset Village. I do not recall your names." Patrick extended his hand to the nearest Jamaican.

"I am David, mon, an' des is my bredda, Henry. How can yah be forgettin' our names mon? We mek business deal wit yah, mon. But nuh need ta trouble yer self 'bout dat, mon. Yah breddas fram de U.S. tell us aw 'bout yer troubles. We are here now, nuh t'ing to worry 'bout, mon. Now we complete da business we spoke of, mon. Irie!" David made a wide grin revealing several rotted teeth on the bottom row and a big gap where his top front teeth use to be. Patrick had told me they were from Cane Valley where there are large cane sugar plantations and I heard about Jamaicans subsisting on diets of mostly pure sugar. I have seen many Jamaican adults with no teeth, young adults in their mid twenties. I wondered what the so-called troubles were that Liam and Luke had concocted for these two gullible Jamaican youth. Patrick glanced at Liam hoping for assistance – Liam got the non-verbal message.

"I told David and Henry all about you and Oliver rescuing the lovely damsels in distress, and that all of your attention had gone to making sure they were okay, and that you fell in love and are getting married very soon." Liam smiled a sheepish grin, proud that the story he gave to them was the truth, but not the reason for Patrick ignoring the so-called business deal.

"Yes, mon. Yah saved de ladies fram distress an' yah are rewarded wit true love. Der is good ta be found in every t'ing mon." Henry's comment brought a look of relief on Patrick's face. Patrick was true to form, quick to recognize an opportunity.

"David and Henry, you are honorable men. I am pleased that you have not forgotten our business arrangement, and I am grateful for your understanding. I see you have brought your ganja with you." David and Henry jumped off the wagon, eager to display their product.

"Irie mon! Jus as we promise. We nuh foolin' yah Patrick wen we talk on de beach dat night. Come and 'ave a look fer yer self, mon." Patrick walked to the back of the wagon. I joined him while Jules and Jamie were busy petting the donkey. Those who were present for breakfast were gathered nearby giving their attention to our guest.

Henry reached under the pile of burlap bundles and slipped out a machete, using it to slice open a bundle, revealing greenish-red buds, some the size of a fist. Patrick let out a whistle.

"Yes mon! Good ganja. De bes' in aw of Jamaica. I n I de best ganja farmers, mon!" David stood with his hands on his hips and his head held high.

"I can see that. Thank you for bringing this to me."

"No problem mon! Wat 'bout de submarine, Patrick, yah mek progress?"

"No. The Navy shut down their military installation in my hometown and sold all the submarines to a foreign country. I have other ways to get ganja to the U.S." I was surprised that Patrick had decided that he was going to buy all of their ganja. I wondered how the hell he was going to pay for it. I'd bet my left nut that he was wondering the same thing.

"I am sorry ta hear 'bout da submarine, mon. Dat was a good idea. How yah be gettin' de ganja ta de U.S., Patrick?"

"We can talk about that later. Would you like to join us for breakfast?"

"I see lots of friendly faces lookin' upon us, mon. Yes I. We eat wit yer frens, mon." David and Henry walked up to members of the community, shaking hands and exchanging names. They made their way to the fire in the center of our community-gathering place. Michelin poured coffee while Harold prepared plates of food for them. Luke told the story of how they met David and Henry on the beach. When he mentioned that they were from Philadelphia, David immediately remembered it was the city Patrick had told him about and asked if Luke knew Patrick. One thing led to another and here they were, at Sunset Village with over a hundred pounds of ganja.

Elijah had joined the group. Patrick introduced him to David and Henry. Elijah wasted no time delving into the nature of their visit. "Wat is yer business here, mon?"

David replied with a respectful tone. "My business wit Patrick."

"I see yah ave lots of ganja. Patrick buy dis?"

"Yes mon! We be mekkin' a deal," David replied.

"I own dis land, mon. I mus' be part of dis business." Elijah sounded a little stern. Patrick was quick to intervene.

"Of course, Elijah. I did not know they would be here today. The business David is speaking of was discussed quite sometime ago, before Sunset Village. We had lost track of each other. Luke and Liam met them on the beach and here they are."

"So wat de terms of dis business transaction?" asked Elijah.

"We have not had that discussion. The original arrangement has changed so we must negotiate," replied Patrick.

"I mus' be part of dis talk!" Elijah insisted. David and Henry looked puzzled and concerned.

Patrick placed a hand on Elijah's shoulder and said, "Of course, Elijah. No disrespect, mon. I did not know they were coming or I would have spoken with you first."

"We mus' mek discussion later. Look at de sea. A big storm soon come." Everyone who was paying attention to our discussion looked at the sea and in the distance there were huge thunderhead clouds. "Dis storm will be very strong. We mus' put de ganja in yer cottage, Patrick, ta keep dry." Then Elijah raised his voice for everyone to hear. "Tropical storm soon come. We mus' mek every t'ing safe. Help put ganja in Patrick's cottage. We mus' put away t'ings dat de wind carry away!"

Everyone got in motion. We unloaded the ganja, which did not take too much time since each bundle weighed approximately ten pounds and there were sixteen of them. David, Henry, Patrick, Elijah and I took care of it within minutes. Elijah told David and Henry where to take the Donkey and wagon and then continued to instruct everyone in their efforts. Norlina and Edward were busy putting the bar stools and tables into their cottage, along with the consumable items – cases of Red Stripe and rum, food etc. The wind picked up to about twenty miles per hour.

As I was busy assisting Norlina and Edward I saw a Rasta man standing on the road by the entrance gate. At first I didn't recognize him, then it came to me, Conric! Michelin's ex-soldier business partner and quasi-romantic lover, which I surmised was based on convenience and lust rather than loving affection. Conric saw Michelin and Harold inspecting the wind rustling the thatched roof of the oval-shaped bar and restaurant. He called out, "Woman! You must come here!" Every woman within hearing distance of his command stopped what they were doing and looked his way.

Michelin had an incredulous look on her face. She stood looking at him for a moment and then briskly, almost angrily, walked toward him. She stood only inches from his body, slightly bending her neck to look up at his towering frame and asked, "Why are your here?"

"Woman, blood clatt, yah 'ave betrayed I!" Conric's voice was loud and definitely threatening. Harold walked stealthily in their direction like a panther moving towards its prey.

"I am not your woman. It was time for my family to move on."

"I n I business an' bodies are bound toget'er. Yah 'ave betrayed I, woman!"

"I have not betrayed you. It was clear that we had a business arrangement that was satisfactory to the both of us and anything else we shared was simply a matter of friendship. The time had come for me to move on with my family. You have no right to be angry with me."

Conric grabbed her arm and said, "You are my woman! I planted man seed in your body. You are mine!"

"I belong to no one! Let go of me." Michelin vainly struggled to free her arm from Conric's grip. She tried kicking him but he swiftly shifted his body to avoid contact, causing Michelin to lose her balance. Conric's hold on her arm kept her from hitting the ground. For a brief moment she hung in the air like a rag doll before her feet found the ground.

Harold, unnoticed by Conric, stood directly behind him. He said in a calm yet threatening voice, "Let her go, soldier man."

A startled Conric flung around, not letting go of Michelin, again causing her to move like a rag doll. She called him a misogynist pig – I didn't know what that word meant but it couldn't be anything good. Conric stared into Harold's face. "It is you, the English woodcarver. Wat concern is dis of yours?"

"She is my friend and the friend of every person you see about you, and you, sir, are treating her in a most disrespectful manner. I must insist that you release Michelin this very moment."

"Blood clatt, mon! Yah speak like de English Masters!" Conric spit in Harold's face. Without a word and with movement so quick I almost missed what followed. In a highly agile motion, Harold dropped to the ground and leaning on one arm and with the rest of his body horizontal with his feet positioned toward Conric, he swept his legs underneath the feet of Conric. As Conric was falling to the ground in an attempt to keep his balance, he let go of Michelin. Harold moved with cat-like speed underneath Michelin and caught her in his arms. Conric jumped to his feet only to be met by Elijah, who held the blade of a machete at his throat.

"No mon come on I land an' treat I n I people dis way. Dis woman is de madda of my woman. I 'ave de mind ta cut off yah head!"

"Elijah! Do no harm to this man. He is simply angry and confused," pleaded Michelin. Elijah's blood red menacing eyes held Conric motionless – along with the sharp edge of steel against his throat. "Elijah, please, do not hurt him," Michelin pleaded again. This time, Michelin placed her hand on Elijah's arm and softly said, "Elijah, please."

All who were present from our community stood breathless as we observed the scene before us. Michael and Lucinda looked particularly stunned. Jamie and I stood by their side and I gave them a quick overview of the history of Conric and Michelin's relationship. Still, the violence was extremely unsettling to them. A few of us knew that Conric was a trained soldier, and all of us were aware of the pride that Jamaican men have of their manhood. The fact that Conric was creating a disturbance on Elijah's land and was posing a threat to the mother of his pregnant woman was enough reason for Elijah to make good on this threat, and Michelin clearly understood this.

"Iffin I let yah go, yah mus' promise ta never return an' ta wipe dis woman an' dis place fram yah mind ferever! Wat yah 'ave ta say soldier mon?"

"Conric stared into Elijah's eyes with his neck stretched and his head slightly tilted back. A small trickle of blood appeared just below the blade. Other's must have seen it too for there were several highly audible gasps.

"Michelin is mine!"

"An' yer life is mine fer de takin iffin yah nuh tek de offer, stupid soldier mon!"

"I n I will burn dis place ta de ground."

"Dead mon do not'ing!" Elijah seethed through his clenched teeth.

"Please, Conric, do as Elijah says. We can still do business," Michelin's pleading was having no affect. I imagined that if Elijah took Conric's life that she would feel responsible. Harold understood this and said as much, "Elijah, Michelin does not want blood to flow on this land. You have created a very special place. She and Helena would no longer feel comfortable living here if you were to take this man's life. It would be a bad omen for your yet-to-be born child. You must let him go."

Elijah continued to ignore the pleas of his family and friends. "Wat yah say soldier mon? Do yah leave I n I never ta return, or I n I send yah ta hell!" It was a stand off and I feared that Elijah would swiftly end it with one quick swipe of the machete. Then, as if the Gods decided to intervene, a brilliant flash of blinding light accompanied by the loudest sound I have ever heard exploded all around us, causing most of us to fall to the ground. Lightening had struck the restaurant-bar and the thatched roof lit up like a torch. For a brief moment the flash of light blinded me – and everyone else. I closed my eyes and when I opened them I looked toward Elijah and Conric – they stood like statues, un-perturbed by the bolt of lightening. Not even the heavens could persuade Elijah from his intentions. Conric spoke, "Jah 'as spoken wit His lightening bolt an' booming voice. Yeah, mon. Jah cursed dis place an' destroy Babylon wit fire. I 'ave nuh need ta burn it down, Jah is doin' it fer I! I nuh longer 'ave need fer dis woman. She is defiled an' has no place by I n I side. I curse her an' yer Bablyon lan'."

Just as Conric finished speaking his face-saving and quite convincing statement, Charlie, who went unnoticed until now, stood behind Conric and with steel vice-like strength took his wrists and bound them with rope. At that moment Elijah lowered the machete. Charlie muscled Conric to the front gate. Without untying his arms, Charlie kicked him in the back forcing Conric to stumble down the road away from Sunset Village. Charlie was a man in his sixties, which made his strength all the more impressive. I watched Conric catch his balance and walk proudly down the road and out of sight. I let out a sigh of relief, fully aware that our community just escaped witnessing what could have been a murder, putting an end to our somewhat utopian community.

The sky had opened up and the rain came pouring down with such force that it almost hurt as it hit my head. Everyone ran for cover, going to their cottages. Jamie and I peered through the slats of one of our shutters at the smoldering restaurant-bar. It had burned quickly – stonewalls that outlined the structure along with the now rain soaked charred wooden beams strewn upon the ground was all that remained of the once beautiful building.

The wind grew stronger, reaching what I guessed to be seventy miles per hour. I was worried that the creaking zinc roofs on the cottages and stone castle buildings would blow off, but they were holding. I heard what sounded like the crash of trees and hoped they did not hit any of the buildings. Then I thought about Karl. Could he still be out at sea fishing? I scanned my mind to determine if he was present when the Cane Valley boys arrived with Luke and Liam and when the incident with Conric occurred, but I did not see his face. I looked through the slats toward the cove and discovered that he must have returned from fishing because his boat was in the cove moored to the large bamboo raft – bobbing and swaying. Then I thought of the sea cave.

"Jamie, we have to try and get to the sea cave."

"Why?"

"I need to see what the waves are doing. The cave, Karl, what if he is in there?"

"He is probably safe within Michelin's cottage."

"No Jamie. He was not present when everything happened or surely he would have intervened to protect his mother."

"Oh no! We have to do something, Oliver!"

"I know what to do. There is a rope attached to a hook on the back of our building. I can tie it around my waist and attach the other end to the knee-high stonewall that runs along the edge of the cliff and make my way to the cave."

"Oliver, that sounds too dangerous."

"I have to try. He might need help - if he is down there."

"Oliver, he is a very smart boy and would know that the cave would flood when the storm arrived – he would have had plenty of warning."

"Maybe not. I saw him go out in the boat this morning but he must have only checked the traps because his boat is moored to the raft. He might have gone night fishing and only went out briefly to check his traps this morning. Perhaps he went back to sleep. You know Karl – he works hard, loves hard, and sleeps hard."

"Yes, you could be right. What can I do to help?"

"Just stay safe and don't come running out after me. I just need to keep my balance in the wind long enough to tie the rope to the wall. I will be heading into the wind so it won't be easy but I have to try."

I retrieved the rope. As I stood behind the cottage I was sheltered from the full force of the wind. I tied the rope around my waist and quickly discovered that I could not stand in the wind. I had to slither along the ground like a snake. Fortunately all of the area I had to cover was paved with smooth flag stone or concrete. I made slow progress in the force of the gale and the pounding rain. I finally reached the wall that ran along the rim of the U shaped cliff. I attached the rope, looping it through an opening in a concrete cracked crevice. The salt spray was blowing hard causing my eyes to sting. I thought that if this were a hurricane, the water would rise above this more than twenty feet high cliff and flood all of the buildings – maybe it was developing into a hurricane but not yet, or else there was no way I could be in this wind – I would have been blown away like a leaf. Once I was confident that I was securely attached to the wall, I decided to peer over the rim to look at the sea cave entrance. What I saw was astounding! The entrance to the sea cave was completely submerged in water. I quickly scanned the periphery of the cove and when I looked directly below where I was positioned, I saw Karl. He had strapped himself in the King & Queen volcanic-stone throne. His arms were outstretched holding a tight grip on the metal handholds. Swells rose over Karl's body, completely submerging him, and then the water receded, exposing Karl's lean muscular naked body. This was happening over and over again in a violent yet rhythmic motion. He was yelling in Danish the same phrase over and over again, *jeg elsker dig,* something like that. Of course I had no idea what it meant. This is exactly what Patrick had in mind when he designed the King & Queen throne that was chiseled out of the volcanic cliff face and smoothed over with concrete. Karl was an adventurer and he could not resist this opportunity, even though it was highly dangerous. I admired him and wanted to join him. I shouted to Karl but he could not hear me – the wind was coming in my direction so it carried his voice toward me. Then, I noticed that he had an erection – unbelievable – this kid was making love to the sea, perhaps he imagined he was making love to a sea god or goddess. The rising and falling push and pull of the sea must have felt like a giant liquid vagina massaging his penis. I decided I had seen enough, not wanting to witness the grand finale. I repeated the phrase he was yelling, *jeg elsker dig,* in my head as I made my way back to the cottage because I wanted to ask Helena or Michelin what it meant.

Returning to the cottage was less challenging since the rain and wind were not pounding my face, still, I had to slither along the stone patio or the wind would blow me away. When I got inside the cottage Jamie wrapped her arms around me. As she held me I told her what I saw and she busted out laughing, and then she asked, "Do you think he could drown?"

"Well if he does it will be during an orgasmic bliss. I don't think so because the sea is rising and falling. Karl can hold his breath for a long time and he is very strong. Even if he got tired of holding onto the metal handles, he was smart enough to tie himself in, and he could easily untie himself and make it up the stairs to safety. Man, what a character he is, wow, that kid has one hell of a set of balls!"

"Making love to the sea, gee, Oliver, that sounds amazing. But I know what is even more amazing."

"What's that?"

She answered with a smile as she pulled her dress over her head and positioned a breast to my mouth. I suckled as I unzipped my cut off jeans – it was all I was wearing – she made stormy super passionate love to me. She whispered in my ear, "You are so brave, and you care so much about people, I love you so, so much, my sweet Oliver."

"Jeg elsker dig!" I shouted as I reached orgasm, feeling silly afterward, particularly when Jamie asked what it meant. For all I knew, I could have cursed at her. She asked me what I had said and I told her it was what Karl was shouting while making love to the sea. She laughed and said it could have been a phrase meant for a male lover.

As swiftly as it came, the storm was over, but it had taken its toll. Jamie and I were the first to venture out of the cottage to assess the damage. We swiftly walked across the stone meditation patio over to the cliff to look for Karl. As we were making our way down the cliff stairs we glanced over at the King & Queen throne – Karl's naked and motionless body was still strapped in the volcanic-stone throne. Fear gripped our hearts as we thought the worst. "What if he's dead? I should have convinced him to get shelter!" I said in a stressful tone. Jamie did not respond to my guilt-laden comment. She was in front of me and reached the throne first.

"Karl, Karl, are you okay?" she said as she shook his body. To our relief he groaned and turned his head to one side, his eyes still closed. His long dreadlock hair, eyebrows and lips were encrusted with sea salt. "Karl, Karl, wake up! Oliver, he needs water."

"He looks water logged to me!" I chuckled. I did find it amusing now that I knew he was alive and most likely just exhausted from getting laid by Mother Nature.

"It's not funny, Oliver, he could be in a coma."

"Nah, he's just worn out." I gave him a moderate smack on the cheek. He moaned. I smacked him again. He opened one very blood-shot eye, and mumbled, "Jeg elsker dig."

"Wake up dude! King Karl, the orgasmic ride is over. We need to get you off your throne." This time Jamie let out a chuckle.

"Ah, so you do see the humor."

"I can't wait to tell Michelin and Helena about this, Oliver. What a story."

"I can't wait to hear Karl tell us about his orgasm." We laughed.

"He's too shy to talk about such things," added Jamie.

"Well, he can deny it all he wants but I saw him with his hard big bamboo thrusting into the sea goddess, and you, my sweet Jamie, see him strapped in his throne naked as a new born baby!"

"Jer elsker dig," Karl moaned again.

"I can't wait to learn what that means. Yo, Karl, what the hell are you saying?" I gave him another firm love-tap on his hairy cheek.

"I love you," he said to me.

"Yeah, we love you too. We are happy to see that you fucked Mother Nature and are alive to tell the tale. So, what does jer elsker dig mean?"

"I love you."

"Yes, we love you too. What do those words mean?"

"Oliver, he is telling you that they mean I love you!"

"OH, wow, that is so freaking far out! You were telling Mother Nature that you love her! Far the fuck out! Man, that is so cosmic."

Jamie left to get water while I untied Karl and sat beside him. He was too exhausted to move and he was definitely dehydrated.

"So, Karl, what was it like making love to the sea?"

"Freya! She is the most beautiful of all goddesses!" he replied.

"Freya? Who is she?"

"Norse goddess of sex and the sea!"

"Wow, like Aphrodite. You really had the divine big bang of your life, Danish boy-king!"

"She is the greatest lover in all the universe!"

"Yes, and I wager that you think you are the greatest mortal lover on earth."

"Ja! I am an elsker!"

"Say what? Ja, elsker? What do these words mean?"

"Ja is Danish for yes and elsker means lover."

"You are so funny. Karl the Danish mortal lover of the Gods! I think you just earned a new title."

Karl laughed so hard he began coughing uncontrollably, followed by puking up what looked and smelled like salt water. "Oops, there goes Freya's cum juices!" Karl laughed again and puked some more.

Jamie arrived just in time with water and some fruit. Helena and Michelin were with her. The two of them immediately took over administering to Karl. Jamie asked if there was anything we could do and they simply said no, and thanked us as they proceeded to speak to Karl in Danish. We decided to leave them alone and continue our survey of the storm's damage.

The restaurant-bar was destroyed and the burned wood continued to smolder, filling the air with a wet burnt smell. The flowers as well as our vegetable garden were decimated, and the ground was covered with leaves and fruit that were blown off the trees. Several of the trees had fallen, and one had demolished two of our outhouses – Harold's fine woodcarving gone to shit. The community worked hard cleaning up the grounds for the remainder of the day. The restaurant-bar would take a lot of time, energy and materials to rebuild.

During the clean up work Jamie and I worked along side her parents and Michelin and Harold. The Starrs were disconcerted over the Conric incident and we assured them that such violence is extremely uncommon and that in fact, that was the first occurrence I had witnessed since arriving on the island. The Starrs had one hell of an orientation to paradise! It was not a big surprise that Michelin and Harold had a lot in common with Lucinda and Michael. The four of them were highly academic with anthropology and religion being areas of mutual interest, and even though Michelin and Harold were younger than the Starrs, they were the oldest members of the Sunset Village community. They launched into fascinating conversations on anthropological studies of indigenous cultures, theories, and in-the-field ground-breaking studies that have been conducted, particularly the work of Margaret Mead in the South Pacific islands. They spoke of Jamaican culture, discussing a brief overview of Jamaican history: most notably the original Arawak Indian inhabitants and their demise, the Spanish, the English, slavery, Jamaican independence, and to my delight, Rastafarianism and reggae music.

I told them of our experiences in the sea cave with Lord Joseph and the Rastafarians, the rituals performed, our interpretations and how they personally affected us. I was intrigued by Lucinda and Michael's fascination with our experience of Jamaican culture and how we had looked at it through our own unique anthropological perspective. They were particularly impressed by both my theoretical knowledge and experience, and more importantly by my interpretations. Lucinda remarked that the manner in which I expressed my experiences suggested that I was attempting to avoid being ethno-centric. Michael commented that we had learned to live a so-called native life-style, although it was not truly native since we were bringing to the experience our own cultural constructs, whatever that meant, to the new world we had created. It turned out that the Starr couple perceived the life that Patrick and I had created with their daughters and our Jamaican friends as an anthropological wonder, and one worth an empirical study and the writing of an academic paper. When they talked of academic studies and publishing papers on our island adventures, it was time for me to leave the conversation, as I was not interested in having my life viewed under a microscope and dissected like a lab rat. I simply wanted to enjoy my life. Jamie felt the same way, and she was far less interested in the academic discussion, since she was raised in a high-powered academic family and community, and had avoided attending college.

After a very long day of hard work, everyone departed to their living accommodations to rest and freshen up. Jamie and I retreated to our cottage sanctuary. "Jamie, when are you going to tell your parents?" I said in a very soft and caring tone, which clearly communicated what I was referring to.

"I am not going to tell them. I had already told Patrick, Julie, and the rest of the community to not tell them."

"Are you sure about this?"

"Yes."

"But why?"

"I love them too much to have them worry. They will learn soon enough when the time comes."

"And you think it will hurt them any less knowing later when it is too late?"

"Too late for what, to endure more months of suffering? They deserve better than that."

"They deserve better? What about what you deserve? Your parents love you and you could use their support."

"Their support would amount to pressuring me to return to Bloomington and doctors, hospitals, radiation treatment, chemotherapy, and possibly putting Julie through another bone marrow transplant. I have been through that hell and I know my disease well, and there is no chance of a cure. I refuse to go through that again, to put my parents through that again. No, this time nature will run its course and I will accept the inevitability of what is to come."

"They have a right to know!" I said emphatically.

"They have a right to see their daughter happy and living an amazing life with the man I love. That is the parting gift I will give to them, not a frail sick body that they will watch disintegrate before their eyes. No, they deserve better than that and so do you."

"We can go back to Bloomington and fight this together as husband and wife with the emotional support of your family and the best medicine available." I was getting very emotional and my voice sounded desperate. Jamie took me by the hand and sat me down beside her on the bed.

"Oliver, my dearest love, I understand how you feel. I appreciate you wanting the best for me. Living out the remaining days of my life, one precious moment after another with you and my sister and Patrick, that is what is best for me. You need to accept what I know. That there is no cure for death, no matter what form it comes in, and what time it arrives. At least I know that it is coming for me soon, and I can live the remaining days of my life as I choose, and I choose to live them with you. If you will have me."

"Have you? I am you! There is no you and I, there is only us – I n I! If I could take this horrible disease from you and dissolve it into my body, then I would." My eyes were tearing.

"And you would be saying to me what I am saying to you. Let's suppose you knew when you were going to die …"

"I am going to die, someday," I interrupted.

"Exactly. But suppose you know the timeframe more specifically, as I do. How would you choose to live your life?"

"I would live it here with you. I would revel in every moment, and live each one as if it were my last, to the fullest."

"I would expect no less from you." Jamie interjected.

"And I would go on as though nothing was wrong. I would live each day as if I would live forever, but with the heightened awareness that each moment could be my last."

"Yes, yes, my sweet love, you do understand."

"Yes, Jamie I do. It is just hard to accept."

"I know. It has taken me almost a decade, most of my childhood, and all of my teenage years to come to this understanding, this acceptance of the inevitable, and now I see it not as a curse, but as a gift."

"You are the most amazing person on earth and in heaven."

"Oh, I bet you say that about all the women you have loved."

"This is now and now is all there is, and right now you are all there is."

"Ah, yes, there were other *now's* in your life. I need not mention her name. A person as wonderful as you had to have had other loving people in your life, otherwise you would not be the person that you are and I would not reap the harvest of the seeds that all those women have sown."

She laughed and pushed me on to my back, stripped off her dress and straddled her knees across me. She unzipped my jean shorts and pulled them down my legs. She eased her sweet soothing warmness on to my body, squeezing me as she slowly gyrated. I reached upward and cusped her breasts, occasionally pinching her hard pink-red nipples. She moaned over and over, and when the pleasure completely consumed her, she lost control and cried out, "I love you Oliver!" She squeezed with all her strength and then gushed forth her warm love juices, pouring over me, across my pelvis and down my thighs. Her back was arched and her ravished eyes looked deep into my own. She reached down and pinched my nipples harder and harder until they almost bled, and then my mind filled with light as I exploded, coating her insides with the cream of my seeds.

"Come with me Oliver – oh we just did – uh, I mean let's join my parents for their first sunset swim in the cove-pool and Oliver, keep your shorts on!"

"And what are you wearing?"

"My birthday suit, of course."

"Then, why can't I?"

"I don't want my mother knowing what you look like."

"Why? You said your parents are nudist."

"They never saw you, and they never will. Some things are meant to be kept private, and your privates are mine and only mine!" She placed her hand over me and gently rubbed. I started growing hard again. We laughed, dressed, and headed for the cove-pool.

The swim was wonderful. Lucinda was an excellent diver and Michael was afraid of heights. We gave them a tour of the sea cave, lighting the torches Karl had set up. We sat in there for a while chatting, describing the land we were going to purchase in Little Bay.

"Let us help you to finalize the deal tomorrow," suggested Michael.

"We need to get to the bank and then over to Little Bay. It will take some time."

"How much time could that be? Where is the nearest bank?" Michael asked.

"Sav-La-Mar. It is about twenty miles away. Little Bay is between Negril and Sav-La-Mar," I responded.

"Well, that shouldn't take long at all," said Michael.

"I suppose we could rent a taxi for the day," I suggested, "that's what Patrick and I were planning the day after our wedding."

"Taxi? We rented a Land Rover," said Michael, "we can take care of this business rather quickly if your Jamaican real estate man is available."

"Wow! Let's do it!" Jamie exclaimed.

The next morning we met at the road on the edge of the property where the Land Rover was parked. We drove to Savannah La-Mar. Patrick had a little hassle convincing the bank manager to give him such a large sum in cash, but with Michael's intervention he was successful. Patrick withdrew $7,000 in all, telling me he wanted money to get the water line put in, possibly the electricity, and to order building supplies. I asked Patrick how he had amassed so much money and he told me that the ganja business he had set up in the U.S. was doing very well. It was then that I learned that Randy and Patrick's sister were now a couple living together in Philadelphia and that they were the distributers of the ganja he and Elijah were mailing to the U.S. I also learned that he worked out a deal with Elijah, David, and Henry to expand their business operation. The Cane Valley boys would provide all of the ganja as well as assist in traveling around the island to different post offices to mail the discreet quarter pound packages. I was amazed that all of this was taking place and that Patrick knew that it was not necessary to involve me in any of it, knowing full well that ganja dealing would not be my forte. I was, however, astonished at the amount of cash Patrick had accumulated in a relatively short period of time, and all without my knowledge. I was a little disturbed by this fact since Patrick and I were consistently communicating our survival strategies. We certainly have come a long way from learning how to meet our basic survival needs in paradise.

Next, we headed for Little Bay. Andy was in his garden when we arrived, and was very surprised and happy to see us so soon. Patrick showed him the money. Andy's eyes popped out of his head as he leaned against a tree to steady his body. "Dat is de mos' money I 'ave ever seen, mon. Dis is Irie!" We went to the post office and took care of all the legal documents. The land was ours!

We gave the Starrs a tour of the property and talked of our plans. Michael and Lucinda were pleased with the land and our plans. Unfortunately, there was no way to take them down to the sandy beach from the land, which was the most amazing and unique part of the property.

"Yah can tek dem in de canoes ta de land, mon," suggested Andy. The parents declined saying they would prefer having snorkeling equipment with them and that they would like to have an entire day, and preferably longer. We asked Andy if he would be willing to supervise the building of our stone castle and if he knew people to hire to do the labor.

"Yes, mon. I am de bes' stonemason in aw Westmorland Parish, mon. I knoh many Jamaicans who be glad ta 'ave work. Yah mus' gi me de plans ta start de work, mon." I told him we would have the plans in the next several days. Jamie, always having her sketchpad with her, took it out and asked Patrick and me to describe what we wanted to build. For two hours, all of us discussed the stone castle and what it should look like in fine detail. Jamie's amazing artistic talent produced superb detail drawings from every perspective, including each room, the verandas, the tower top, and the staircase that started at the top of the tower and wound all the way around the castle to its base, connecting with the carved cliff staircase that descended to the sand beach cove.

Andy was amazed! "I 'ave never seen anyone draw like dat! Irie! Lovely, mon. It be de best building ever made by dese 'ands! Next we mek a list of materials needed an' order dem right away. I will 'ire de young men an' we start as soon as de materials arrive. Yah be very pleased, mon! I will 'ave de government run de water pipes, an' I find out 'bout de electricity, an' file de proper papers, mon. No problem, mon. I tek care of everyt'ing!"

Andy insisted that we smoke ganja with him in celebration of our purchase. He used his hand carved bong instead of rolling spliffs. Again, I was surprised that Jamie smoked ganja, and I noticed her mother looking at her with a curious eye. She must have known that Jamie had kept her body pure and had to be wondering why she was no longer cautious. This was the second time in two days that I saw her smoke ganja, and I suspected she was smoking when I wasn't around. I made a mental note to ask her about it when her parents were not present.

"Oh, we never told you, Andy, the four of us are getting married tomorrow!" I announced.

"Yah be jokin' wit me now!"

"No joke, Mr. Andy. That's why my parents are here. You must come to the wedding," said Jamie.

"I'd be 'appy to atten', mon. Congratulations! It is an 'onor ta sell yah de land fer yah new 'ome. An' I be buildin' yah dream castle! Dis is a wonderful t'ing, yes a wonderful t'ing. You mek an ole mon very happy."

"You can come with us now, if you can. We have room in the Land Rover," offered Michael.

"I will do dat, mon. I gatter me t'ings an' be wit yah shortly.

It was sunset time when we arrived back at Sunset Village and the community was not on the cliff meditating, they were mingling around the campfire circle chatting and preparing food. I asked Harold why they were not meditating and he said to go look at the cliff. I did. There was a huge painting of a lotus flower on the concrete pad.

"It is beautiful, is it not?" said Harold.

"Yes. Michelin painted it, right?" I responded.

"She sketched it out and several people assisted her in the painting. We finished painting just before you arrived. It is for the wedding ceremony." Harold beamed.

"It is quite beautiful," I said. The Starr family and Patrick came over to have a look. They were impressed.

"Michelin is a talented artist," said Lucinda, "and based on our conversations, she is quite a scholar as well."

"She is that and much more, Ms. Lucinda. I am a very fortunate man to have her as my friend. However, she is a hard-headed woman and does not believe in marriage in any form, otherwise the marriage ceremony would be a greater communal event."

"You asked her to marry you?" I asked.

"Yes. And she refused, giving me a very long scholarly anthropological and feminist oratory on justifications for her disrepute of the institution of marriage. It is quite interesting to me that I would come to love a very beautiful and intelligent woman who challenges the very core values of my belief system and worldview. Ah, the price we must pay for companions of the heart!" Harold lamented.

"Harold, you have met your match," said Michael.

"Match indeed! She is more akin to a torch, I do say!"

We laughed as we walked together back to the campfire ring. Karl, Luke and Liam had returned from a very successful fishing trip. They had come upon a school of tuna and were able to bring in several large fish. We ate our full of tuna steaks. We learned that the community was quite busy all day preparing for the wedding, and the painting of the cliff was only one part. Flower decorations and food preparations were attended to as well. Most of the burnt wood from the destruction of the restaurant-bar was gone, only the blackened stonewalls remained and most of the stones were scrubbed clean. Everyone was tired and there was little energy for playing music and staying up late. The trip we had taken that day to purchase our land had zapped our energy so we retired early as well. We set Andy up in one of the spare tents we had available for guests and as potential tourist rentals. Shannon had suggested that Julie, Patrick, Jamie and I move into the stone cliff tower since we were to be married. We eagerly accepted her offer. Shannon also invited Jonathan to move into her concrete cottage, saying it would be more comfortable than his tent. He thanked her and politely refused.

The stone tower had two floors. The only access to the tower top was from the second floor bedroom. We flipped a coin and Jamie and I won the toss, choosing the top floor, of course. Jamie and I went to the tower to look at the night sky and the sea. There was a light breeze blowing, chasing away the muggy feeling that came with the humid air.

"Jamie, I noticed that you have been smoking ganja lately," I said.

"Yes, I wanted to speak to you about that but it slipped my mind. I decided a few days ago to try it to see if it would increase my appetite."

"Has it helped?" I asked.

"Yes! It not only gives me the munchies, it helps with the, with the, well you know, the pain I sometimes feel." A chill ran down my spine. The mention of pain hit me with a hard dose of reality.

"How much pain are you in?" I asked, in a slightly shaky voice.

"Not bad. Not bad at all. It comes and goes and it isn't excruciating or anywhere near it. The ganja does help minimize it. You know, I wonder why the medical benefits of marijuana are not utilized and researched by the pharmaceutical industry?"

"I wish I could feel your pain for you," I said.

"I know, love, and if you could, you would take the disease as well. I would do the same for you. But things are what they are, and I would never give this disease to you."

"I have been hoping for a miracle."

"Thank you. I do not believe in petitioning a higher intelligent being for favors. If that were possible, I expect people would be healed of illnesses all the time and there would be no wars or disease of any kind. I do not subscribe to such fantasies."

"I know how you feel about the concept of God. I, too, would not have faith in supernal intelligence and eternal life had I not experienced psychological healing from those very entities."

"Your epiphany is a beautiful story, Oliver, and I do not dispute the reality of it. I only know what I know based upon my own experiences. I accept the possibility that there may be a personality being that some call God, Christ, Buddha or whatever, but it has not been my experience. What I have experienced is a Universal Love, the oneness of all things. This One Love is what I think is the only experiential reality that can unite all of humanity. I find religious doctrine and creed too laden with cultural bias and therefore prone to conflict, resulting in division that results in violence. No, I choose to wear no cultural garments of religious dogma."

"What about spiritual healing?" I asked.

"You told me you have experienced such healing, so yes, I do believe the super-conscious part of our mind is capable of healing our emotional distresses through meditation and positive thinking. I am not convinced that it can heal the body, or that it has to do with intelligent spiritual entities intervening in natural processes."

"What about life after death?" I asked.

"Well, we'll know when the time comes, won't we," she replied matter-of-factly.

"Jamie, my sweet, sweet Jamie. I want to spend eternity with you. I know that we live on forever and I wish I could impart that knowledge to you."

"Oliver, I honestly hope you are right. I cannot dispute your claim, no more than you can substantiate such beliefs with anything other than your professed experiences. You are my soul mate, and I do sense, experience, that I have a soul, an entity that lives on after this body changes back to inanimate matter, but I do not know if my personality – my identity known as Jamie, will live on."

"Then, I am asking you to trust me. There is life after this world and you and I will know each other throughout all of eternity. This is a much better thought system than the one you currently hold. What you believe is just that, a belief, and so why not choose one that is more uplifting?"

"Because I do not believe in fairies, or Santa Claus, or the Easter Bunny. I cannot believe in things that are outside my realm of direct experience, no matter how pleasant a fantasy may be, it is still a fantasy."

"The power of positive thinking is something you have experienced as producing results, is that correct?"

"Yes."

"All I am saying to you is that we can know of things that exist beyond the realm of our senses through the most powerful form of positive thinking there is, and that is faith. We experience the Divine when we believe in the Divine. Faith, my love, is the key. Without faith, we cannot see clearly into the spiritual dimension of life, the super real."

"That is a very valid point, Oliver. I do not know how to have faith. I wonder if faith is no more than the human mind's tendency for delusional thinking, and I refuse to delude myself. Resisting reality only enhances emotional pain. I choose to accept what *is,* and to live each moment to its fullest, you know this about me, we have talked about this many times."

"Oh, Jamie, my love. I truly wish I could place inside your heart the faith that fills my heart and opens my mind. This challenge we face together would be less, less, hurtful."

"Oh, my dear Oliver, I do have faith. I have faith in you. I have faith in universal love as the substance of all that is. If eternal life is real, and if I am to live on forever in the form of an infinite self that is distinctly some essence of Jamie, then that is what will be with or without your petitions – or my belief."

"Maybe it will happen only if you ask for it."

"Oh boy, now you are sounding sanctimonious. Let's not go there, my love."

"You're right. I am sorry."

"Oliver, I know you want what is best for me, and you already are doing that by sharing your love with me. If there is eternal life, than we will share our love in eternity. What difference does it make whether I believe in eternal life or not? The only thing that truly matters is what we share here and now, and that, for me, is what eternity is, the here and now!"

"You are so wise."

"You are sexy!"

"You are horny."

"For you, always."

"Jer elsker dig, sweet Jamie."

"Jer elsker dig, handsome Oliver."

We made love on the tower beneath the firmament of heaven and earth, and the entire universe witnessed the beauty, goodness, and truth of our love for one another, our eternal universe of love.

I n I, ONE LOVE, ONE HEART

We slept a little later than usual. On our way down the stone cottage stairs, we woke up Patrick and Julie. Most of the community was already meditating. The lotus flower painting had dried. I saw Andy walking towards us. I invited him to sit beside me. He looked puzzled, obviously having no idea what everyone was doing. I whispered in his ear that people were quieting their minds to rid their thoughts of Babylon. He smiled and nodded indicating that he understood.

Lucinda stood up and spoke, "Today my daughters are going to be married. I am overwhelmed with joy. It is quite significant that this community chose to paint the lotus flower upon this site. It is one of the most ancient and deepest symbols of our planet. The lotus flower grows in muddy water and rises above the surface to bloom with remarkable beauty. At night, the flower closes and sinks underwater, at dawn it rises and opens again. Untouched by the impurity, the lotus blossom symbolizes the purity of heart and mind. The roots of a lotus are in the mud, the stem grows up through the water, and the heavily scented flower lies pristinely above the water, basking in the light. This pattern of growth signifies the progress of the soul from the primeval mud of existence, through the waters of experience, and into the bright sunshine of enlightenment."

"Hey, man, that is exactly what it means to be a Ghetto Flower! We came up from the mud of the city streets and through special experiences that shined light on our minds, we have grown into flowers in paradise," said Luke. I was amazed by what he said and felt very proud. The Ghetto Flowers looked around at each other and smiled with looks of acknowledgement and appreciation.

I was feeling both excited and nervous. And, as was my usual state of mind at the beginning of meditation, my thoughts were zooming through my head. The most prominent thought-feeling I had concerned Jamie's illness and her decision to not tell her parents. I was worried that her parents would overhear a conversation between other community members discussing Jamie's illness. I would prefer they learn of the return of her cancer directly from Jamie. However, I understood Jamie's position and respected her decision. Then, grief overtook me as my thoughts of Jamie's illness and inevitable death sunk my emotions into the depths of sorrow. I cried silently but apparently many noticed as I saw several people looking at me with expressions of concern. Jamie began weeping too, and then, to my surprise, so were many others. I sensed that the community was bearing the weight of the grief that we were experiencing. It occurred to me that when people join together in ritual, that there is an energy phenomenon that takes place that is indeed communal in nature. To me, this was proof positive of the existence of higher planes of consciousness that is possible to obtain as a community, regardless of the varying belief systems of each member. It is the collective consciousness based in the reality of love that makes such an experience possible. The communal sharing of tears lifted the heavy burden from my heart, and it had worked for Jamie as well. She took my hand and looked me in the eye and whispered, "Perhaps there is a spiritual world, my love." Joy filled my heart at the sound of these words. The truth is, what Jamie had said to me the night before was comforting. She believed in the eternal now, and by sharing love we are fully present in the moment. This was, according to my thinking, the goal and purpose of our meditations. It is to become one in the presence of love, and that is exactly what had just happened.

Michael stood up and spoke. "I do not know the meaning behind this communal expression of tears. I do understand that for a common experience of such magnitude to occur, there must be strong communal love present. My wife and I have been meditating for years, and we have instructed our daughters throughout their childhood to share in this practice. I am delighted, and amazed, that such a practice exists here among you."

Julie stood up and spoke, "Father and mother, you have taught Jamie and me to still our minds so that they may be all the more receptive to the higher nature of our being, which we have learned is love. For this we are grateful. Your daughter, Jamie, is to be thanked for being the impetus for developing our practice of communal meditation. Thank you, sister, for being my dearest friend." I was moved by Julie's words. She spoke the truth. There is a quality to Jamie's character that inspires all of us to engage in the practice of meditation, and from that inspiration we have grown into a strong community. I knew that every member of our community was aware of Jamie's exceptional personality quality, the spiritual drawing power that she possessed, and she would be the first to deny the possession of such a gift.

Jamie stood up, leaned over and took both my hands, gently guiding me to stand with her. She walked me to the front of the arc formed by the group facing the sea. I was calm although puzzled by what she was doing. She turned and faced me, took both my hands into hers and looked at me with those incredibly beautiful rich chocolate illuminated eyes and said:

"Today is the day that I publicly profess my eternal love to you, Oliver. I give all that I am to you. My soul embraces your soul. I am you, and you are I."

She continued to gaze into my eyes. Within my mind, I called upon my heart to speak in poetic verse:

"Jamie, my earth angel, the lovely infinite vastness of the birth of our universe spreads out before us. It is our playground for sharing the gift of Love - expressions of truth, beauty, and goodness"

Jamie responded, *"I embrace you, hold you, comfort you, and strengthen you. I energize you with all you need to navigate through life's temporal challenges."*

I looked deeper into Jamie's eyes and said, "*Together, we shall unfold into the holiness of our love relationship. Know that I am with you all the time. We are soul embracers. Neither time, nor distance, nor circumstance, can separate us, for we travel side by side on a pathway throughout eternity.*

Jamie leaned forward and lightly kissed me, then, stepping back she said, *"Take my soul into your soul, embrace me as I embrace you, and together we shall live in the mind of, the heart of, the spirit of, Our Universe of Love."*

I repeated the last words, *"I take you into my soul and embrace you as you embrace me, and together we shall live in the mind of, the heart of, the spirit of, Our Universe of Love."*

We kissed, and hugged, and everyone clapped and cheered. Lucinda and Michael stood up and embraced us. Then, Julie stood up and said:

"It is an honor for me to witness the marriage of a sister who is also my best female friend. This is indeed, the happiest day of my life. Sister and brother Oliver, I bless your marriage. Mother and Father, I now present to you my beloved and we too shall receive your blessings and those of our community of friends."

Julie invited Patrick with a gesture of her hands to stand up and take his place in front of her. She spoke these words to him:

"Patrick. There has never been a man in all my life that understands me better than you. I feel deeply respected, appreciated, and loved by you. When I first met you, I knew that we would become, well, at the very least, playmates. I never imagined in my wildest dreams that you would turn out to be the man I never knew I was looking for. You have captured my soul with your

kindness and intelligence ... and very good looks! I give my life to you, and together we have created new life, something I never thought I would do until I met you. I am proud to be your life partner and the mother of your child."

Julie closed her eyes as tears rolled down her cheeks. Patrick kissed her tears and placed his hands upon her swollen womb, then spoke these words:

"Julie, my dearest, dearest love. Your courage, strength and matchless beauty have accomplished what no other woman on this earth could possibly obtain. You have so completely embraced my heart and it has become one with yours. I, too, originally thought of you as a potential friend. In my wildest dreams I never imagined that not only would you become my best friend but also the greatest love of my life. Together, we have performed the most revered human act, the creation of life. I stand before the mother of my child and the woman that I trust with all my mind, heart, and soul. To you and to our unborn child, I give my life forevermore. I n I."

Julie spoke the final words of joining two into one, *"I n I, my dearest lover, I n I One Love, One Heart."*

Julie and Patrick embraced and kissed a long passionate kiss. Once again, everyone clapped and cheered. The parents embraced the couple and then Jamie and I joined them and we had a family hug. Then, the entire community stood up and closed in around all of us, becoming one large mass of bodies, creating a community hug in the center of the lotus blossom. Jonathan broke out in song, singing: *Dear friends, dear friends, let me tell you how I feel, you have given me such treasures. I love you so!* He repeated these words and on the third chant everyone joined in. It was beautiful beyond belief!

Elijah immediately took off to get Millie and Charley, who were not present because no one knew that the marriage would be taking place that morning, including the brides and grooms. It was an act of pure spontaneity. It was decided that the entire day would be spent in celebration, keeping in sync with the tone set by Jamie's spur-of-the-moment initiation of wedding vows. Elkannah and his family were invited, and to our pleasant surprise, Lord Joseph and his nephew, Levi, came as well.

No one had their morning coffee, so breakfast was the first thing we all did, while smoking copious amounts of ganja, followed by a community swim in the cove-pool. Millie had prepared banana bread laced with ganja the day before, and, to the delight of many, she also made a very large vat of extremely potent mushroom tea. It had become a hallucinogenic tainted celebration that lasted into the wee hours of the following morning. Music, dance, poetry, storytelling, sailboat rides, swimming, abundant food, and lovemaking were all part of this festive day.

Michael and Lucinda Starr remained at Sunset Village up to the day before they were to resume their teaching duties at Indiana University in early September. During their stay, they did all they could to assist their daughters and son-in-laws in the creation of the Sand Cove Castle in Little Bay, traveling frequently in the Land Rover between Sunset Village and Little Bay. Before they left, they gave the four of us a single wedding present - a medium sized catamaran sailboat with a small motor that they had bought in Montego Bay and had delivered to Little Bay. This boat made travel on the sea between Sunset Village and Sand Cove Castle comparably swift, especially when the wind was in our favor. Still, Patrick and I were partial to our handmade sailing and fishing craft, and used it whenever we had the opportunity. The catamaran was used occasionally for fishing, when Patrick wanted to speedily get out to deeper water to spear bigger game, which required someone to accompany him.

Additionally, as I later learned, the parents opened bank accounts for their daughters and deposited a considerable amount of money, adding to the inheritance they had received from their grandparents. Jamie and Julie's basic financial needs were secure, a phenomenon that Patrick and I naively had no idea was even possible, coming from families that had known mostly poverty, and we were continually finding ways to meet our needs that best suited our lifestyle throughout our lives, which was true in Philly, Wildwood, and Jamaica. Michael and Lucinda Starr returned to Indiana, never learning that Jamie's cancer had returned. They planned on coming back to Jamaica to be present for the birth of Julie's child, which was expected in late December or early January, when the University would be on break. They had come to Jamaica and witnessed the marriage of their children and would soon return to participate in the birth of their grandchild. As they were leaving, the thought came to me that it is parents and grandparents who truly understand the meaning of the concept of One Love and One Heart.

POSITIVE VIBRATIONS ON THE WINDS OF CHANGE

Patrick continued his smuggling operation, enlisting the assistance of Andy for delivering the small envelopes to post offices. Since he was a well known and respected elderly man, no one suspected him of illegal activity. Patrick was amassing considerable wealth, which he continued to assert was mine as well, and much of it he was pouring into the castle and the development of the land to enhance its modest agricultural production. Michael and Lucinda Starr never asked about our source of money and we never gave them details of our economic background or financial dealings.

Initially, Jamie and Julie spent little time at the new land, preferring the tranquility and camaraderie of the Sunset Village community to the noisy bustle of castle construction, which, in the early stages, was filled with the sound of jackhammers carving our collective dreams out of the jagged cliff. Patrick and I, and when necessary the gifted architect-engineer Karl, traveled to Little Bay frequently, overseeing as much of the construction as was necessary. We would often stay on the property for many days at a time, adding our skill, labor, and most importantly, vision to the reshaping of the land. Andy proved to be an exceptionally gifted stonemason, and his eager young Jamaican employees were competent workers. Much to the delight of everyone, Andy discovered a cavern several feet below the cliff top surface that made it possible to jackhammer an opening that led directly to the sandy beach cliff overhang. He said he could construct a set of steps that led from the center of the castle directly to the white sandy beach. This discovery altered the original design of the castle to include a spiral staircase that descended from the very top of the castle through its center leading directly to the sea – an amazing architectural wonder that required the intelligence and talent of Karl to design and the skilled guidance of Andy to build.

During the time period of the construction of the castle, we witnessed a dramatic influx of hippie tourists into the pristine unsuspecting, Negril Village. They came from the United States, Canada, and countries throughout Europe. This little fishing village was experiencing an alien invasion of young idealistic paradise seekers that found rustic accommodations on the pristine seven-mile beach and in the gardens and homes of Jamaicans all along the West

End cliffs and Red Ground areas. This wonder seeking generation with their minds and hearts full of ideals for the creation of a new world, in search of the Garden of Eden, along with their penchant for pleasure seeking and mind exploration through the use of ganja and hallucinogenic substances, had infused this once quiet fishing village with their values and varied cultural influences. Unbeknownst to these young counter-culture hippies, the most powerful influence was their money, and they had lots of it. Even though this adventure seeking generation, for the most part, wanted to live a simple and inexpensive life, which was quite possible in Negril, their money was the precious commodity that would be the driving force that would change Negril forever.

Sunset Village was prepared to receive these young and multi-talented paradise seekers. It was what Patrick and I, along with the vision and entrepreneurial ambition of Elijah, had foreseen and much of what we did at Sunset Village was in preparation for this occurrence. The cottages and tents became filled with new guests and, at first, they were easily assimilated into our community, and their idealistic energy added much to our village. The community was strong and resilient and we were adequately prepared for the initial wave of these newcomers. Indeed, Sunset Village was designed for this purpose. Yet, it would inevitably bring change to the intimacy that the original creators of this village had cherished. New personalities meant changing interpersonal relationship dynamics, some welcomed and some not. Gradually, there developed a transitional element to the community. Some of the new people stayed for short periods, bringing their hopes, dreams, pleasure seeking hedonism, talents, and money, and then they would simply vanish as if riding in on the force of one wind and in an instant, were gone on another.

And, there was the fact that the four newly weds were making a new home in Little Bay, and it was just a matter of time before we would sail away on the winds of change. Everyone knew this and even assisted us in the process. Jamie continuously reminded the community that change is constant, and that the love we create is eternal. For all of us, Jamie was the embodiment of this indelible fact of life, and in a sense, because of the process she was going through with her body, she had become a powerful teacher prompting us to learn the all important lesson of the conscious acceptance of the reality of the inevitabilities of life, which is the unceasing process of change. Jamie's personal assertion, adaptation, and maybe even contribution to Buddhist teachings was the concept of the eternalness of love and that each one of us is a love creator to this eternal supreme reality. It was a wonderful teaching that provided a way for all of us to feel that how we live our lives really does matter, that our loving one another is how we contribute to the continuation of life everlasting. I continued to share with her the concept that we experience eternal life as succinct personality entities as well as making contributions to the supreme eternal reality of the oneness of love, although she remained reluctant to accept the idea of personality survival.

Luke, Liam, Roseann, and Donna were the first to bring tourists to the community. For a spell, the four of them were living in Lord Joseph's cave where they met a young Rastafarian musician from Kingston who brought with him three young tourists who were from Germany. His name was Tafari Jacobson, and he was a tall, handsome twenty-two year old exceptionally talented musician. He was from the Kingston neighborhood of Trenchtown, the birthplace of Reggae music. Tafari was strongly influenced by the music of Bob Marley and the Wailers, and he brought with him the powerful positive vibrations of their music – the message of One Love and One Heart. Tafari represented to the Sunset Village community the cultural embodiment of what was becoming Jamaica's greatest artistic contribution to the world. His singing and guitar playing talents were equally matched with a charismatic personality. Everyone took an instant liking to him as he spread the message of reggae music and Rastafarianism to the Sunset Village community – positive vibrations, indeed!

The Ghetto Flower foursome came strolling into Sunset Village with Tafari and the three German travelers, introducing them to our community during a sunset meditation session. Tafari, after sitting with us for half an hour stood up, and without introduction began strumming his guitar and sang a rendition of a song he said he had heard Bob Marley playing during a jam session with a gathering of Rastafarians in Kingston. I later learned that the song had not yet been recorded. Tafari called the song, *One Love, One Heart,* and he sang it like an angel.

"Greetings, I n I. Tafari Jacobson is mi name. I n I pleased ta be wit de good people of Sunset Village. Yeahmon, positive vibrations are aw around. Irie! One Heart is beatin' wit de rhythm of de One Love of Jah. Selah!"

His singing and his introduction astounded us. The winds of change just blew into our community a cultural force that was just beginning to break loose upon the world. Our community was full of talented musicians who quickly assimilated Tafari Jacobson into their world. The two people who were most influenced by Tafari were Shannon and Jonathan. Shannon and Tafari developed a romantic relationship, living together in one of the stone cottages, and she embraced much of his cultural and religious practices, although she did not accept all of the Rastafarian creeds. Shannon took readily to the Ital diet and the central message of One Love, which was consistent with her own spiritual experiences and worldview, and they loved singing together. What she did not accept was the teaching that King Haile is a messiah – a divine being from a long succession of prophets including Jesus. Tafari, in essence, was teaching the message of One Love and One Heart, which was well received by our community, especially, as Tafari had originally experienced within the first moments of his arrival, One Love was a reality we were living.

Tafari immediately recognized the talented and spectacular voice of Jonathan. The two of them, along with Shannon, sang together frequently, and Tafari taught Jonathan how to play the guitar, which he picked up quickly, since he has an amazing ear and long nimble fingers. This brought about the much needed healing between Jonathan and Shannon and their lifelong friendship once again had been renewed. To my delight, and to that of everyone who knew of the hurt that existed among our friends, Tafari encouraged Karl to play his congas with them. Karl's drumming provided the driving beat that completed the reggae sound. Playing music was a new way for the three of them to resume their relationship without the complications of sexuality. The four of them played up and down the cliffs and along the beach of Negril, and most often at Sunset Village. Their performances at the village brought lots of tourists to Norlina's newly restored bar and restaurant. Sunset Village had become the main hippie hangout along the West End cliffs. Patrick and I had no time for such creative expressions and hedonistic pleasures as we were fully engaged in the responsibilities of our family and castle building. In large measure, the Sand Cove Cliff Castle was our way of avoiding the commercialization of Negril. We were intent on living the native life, although quite extravagantly – like native kings and queens.

Julie's womb was growing quite large, and Michelin, the grandmother-to-be midwife, was the first to learn that her daughter was carrying twins, an immensely joyful revelation. Jamie and I continued working together to manage her disease. She stopped smoking ganja but continued eating it on a regular basis as it had several medicinal qualities that enhanced her appetite and relieved her occasional bouts with extreme nausea. The somewhat euphoric quality of ganja aided her mood as well. Occasionally, she and I would take hallucinogenic mushrooms, hoping that its medicinal properties for the mind would extend to her immune system and we had reason to believe that it had, for the progression of the leukemia had slowed down almost to the point of remission.

Time passed both slowly and swiftly, as is the nature of island time. December was upon us, and Michelin said that Julie could give birth any day. The castle was almost complete, and Julie hoped that it would be ready for us to move into so she could give birth to the twins in our new home. On December 15th, Lucinda and Michael Starr returned, and they did much to speed up the process of readying the castle. By December 29th, the castle, although not complete, was ready to move into. Many of the original members of Sunset Village had decided to stay at Sand Cove Cliff Castle to await the birth of the twins. The castle was not large enough to accommodate everyone, so tents were brought along. Norlina, Edward, Elijah and Helena (who was close to giving birth), had to keep Sunset Village operating at the height of the tourist season, so they were unable to attend.

Everyone loved the castle! It was an architectural wonder that embodied the dreams and inspirations of many. Julie and Patrick moved into the top floor. Their room had a large arched window facing the sea. Julie had set up her bed facing the arched window and it is there that Julie gave birth to fraternal twins, a boy and girl. Patrick caught each child as they came through the birth canal, with Michelin and Jamie on each side of him for assistance. The children were small, weighing just above four pounds each. Julie and Patrick announced their names: *Jamie and Oliver*. It was a tremendous honor bestowed upon us by our dearest soul friends and family. Michael and Lucinda were very, very happy. The village members stayed on the property for the following week, enjoying the beauty of the castle, the cove, and our varied and abundant fruit tree garden. Jamie radiated with so much happiness that I was convinced that one filled with so much joy could not possibly retain a hideous disease coursing through her veins. I had hoped that she was healing - that she had healed.

Our friends returned to Sunset Village and two weeks later, Michael and Lucinda Starr returned to Bloomington, Indiana and their teaching duties, promising to return during spring break and summer. They made arrangements to go on sabbatical for the following school year so they could live at Sand Cove Cliff Castle. Julie, Patrick, Jamie and I had left Sunset Village forever, only to return on occasion to visit with our friends. The twins both had thick curly auburn hair, like their mother, and they had blue-green eyes that reminded me of the Caribbean Sea.

Helena bore a lovely girl. The infant had Elijah's beautiful caramel skin tone, and she had light green eyes and platinum blonde hair, a very unusual and gorgeous combination. Elijah and Helena held their *creation of life* ceremony that had the feeling of being a wedding celebration. Everyone attended, including Lord Joseph, Elkannah's family, and of course Millie and Charley. Michelin was a very proud grandmother, and she was the one who delivered the baby. Helena and Elijah named her Loletta.

Tafari and Shannon left for Kingston where Tafari hoped to launch a music career. Jonathan returned to Philadelphia with plans to pursue a career in music as well.

Michelin and Harold moved onto the land that Harold owned on the beach at Bloody Bay, not far from where Michelin and her children had camped with Conric. I was surprised to learn that the land Harold owned was beach property in Negril, a fact that he never mentioned while we were living together at Sunset Village.

At first, Karl was content to continue his native fishing lifestyle, residing in the cave at Sunset Village, occasionally sailing to the castle and to Bloody Bay. He became good friends with Lord Joseph and even declared, at one point, that he was a white Rastafarian, and he spent time in the Blue Mountains with Lord Joseph and his Rastafarian community. Karl's devotion to the religious philosophy was short lived as he became disillusioned with its restrictions and crystallized doctrines – he was simply too much of a free spirit to adopt any prescribed way of life. Karl continued his explorations of Jamaica, sailing around the island, living the truly, free native island boy lifestyle that Patrick and I once lived in Negril. Every once in a while, Karl would show up at the castle to spend time with us, share stories of his adventures, and then move on.

Luke, Liam, Roseann, and Donna remained at Sunset Village, taking up semi-permanent residence in one of the stone cottages while Helena and Elijah lived in the other. Along with Norlina and Edward, they became the core of the village, continuing the legacy of this unique community, including the meditation sessions, which were frequently attended by hippies throughout Negril. The four of us visited Sunset Village and Bloody Bay on special occasions, maintaining our close ties to our dear friends and they too visited the Sand Cove Cliff Castle and the lovely baby twins.

As promised, Michael and Lucinda Starr returned during the late March spring break, and then again in June with the intention of staying a full year. They helped take care of the baby twins and they worked steadily in the gardens, making considerable improvements on the beauty of our land. An addition was added to the castle to provide comfortable living accommodations for the grandparents.

It was during the month of November of that year that Jamie's leukemia came raging back with fury. The parents were alarmed, and as Jamie had predicted, they wanted her to return to Bloomington to undergo traditional medical treatment. Jamie was persistent in refusing to succumb to a process that gave her less than a 2% chance of survival, eventually convincing her parents that living out the final days of her life with her family around her was the right decision.

Jamie's love for life, her ability to live each moment to its fullest, and the strength of her love for others, was an inspiration for all of us. She never complained of her disease, and she did her best to conceal her physical pain in an attempt to minimize the suffering of those of us who loved her so dearly.

She struggled on valiantly into the spring months, and finally, on the night of May 5th, Jamie died in my arms underneath a canopy of stars on the top of Sand Cove Cliff Castle.

A funeral ceremony was held for her at Sunset Village on the Lotus Meditation Cliff, where Jamie had started the tradition of communal meditation that had made a lasting spiritual contribution to all who participated during and since. In addition to the original core members of the Sunset Village community, over a hundred people attended, including students and their families from the Negril Elementary School. We meditated at sunset, and during the meditation, one by one people stood up and gave deeply personal expressions of their love for Jamie and the inspiration she had contributed to their lives. Songs were sung and poetry recited, and tears flowed like spring rain. Yes, there was much sadness for we all missed her physical presence immensely, and yet there was joy as well, for we all knew that Jamie's love would live on eternally both within our hearts and within the very fabric of the universe which she so ardently believed was made of love and sustained by the love that each individual life contributes.

During the height of what I had chosen to call *Jamie's Ascension Ceremony*, I stood up and recited a rendition of what Jamie and I had vowed to each other on our wedding day.

My beloved Jamie, you travel forth into Our Universe of Love

The lovely infinite vastness of the birth of our Universe spreads out before you
Our playground for sharing the gift of Love
Expressions of Truth, Beauty, and Goodness
I embrace you
Hold you
Comfort you
And strengthen you upon your journey

My spirit energizes you with all you need to navigate through life's eternal challenges
Together we shall continue to unfold in our holy love relationship
Know that I am with you all the time
For we are soul embracers
Neither time
Nor distance
Or circumstances
Even physical death

Can separate us for we travel side by side on a pathway throughout eternity
You have taken my soul into your soul, and we have forever become One
Eternally I embrace you as you embrace me
And forever we live together in
The Mind of
The Heart of
The Spirit of
Our Universe of Love

I Love you, my dearest friend and lover, forever more. You have not left me, you cannot leave me, we cannot leave each other, and I know that you now know, that your personality lives on forever, and one day you and I will once again occupy the same time-space within Our Universe of Love. I am with you my friend, I am with you my love, I am with you my lover, I, I ...

I fell to my knees crying soulful tears, surrounded by the physical and spiritual comfort of our beloved friends and family.

As was our custom, we spent the night playing music, although with sweet sadness, and we told stories, mostly fond memories of Jamie and the variety of ways she had touched the lives of so many people. Patrick, Julie, their twin babies Jamie and Oliver, Michael and Lucinda Starr, Michelin, Harold and all the other original members of the community, remained at Sunset Village for the next several days. Harold presented us with a life-sized wood carving of a perfect likeness of Jamie sitting in her lotus meditation position, carved out of a Jamaican Cedar tree that was on the property of the Negril Elementary School, where Jamie taught many of her art classes with the children. The school had donated the tree upon the request of Michelin and Harold. The statue was placed on the cliff at the very center of the lotus blossom. Jamie's body was taken to a crematory in Kingston. I placed the ashes inside the statue in the place carved out for this purpose by Harold – in the position of Jamie's heart.

After I deposited the ashes in the statue, I felt a hand on my shoulder, and the gentle voice of Harold graced my ears, "Oliver, I must share with you my thoughts concerning the experience of disappointments, of the dissolution of our fondest hopes and dreams. Our spiritually immature minds build castles in the sands of time, which will inevitably be washed away by the tide of successive events. On the other hand, our true spirit-personality is of God and therefore is infinite, which means that we are not bound by the limitations of time. The immature human self, the ego, identifies its existence with the experiences of this world and not the eternal cosmological view of the spirit personality, and is therefore prone to severe disappointment when our sand castles are washed away. As faith children, we know that this world is but one short scene in an eternal movie that is our ascension career, therefore, when our fondest dreams and hopes, sand castles, are dashed on the rocks of temporal existence, we are able to weather them without damage to our psyche - and we see them as containing lessons in love. Learn this lesson my brother and the sorrows you bear in time will become gems of wisdom for all eternity." Harold hugged me and went on his way.

For the rest of the spring and summer months, I lived at Sand Cove Cliff Castle with my family. I spent my days fishing and sailing, and thinking of Jamie. I missed her terribly! Even though I knew with absolute certainty that one day she and I would be in each other's physical presence once again, I continued to ache for her. I wanted to make love with her, to watch sunsets and sunrises with her, to talk and laugh and to live out our lives into old age. I imagined Jamie comforting me, saying that I was causing unnecessary suffering by resisting the reality of what is, and yet these imaginary conversations gave me only temporal comfort. The truth was, I was heartbroken and I wanted, needed Jamie to be with me not only in spirit but also in actual physical form. I shouted my grief and anger out to the cosmos, and in all too brief moments, I was reassured by my faith in the truth that Jamie and I would once again be reunited – yet doubt and anger and anguish and unbearable loneliness coursed through my veins.

August soon arrived and Michael and Lucinda had to return to Bloomington, Indiana and their teaching careers. They invited me to visit, indeed to live with them at any time of my choosing. The twins were now eight months old and I was convinced that little Jamie was an exact duplicate of her Aunt Jamie. Little Oliver was a carbon copy of my dear friend and island boy co-adventurer, Patrick O'Malley.

My heart was restless. I spent more and more of my time alone, sailing along the cliffs, swimming, fishing, including revisiting Lord Joseph's sea cave and Conch Island. I soon realized that I was reliving my memories of the times I had spent with Jamie. I forced myself to spend time with others, visiting my Ghetto Flower friends at Sunset Village, Michelin and Harold at their home on Bloody Bay beach, and I spent time sailing along Jamaica's lovely coast with Karl. Yet, I still felt a deep emptiness, an aching loneliness that reached to the very core of my being.

One day, I visited Sunset Village to meditate with the new group of hippies and my friends. I sat beside Jamie's wooden statue. I recited in my mind Jamie's now famous meditation instructions. As a sense of calm finally came over me, I saw the image of my mother wading in the surf at the Jersey shore. She waved her hands in a manner that beckoned me to come to her and she said, *"Come back home, my son."* In that moment, I knew that I had to return home.

Patrick was skeptical of my returning home. We were sitting on top of the castle tower watching the sunset when I told him that I was going home. "Oliver, you are home. What you and I have created here is more of a home than the redbrick-concrete-asphalt-steel-glass ghetto jungle of our childhood. We are your family. Jamie, in many ways is still here. Can you not see her every time you look at Jules and little Jamie? They are carbon copies of her. The loneliness and hurt you feel will pass with time. Stay here and help me raise my children, your children, Jamie's flesh and blood, please. There is nothing for you in Philadelphia!"

"I have to go. I have tried, Patrick. I feel a calling to return to Philly. We have left our roots behind, yet there are people we love who are still there. I must see my mother and tell her about Jamie. Perhaps time away from Jamaica will help me with the unbearable loneliness I feel. I honestly don't know if I can shake that, or if I really want to. In a strange way, it keeps me in touch with Jamie."

"Well, Oliver, you have always followed your heart and it has never failed to lead you to beautiful places. I trust that about you, always have. It is one of the main influences that helped us create the life we now share. I can honestly say that if it were not for you I would not have Jules and my lovely twin children. Thank you, brother!"

"You are welcome. Man, we sure have come a long way from the streets of Philadelphia. Ha, Ghetto Flowers in paradise – who would have ever thought that we would have such an adventure? Patrick, we sure are a dynamic duo!"

"That we are, Ollie, and much more! I remember that summer when we stayed in Wildwood into late September. I recall you saying that it would be great to live a lifestyle like Native Americans along the seashore, ha, and lo and behold, less than a month later we are on our way to Jamaica. That says a lot about the power of dreams."

"Yes, it does, and a lot more about the power of a good friendship. I also remember you saying something about creating a psychedelic spiritual community with naked babes. You got your wish, we both did."

"It is amazing – the power of thoughts and dreams and friendships. You know, I never really went for the spiritual stuff the way you did, Ollie. I took all that religious stuff with a grain of salt. You know, I think it is something that is a part of people's lives for a variety of reasons, but it never really meant that much to me."

"More like a bud of ganja than a grain of salt, Patrick." We laughed. Patrick opened his leather pouch and took out a spliff. He fired it up and said, "How about a little religious sacrament? One more mind cleansing of Babylon before you go on your way." For some reason his comment made me laugh so hard it caused me to cry.

As we smoked the spliff we reminisced about our adventure – the life we created. At first we thought of the experience with the Jesus Freaks on the Wildwood beach as the origin of our journey, but upon further reflection we realized that it began when we were kids roaming the streets of South Philly, involved in a variety of mischievous activities. Our street smarts had prepared us for adapting to the survival requirements for living in Jamaica with very little money, our resources being our flexibility, our adaptability, and most important, our friendship. We concluded that it was all those years of dealing with challenging and oftentimes very threatening circumstances during our childhood that strengthened our friendship, teaching us to rely upon one another, and developing the confidence that we could survive anything. In reality, surviving in Jamaica was fun and was never so-called life threatening – it was a more resourceful playground than the city streets for two inner city kids to do their thing – actually to grow into manhood.

"You know Ollie, the most amazing thing about Jamaica is its people - their generosity and kindness, which paved the way for us to do so well. Elkannah taught us how to fish and gave us the use of a canoe, which was the key to everything that followed. And man, Lord Joseph was one heck of an intro to an aspect of Jamaican culture that is truly homegrown indigenous, 100% genuine Jamaican – and that sea cave, whew, what a natural palace that is!"

"Yeahmon, we were fortunate to know some really cool people. I wonder how many folks in this world would be as generous as Elijah and his family to open their home to us and give us so much leeway in influencing the development of their land into becoming a thriving community?"

"Not many, I suspect. They really are one-of-a-kind, Ollie. Or maybe most Jamaicans are like that, and if not, well, we sure were lucky."

"I get a real kick out of Harold the Woodcarver – a Kingston Jamaican born dude who has an Oxford education, a cultural crossbreed of Rastafarianism, Christianity, Jamaican and English culture – wow, what a combo that dude is! I love the fact that he and Michelin are an item, and that Helena had a kid with Elijah – and Karl, wow, talk about multi-talented people, that kid is amazing! You know, Patrick, Harold understands the way my mind works better than any person I have ever met."

"Hey, I thought I had that honor – just kidding. Including Jamie?"

"Well, that's different. I suppose when it comes to my spiritual perspective on life, yes, more so than Jamie, which is not easy for me to say. Jamie and I are, I mean were, no are, super compatible in every way and we had a deep respect for each other's philosophical and, I guess you could say, spiritual outlook on life. But Harold and I have very similar experiences and interpretations of what we consider to be spiritual realities."

"Hmm, I guess that's why we need a variety of people in our lives."

"Yeah, you got that right, Patrick. There are many dimensions to our personalities and each relationship strums an important chord."

"That's a good way to put it. I like that. And I think you and I strike the chord of friendship, of pals between two guys that is quite special. You know, sort of like a harmony thing, like we balance each other."

"Yep, Patrick – it sure has been one hell of a high-wire balancing act throughout our lives, that's for sure!"

We had good laughs over many of the events that had occurred since our Jamaican adventure began. The hitchhiking trip to Florida was a hell of a roller coaster ride through the Southern States. We both agreed that one of the most memorable highlights, actually pleasurable indulgence of our adventure, was with our Playboy Bunnies, Penny and Jenny – besides meeting Jamie and Jules, of course. Patrick said that while making love to Jenny, he had experienced sexual healing over the loss of his adolescent lover, Chrissie. His mentioning of Chrissie brought up the topic of Sandy. "Speaking of loved ones in Philly, do you plan on seeing Sandy?"

"Whew! That's a tough one. Not sure. I think I will leave that one up to fate. It is interesting that I continue to feel guilt over leaving her and avoiding communication about everything, even after all these years. Whew, that was another lifetime, another world."

"Well, Oliver, I recall you once saying, *love never dies, it just hides behind changes.*"

"Hmm, I thought it was you who said that, Patrick."

"Ha, maybe it was. Sometimes I can't tell where you begin and I leave off – strange, isn't it Ollie?"

"Not really. We have shared so much together and our dreaming, thinking, doing, and learning had a great deal of overlap. I mean really, Patrick, we married twin sisters and before we left Philly our childhood sweethearts were twins. It is incredible when you think about it."

"Yeah, one hell of a serendipitous friendship that's for sure – ah, almost spiritual, Oliver – ha!"

"Well, I suppose spirituality is a word we give to our most amazing life experiences, in that sense, Jamaica has been one hell of a spiritual trip, and that makes you a very spiritual person, Patrick."

"If you say so, Ollie."

"I know so, Patrick."

Patrick offered me money that I was initially reluctant to accept. He reminded me that everything we created in Jamaica we had created together, what was his was mine, what was mine was his. He said that as long as the business was generating a profit, I was entitled to my fair share, even though I had nothing to do with it. He reminded me that I am part owner of the castle. It dawned on me that I had let go of the surviving in Jamaica mentality - it must have been because I became hyper focused on Jamie. I told him I would check in on Randy and his sister and make sure the business operations were running smoothly. He laughed and said there was no need to keep tabs on the business, that that was solely his concern, my part was simply to accept periodic cash deposits in a bank account he had set up for me through his sister. He asked me to deliver pictures of the twins, Jules and the castle to Randy and his sister – and to smoke a spliff with them.

I informed my family and friends that I had a journey that I must go on, a path I must follow, and that eventually it would bring me back to them. It was early October when I left Jamaica, around the same time Patrick and I had arrived three years ago. I bought a one-way ticket to Philadelphia, not knowing when I would return to Jamaica.

When I arrived in the Philly airport, I took a taxi to my home. It was late in the evening. My father and brother were asleep in their beds. Mom was asleep on the sofa. The house looked ridiculously small to me, as did the street and the neighborhood. I knelt beside my mother. She was wrapped in covers and her face was turned toward the pillow. I placed my hand on her shoulder. She moaned. I leaned forward and kissed her on the cheek. She felt cold, and her cheek was flesh and bone – it was then that I realized she had lost a great deal of weight. She stirred, turned her head and opened her eyes.

"Oliver, oh my God. You are home!" She turned her body to hug me but it pained her to move. She coughed and wheezed. The covers fell off her shoulders revealing arms that were frightfully bony. I placed my arms around her and turned her frail body towards me.

"Mom, you're sick. What happened to you?"

"I am so happy you are home, Oliver. I have been so worried about you. I thought I would never see you again. You have been gone such a long, long time. I missed you so much." Tears welled up in her eyes. I hugged her, gently, careful not to cause her pain. My mother had suffered from rheumatoid arthritis from the time shortly after she had given birth to me, her second and last child. The arthritis had caused the joints on her hands and feet to swell and her fingers and toes were twisted and a constant source of pain throughout much of her life.

"What happened to you?" I repeated my question.

"Oh, Oliver, everyone thinks I have some kind of rare disease and they want me to go to the hospital but I refuse to go. I have no disease. I am simply tired of life, of this body filled with so much pain – I do not want to go on any longer."

"What do you mean, not go on any longer? No! You can't give up, not now. I am home. You are going to be okay. I will take you to the best doctors and we will find out what is wrong with you." I pleaded.

"I told you, there is nothing wrong with me that doctors can fix. I simply do not want to live any longer. Please understand, Oliver. You are the only person I could ever talk to. You are the only one who understands me and knows how hard life has been. I have lived long enough. I need your blessing."

"No, Mom! No! You can't give up. You are too young. I have lost too much already, I can't lose you too."

"Lost what?" she asked in a weak yet alarmed voice.

"Mom, I was married to the most amazing woman. You would have loved her as I loved her."

"Married, you. How? Who? When? Why didn't you tell me? I don't understand."

"Oh mother, I am oh so sorry. You didn't get my letters? Jamie, my beloved Jamie, Mom, you would have loved her so much." My mother, father, and brother were illiterate. I was disheartened that I never received communication from them, and that they did not respond to my letters. I felt guilty that I had allowed so much distance to develop. In so many ways I had cut loose of my past and here I was face-to-face with the life I had left behind.

"Where is she? Why didn't she come with you?"

"Mom, she died not too long ago."

"Oh my God. Oh my dear, dear Oliver. I am so sorry. Come closer." She placed her arms around my shoulders and pressed her cheek against my face. We cried, our tears mingling. I explained to her the cause of Jamie's death.

"Mom, please don't go. Please don't leave me. I can't lose another heart. I can't!"

"I am so, so sorry my son. If I could continue in this life I would, but my time has come. If I could, I would stay here for you forever and a day. You must accept, as I have, that it is time for me to go."

"No Momma, please, please, do not leave me alone. I can not continue to face this world alone."

"Oliver, listen to me. You know how I don't like to talk about religion. You know that I have never even been inside a church with you. But this I do know: this world is not all there is and I will know you forever!"

"Momma, my dearest mother, that is what I told Jamie when she was dying. I believe that, no, I don't believe that, I know that. If it were not true this life would be meaningless, without purpose. What am I saying? No, you are not going to die!"

"Oliver, that is why I prayed for you to come home. I am dying. I am leaving this world as we speak."

"Pray? You? No, Mom, no, I can't take this, no!"

"Son, you know what my life has been like. I have lived with terrible pain for such a very long time, ever since you were born. This body has become a curse to me."

"I should have never been born, then you wouldn't have gotten sick! It is all my fault."

"No, Oliver, no, you must not think like that. You are the most precious gift of my life. I would have never lived this long if I did not have you in my life."

"I should have never gone to Jamaica, if I stayed home you would not be this way. It is all my fault. Now that I am home you will get better."

"Son, you must never think that anything you have done has caused me harm. Yes, you were a pain in the ass at times, but never the cause of illness, and you have nothing to do with my dying. Well, now that I have gazed upon you, touched you, have spoken with you - I am free to leave this body once and for all."

"What? Damn, I should have never come home then you would live on in hope that I would one day return. Oh, hell, this is so crazy. I feel like I am going crazy. I am a curse to your life, Mom. I am so sorry that I have hurt you."

"Stop this nonsense. You have not hurt me. Well, I would have preferred that you didn't go off to some silly island in the middle of nowhere and leave that lovely girlfriend of yours behind. That was stupid of you, but no, you are not the cause of pain in my life. You have always been my greatest joy."

"Mom, Mom, you have to listen to me. If I am your greatest joy and you have no disease, and now that I am home, you can live Mom, you can live!"

"I know how hard this is for you son. I am so sorry you lost your, your wife – what was her name again?"

"Jamie."

"I am sorry you lost Jamie. Oh my God, what a terrible, terrible thing that must be for you, and now I am leaving this world too. Oh, life can be so cruel."

"Yes, yes, life is so cruel, and we can fight back. You and me, Mom, we will kick the shit out of life!" She actually chuckled.

"I love your spirit, Oliver. I once had such a feisty spirit."

"You still do. It is who you are, Mom. You are the Momma Panther of Grays Ferry!" again she chuckled.

"Oliver, oh Oliver, you are so much like me, and thank God you are nothing like your father. He has been worse than a child during all of this. Drinking and crying all the time, and getting angry and cursing up a storm. Can't say I'll miss him when I am gone. As for your brother, well, he has his challenges but he is a hard worker, that boy is, so he'll be all right. It was you I always worried about with your dreams and wild schemes."

"You don't have to worry about me anymore. I will live here and take care of you. I will get a job and go back to school. You'll see. I will make it all better. Now that I am home you will get better."

"Son, son, you must understand and accept that it is time for me to go. I want to go. The only thing left for me to do was to see your lovely face one more time, and I have. Come here, lay down beside me and let me hold my boy again." I snuggled against my mother's body. As we held each other I could feel the sickness coursing through her body, as she moaned with pain. I felt a deep sadness and a deep love simultaneously. I imagined my love for her seeping into every cell in her body, embracing her mind and heart. And then I felt her love for me pouring into every fiber of my being, her sweet maternal affection for her son. Our tears of sadness, tears of love, mingled on our cheeks. I kissed her forehead over and over. She clung to me with all the strength she had left in her frail body. We fell into a deep restful sleep.

I woke up. My mother had died in my arms. A strange calm and peace came over me. I gently kissed her face over and over again. Mom had given me all that she had left to give – she had transferred her life force into my heart. She had shared the last of her life with me – she who brought me into this world had left the world giving me all that she had left to give. Yes, I felt a deep loss – and, more so, I was given a wonderful gift.

I thought of waking my father and brother and for some reason I could not bring myself to do it. The image of my mother holding me in her arms when I was a two day old infant while standing at the water's edge in Stone Harbor during the sun rise came clearly into my mind – a story she had recited to me many times. I felt a powerful stirring in my heart to drive that very moment to Stone Harbor, New Jersey to revisit the place where my mother had given thanks for my creation. I wanted to hug my father and brother and tell them how sorry I was. Then, I recalled the image of Mom that I had during my meditation at Sunset Village – she was on Stone Harbor beach, and not in South Philadelphia. I felt a strong compulsion to go to Stone Harbor, so strong that I was willing to leave my mother's body without telling my family that she had died. Quietly, I went into my bedroom and retrieved the keys to my Volkswagen Bus. I moved as if I was in a dream, feeling like I was in an unreal or super real time-space dimension. My actions almost felt as if something else was guiding me or that my deeper intuition was leading the way.

I had to pour a little gasoline in the carburetor and pop the clutch to start the engine, since it had been sitting for so long. I loved hearing the purr of its lawnmower-like motor. It was eerie driving through the streets of my old neighborhood. It felt as though I had taken a trip back in time to an ancient world that in many aspects no longer existed for me. Although, the many people there that I loved so dearly, especially Sandy, kept me strongly connected to this world. The thought of her stabbed my heart with guilt, a feeling that I could not deal with in my current emotional state. I shook off thoughts of her as I drove over the Walt Whitman Bridge and on to the Black Horse Pike. During the drive to Stone Harbor my mind was in a foggy haze. I was exhausted from the sequence of events and the long period of travel. Yet the adrenaline from the death experience with my mother drove me on. I rehearsed my life with my mother, a walk through the corridors of my mind – emotions of guilt, remorse, fear, and love came in powerful waves crashing upon my psyche. I turned my thoughts towards more positive events in my life, especially the times I had spent with family and friends at the Jersey seashore. I thought of my beloved dog, White Shepherd, and the fact that she was living in Stone Harbor with my friend and mentor, Ellen, the schoolteacher and lifeguard. Perhaps I would visit them this day.

I arrived in Stone Harbor well before the sun would rise. I parked the Magic Bus on 88th Street, near the beach pavilion where I had spent many nights playing my flute. I took my flute to the pavilion and played a sad, haunting soulful melody that originated from the deepest cavern of my being. The sound was lovely, and yet it revealed to my conscious awareness the fullness of my emotional pain. The melody was a prayer – a prayer for Mom – a prayer for Jamie, a prayer for me. I realized that I had not played a flute prayer since Jamie had died, when she had asked me to go to the castle tower with her and play beneath the stars. It was in the early hours of the next morning that she had died.

When I finished playing my flute-prayer, I took a walk along the beach. I walked to the very tip of Stone Harbor, the end of the seven-mile island beach to Hereford Sound, the opening to Stone Harbor Bay where I had spent so much of my youth fishing and crabbing. I sat on the sand looking at the lights from Wildwood, the seashore town on the other side of Hereford Sound. I became aware of my physical weariness. The previous morning I had left Sand Cove Cliff Castle and here I was sitting on the beach of my childhood summer playground. I stretched out on the soft cool sand and looked up at the starry sky and thought, wow, what a big universe. I spoke to Jamie, "I know you're out there somewhere, and somehow, someway, someday, I will find you. I promise Jamie, I promise! I called out to my mother, telling her that one day I would be with her again." Emotionally and physically exhausted, I drifted off into that mental space somewhere between wakefulness and sleep, where the mind drifts in a semi-conscious dreamy state *… the mist of pre-dawn surrounded me. The sun would soon come up and the first light of dawn was sending rays of light through the shrouded mist. I sat up and looked down the beach. I saw in the distance a figure walking along the water's edge coming in my direction. She was wearing a long flowing gown. I could not make out her features, yet I had a strong feeling that I knew this woman. I stood up and walked toward her.*

I felt the wet sand beneath my feet and the cool salt water lapping my ankles. The mist continued to prevent me from seeing the features of the person clearly. I could only make out a light hazed form, although, I was able to feel quite strongly the personality presence of this woman, someone familiar and emotionally close. As we came face to face, I saw that she had beautiful auburn hair and bright chocolate eyes shining with radiant intelligence. She wore a blue dress and a necklace of clear quartz stones – Cape May diamonds. As we stood looking into each other's eyes, she gestured for us to sit upon the sand and doing so I became aware of a tray of fruit lying before us. We shared the fruit, feeding it one to the other, as we exchanged the emotional energy of having always known each other. In one moment, I thought she was Jamie, then in another moment it felt as though she was my mother, and then Ellen, and yet again, Sandy – and each time I felt that she was each individual woman that I loved so dearly, her eyes would take on their respective color and unique personality. Then, I thought that perhaps she was all of the women I have ever loved and still love. This was happening without either of us speaking a word and yet we were having a profoundly intimate conversation where nothing was said and yet all was communicated. It was quite pleasant.

I became aware of a cumulus cloud floating just a few yards away above the ocean. I looked at it for a while, finding it rather interesting to be sitting there. We continued our silent communication when I felt the need to return my attention to the cloud. I stared at it for a long time and then it occurred to me that the cloud wanted me to come to it. I looked at my friend and she nodded, as if commenting with reassuring brightness in her eyes, "Go Oliver, it's okay, we cannot leave each other." I walked into the ocean and reached the cloud just as the water was slightly below my knees. I stepped on the cloud and it felt soft and fluffy yet consisted of a firmness that easily supported my body. I comfortably sat in the center of the cloud and it began to move. Out over the sea we went, gradually increasing our elevation. A marvelous excitement came over me as I looked out in the direction of the eastern horizon and beheld the tip of the sun rising from the sea, lighting the sky in rays of deep orange-gold. As I looked upon the beauty of this seascape, the ocean had the appearance of a silver sea of shimmering glass. Upon the surface, I saw images of episodes in my life, an oceanic cinema rolling upon the gentle waves. I saw myself as a little boy running through the narrow alleyways of my neighborhood with slingshot in hand chasing feral cats. I saw a scene of my childhood friend Liam and me stealing money from the home of a greedy mean old lady and giving it to charity, only later to discover that the home of the old lady, and indeed all of her possessions actually belonged to Liam's family – it was when we referred to ourselves as soul-saving thieves. Then, I was in camp with my ghetto flower friends, fighting bullies and attempting to rescue our girls from the evil clutches of camp counselors. Ellen, my Stone Harbor mentor was sitting with me among the dunes of Avalon, telling me that I am her young ghetto flower. I saw Sandy and scenes from the many intimate times we had shared. Then, there appeared scary images of gang racial violence and drug abuse and friends and family members dying of drug overdoses. I saw my cousin Butch's and brothers of my friends' coffins - all killed in Vietnam. I saw myself sick with hepatitis inside a Catholic Church screaming in agony at God over the insanity that was my life, and I saw the epiphany that soon followed. I saw priests reaching out in the neighborhood to help the youth being cut down by drugs and violence and the role I played in assisting them. I was in a classroom at college learning of the social and psychological constructs of my own psyche and that of my family and neighborhood. And I saw Patrick and me hitchhiking and then arriving in Jamaica and having our adventures. I saw Jamie and Julie along the road in Negril where we had first met, followed by scenes of the many loving, precious moments we had spent together, especially our wedding day. I saw the smiling faces of the little twins, my niece and nephew Jamie and Oliver, looking at me lovingly.

And then I was with Jamie dying in my arms as we sat under the canopy of stars atop the castle tower on that fateful night when she told me she wanted to look out into our starry universe one last time, as she whispered these words from her lovely lips, "I love you my sweet dear husband, Oliver." I looked in her light fainted eyes and said, "Jamie, my love, I need you to know that this life is but a short and intense experience that primes our eternal embryonic soul for life everlasting. You have taught me that this entire material world is impermanent. I want you to accept that you are not. I know this from faith-experience and not from mere belief – it is a fact that you and everyone you love will live forever and you will have an eternity of adventures to share with them. As emotionally and physically painful as this experience is for you, know that it is only a metamorphosis and that you will enter into a new and glorious body in a world of unimaginable beauty. The time we spend on this earth is only the beginning of an eternal ascension career and I look forward to having many adventures with you. In just a very short period of time, I will greet you in that beautiful world and say, I told you so!!!" She smiled and responded, "That is such a beautiful vision, my love, and for us I will take it with me on my journey into our universe of love, and I trust with all my heart that you speak the truth." She closed her eyes for the last time and breathed no more, I kissed her lips ever so gently but I refused to say goodbye.

Upon seeing this scene, I suddenly became aware of not feeling afraid, that none of the emotions stimulated by these scenes were threatening to me, they were the story of my life, the journey I had taken, the feelings and the scenes were not bad, they were of a richly lived life full of adventure and remarkable relationships. Then, the thought came to me, 'I have no need to look upon my past anymore with remorse, I am finished with this, it is done, and it is time to move on.' The cloud, as if hearing my thoughts and acknowledging the truth thereof, reversed its direction and moved back towards the shoreline. As I came closer to the beach, I saw a child of seven years standing at the water's edge. A feeling of apprehension gripped me, sensing that the child was I. I was afraid to see me as a child, yet I could do nothing to stop what was happening. I expected to see the child as frightened and tormented. I reminded myself that I no longer needed to look upon such things, that I just decided it was all okay and that I must move on with my life. So why was this happening to me? When I stepped off the cloud, my child-self ran towards me and then stopped within a few feet and looked into my eyes. And I beheld that the boy was not frightened or sickly, and quite to the contrary, he was beaming with happiness. Seeing that I was pleased, he ran to me and we embraced in a long, warm, joyful hug. I, the adult Oliver, and I, the child Oliver, had embraced and became one and merged and again I was standing alone. In this moment, I felt reassured that all along the path of life, my true self was kept safe and unaffected by the sufferings of this world, and that much of my perceptions of the past, of my identity, and perhaps most important of all, my relationships, had been healed. I turned to gaze upon the horizon, and there I saw my female friend-lover-wife-mother-spirit standing upon the ocean holding a babe extended in her arms toward the morning light of the rising sun - she was giving thanks for the birth of a new life.

"Oliver, Oliver James, open your eyes." I felt a hand on my shoulder shaking me as my name was repeated over and over again. Something wet was touching my face. I turned my head in the direction of the voice and there she was kneeling beside me.

"Sandy? Oh my God, it is you … and White Shepherd! Where's Patrick?"

Author's Note

Novels in the Ghetto Flowers series:

GHETTO FLOWERS
The Early Years

GHETTO FLOWERS
Dark & Light

STONE HARBOR DREAM
Short Stories

ABOUT THE AUTHOR

Francis O. Lynn was born in South Philadelphia and lived there for the first nineteen years of his life. The experience of growing up in a unique inner city community contributed significantly to his commitment to the education and development of people of all ages. He was inspired by his students to write the stories he told about the inner city and other experiences. The *Ghetto Flowers* novels are the fruition of that inspiration.

Francis received his undergraduate degree from Indiana University, concentrating his studies in psychology, anthropology and education. He received his Masters degree in education from The College of New Jersey. He began his professional career working for the South Bend, Indiana Community School Corporation developing peer influence programs in several high schools. Francis created and directed the Youth Enrichment Program for the city of Bloomington, Indiana and served as a counselor in a shelter for runaway teenagers. He taught high school social studies and served as a counselor at the Harmony School, an independent K-12 school in Bloomington, Indiana. Francis served as Youth Programs Director at Powell House, a Quaker education and retreat center in Old Chatham, New York. There, he facilitated conferences designed to create a positive youth culture within the tradition of the Religious Society of Friends (Quaker) for youth from multiple cultural backgrounds. As part of that work, Francis conducted trips to Costa Rica, England, Native American Reservations, and other areas of interest throughout the United States, introducing young people to principles of ecology and cultural diversity. Francis currently teaches language arts, math, science, social studies and leads education adventure programs for young people and adults. He lives in Princeton, NJ with his wife and four children.

ISLAND ODYSSEY
Ghetto Flowers in Paradise

Francis O. Lynn

Made in the USA
Middletown, DE
12 November 2015